CW01019822

*About the author: I live in Cumbria I have been writing for many years.*
*My novels are a mix of romance, drama & comedy.*
*My interests are music, writing, reading, theatre, films & travelling around the UK.*


*You can find me on Twitter AlexStone@glitter452*
*Instagram solsburyhill355*

*Also available by the same author*

*English Girl Irish Heart*
*Glamour Girl*
*Spotlight*
*Love*
*American Dreams*
*Chasing Rainbows*
*Rainclouds*
*Harmony*

# Family secrets

## Christmas 1990

*As Corey arrived at her father's house she looked up at the Christmas wreath on the door it had green holly leaves. And a red bow in the middle she thought it looked pretty. It had begun to snow the temperature was below freezing. As was usual at that time of year she could smell the familiar scent of alcohol her mother seemed angry. As she always was everytime they went there. Her father opened the door 'Marie come to say hello'. 'I've nothing to say to you!' 'good if I had my way I'd never see you again!' 'good luck with that!'. 'Since we have a son together and Corey you said you wanted her she's yours!' 'what!'. 'You said you can do a better job bringing up a child'. 'Mammy' 'Corey you're going to be living with your father' 'I want to live with you!' 'you can't!'. Corey began to cry confused at what was happening. A little girl being taken away from the only mother she'd ever known 'no mammy!' 'listen Corey' her father said. 'I love you you can still see your mammy in the holidays'. 'But you'll be living here with me we'll have fun go places together the cinema bowling whatever you want'.*

'Your my little girl' Corey felt a bit better why couldn't her parents live together? 'what about Nicky?' 'Nicky'.

'She can still see her can't she' 'yes Corey we'll still see each other you'll just be living at another house right'.

'She's all yours' her mother said her mother left a suitcase of clothes Corey held her favourite teddy bear.

'I'm going I'll see you soon' she cried again sad her mother's car drove off she didn't look back once.

Didn't she love her anymore? what mother would abandon her own daughter without a second glance.

'Good riddens!' her father said as he looked through the suitcase of clothes she had left 'there's some good stuff'.

'But some of this...anyway I'm gonna take you shopping'.

'Buy some new things how would you like that'.

'Dresses T-shirts whatever you want only the best for my little girl' Corey smiled 'it's me and you now Daniel'.

'We'll be a family the three of us everything will be good'.

'I promise' she believed her dad after all he loved her. Everything would be ok she'd see her mother in the school holidays and her sister.

That Friday evening they heard a knock at the door. Her father opened it was Nicole Marie's other daughter.

She was eleven pretty with blonde hair shoulder length. And wore a blue alice band and a navy school jumper grey skirt 'I came to see Corey is she in?' 'maybe'.

*'I came to give Corey her favourite doll she never goes to sleep without it' Nicole handed over a plastic Sindy doll. 'Where's it's clothes?' 'the dress came off I'm sure they sell clothes for it' 'I'll make sure she gets it' 'thanks'. 'Can you say hi to Corey for me?' 'yes' 'tell her I'll see her soon' 'course I know how hard this is for everyone'. 'Families separating everything will go back to normal'. 'Me, Daniel and Corey you and your mam and what's his name?' 'Clive well I'd best be going' 'bye'.*

*Nicky didn't much like Corey's father she hoped her younger sister would be happy with him.*

*She was missing her already she would read stories to her and play games now she wouldn't be there anymore.*

*Her mother hated her ex-husband there was eight years between them he'd been twenty two when they'd met.*

*She was thirty she was with another man the love of her life she'd fallen for a younger man a charmer.*

*Once they were together he'd done nothing but drink.*

*Even hitting her occasionally now she'd had enough.*

*And was moving on with her life their mother was now forty two they'd separated years ago.*

*With the kids going back and forth between the two homes.*

*Never did Nicole think she would be separated from her siblings 'who was that?' Corey asked 'your sister'.*

*As she watched as her dad threw her Sindy doll in the bin.*

She knew it was hers it had lost it's clothes.
'My Sindy doll! 'so what if it is!' 'it's mine!' 'leave it!'.
Corey began to cry 'is this all you do is cry it's a piece of
plastic it's not real!' 'yes it is!' 'I feckin hate dolls!'.
'My sister has a doll shop no child of mine is playing with
dolls your living with me now not your mother'.
'Remember that!' suddenly Corey was scared of her father
for the first time 'listen to me I'll get you other toys'.
'Better toys' she didn't want other toys she wanted her
favourite doll her father brought her a big white panda.
For Christmas it was lovely but she was still upset.
As she always wanted to be allowed to play with dolls.
Later Tiny Tears were also banned Corey grew up jealous
of other girls she snapped out of her memories.
She was in the supermarket shopping it was the
beginning of September she spied some shortbread.
With a Santa on the tin the Christmas confectionary
was already on the shelves.
Corey knew her sister loved shortbread as she put it
into her basket she couldn't wait for Christmas.
She just needed to get her dad's funeral out of the way.
He had died recently she was surprised it had taken
so long he was an alcoholic and had been all his life.
Her childhood ruined by his drinking Corey had never
known a time when he didn't drink.

*Corey had tried as a teenager to get him to give up*
*and his ex-girlfriends or at least cut down.*
*There was no chance some people were funny drunks.*
*Her dad had always been aggressive cruel physically*
*and emotionally abusive to her throughout her life.*
*He had made her feel like nothing worthless like she*
*was never good enough 'you're a stupid woman'.*
*'What do you know!' he'd shout at her when she tried*
*to talk to him about his drinking.*
*He'd tried to take her money from her told her she wasn't*
*allowed a part time job at College like other teenagers.*
*Not because it would interfere with her studies but*
*because he wanted her money so he could drink it away.*
*Strangely he'd never cared she was a lesbian.*
*He had never made much of an effort to make Polly*
*feel welcome in the family or her mother.*
*Not that she ever had much of a family her father*
*had looked down on Polly.*
*Because of her glamour modelling past he'd never*
*been much of a father to her her or even tried to be.*
*Her uncle Tommy was more of a father figure he always*
*looked out for her gave her good advice.*
*Paid for her to go to College her father only wanted her*
*money especially when she became a successful singer.*
*It was sad to admit he never really loved her.*

*Not the way a father should the truth was he should never
have been a parent he was incapable of loving anyone.
But himself Corey had always felt jealous of Polly's close
relationship with her dad they were so close.
He would never have asked her for money he loved her.
And he was there for her Corey knew it wasn't her fault.
That she had been born into that life she also felt anger.
At her mother for leaving her with her father knowing
he was violent now both her parents were gone.
She had to let those feelings go move on with her life she
tried to be the best parent she could be to her children.
Trying to be the parent she had wanted her parents
had failed her she knew that now she was older.
Her mother had paid for her to go to private school.
But she had never loved her never showing her love
judging her for her sexuality saying cruel things to Polly.
Choosing her sister Nicky over her now her she was gone.
Corey didn't have to think about her anymore she was
dreading her father's funeral.
Having to listen to her father's friends say what a
wonderful man he was having to see her brother Daniel.
She hadn't seen him in seven years the occasional message
passed on between them her brother had changed.
He wasn't the person she'd grown up with kind and caring
he'd become someone else drinking heavily.*

*Like their father becoming nasty he had assured her he'd*
*stopped drinking maybe they could make it up maybe not.*
*Corey didn't know she had been curious about what*
*he'd been up to since they'd last seen each other.*
*As Nicky walked through the shopping centre she spied*
*a porcelain doll she had to buy it for Corey.*
*She already had one a gift from many years ago she*
*had told her how she wasn't allowed to play with dolls.*
*As a child as her father hated them Nicky felt sad guilty*
*almost she had a good childhood.*
*With love from her mother she hadn't gotten along*
*with her dad Clive he never seemed to like her much.*
*Never had time for her hated any affection but it didn't*
*matter that much at least he never hit her.*
*Like Corey's father and he only drank occasionally*
*when he had friends round a selection of the best wines.*
*And whisky in the drinks cabinet they were reasonably*
*well off she'd been jealous of her sister.*
*As she'd gone to private school she knew from their*
*mother Corey wasn't a straight A student.*
*She was a C average B at best who even needed help with*
*some of her classes she had been a straight A student.*
*Top of the class nothing less would do for her mother.*
*Nicky felt like she'd let her down when age sixteen she got*
*pregnant with her son Regan somehow she'd forgiven her.*

*Corey never got on with their mother any of them there*
*was always a row whenever Corey visited the house.*
*By the time she left school she stopped coming.*
*Nicky felt guilty now Corey was older for not making*
*more of an effort to keep the family together.*
*She had loved her sister when she was younger.*
*By the time she was thirteen fourteen she didn't want*
*her sister around they had drifted apart.*
*Corey was four years younger who wanted their younger*
*sister around when you were trying to be cool.*
*In front of your friends Nicky remembered one day*
*she'd told Corey they were in the shopping centre.*
*That she didn't want to see her anymore 'me and mam*
*don't want you around anymore' 'but why?'.*
*'You've got your own family to go to mam doesn't love*
*you like she loves me it's the way things are'.*
*Nicky watched as her sister cried later she played back*
*that day in her mind regretting what she'd said.*
*That she'd ruined their close relationship they'd once had.*
*By the time Corey was a teenager their relationship was*
*virtually non-existent she didn't even like her.*
*Nicky regretted not supporting her over her sexuality.*
*Calling it a phase they were close now as adults but she*
*would always feel guilty Nicky brought the doll.*
*As she made her way to Corey's house Nicky rang the bell.*

Corey opened as she came in her sister's Christmas
present safely in it's brown paper bag 'it's a present'.
'Who for?' 'you for Christmas one of them' 'already'.
'I like to start early it gets too mad at Christmas'.
'Your telling me I can't wait I've not started shopping
yet probably end of October tea?'.
'Any of that nice lemonade?' 'ice' 'yes lots of it'.
Corey poured them a glass cinnamon biscuits' 'lovely'.
'Homemade' 'their lovely we should sell them in the
restaurant' Nicky said 'I agree'.
'It's always good to expand our dessert range'.
'how's things?' Nicky asked 'fine just the funeral'.
'Coming up' 'I'm sorry' 'don't be just be glad he wasn't
your dad' 'well mine wasn't exactly the greatest either'.
'But at least he never hit me I always felt guilty'.
'That mam left you and Dan with him' 'don't be it wasn't
your fault mam said she never knew he was violent to us'.
'But she must have known if he was to her' 'that's what
I mean you were seven Dan was six why would she'.
'I guess she had to leave him but why didn't she leave
you with us the family was broken' 'we're close now'.
'But we weren't as teenagers' Nicky said sadly
'I was jealous of you blonde a glamour model'.
'It seemed more exciting than my life and you got to grow
up with a mother I hated you for it' 'I was jealous too'.

'Me why?' 'you went to private school I hated my school'.
'And you got to travel round Ireland in a caravan in the holidays you seemed more confident than me'.
'No I wasn't all the other girls at the school were rich'.
'Straight A students and I was the only lesbian in the school I felt out of place different' 'you never said'.
'I just assumed you were having a great time' 'I did'.
'But you know' 'you never told me things' 'I thought you hated me that you preferred Dan'.
'We could have been so close' 'we are now' Corey said.
As Nicky hugged her 'love you' 'you too' 'so how are you feeling about the funeral?' 'you know'.
'They'll be saying what a great person he was loved by everyone that time he asked me for money in jail'.
'I refused to give him any' 'good I would have too'.
'He said he was dying of cancer' 'I doubt it why has he only just died then that was fifteen years ago'.
'What if his friends get funny with me' 'I'm here'.
'Uncle Tommy Polly and you're his daughter' 'I know'.
'For years he drank all his life always getting thrown out of pubs for being drunk starting fights with people'.
'I knew the day would come I tried to stop him drinking'.
'I know you did and Cora his ex there's nothing you could have done or Dan he was a waster who drank'.
'All his money away who treated his kids badly'.

'I thought I'd be upset I feel nothing maybe it's my autism like if he wasn't my father I wouldn't be going'.
'I wonder how Dan feels' 'why don't you ask him'.
'Come on make it up whatever this falling out was about he's your brother our brother it was probably nothing'.
'Seven years you haven't spoken to him' 'I know at the time it was for the best' 'make it up for me'.
'Then we can be a family again even though we're not blood related it makes no difference'.
'I still think of you as my step-sister' 'me too'.
'I'm sure Dougie wants to see you make it up'.
'Imagine if anything happened to Dan you'd really regret it' 'I guess ok we'll talk no promises' 'good thanks Cor'.
'Dan hardly drinks now he looks great he's got a girlfriend their engaged' 'I'm happy for him'.
'He always asks after you' how could she tell Nicky her own brother had sexually abused her.
Maybe they could talk about things maybe he was a different person maybe it was the drink.
That made him attack her she had tried to put it out of her mind ever since that night she still had flashbacks.
That September morning Corey got ready to attend her father's funeral she wore a black dress and jacket.
A silver cross necklace the funeral was at 11am she applied her make-up she didn't know if she'd cry or not.

*She had little feelings left for the man she thought of*
*as her father 'ready?' Polly asked 'yeah I am'.*
*'See if the bastard's really dead' she joked she already*
*had a few days ago they had put make-up on him.*
*She felt nothing as if she was looking at a mannequin.*
*Corey was done with him hopefully he'd be a nicer person*
*in the afterlife it was time for her to move on with her life.*
*Polly handed her a pack of mini tissues she put in her*
*pocket in case she cried.*
*Their daughter Susan had insisted on coming as fourteen*
*year old girls tended to idolise their grandparents.*
*Whatever they had done Corey told her little about*
*her dad other than he had been in prison.*
*And involved in crime she could find out the details*
*when she was older Marie was working.*
*And didn't want to come Corey didn't blame her funerals*
*weren't exciting for a teenager the protocols.*
*The arrival of the funeral cars the wearing of black.*
*Families often divided and on different sides of the church.*
*The speeches the crying the wake the leaving hoping you*
*had enough time left in your life.*
*To accomplish all the things you wanted to do Corey*
*told herself funerals were a part of life.*
*Especially as you got older it didn't make it any easier.*

*As she walked up to the church a taxi had brought them there she wasn't going in any funeral cars.*

*She didn't think it was appropriate when she had been estranged from her father since her mid-twenties.*

*Corey was now forty two but looked ten years younger .*

*She'd given up smoking years ago age twenty one it had obviously worked as she still looked good for her age.*

*As she linked arms with Polly as they arrived waiting outside the church they looked around at people arriving.*

*In different black outfits members of the gypsy community and other friends of her father's her uncle Tommy arrived.*

*'Hi darling' he said greeting he 'hi' he kissed her on the cheek 'you ok?' he asked 'fine' they watched.*

*As a large black hearse pulled up as well as four grey horses a wreath read 'dad' obviously from Daniel.*

*She had played no part in arranging the funeral leaving it to him since they weren't talking as Corey looked closer.*

*As she realised the coffin was gold anyone else she would have liked it not her dad.*

*All his life he had treated people badly be a bad person and you'll be rewarded with a £12,000 gold coffin.*

*At your funeral 'have you seen that coffin?' Polly said.*

*'Prince Of Egypt my dad' 'the bastard deserves nothing!'.*

*Tommy said overhearing their conversation.*

'Probably paid for by his ex con mates' 'if you can afford it anyone else I would have said fine' Corey said.
'I'll never forget how he treated you his daughter'.
'Thanks' she saw her brother one of the pallbearers.
He had no choice it was tradition the male members of the family must carry the coffin 'is that uncle Daniel?'.
Susan asked 'yes' 'is that coffin heavy?' 'probably'.
They went inside the church as Westlife's You Raise Me Up played as they took their seats on the third row.
Corey knew she should have been sitting in the front row.
Dan was sat there with his girlfriend her father's two sisters and his best mate one of her Aunt's sobbed.
She felt strangely unemotional how could she over a man who never cared about her.
Who only ever wanted to hurt her 'we are gathered in the presence of god to remember the life of Terry Rooney'.
'Taken from us too soon let us begin with a hymn' they sang 'now we will hear from his best friend Charlie'.
'Terry this is hard he was my best friend I loved him like a brother he was my everything he was a great man'.
'Who loved his family his children things won't be the same without him'.
'Be a better place without the likes of him' Tommy said quietly to Corey a woman behind him gave him a look.
It was Corey's Aunt Matilda who she had always hated.

*Her dad's sister 'Terry I'll miss you I know you'll be looking down on us' 'he was a wonderful father'.*

*'Not always appreciated by those close to him'.*

*Matilda said looking at Corey and Tommy.*

*'To bring up two children by himself he made sacrifices'.*

*'He never brought us up we looked after ourselves most of the time' Corey was angry at her Aunt.*

*Charlie stepped down from the podium as the service continued 'she's talking rubbish and we all know it!'*

*Tommy said to Corey she felt better having him there with her she wished he could have been her father.*

*Finally the service ended as You Raise Me Up was played again she was slightly amused her dad hated Westlife.*

*Five poofs on stools he called them she didn't mind Swear It Again one of her favourite songs she spied her Aunt.*

*Who looked at her 'if you've got something to say say it to my face! you know nothing about my upbringing!'.*

*'The way you abandoned him! in his hour of need'.*

*'What about my needs being smacked about by my own father! I tried to get him to stop drinking we all did'.*

*'Corey's right the man was scum and you know it! we all know it and he didn't deserve a gold coffin!' Tommy said.*

*'Then why are you here! why are any of you here!'.*

*'For the wake the free food!' 'she's his daughter'.*

*'She's got a right to pay her respects and her kids'.*

'Terry's grandchildren' 'he had other kids a son and a
daughter I heard' 'then where are they? 'I don't know'.
'I don't care if my father had other kids by other women'.
'We grew up with him and they didn't have to put up with
what we did!' 'she's here to pay her respects what a joke!'.
'Respect this!' Tommy said as he tried to go for Matilda
being restrained 'Tommy's right my brother was scum!'.
'Daniel and Corey would have been better off without
him!' Corey's uncle Tony had joined them.
'You're a disgrace! all of you!' 'cause it's the truth!'.
'You're the disgrace making him out to be something
he wasn't!' Tony said 'I'm going!' 'what's going on?'.
Daniel asked joining them 'nothing just the usual drama
in our family' Tommy said Corey looked at Daniel.
They were together for the first time in seven years.
'You look good' he said 'you too' Corey replied 'listen
no rowing at dad's funeral whatever he was like'.
'It's still a funeral' 'Dan's right' Corey said 'let's go to the
wake' 'Corey can we talk?' Daniel asked 'ok' 'in private'.
He followed her outside Polly watched from afar
'I've missed you tell me you haven't missed me too'.
'Of course your my brother' 'I'm sorry about that night'.
'I was drunk it wasn't me if I could take it back I would'.
'What happened you know I love you I want you in my life
again your my sister my best friend'.

'I only ever wanted to be your brother things went too far
I'm not the same person I was back then'.
'You think you can manage that?' 'I can try please can we
start again? forget the past have a normal relationship'.
'Ok but if anything like that ever happens again' 'it won't'.
'I promise' he hugged her tight 'I was scared that night'.
'I don't ever want to feel like that again' 'please forgive
me' 'ok' 'really?' 'yes' 'I hardly drink now'.
'I'm a different person I'll see you at the wake'.
'Isn't it great Dan and Corey talking again' Nicky said.
To Polly she realised Nicky obviously didn't know
about the night Corey was attacked.
And a funeral wasn't the right place to tell her.
'We can be a family again' Nicky said happy they
soon arrived at the wake at a nearby hotel.
Polly helped herself to food she spied Daniel 'hey' 'hi'.
She said she knew she sounded frosty no more than he
deserved 'I saw you and Cor talking' 'yeah'.
'We've made it up only took seven years' 'just so you know
I've never forgiven you for what you tried to do to Corey'.
'I never did anything! I was drunk' 'only cause Carol
came back in time' 'yeah we're talking again'.
'If Corey can move on so can you' 'I've been a sexual
abuse victim I know how it feels!' 'I never did anything!'.
'I apologised' 'Corey told me you date raped her'.

'The details weren't clear but she knows you did'.
'I wouldn't go around accusing people of things if
I were you! I'd be careful I know your big secret'.
'What big secret? I've released two biographies the
public knows everything about me' 'not everything'.
'How about your sister how she's not really your sister'.
'You were drunk one night Cor was in bed Louie was too
drunk to remember' 'your little confession' 'I was drunk'.
'You were crying' 'you don't know anything!' 'here's
a deal you stay out of my relationship with Corey'.
'And I might not tell anyone about your sister'
'I remember when you used to be a decent person'.
'I still am you read too much into that night a drunken
mistake nothing else' 'if you say so!'.
'Yes or no to our deal?' 'maybe' 'that's a yes then enjoy the
wake' Polly was upset angry she'd liked Daniel for years.
Whenever she rowed with Corey's mum he stuck up for her
her former brother-in-law now she hated him.
How could Corey even think of making it up with him
she was worried in case he tried something again.
It probably wouldn't happen since she and Corey's
inner circle knew about the night he tried to rape her.
Dan knew her biggest family secret the one she'd tried to
hide.
She'd spent her whole life forced to keep locked away.

*Polly was glad when they left the wake she decided not to talk about Dan she and Corey were back together.*

*Happy she didn't want them to row the following afternoon Polly logged on to the internet.*

*As she clicked on the blind item gossip website.*

*A way of catching up with what her fellow celebrities were up to and providing some entertainment.*

*Celeb gossip items that didn't mention the celebrities names.*

*i.e this actor had an affair with his younger co-star'.*

*A new item had appeared 'her sister is her mother'.*

*Polly read on 'this is one of the most shocking blind items we've ever published' she was curious.*

*'This A list actress/singer grew up in care her drug addict/alcoholic mother was unable to care for her'.*

*'She talked about the abuse she suffered as a child in care'.*

*'What you might not know is when she was only a month away from her twelfth birthday'.*

*'She gave birth to a baby daughter it was agreed because of her age and the situation'.*

*'That instead of getting the baby adopted she would be brought up by the mother and her family'.*

*'The celebrity's Aunt and husband brought the girl up'.*

*'As the mother was unable to get custody until she was a teenager the child never suspected anything'.*

'She has no idea her sister is really her mother in recent years the celebrity has wanted to tell her the truth'.

'Her mother has never allowed it worried her close bond with her granddaughter will be broken'.

'The celebrity is desperate to tell the truth the mother says if she does she will never speak to her again or the family'.

'Celebrity? what should she do? we will give you part two in a few days' Polly finished reading the article.

'What's this blind gossip' Corey said appearing behind her 'let me read that's shocking'.

'I guess it's like what happened with me and Dougie only I wasn't sexually abused'.

'I mean I thought he was my brother I wasn't in on the secret mam never told me who do you think it could be?'.

Corey scrolled down the guesses 'why are they saying you?' 'because I grew up in care and I talked about it'.

'On Oprah and This Morning' 'well it's not' 'maybe it's a good thing whoever it is can get their secret out'.

'And no more lies that website depresses me the amount of celebrities cheating on their partners or doing drugs'.

'I know your right' 'I'll get you a drink lemonade'.

Corey said 'love one' she'd almost been caught out.

Polly had come close to telling Corey so many times.

When Kaleigh turned eighteen then when she was twenty one now she was thirty one.

*It had never been the right time Kaleigh had gotten*
*famous after appearing on a talent show.*
*Then she'd married Stacey what would she think of her?.*
*They'd known each other all of their lives since they were*
*thirteen Stacey would be angry she'd kept it a secret.*
*Polly knew she'd had no choice as far as Kaleigh*
*was concerned her dad Simon was also her dad.*
*She wished he was Polly knew it didn't matter adopted*
*kids were brought up by other people.*
*Who weren't their real parents were they any less their*
*mother or father.*
*Kaleigh called her the best sister in the world they were*
*so close why shatter that illusion everything was fine.*
*She'd occasionally have a cry wish that she could tell*
*Kaleigh the truth.*
*That Luke and Louie were her half-brothers.*
*Not her nephews that she was her mother not her sister.*
*But it would destroy her life everyone in the family would*
*hate her they might even accuse her of lying.*
*They would never speak to her again Sarah was her*
*mother the only one she'd ever known.*
*Even if she hadn't brought her up till Kaleigh was fifteen.*
*She was her biological grandmother she had been the*
*right age to be her mother twenty five.*
*When she'd been born Polly had not even been twelve.*

*The scandal if it had come out and the local or national papers had found out an eleven year old getting pregnant.*

*It wasn't her fault she'd been a child abused in care at the mercy of men much older to abuse how they wanted.*

*Until she moved to Ireland age thirteen even then she'd been groomed by her teacher.*

*It was a time in her life she had tried to forget talking about it in her early twenties to help other women.*

*Occasionally it would come up in conversation with Stacey when talking about their time at private school.*

*Otherwise it was a box to be shut away never talked about it was the only way she could have a life.*

*It was the same with Corey she didn't want to talk about her father and the terrible childhood she'd had.*

*And Polly didn't want to talk about being sexually abused.*

*So they never did she never wanted Kaleigh to find out how she'd come into the world.*

*Polly had spent her whole life keeping things a secret.*

*She told herself it was too late even if Kaleigh found out the truth she would never see her as her mother.*

*Then if she found out their father wasn't even related to her she might go off the rails yes she was an adult.*

*But she might not deal with it well hate her never talk to her again it was better just to carry on as she always had.*

*No matter how hard it was sometimes she was Kaleigh's*
*sister it was the way it had always been.*
*Sometimes Polly would dream that one day she could tell*
*her that Kaleigh would hug her tell her she loved her.*
*That it didn't matter that they could all be one big happy*
*family but it was a dream that would never come true.*
*Whenever she thought about it for too long she felt sad.*
*Polly switched off her laptop trying to forget what she'd*
*read but couldn't.*
*She only hoped Kaleigh didn't read the blind gossip*
*websites as she Corey and Stacey did.*
*Corey was doing a speech at a function to help women*
*in Dublin who'd suffered domestic violence in a hall.*
*In the town centre it was something she wanted to do.*
*Polly was helping her practise her speech anything*
*to take her mind off things.*
*Corey was looking forward to helping other women who'd*
*gone through what she had that afternoon they arrived.*
*For 1pm Corey was nervous she toured with the band*
*and as a solo singer but doing a speech would be hard.*
*But she was determined she could do it just once to help*
*other women Polly took her seat near the front of the hall.*
*As she was introduced 'ladies and gentlemen welcome*
*to our charity function in aid of our charity'.*
*'Action against violence for women and men in Ireland'.*

'Today we have a few guest speakers who will be sharing their stories I am excited about our first guest'.

'She is a successful singer, songwriter and actress'.

'Who has spoken in the past about her upbringing and the violence she suffered and she is here today'.

'To share her experiences please welcome to the stage Corey O'Hanlon' they clapped.

Giving her a warm welcome 'hello everyone I'd never done a speech before if I go wrong I'm sorry'.

'I'm happy to be here for such a great charity I'll tell you a bit about my life and what happened to me'.

'And maybe I can help others when I was seven I went to live with my father I thought it would be great'.

'My mother she said it would be ok that we'd see each other in the holidays but it was me and my brother'.

'Daniel my father he shouldn't have been a father he was an alcoholic till the day he died he was violent'.

'The day my mother left he said he'd take me shopping'.

'Buy me new clothes and toys that we'd be a happy family just the three of us'.

'The day after my older sister Nicky gave me my favourite doll I'd left it at mam's it wasn't in the best condition'.

'But I loved it a Sindy you know when you're a kid and you get obsessed with certain toys I loved dolls'.

'My dad hated them he threw it in the bin he said dolls
were banned he started being aggressive towards us'.
'He'd shout get angry if we didn't do what he asked I was
nine when he smacked me not just a light smack'.
'Across the face every now and then it was the belt me
and my brother he'd smash bottles against the wall'.
'Sometimes he'd shout down the phone at his girlfriend's
we'd hear him in the kitchen try and hide in our room'.
'Till he'd calmed down one day he'd be the best dad in the
world the next we hated him I learned not to argue back'.
'It was for the best an easier life I thought when I got
older things would get better they never did'.
'When I was almost thirteen I got pregnant I had a
boyfriend we wanted to try sex it was wrong I was a child'.
'I hid my pregnancy we all did then when the baby was
born my son I wanted to keep him'.
'Dad said he hated the noise that he hated him I knew
if I kept him he'd be in danger so he went'.
'And I felt heartbroken my dad didn't care one Christmas
it was the worst we asked to see mam'.
'Then we would come back he got angry he got out his
belt he belted me so hard I wanted to die'.
'I wanted someone to rescue me but we couldn't tell
anyone Daniel was my best friend we were afraid'.
'Of being separated put into care so we made out
everything was ok even when family relatives visited'.

## *Old Lovers*

'Another time dad went to Vegas with a girlfriend we were left alone it was normal we never expected anything'.

'He wasn't much of a father to us one time I went to Stacey's for Christmas with Daniel it was nice normal'.

'She had a normal family a dad who cared he would never have hit her he loved her'.

'And I knew I could never have that I planned when I left school I'd move out I got a part time job he found out'.

'Dad hated me working it was a coffee shop in the Art gallery I liked it then I needed some money to escape'.

'So I became an escort girl slept with women some older'.

'We met in hotels even when I got my own flat me and my brother I was worried he'd find out where we lived'.

'When I was eighteen and a half I moved to London that way he wouldn't find me and for my music career'.

'But I missed home I worked as a dominatrix and did pole dancing I was like nineteen twenty'.

'I should have had someone looking out for me I didn't'.

'My brother was back here and mam didn't care about me she made it clear my sister Nicky was the favourite'.

'I understand why she grew up with her I didn't but I felt like my parents failed me like other kids'.

'What I'm saying is if I'd have had a proper family who loved me a support network it would have been different'.

*'A few years later I started seeing my dad occasionally'.*

*'I thought now I was an adult too things would change'.*

*'He came to my wedding to Polly he was drunk and we argued and he smacked me in the face'.*

*'And I couldn't tell anyone my father hit me I told Polly'.*

*'And Stacey and all my other friends and I felt better'.*

*'Like I didn't have this secret anymore and you know living with an alcoholic parent is hard'.*

*'You feel you have no-one to turn to and at school I had to pretend everything was ok I went to a private school'.*

*'An all-girls school the other girls had perfect lives'.*

*'I had to pretend to be now I realise it's ok not to have the perfect life no-one has the perfect family'.*

*'I don't want anyone to go through what I did so if you suspect anything think a child's been beaten up'.*

*'By their parents or a friend or someone who has an abusive partner tell someone and that's it' they stood up. Clapping as Corey stepped down from the stage she'd done it 'Cor that was amazing!' Polly said 'no' 'yes'.*

*'You were great' the woman from the charity approached them 'Corey thankyou it was a great speech' 'thanks'.*

*'See you later' the speeches continued for an hour after they chatted 'the speech was so inspiring I'm Melinda'.*

*'Polly I'm such a big fan of yours' 'thanks' 'you two make such a great couple I'm so glad your both here'.*

'Supporting us we wouldn't have missed it' Polly said
they looked over as a group of teenage girls appeared.
In the hall with different coloured hair 'another charity
do' 'which charity?' Corey asked Melinda.
'It's a new charity to help gay and lesbian teenagers
who've been made homeless' 'sounds like a great cause'.
'It is they do great work you should stay' 'we'll stay for
a bit longer' Polly said they all made their way outside.
As people came up to them Polly went to the ladies
as Corey waited outside 'ready to go' she asked.
'Just give me a minute and we'll go' Corey said as
she checked her appearance in the mirror.
She was wearing a navy jacket with gold buttons and
a just below the knee navy skirt and a silver locket.
A gift from Polly Corey thought she was dressed
right for the occasion serious but not too serious.
Her hair dyed dark copper red the toilet cubicle opened.
A blonde woman appeared she appeared to be dressed
almost identically she came up behind her 'Corey' 'Amy'.
'This is a surprise how are you?' Amy asked 'I'm great'.
'I saw your speech it was so inspiring' 'thanks' 'I wish I'd
known about everything when we were together' 'it's fine'.
'It took me a while to tell Polly' 'it's gonna help so many
women out there' 'hopefully you know'.
Corey was lost for words she didn't know what to say.

'You look great Cor you still look twenty five' 'I look after myself I don't smoke and I have facials Polly does too'.
'She seems nice' 'she is you'd like her' 'I'm sorry'.
'About what happened between us' Amy said 'it's ok'.
'It was a long time ago twenty four years ago'.
'Well it doesn't feel like that long' Amy said 'Polly says age is just a number' 'I agree' 'you look great too'.
'Thanks' 'Cor' she heard Polly calling 'I have to go nice seeing you again' Amy said 'bye' Corey shut the door.
She couldn't believe she'd just seen Amy again after so many years she was in shock 'you were a long time'.
'I saw an old friend' 'oh right' 'let's go home' Corey said.
'Ok darling' they walked by everyone Corey saw Amy chatting to a lesbian teenager she was curious.
As she remembered how Amy had hidden her own sexuality two years they'd been together.
Corey had been left heart broken Amy had ended their relationship calling it a phase it had hurt her so much.
A phase was a few weeks not two and a half years she knew it had been the influence of Amy's parents.
Who didn't want their daughter to be a lesbian.
Amy had insisted she wanted to get married have children like other women.
And that she couldn't do that if she was gay how Corey had hated her for giving in to what her family wanted.

*Not being true to herself she'd been so angry she'd*
*dumped her stuff into a black bag outside the flat.*
*They shared soon after she moved to London for*
*a few years trying to forget everything.*
*And focus on making it as a musician having one night*
*stands never relationships until Polly.*
*That's how much she had hurt her all these years later*
*she still felt the same she'd always wondered about Amy.*
*Corey had secretly spied on her on Facebook there was no*
*clue about her relationships only that she lived in Dublin.*
*And had dogs no mention of any children like she had*
*planned Corey hoped she was happy in her life.*
*She decided not to tell Polly about their meeting.*
*Corey knew she wasn't really the jealous type even so*
*Amy was her past Polly was her present.*
*Ever since they'd gotten back together it had been great.*
*They were more in love than ever and her dad's funeral*
*was over with it would be Christmas soon.*
*The next day Corey went into town Polly had a chill out*
*day at the house the car was in service.*
*So she took the train as she spent a few hours in town*
*before going to the train station she was early.*
*The train would be arriving in ten minutes she waited.*
*'Corey' 'Amy hi again' 'hi waiting for a train?' Amy asked*
*'yeah cars in the garage' 'oh I don't drive'.*

'Polly doesn't either she had a few lessons she was terrible she'll hate me saying that' 'I like the train'. 'I'm sorry if I seemed you know..it was a shock'. 'Seeing you after so long' Amy said 'I know what are the chances of us bumping each other' Corey said. 'Your speech was great' 'thanks why were you there?'. 'I was helping a charity gay and lesbian teenagers who are homeless' 'I heard something about that'. 'It's a great charity' 'so are you married?' Corey asked. 'I was when I was twenty one till I was twenty six'. 'Too young' 'yes I wanted to be like my friends get married have a baby by the time I was twenty five'. 'So I got married for all the wrong reasons he wasn't the right person we were never in love'. 'He wanted me for arm candy' 'older?' 'much older'. 'Ten years and he had money I suppose I thought I could have stability he was into horseracing and polo'. 'And it wasn't my scene I made a mistake' 'did you re-marry?' 'no I'd like to if I met the right person'. 'I'm sorry that time I put your stuff outside the flat'. 'I deserved it' 'you were eighteen I mean I knew my sexuality by the time I was thirteen'. 'But some people have same-sex relationships and their straight so I was hurt and upset' 'you were right'.

'Everything you said was right how I was trying to please my family that's why I got married'.

'I thought I could be happy being straight be like everyone else marriage and kids a normal life I hated it'.

'I thought I could make myself straight but I couldn't'.

'I hated having sex with a man it didn't feel right'.

'You're a lesbian?' 'yes I knew from when I was sixteen'.

'I loved you you were my first love I wanted to be something I wasn't I wish I could have been like you'.

'Strong enough but I wasn't and my parents they hated it when they found out so I said it was a phase'.

'That I thought I was bi-sexual they were happy me being with him my ex-husband he made them happy'.

'I was normal then when I was twenty six I left the marriage and I was gonna be me come out'.

'They hated gays and lesbians I thought I'd get another boyfriend a cover for who I was'.

'But he wasn't a nice person I mean I thought he was we dated for six months I couldn't do it lie anymore'.

'I had to be me so I came out' 'what did your family say?'.

'They pretty much disowned me' 'I'm sorry' 'and my so called best friends they couldn't handle it anyway'.

'Then I realised I wanted nothing to do with them if they couldn't accept who I was it was hard being alone'.

*'For a while' 'what happened next? I mean do you have a girlfriend?' 'yes' 'how long?' 'like ten years' 'that's good'. 'Better than living a lie' 'I know I'm happy I'm a big fan of Polly's and yours I came to see you live' 'really' 'yes'. 'A few times here in Dublin' 'you should have said'. 'You're a great singer and the rest of the band are great'. 'Thanks' they looked as the train arrived 'listen follow me on Twitter' 'I will' 'see you again maybe' Corey said. As Amy waited 'definitely I'm on the next train' 'bye'. Corey said going to the train Amy didn't tell Corey she already followed her on Twitter. But had changed her surname she also didn't want to come across as a stalker she was happy. With her girlfriend but had always wanted to apologise for what had happened when they were together. Now she felt better Corey returned to her house she didn't tell Polly about seeing Amy again 'hey Cor'. 'You know what do you say we never visit another shop ever again and do all our shopping online'. Polly suggested 'good idea maybe but what about clothes and shoes we'd end up sending half of the stuff back'.*

## Sisters

'I know just an idea' she didn't want to tell Corey
she'd been thinking about things.
Kaleigh how things could have been different.
Polly knew Corey would understand maybe she should
have told her the blind gossip item was about her.
But she couldn't it would ruin things in the run up to
Christmas it was supposed to be a happy time.
'I found that bike Marie's on about on Amazon in hot pink'
Polly said 'oh good she'll be happy'.
'And it's good exercise we'll have a great Christmas'.
Polly said happily a few days later Corey had decided
to go and visit her Aunt Matilda she hated her.
With a passion even as a child she'd never warmed to her.
And the fact she seemed to think her father was wonderful
and could do no wrong.
If she had a choice she would never see her again.
Corey wanted to find out more about her half-brother
and sister she'd heard about having a brother before.
That he'd been in prison like her father and had a
drug problem but she'd never really been interested.
Corey hadn't taken drugs since her early twenties.
And didn't want to get mixed up with someone like that.

*When she asked her father he said not to bother thinking about him that they were his family.*

*But it had never stopped Corey being curious the fact that her Aunt had mentioned her father having a daughter.*

*Made her even more curious it was the first she'd heard about it now her father was dead.*

*There was no harm in finding out a bit about her she'd have to suck up to her Aunt.*

*Otherwise she wouldn't be able to find out anything.*

*She would have to apologise for what happened at the funeral but she had no choice she was an actress.*

*Corey told herself she could fake being nice to her Aunt for an afternoon she got the address off her Uncle Tony.*

*As Corey arrived that Tuesday afternoon she hoped she'd be in she knocked on the door.*

*She didn't know her Aunt very well what if she asked her to leave it would be a wasted trip the door opened 'Corey'.*

*'This is a surprise' 'hi listen I'm sorry about what happened at the funeral the other day' 'really'.*

*'You're telling me you came all this way across town just to apologise what have you come to see me about?'.*

*'Your right but I still am sorry things went too far'.*

*'Your telling me' 'whatever my dad did I still always loved him he was my dad' 'that's true come in'.*

*'So why have you come to see me then?' 'I was curious'.*

'About my half-brother and sister' 'sit down' Corey sat
on the sofa her Aunt hadn't asked her to leave so far.
A good sign 'what do you want to know?' 'how old they
are and what jobs do they do' 'your brother died'.
'A few years ago' 'from what?' 'he was a drug addict'.
'I heard he was but I never knew anything about him dad
wouldn't say anything to me' 'he was a waster Calum'.
'On drugs his whole life went to rehab but never
stayed off them he dealt drugs he burgled houses'.
'To pay for his addiction' 'how old was he when he died?'
'twenty eight surprised he lasted that long'.
'We're talking class A hard drugs cocaine heroin your dad
was close to him for a while but they drifted apart'.
'His mother was the same drug addict lots of kids by
different men so there you go' 'did he look like me?'.
'For all he knew he might not have been his never got
round to doing a DNA test she said he was his son'.
'Who knows what the truth was' Corey was beginning to
wish she'd never bothered asking about her siblings.
'Was my sister a drug addict too?' 'not as far as I know'.
'What was her background?' 'your father had a
relationship with her mother the same time as Marie'.
'She told him he had to choose between them he chose
your mother massive mistake we all know they split up'.
'And anyway they weren't right together' 'I know'.

'So my sister's mother she went off with someone else'.
'Yes he knew about the baby Marie was pregnant at the
same time it made things hard as you can imagine'.
'Did he keep in touch with her?' 'no he chose his family'.
'He never had anything to do with your sister or the
mother I mean he saw her round town'.
'It was easier that way' 'so she's the same age as me' 'yes'.
'I don't know much about her the mother's name was
April Hutchings she married a politician'.
'They had a big house I'm sure your sister wanted for
nothing so everything worked out well in the end.
'What does she do my sister as a career' 'I don't know'.
'All I know is April runs a designer wedding shop in town'.
'She's a dress designer your sister was called Victoria'.
'But once she started school they lost touch your dad
and April so that's it' Corey suddenly had a thought.
'You said her name is Victoria' 'yes' 'really your sure?'.
'Yes I wouldn't be telling you all this if I wasn't sure'.
'I have a friend who I went to school with her name's
Victoria her dad's a politician'.
'And her mother is a fashion designer she has a dress shop
in town and your said her name's Hutchings'.
'Yes you think it's her' 'it has to be it's too much of a
coincidence' 'this is interesting' 'you won't say anything'.
'No why would I I've not seen her since she was a baby'.

'Anyway thanks' 'glad I could be of assistance but I'm expecting a neighbour for afternoon tea' 'course I'll go'.
'Well I'd say see you again but we know that won't happen' Corey left trying to take in the news.
That her close friend may be her sister she went over the details but she knew there was only one dress shop.
In town with the name April Hutchings she'd passed by it so many times it was called 'Wedding Dreams'.
They even had a Twitter page she followed Victoria had asked her to saying it was her mum's shop.
Her mother was one of the owners and she'd married a politician Victoria's father who she was estranged from.
Like her own father he'd not been there for her preferring to have his string of girlfriends for company.
Than take any interest in his own daughter she couldn't tell Victoria yet what if it ruined their friendship?.
Or she thought she was lying she posted things on Facebook about her sister Katie they seemed close.
Going out for shopping trips and to the theatre.
What need would she have for another sister? maybe it was better not to say anything.
That night Corey went over the conversation with her Aunt in her head replaying every word.
Corey thought of an idea maybe she could talk to April.

*See what she said about it she wouldn't say anything to*
*Victoria Corey decided she couldn't even tell Polly.*
*Until she'd gone to see April in case Victoria found out the*
*truth that Friday morning it was a beautiful autumn day.*
*The sun was shining as Corey ventured into town feeling*
*slightly apprehensive.*
*She could have quite easily left things as they were*
*but she'd found out a family secret.*
*Although it appeared to be no longer a secret since her*
*Aunt had told everyone at her father's funeral.*
*She'd been good friends with Victoria for years.*
*Since she'd left school going to visit her every Saturday*
*when she worked in a designer clothes store.*
*Hanging out going to the cinema & the theatre.*
*Even when she moved to L.A they kept in touch how*
*could she tell Victoria the truth.*
*She might not want to be friends anymore Corey knew*
*she'd been scarred by her childhood as much as she had.*
*Victoria had been abused by her uncle for years*
*abandoned by her mother and father.*
*Left to be brought up by housekeepers and maids and*
*any other family relatives who would occasionally visit.*
*The castle she lived in as a teenager Victoria had even*
*waited to have children till her early thirties.*

Due to her upbringing she had a ten year old daughter
Sapphire.
Now she was back in touch with her mother and sister.
Victoria had the family she'd always wanted Corey
decided discretion was the best move.
As she passed by the shop window which had a pale pink
beautiful dress on a mannequin and a silver tiara.
She entered the shop it was 11am there were
a few women looking at dresses.
An assistant wearing a navy suit approached Corey.
'Can I help you?' 'yes I need to speak to April' 'I'm afraid
she's busy at the moment' 'please it's really important'.
'I can wait tell her it's Corey' 'ok give me a minute'.
Corey sat down she watched as April chatted to a client.
A woman and her mother Corey looked at some outfits
around the shop maybe she could come here.
If she and Polly decided to ever re-marry the assistant
returned 'she'll be a minute and she'll come over'.
'Thanks' Wedding Dreams did made to measure couture
dresses as opposed to some wedding shops.
With a variety of dresses that people just chose from.
Which was why most of the women there were between
a size six to twelve Victoria worked in retail herself.
Obviously she had inherited her mother's love of fashion.
April came over 'Corey it's great to see you' 'and you'.

*Corey knew April as she had been a teacher at her*
*primary school many years ago.*
*'So what can I do for you? you and Polly getting*
*re-married' 'not yet' 'someone else?'.*
*'I need to talk to you in private?' 'is something wrong?'.*
*'I found something out family information and...'.*
*'Let me finish this sale I think I may know why*
*you're here' Corey watched as April went to the till.*
*Ringing through the sale for the wedding dress & mother*
*of the bride outfits he returned 'follow me'.*
*'In the back room' April shut the curtains as they stood*
*near rails of wedding dresses 'Corey'.*
*'You tell me what you want to say' 'my Aunt at my father's*
*funeral we were chatting and she said I had a sister'.*
*'And I asked for information and the name she gave was*
*Victoria's she said my sister's surname was Hutchings'.*
*'And that her dad was a politician and that your name*
*was April and you ran a dress shop in town'.*
*'And I think it's too much of a coincidence so I think*
*I'm Victoria's sister half-sister'.*
*'I mean we might need a DNA test I thought I should talk*
*to you first because I know Victoria has a sister'.*
*'And I wouldn't want to ruin things between them'.*
*'And we're such close friends' 'I know about you me and*
*your father we had a fling years ago I was twenty'.*

'I had Victoria he wasn't really interested he was seeing someone else Marie who he married'.

'And I later found out he did bad things criminal behaviour I once asked him if he wanted to see Victoria'.

'He said no so I married someone else and I guess I forgot about him then years later I saw him in town'.

'You must have been like eight with your brother'.

'It was Christmas he was buying you toys then later I recognised you when I taught at your school'.

'I wanted to hate you because he'd chosen his kids over Victoria even though I knew he wasn't right for me'.

'But I couldn't you were sweet and one time you told me you weren't allowed to play with dolls'.

'Because you said your daddy hates dolls and you would make him angry and then years later I found out'.

'That he was abusive that he hit you and I wished I knew back then I would have done something' 'it's ok'.

'No it wasn't every child deserves a good childhood'.

'Anyway Terry really didn't mean that much to me I never really thought about him much I followed your career'.

'When you were on TV I thought about telling Victoria the truth'.

'That she had a sister but we had this solid family unit and then Katie as well I suppose I was angry at him'.

'The way he used me then ignored his daughter'.

*'And you were happy with your brother so I didn't see the point in rocking the boat'.*

*'And then I had to leave the family home because of my husband he hit me and Victoria was his favourite'.*

*'So we split it made things even harder so I'm sorry'.*

*'I never told her about you' 'maybe it's for the best'.*

*'She told me she was lonely growing up that she wished she had a sister you could have maybe seen each other'.*

*'I was thinking maybe we shouldn't say anything she's really close to her sister maybe she doesn't need me'.*

*'I mean as a sister' 'is that what you want?' 'no but we're really good friends what if she finds out and isn't happy'.*

*'Listen we will tell her not right now we'll find the right time maybe in a few weeks or months' 'your right'.*

*'So we are real sisters?' 'yes' 'do you think we look alike?' 'a bit' 'I'll go now I'll see you round'.*

*'I follow you on Twitter' 'maybe I can message you'.*

*'Ok that would be great' 'bye Corey'.*

*She knew why April had kept Victoria away her dad was a bad person the fact he wasn't interested in his own child.*

*Didn't surprise her he'd never been a great father.*

*At least she knew Victoria was her sister Corey left the shop feeling better about things.*

*At least she knew the whole story and understood why April would have wanted to keep away from her father.*

*He was hardly the most reliable person but Corey*
*also wished they'd grown up together.*
*She thought of the fun they could have had but also*
*knew everything happened for a reason.*
*As she walked down the road she spied a familiar face*
*coming towards her it was Amy 'Corey hi'.*
*'Fancy seeing you here again' 'I know' 'are you getting*
*married?' 'no I mean we might'.*
*'But I know the woman who runs the shop April'.*
*'I'm engaged and we're looking at dresses the shop*
*looks good' 'it is the best it's made to measure'.*
*'Oh my other half is a size eighteen so it might not be*
*a good idea but I can look for myself'.*
*'I really want a pink dress' 'they have one' 'really'.*
*'It's really nice' 'I'll have to have a look oh if you and*
*Polly ever want to come round you could meet Melanie'.*
*'If you wanted' 'I'd love to' or you could come to ours'.*
*'Would Polly be ok with that?' 'course' 'she knows about*
*us our past' 'yes she's fine she's not the jealous type'.*
*'That's great' 'maybe tonight we could get takeaway'.*
*Corey suggested 'sounds great' 'how about Chinese'.*
*'I haven't had one for ages' 'me either' Corey agreed.*
*'What time should we come round?' 'six' 'sounds great'.*
*'What's your address?' Amy got out her I phone as she*
*keyed in the address they had arranged a dinner date.*

*As she returned home she looked through old photographs*
*of her and Victoria their school photos.*
*On holiday in Greece when she was a teenager.*
*And at Polly's birthday party so she could see if they*
*looked alike.*
*Corey definitely thought they had the same facial*
*expressions and chestnut brown hair.*
*Although she often dyed it copper red Corey liked*
*the idea of having another sister.*
*Victoria would have to know the truth sooner or later.*
*In the meantime she had a dinner date to get ready for.*
*'Cor did you have a good time in town?' Polly asked.*
*'The best' 'how come you were looking at old photos?'.*
*'It's a long story' 'tell me' 'ok you know at the funeral'.*
*'My Aunt said I had a half-brother and sister I was getting*
*details like what happened' 'you might meet them?'.*
*'My brother died of a drugs overdose he was in and out*
*of prison like dad' 'not good news then' 'I never met him'.*
*'Dad never took a DNA test my Aunt thinks he might not*
*even be dad's son'.*
*'Does that mean your sister isn't related?' 'no she is'.*
*'How do you know?' 'I just do there's too much*
*information' 'tell me about her?' 'where do I start?'.*

'Ok so we're chatting and my Aunt says her mother has
a dress shop in town and that her name is Hutchings'.
'And her dad's a politician and you know where this is
going' 'not Victoria' 'yes' 'oh my god! she's your sister'.
'I went to see April Victoria's mam' 'what did she say?'.
'That they had a fling April and my dad he was also
seeing mam and that he wasn't interested in Victoria'.
'And she said because I was happy with my brother'.
'And she lived with her sister Katie that she thought
it was better to leave things as they were'.
'And the problems Victoria had with her parents'.
'Her dad not being interested and not being in contact
with her mother so that's why everything happened'.
'I can't believe it' 'neither can I' 'are you gonna tell her?'.
'I can't' 'why not?' 'she's really close to her sister'.
'They post photos together on Facebook they seem really
happy she wouldn't need another sister would she'.
'April said I should wait a while to tell her'.
'All she ever wanted all her life was to be reunited with
her mother and sisters and now she has her daughter'.
'And her fashion business and she's one of my best friends
I think I should leave things how they are I will tell her'.
'When the time is right not now' 'ok I understand'.
'You won't say anything?' 'no I won't it's for you to do'.

*'Oh I invited someone to dinner' Corey said 'who?' 'Amy'.*
*'My ex-fiancée I promise it's all in the past she's with*
*someone else engaged to be married we got chatting'.*
*'The other day at the railway station and then I saw her in*
*town' 'is that the one you threw her clothes into a bin bag'.*
*'When she cheated on you' 'yes but it was a long time ago*
*I think she's changed she tried to be straight'.*
*'In her late twenties she came out as a lesbian but her*
*family disowned her you don't mind her coming?' 'no'.*
*'I don't know her' 'I think you'll like her we're just friends*
*nothing else' 'I know it's fine is it just her?'.*
*'And her fiancée I said we could have a Chinese'.*
*'Sounds good' 'she was at that charity day' 'the one where*
*you gave the speech' 'yeah she works with this charity'.*
*'Helping homeless gay teenagers I said to come over for*
*six' 'we'd better get ready' Corey was happy.*
*Polly was ok about her inviting Amy and her fiancée over*
*Polly had to admit she was slightly jealous.*
*But also curious she'd heard bits of information over the*
*years all she knew was they had been a couple years ago.*
*When Corey had been at Art College that Amy had broken*
*her heart and said it had taken years to get over.*
*Polly carefully selected some glasses as she prepared*
*the table she had an hour and a half to get ready.*
*She felt slightly nervous as she had never met Amy before.*

*Finally Amy arrived at quarter to six she was wearing*
*a long black coat suede boots.*
*And had long blonde straight hair and was pretty Melanie*
*had long red hair she wore a blue chequered sparkly shirt.*
*And blue jeans Corey greeted them 'Polly hi I'm such*
*a big fan' Amy said 'thanks' 'I really like your films'.*
*'Thanks come in we've got the menu' Polly said as they*
*sat down they chose what they wanted.*
*As they put in an order 'I love your outfit' Polly said*
*admiring Melanie's outfit 'thanks I do line dancing'.*
*'Hence the cowboy boots' 'love them' 'I like dressing up'.*
*'I tried to get Amy to join in but it's not her thing'.*
*'I like country myself in fact one of mine and Corey's first*
*dates was in a country bar in London' 'I remember'.*
*Corey said 'we danced to country music in a fifties style*
*diner' 'sounds romantic' Amy said 'so do you live here?'.*
*'In Dublin?' Amy asked 'yeah but I have a house in*
*The Wirral as well it's half an hour away from Liverpool'.*
*'Near the sea I divide my time between there and here'.*
*'I lived in London when I was younger but it wasn't for*
*me' 'I know tell me about it great culture'.*
*'But can't move for so many people' Melanie said.*
*They heard a knock at the door it was the takeaway*
*delivery 'how much?' Polly asked.*

*'Your not..Polly Patterson' 'I am' 'could you sign an*
*autograph?' 'course' Polly signed a piece of paper.*
*'Thanks enjoy your food' 'we will bye' 'you must get asked*
*for autographs all the time' Melanie said 'it depends'.*
*'I should be glad of the attention now I'm in my forties'.*
*'You look great on it' 'thanks' 'I'm thirty five Amy's forty*
*two' Melanie said Polly decided she quite liked Melanie.*
*Amy was quiet but she seemed nice 'so it sounds really*
*good this charity you work for' Polly said 'yeah it is'.*
*'I help homeless teenagers you know some families still*
*aren't as accepting of being gay or bi as they should be'.*
*'Some come from religious background's or they just get*
*thrown out on the streets they have nowhere to go'.*
*'We provide them with shelter and counselling and advice'.*
*'I really love working there' 'did you always do charity*
*work?' Polly asked 'no I worked for years in an office'.*
*'I hated it really it was expected of me now I paint for a*
*living I sell my own paintings' 'sounds great I love Art'.*
*'Corey got me into it' 'wo's your favourite artist?'.*
*Amy asked 'I couldn't pick one but I like Jack Vitriano'.*
*'Renoir' 'I love those people too' 'do you have a Twitter*
*page?' 'yes I post new paintings and I have a website'.*
*'I love it being self-employed and Melanie is a DJ'.*
*Polly served the food poured drink as they sat down.*
*'Is this glitter?' Melanie asked looking at her drink.*

'J20 glitter berry with edible glitter' 'so cool I'm really into trying new drinks' 'me too' Polly said 'and Cor'.

'We got this Soda Streamer recently you know from the nineties' Corey said 'I love retro things' Amy said.

'Last Christmas I got a Frosty The Snowman I was never allowed one as a child' Amy confessed.

'I was never allowed to play with dolls' Corey said 'snap'.

'I was never allowed a Tiny Tears don't you hate that like it ruins your whole childhood' Melanie said 'agree'.

Corey said Polly was enjoying herself more than she thought she would.

To her surprise she liked both Amy and Melanie.

And it was nice meeting people who weren't celebrities.

'That Chinese was the best' Melanie said 'I know good to treat yourself now and again' Polly said.

Polly served homemade fairycakes for dessert as they sat in the living room watching TV and chatting.

Amy looked at a photo on the mantlepiece of Corey.

'Is that your brother?' she asked 'Daniel yes we didn't speak for years but we've made up recently'.

'Can I ask why?' Amy asked 'it's a long story my sister Nicky wanted us to I had a good reason'.

'Why I didn't speak to him we're taking it slowly I also found out recently I have a brother and sister'.

'That's great' 'my brother died of a drugs overdose'.

'I never met him but I know my sister' 'what Cor means
is our friend Victoria who's the same age as us'.
'She found out she's her sister but she doesn't know'.
'I don't know if I should tell her' 'why not?' Amy asked.
'Because she has a sister Katie who's younger they were
estranged for years her mam April kept her sister'.
'While her father got custody of her and then she was
raised by maids and housekeepers her dad's really rich'.
'A politician it turned out her father hit her mother'.
'Which is why she left they got reunited and everything's
great between them'.
'And if she found out I was her sister she might hate me'.
'Blame me for everything' 'why would she' Polly said.
'Because my dad and April had a fling and maybe that's
why she ended up with Victoria's dad'.
'In a bad relationship' 'you don't know that' 'I agree with
Polly neither of you asked to be born into that situation'.
'And just because she has a great relationship with her
sister doesn't mean she wouldn't want another one'.
'Amy's right' 'maybe I quite like the idea of having
a sister' 'then tell her' 'I'd love a sister' Melanie said.
'I hated being an only child you should talk and let us
know how it goes' Corey thought maybe they were right.
Maybe Victoria would be happy to find out she was her
sister.

## Pushed to the limit

*It was a rainy September day as Polly got ready to leave the house she'd eaten lunch.*

*Had watched a bit of Loose Women and was now ready to go she was clutching a pink umbrella.*

*As she got into a taxi she had never got round to learning to drive the few lessons she'd had had been a disaster.*

*And Corey was a good driver so it wasn't necessary she was going to see her son Luke they didn't get on.*

*Polly never really knew why he'd always been distant.*

*Ever since he became a teenager accusing her of not being there for him as she was away in America.*

*Making movies despite the fact it meant he had been able to go to a good school wear designer clothes.*

*He seemed to have nothing but contempt for her.*

*Her mum had brought him up in Liverpool away from Hollywood the way she wanted.*

*Polly knew what happened to L.A rich kids they grew up spoiled drinking and taking drugs.*

*And now her son had become that anyway she knew Luke did drugs he even posted photos on social media.*

*Polly was anti-drugs as she'd been raised in care due to the fact her mother had been a drug addict and alcoholic.*

*Now her son was going the same way she blamed herself.*

*That maybe it was in the genes or that she'd not warned*
*him enough about drugs she knew her mother had.*
*According to her he was only an occasional user that's*
*how addictions started didn't they occasionally doing it.*
*Before getting addicted Polly knew he was now twenty*
*nine not a teenager anymore.*
*But she couldn't help being concerned he also seemed*
*to spend his days playing computer games.*
*Hanging out with undesirables she'd paid for him to*
*have a good education so he could be someone.*
*Where had things gone wrong? things had started*
*well enough attending a good school.*
*Then studying computing, media and music production*
*at College for three years then things changed.*
*Luke had started hanging out with different people.*
*Clubbing more dropping out of his course before it*
*finished going through a variety of girlfriends.*
*Worst of all hating her for no reason accusing her*
*of being a bad mother not being there for him.*
*She'd tried to make Luke understand that everything*
*she did was for the both of them.*
*She had such a good relationship with her two daughters*
*with Corey as well as her step-son.*
*It had got to the point where nothing she did was good*
*enough but she had to try and repair their relationship.*

*Stacey told her to walk away that nothing was worth all*
*that trouble that many parents and kids were estranged.*
*That she had been the best mother she could be in the*
*circumstances as a teen mother she'd had great support.*
*From both her dad & step-mum they'd been so close.*
*When Luke was a child it had been her idea to have her*
*mum bring him up she didn't regret it.*
*Maybe Stacey was right some parents had children*
*that were determined to ruin their own lives.*
*And nothing the parents did would change that Polly*
*looked at her watch it was 2pm.*
*She wasn't a morning person but she knew Luke went to*
*bed around 3am probably from playing computer games.*
*Polly knocked on the door waiting for a reply he opened.*
*'It's me' 'hi Polly or is it Susan?' 'why can't you just call*
*me mum like my other kids' 'cause'.*
*'It's the way it's always been you never raised me not*
*really' Luke had said the same thing so many times.*
*That she no longer responded to it keeping calm.*
*'I do know that I thought we could talk' 'about what?'.*
*'Stuff be civil to each other' 'maybe drink?' 'ok'.*
*'Orange juice' 'great yeah' Polly sat down as she did she*
*spied a dish on top the table it had white powder in.*
*And it didn't look like icing sugar Polly decided she*
*didn't want to start a row Luke was an adult.*

*She couldn't stop him doing drugs she looked round*
*his apartment it wasn't tidy Polly felt angry.*
*It had cost her a lot a posh apartment overlooking the*
*Albert Docks in Liverpool and her son didn't even care.*
*That she'd given him a good life a high standard of living.*
*He could have been renting a two bed terrace or flat like*
*some of his friends 'so been up to anything lately?'.*
*She asked 'the usual clubbing watching TV' 'have you*
*got a job yet?' 'yeah not a nine to five' 'tell me'.*
*'I sell cannabis' 'it's a class B drug' 'so some people need*
*it people with health problems even some kids'.*
*'With special needs I'm doing people a favour helping*
*society' 'can't you get yourself a normal job' 'like you did'.*
*'Taking your kit off for a living!' 'how do you think it'll*
*reflect on me selling drugs!' 'I don't care about you!'.*
*'Sarah's always been my mum always will be' 'what am I*
*then!' 'someone who gave birth to me'.*
*'You know why don't you get yourself a good career!'.*
*'As a DJ you were good at it once' 'still am' 'then why*
*don't you do that instead of wasting your life'.*
*'Playing computer games and doing drugs!'.*
*'Why don't you stay out of my life! you had your chance*
*as my mother and you f\*\*\*d it up!'.*
*'Tell me why you hate me so much?' 'you know why'.*
*'Oh because I actually paid for you to have a great life'.*

'Lots of other celebs work away touring or on film sets they don't get treated like this!' 'my heart pines for you!'. Polly couldn't believe how cruel her son could be.

'I'm doing panto here at the Empire Theatre for a month'. 'I thought maybe you could come' 'I don't think so'. 'A theatre packed full of kids shouting oh yes he is oh no he isn't not my cup of tea'.

'Why do you have to be like that!' 'like what?'. 'It wouldn't take much for you to come and support me'. 'Oh yes it would' 'funny' 'I'll check my diary' 'dates are on the theatre website' 'I'll think about it' 'you do that'.

'Oh I've been in contact with my dad' Luke said 'James'. 'Yeah' 'how come?' 'I'm almost thirty thought I should get to know him found him on Facebook'.

'What do you chat about?' 'things' 'me' 'not really your not as interesting as you think you are'.

'He works as a drag queen in gay bars in Dublin'. 'Change of career he worked as the school caretaker when we were together' 'I know he makes more money'. 'I'll have to check him out online I'd better be going you've got my new number' 'course I'll see you round'. Luke didn't even seem bothered she'd cut her visit short. Polly decided there was only so much abuse she could take and it was the final straw in their relationship.

*As far as she was concerned if her son was going to*
*make life difficult refuse to even be civil to her.*
*Then they couldn't have a relationship anymore.*
*He wasn't the same person he'd been as a child &*
*teenager he was a nasty piece of work.*
*Who had no ambition and no respect for her he didn't even*
*care when he found out she'd been abused as a child.*
*Groomed by her teacher no sympathy nothing she knew*
*Stacey was right she had to let go walk away.*
*No matter how hard she would always care for him.*
*But they couldn't have a relationship she knew that now.*
*Polly knew it wasn't her fault anymore she'd done all*
*she could to be a good mother.*
*Since she had such a good relationship with her other kids*
*she had to focus on them now especially her son Louie.*
*Who was only eight years old the following afternoon*
*Polly called round to see her gran.*
*She might be able to give her some advice put things*
*into perspective she was seventy seven.*
*Despite getting older she was on the ball with no memory*
*problems Polly had always loved her.*
*And come to her all her life about any problems she had.*
*Her gran had been the one who insisted she go to live in*
*Ireland when she was thirteen for a few years.*
*To get a better education at private school.*

*And get away from all the bad things that had happened to*
*her if she hadn't who knows what would have happened.*
*Polly rang the doorbell 'Susan' 'gran' they hugged.*
*'Come in you look great' 'thanks not bad for forty two'.*
*'Try being my age I'll get you a drink 7 Up' 'love one'.*
*Polly took off her coat as she looked round the*
*living room her gran had some new photo frames.*
*Above the fireplace she brought her drink along with*
*some homemade madeira cake 'thanks cake looks nice'.*
*'I try my best if Mary Berry can still cook and she's older*
*than me then I can how's Corey?' 'great'.*
*'I told you about Victoria being her half-sister'.*
*'It's great siblings I was close to my sisters and brother'.*
*'But my biggest regret is my kids what happened Charlotte*
*dying of a drugs overdose Brian less said the better'.*
*'And your mum getting addicted to drugs Sue being*
*estranged from your mum'.*
*'And then your mum's falling out with Sam a few years*
*ago I feel like I failed as a mother' 'no gran'.*
*'You couldn't have known two of your kids would end up*
*doing drugs there wasn't the awareness back then'.*
*'And Sam would have moved to L.A whatever his*
*relationship with Sarah' 'I guess your right'.*
*'Sue's close to Sarah again which I never thought would*
*happen and Sam if it wasn't for my grandkids'.*

'You Adam Kaleigh' 'your not gonna like this'.
'I can't go on the way things are with Luke I don't
have it in me the rows the stress I've tried'.
'But he's always hated me since he was a teenager I mean
I'll always care about him but I can't do it anymore'.
'I keep getting rejected so...' 'go on' 'I went to see him
yesterday to sort things out' 'what happened?'.
'He acted like I wasn't even there he's selling drugs
playing computer games till three in the morning'.
'I said he should be a DJ get a career he's not interested'.
'I could talk to him' 'I wouldn't bother trust me gran'.
'He's in contact with James his dad on Facebook I don't
know what they chat about he works as a drag queen'.
'In Dublin Luke said how I'll never be his real mother'.
'That he'll never think of me as his mother' 'he's a
disgrace! treating you like that!' 'that's what Stacey said'.
'I've decided to go no contact' 'if you think it's for the
best' 'it wasn't an easy decision'.
'I can't help him anymore I'm not providing him with
a lifestyle a nice apartment designer clothes money'.
'For him to blow it on drugs and computer games he
doesn't treat me like he should so that's it sorry gran'.
'Your right you shouldn't have to put up with his
behaviour I'd do the same' 'thanks gran'.
'Oh I think Corey's close to finding out about Kaleigh'.

'How?' 'the internet this website it talked about a celebrity with a secret daughter it didn't name me'.

'But it made it obvious it's me I think it's a matter of time'.

'Is that a bad thing?' 'Kaleigh would never accept me as her mother it would ruin her life' 'how do you know?'.

'It would it's too late' 'Polly what if you died tomorrow or Kaleigh she'd never know the truth'.

'I sometimes dream that she knows and she tells me she loves me anyway it's just a dream she'd be angry at me'.

'Hate me for lying all these years' 'it was Sarah's idea'.

'It was right at the time we couldn't have done anything else' 'Kaleigh's in her thirties now'.

'She's not a child anymore' 'I can't do it I couldn't risk her never speaking to me again' 'I understand'.

'I think you should' 'I'm her sister that's how she's always thought of me I'll never be anything else to her'.

## Reconnected

'Even if I want to be I have two kids who don't think of
me as their mother I've screwed up more than you'.
'We both have none of this was your fault being born into
a life you shouldn't have and you did the best for Luke'.
'And what happened with Kaleigh wasn't your fault'.
They heard a knock at the door Polly answered 'hi'.
It was her Aunt Sue 'hi Polly is your gran in?' 'of course
cake?' her gran offered 'love some' Sue sat down.
'We were just discussing Kaleigh' 'anything I should
know' 'whether Polly should tell her the truth'.
'I said I can't that it's too late' 'and I said if anything ever
happened she wouldn't know you're her mum' 'I agree'.
'Too many secrets in this family what happened with
Harmony and Steven' 'I couldn't deal with it'.
'If she hated me for lying all these years' 'but it wasn't
your fault it was Sarah's idea' 'mum for all her faults'.
'Knew it was the best thing to do at the time' 'maybe it
was but your both adults now'.
'I don't know how you lived with this for so many years'.
'I blocked it out it was the only way I could so many times
I wanted to tell Kaleigh the truth'.
'It was never the right time then when so many years
passed I knew she'd only ever think of me as her sister'.

'That was ok but it was never the truth mum was
the person she thought of as her mum'.
'And if she found out that dad wasn't her real dad she'd
have to find out what happened to me' 'I understand'.
'Thanks' 'Polly I'm sorry I never adopted you' 'it's ok'.
'No it was Shaun he said he didn't want anymore kids'.
'And Kaleigh was only a baby he controlled me everything
I did I was dating this guy I was twenty three'.
'He was lovely and Shaun was around he said it's me
or the other guy and I chose Shaun'.
'And it was the worst mistake of my life and then later
when I found out he raped Kaleigh and I hated myself'.
'Because it was my fault' 'you couldn't have known'.
Polly said 'I should have I wondered why he was always
going off to chat to her she was like my daughter'.
'My little girl and he abused her she told me it was
some lad from school and I was angry'.
'If I'd have known the truth I would have asked him to
leave and then years later Steven told me he abused him'.
Sue began to cry 'I'm a terrible person they were my kids
and he did those things I should have known about him'.
'It wasn't like now twenty years ago there wasn't the
awareness of child abuse as now'.
'People didn't talk about it' Polly said trying to make Sue
feel better 'and he controlled you like you said'.

Her gran said 'it's no excuse I should have been there for my kids' 'don't be so hard on yourself' 'gran's right'.

'We all know Shaun's a bastard' 'he used to beat me and I think back Steven and Kaleigh probably heard us rowing'.

'They stayed in their room Kaleigh used to ask me why I never left him I said I loved him it sounds so pathetic now'.

'He checked my phone said what clothes I could wear'.

'People used to think because we had a nice house some money that I had the perfect life it wasn't like that'.

'I couldn't have a life like other women I had to pretend to everyone we had the perfect marriage'.

'When he made Kaleigh give Harmony away I should have said no left him got a divorce'.

'Every time I tried to leave he would start acting nice'.

'He knew all the right words to keep me there stop me leaving' 'when did you leave?' Polly asked.

'When we went to Spain to open up a bar Steven wanted to come home and Kaleigh went to stay with Hilary'.

'It was after that when they'd left school I realised I was all alone that all my friends had left me'.

'It was me and him' and I didn't want that life anymore'.

'But for years Steven didn't want anything to do with me'.

'And I felt like Kaleigh wouldn't either so we were all estranged and it was my fault' 'he's not around anymore'.

'And your back in contact with Steven and Kaleigh'.

'So it's ok' Polly said trying to make Sue feel better.
'I know I still see him round town I try and hide'.
'So he doesn't see me and I'm with someone else now'.
'I'm glad you left him' 'me too mum' 'now you enjoy that tea and cake'
'So Polly what's this about you seeing your old foster parents' 'I got a message on Facebook' 'that's exciting'.
'It's all the kids they fostered it'll be great we can swap stories I might get emotional' 'I'm sure you will'.
'I can say thanks for all they did for me' that evening Polly went online as she read the Facebook post.
About her foster parents she'd only briefly glanced at it.
After receiving a message from someone they'd looked after her for two years as a child.
From the age of nine till she was eleven they had lived in Lytham St Anne's near Blackpool.
After her foster dad got ill she returned to Liverpool.
It had been two great years her early childhood had been spent being emotionally abused in care.
After she'd left her foster parents it had been the worst few years of her life being abused by her uncle, foster dad.
And foster brother she always tried to block things out.
Otherwise she wouldn't be able to function she always looked back on her time in Blackpool with fondness.
Her foster parents had been kind caring loved her.

When no-one else did except her gran who'd always been
there for her Polly knew she had to see them again.
Tell them how much they'd been there for her protected
her been a family she re-read the message.
'To celebrate looking after foster children for twenty five
years Mr & Mrs Hill are inviting anyone who has been
looked after by them'
'Over the years of any age for one big celebration at
Liverpool's St George's Hall'
'On September 25th 1pm there will be free food great
music and laughter so come alone can't wait to see
everyone & reconnect no need to RSVP or message just
come along x' Polly couldn't wait to go she was excited.
It would be a welcome relief from her recent issues with
Luke something to look forward to.
That September 25th Polly left the house in her taxi.
She was wearing a black jacket and matching pencil skirt.
A gold heart locket as she approached the hall she did feel
slightly nervous but told herself it would be great.
And that everyone else would be feeling the same way.
Outside she noticed someone with a camera Polly told
herself someone had probably found out from the press.
That she would be there she didn't mind and it might raise
awareness of fostering children she stepped inside.
Polly couldn't wait to see her foster parents catch up on
old times meet other people who'd been fostered.

*While in care as Polly stood at the edge of the hall*
*she couldn't believe how many people were there.*
*Usually she would have been spotted by someone for*
*being a celebrity but there were so many people.*
*She had no idea how many people had been fostered*
*suddenly she realised some were members of the press.*
*Journalists with recording devices she felt confused.*
*Were they there because of her? no-one had approached*
*her yet what was going on? Polly stood by observing.*
*As people chatted she asked a nearby journalist.*
*'What's going on?' 'what do you mean?' 'all these people*
*I mean I know all the old foster kids are meeting up'.*
*'But why all the cameras?' 'you don't know their receiving*
*an award for twenty five years of fostering'.*
*'We're all the local press people love these kinds of*
*uplifting stories' 'yeah'.*
*'Thanks' suddenly Polly realised she'd made a mistake.*
*She'd assumed it would be a nice afternoon swapping*
*stories having a nice chat with everyone.*
*Not that she might end up being on camera and that she*
*might not even get a chance to talk with her foster parents.*
*Due to so many people being around she felt sad how*
*could she have thought it was a good idea.*
*What if they didn't even remember her how many kids*
*must have passed through their house.*

*She was one of many Polly decided she'd have a drink
then go a man approached her he looked around thirty.
'Hi are you...Polly Patterson?' 'yeah it's me'.
'I knew you grew up in care but not that they'd fostered
you' 'for two years' 'I was there four years I'm Neil'.
'Polly' 'pleased to meet you did you know all these
cameras would be here?' he asked 'no I had no idea'.
'I thought it was a small get together I wanted to thank
them personally for everything they did for me'.
'But looks like I won't get a chance' 'me either' he agreed.
'Does that sound selfish?' Polly asked 'no I feel the same'.
'I'd rather talk to them alone without the cameras around'
'same it's great about the award' 'yeah well deserved'.
'I couldn't do what they do' Neil said 'I bet they had some
kids with real problems that no-one else would take on'.
'I agree' Polly said 'how long were you in care for?'.
Neil asked 'from five till I was thirteen it was hard'.
'My gran wanted to take me on but you know
social services' Polly said sadly.
'I guess it's hard deciding to take a child away from
it's parents sometimes they have to other times...'.
'My dad was once in a gay relationship they wouldn't let
him adopt me it's not like now I always think if they had'.
I wouldn't have been abused by older men' 'I'm sorry'.*

'I was lucky I wasn't' Neil said 'my wish is one day kids in care are looked after properly by everyone' 'me too'.

'So are you staying?' Neil asked 'I don't even know if they'd remember me' 'but your famous'.

'Look how many kids they fostered and it wouldn't be appropriate to talk on camera'.

'About someone I've not seen for years' 'I understand'.

'Hopefully we can both see them again without all the camera's' 'that would be great listen I'm gonna go'.

'But I don't know if you want to message me on Facebook or Twitter' 'I'd love to I'll add you as a friend' Neil said.

'Course chat online bye' 'nice meeting you' Polly had enjoyed meeting Neil.

The day hadn't gone as she'd hoped but she'd made a new friend Polly left the building thinking about things.

Had she made the right decision? what if she didn't get another chance to see her foster parents.

As Polly walked along the street she saw a familiar face coming towards her it was Luke.

So much for going no contact every time she saw him she felt a sense of dread what he'd say to her.

What he'd be like the more she thought about it the more she realised going no contact was the only option.

And she didn't want drugs around Louie he acknowledged her 'thought anymore about panto?' 'when's it start?'.

Luke asked looking disinterested 'December through to the start of January' 'I'll think about it'.

Have you heard from your dad?' 'you know we're in contact' 'look I know it's none of my business'.

'And you've every right to see him but the thing is...'.

'I was thirteen when we met he was twenty nine' 'so'.

'The more I think about it the more...I realise it was an inappropriate relationship' 'did he force you have sex'.

'No I wanted to' 'exactly I bet you were well up for it'.

'You can't say he's a you know you said yourself you were more like a sixteen year old than a thirteen year old'.

'Experienced in sex you even said he was a great friend to you at school' 'he was but in recent years'.

'I've been thinking things through I don't hate him I just... think it should never have happened'.

'I'm sure if my headmistress had known she would have stopped it' 'I actually wonder if you made all that up'.

'About your history teacher' 'what? Mr Cleves why would I do that!' 'because if you were putting yourself about'.

'With dad the school caretaker then it makes sense'.

'You did that with other older men' 'what are you saying?'.

'Maybe it was wrong but you're hardly the innocent party dad said you were promiscuous men and women'.

'So was your dad with men even Corey said I found out later I even had an HIV test' 'doesn't everyone'.

'I was just saying how I feel about things now' 'I'm not stopping chatting to my dad' 'I never said you had to'. 'If you want to see him it's your right you know'.

'Maybe if I'd have been in contact when I was younger'. 'I wouldn't have turned out like this' 'he never took an interest' 'I bet you never let him!'

'Too many women think they can stop men seeing their own kids!' 'it wasn't like that! I married Andy'.

'Then when we split I thought it was best you lived with mum' 'I understand you palmed me off to someone else!'.

'Nothing I say ever makes you happy' 'why don't you just admit you never loved me or wanted me'.

'I was an inconvenience you were a teenage slag!'.

'You got pregnant and wanted me gone you were probably too far gone to get an abortion so you had to have me'.

'Or maybe once I grew up you lost interest!' 'you don't know anything! I never wanted to have an abortion!'.

'You did with Andy's kid'. 'that was different I was forced to by management' 'no-one forced you to do it'.

'You were eighteen not a kid' 'what's that got to do with anything! it was years ago' 'I'm just saying the truth'.

'You know f**k all about the truth! nothing I say is good enough!' 'you judge me taking drugs not having a job'.

'Some of us have to struggle in life' 'aren't you lucky you never got abused in care' 'here we go again!'.

'No-one cares you grew up in care nothing but an attention seeker and a hypocrite when you went to rehab'. 'For alcohol addiction when you were younger' 'I wanted to be a better person' 'not like me a disappointment!'.
'Yeah you are! I paid for you to go to a good school'. 'College nice apartment flash car anything you ever wanted I got nothing in return! I tried to love you'. 'Be the best mother I could but you always hated me just because I was working in Hollywood'.
'To fund your lifestyle!' 'what lifestyle! hardly living in a mansion am I I don't need your money! I needed you'.
'Your pathetic! my daughters never complained when I worked away in fact they were happy to see me'. 'Didn't Corey look after them when you split up'.
'F**k you! no mother is perfect but I've always loved my children tried to do the best I could'.
'I've had enough of being treated the way you treat me!'. 'I want nothing to do with you anymore unless it's family business Stacey said for years I should give up on you'. 'But I never did until now' 'she's a stuck up bitch!'.
'She's a better person than you'll ever be!' 'you want nothing to do with me well I want nothing to do with you!'. 'And I never did!' 'at least that's something we can agree on' 'yeah and I don't want you calling by my apartment'. 'Ever again! or contacting me on Facebook we're done!'.

'Your not my mum never were Sarah's my mum!'.
'She's your grandmother' 'so never stopped you did it!'.
'What's that supposed to mean?' 'I know' 'know what?'.
'About Kaleigh' 'how?' 'mum told me ten years ago'.
'I overheard a conversation by accident makes sense'.
'What does?' 'why you love her more than me' 'I've tried
loving you and you push me away every time'.
'Kaleigh is a good person and you don't need to be jealous
of her' 'as if! you might not be mother of the year'.
'But at least your educated she's not the sharpest tool in
the box and at least I can string a sentence together'.
'And don't get the shakes' 'please tell me your not
referring to her epilepsy' 'it was a joke'.
'So your sister aunt whatever has a life threatening
condition and you think it's funny' 'your so highly strung'.
'You're a nasty piece of work! and I'm ashamed to call
you my son!' 'I'm ashamed to call you my mother!'.
'Your not to tell Kaleigh the truth she can't find out'.
As Polly said the words she hated having to say them least
of all to her son who she now hated 'I'll think about it!'.
'I've always protected Kaleigh so she can have a good life
'what about my life!' 'I've said all I've got to say'.
'I'm not brawling with you in the street let's say goodbye
and I never have to see you again'.

*Polly watched as Luke walked off how could he have*
*kept it a secret that he knew about Kaleigh.*
*Was that why he hated her so much? then she told herself*
*he'd always been that way since he was a teenager.*
*She felt sad the way their relationship had turned out*
*but that was down to him.*
*A few days later Polly headed down on the train to*
*London to see Louie one of her closest friends.*
*They'd now been friends for fifteen years she didn't know*
*what she'd do without him he was funny camp.*
*And always made her feel better if things went wrong*
*in her life she needed to talk to someone about her son.*
*No-one else understood what she was going through.*
*Polly was still upset over the cruel things he'd said.*
*Accusing her of making up the fact she'd been abused*
*by her history teacher calling her a teenage slag.*
*Bringing up the fact she'd had an abortion when she*
*was eighteen something she tried to forget.*
*Slagging off Kaleigh how could Luke be so cruel her*
*own son she had done the right thing stopping contact.*
*She had nothing to say to him if that's what he thought*
*of her Polly arrived at Louie's Soho apartment.*
*As she went up he seemed happy to see her 'darling you*
*look great have you lost weight' 'for the time being'.*
*'You know I'm a yo-yo dieter' 'drink?' 'yeah please'.*

'I have Fentiman's Victorian Lemonade' 'sounds great'.
Louie poured her some 'and orange and lemon cake'.
'You're a great host' 'only the best for my friends so
how's things?' 'ok' 'just ok?' 'could be better'.
'But you don't wanna hear about my problems' 'yes I do'.
'Tell me' 'it's Luke' 'still estranged?' 'I was hoping we
could sort things I went to his apartment'.
'The one you paid a fortune for' 'that's the one'.
'He's doing cocaine I saw a bowl in the apartment
and he says he's selling drugs cannabis'.
'According to Luke he's helping the community with health
problems if it was anyone else it might be believable'.
'He's in contact with James his dad I said I look back
and regret our relationship that it was inappropriate'.
'He thinks I'm overreacting that it's my fault because
I wanted to have sex is he right? I know he was older'.
'I thought it was fun at the time and he was gay so it was
ok now I'm not so sure' 'how old was he?' 'twenty nine'.
'I was thirteen fourteen' 'gay or not it was wrong'.
'Luke doesn't see it like that he says I was a teenage slag'.
'No-one should take advantage of a teenager'.
'Especially when you'd come from living in care'.
'Their in contact on Facebook he works in Dublin as a
drag queen Luke won't tell me what they chat about'.
'He says if he'd had a father growing up you know'.

'That I ruined his life' 'he had Stacey's dad Paul
he was like a step-dad it's not like he had the life you did'.
'He doesn't see it like that he hates me' 'I don't know why'.
'You're a great person' 'he says he'll always see Sarah
as his mum even though I said she's his gran'.
'I thought it was for the best mum looking after him'.
'Anyway I think he would always have turned out how
he is I don't know what went wrong'.
'I tried to be a good mum' 'you are he had your dad'.
'Your gran yeah you worked in Hollywood but you always
saw him as much as you could' 'I saw him the other day'.
'I asked him if he might come see me in panto at
Christmas he said he wasn't interested'.
'Then we got into a row he said I was an attention seeker'.
'And a bitch he said he was ashamed to call me his
mother he hates me so much and I never knew why'
'He called Stacey a stuck up bitch was mean about
Kaleigh' 'why what have they done?'.
'Stacey said I should give up on him she was right'
'And Kaleigh she's his Aunt' Louie said Polly thought
for a moment whether to tell him about Kaleigh.
She decided the time wasn't right 'I've decided to go no
contact I'm fed up the way he treats me' 'good for you'.
'I know he's my son but I can't put up with his behaviour
anymore' 'I agree you're a great person'.

'You did your best none of this is your fault I can't begin to imagine some of the things you went through as a child'. 'You've no idea' 'he should be supporting you not accusing you of lying' 'your right Louie' 'I know I am'. 'There's no rule book that says families have to be perfect'. 'So how's things with you?' 'they've been better'. 'What's wrong?' Polly asked 'I found out I'm HIV positive' 'I'm sorry' 'it's not me I've always been faithful to Lance'. 'And I took a test before we got together it means he's been seeing other men' 'I'm sorry'. 'When I got married I wanted it to be a proper marriage'. 'I know a lot of gay couples have an open marriage'. 'I didn't want it to be like that' 'did you talk to him?'. 'We're separated' 'you should have said' 'he didn't deny it he said he'll take a test I don't know if he has'. 'I still love him but I can't be with someone I can't trust'. 'Are you on medication?' 'yes I feel ok it was a shock'. 'I cried for days I try not to think about it' 'it's not like years ago people with HIV can live as long as anyone'. 'If you need anyone to talk to with my sister having it'. 'Thanks Polly you're the best' Louie said his voice quivering 'it's ok how's ragdoll?' Louie asked. 'Cor's great I met her ex-fiancée Amy from her College days anyway Corey invited her round I was jealous'.

'I had to pretend I was ok about it she came with her fiancée Melanie they were nice we ate Chinese'.
'We had a great time it was nice to spend time with another lesbian couple she's an artist'.
'And Melanie's a DJ' 'that's good you made some new friends mine will probably abandon me'.
'When they find out I have HIV' 'then their not your real friends so you haven't told anyone?' 'not yet'.
'Apart from Rod he won't tell anyone he's great'.
'How is your brother?' 'Rod's been fired from his job as a chef ten years he worked he's a great cook' 'why?'.
'They found out about his criminal past new management did a check on all employees' 'they didn't know before'.
'No Rod knew he wouldn't get a job if he told the truth'.
'He changed his surname' 'can't he sue for unfair dismissal?' 'no because of his criminal past'.
'But he worked so hard to turn his life around can't he get another chef job?' 'he can try you know how it is'.
'If you've been to prison he's gonna try and get some temporary Christmas work just until he finds something'.
'Anyway looks like we're all gonna have a rubbish Christmas' 'no Louie not if I can help it'.
'Even if you and Lance aren't together you'll have me'.
'Cor we can come to you or you could come to Dublin'.
'Or the Wirral' 'thanks what would I do without you'.

As Corey walked through the streets of Dublin it was
a cold Autumn day the leaves had begun to fall.
She was meeting Kitty they were going shopping.
As one of her oldest friends they had the kind of friendship
where they might not see each other for weeks.
And it didn't matter things would click into place.
They always texted and kept in touch even when they
weren't working together they'd met around age nineteen.
As bandmates despite spending so much time together
they got on well Kitty knew all of Corey's secrets.
And had been there through everything marriage
and children her problems with her brother.
She didn't know what she'd do without her Corey
waited outside of her favourite shop she spied Kitty.
In the distance she was wearing a teal green coat which
looked good with her blonde hair 'Cor you look good'.
'You look better I like the coat' 'thanks it's new'.
'Julian McDonald' 'I love his stuff especially those
Star photo frames' Corey replied 'let's go to Annie's'.
'Have a milkshake' Kitty suggested 'love one' Annie's
was one of their favourite coffee shops.
Despite being from London Kitty knew Dublin well.
Aside from the time they spent their touring she was
also married to bandmate Mike Corey's cousin.
And divided her time between the UK & Ireland.

They sat down inside as they ordered their favourite coffee cake and chocolate milkshakes 'so any gossip?'.

Kitty asked 'Polly's estranged from her son'.

'I thought they had been for years' 'I mean for good this time' 'how come?' 'he's been treating her badly for years'. 'He slagged off everyone keeps saying what a bad mother Polly was he deals drugs cannabis' 'really'.

'He jokes that he's helping people he doesn't want to do anything with his life'.

'Except hang around with other criminals you should hear the things he says about Polly'.

'And he made fun of Kaleigh she said for having a stammer and having epilepsy anyway Polly says that's it'. 'Their relationship is over' 'he doesn't sound like a very nice person' 'he's not and we had dinner with Amy my ex'.

'You and Polly how did that happen?' 'I saw her in the street and I ended up inviting her over to our house'. 'I always felt things ended badly years ago we had dinner with her and her partner Melanie' 'how did Polly feel?'.

'I thought she'd hate it but it was great we had Chinese'. 'I think I'd be jealous if it was Mike's ex so are you and Polly gonna get remarried?' 'I don't know I'd like to'. 'But things are great between us' 'I guess let me know if you do and please can I be bridesmaid' 'of course'.

'So what about you?' 'not up to much just getting ready for Christmas Mike's looking forward to it'.

'He's good at talking about things like when the stuff with Daniel happened he's always been there for me'.

'Have you seen him since the funeral?' 'not really'.

'He messages me on Facebook' 'if it was me I wouldn't give him the time of day' 'I know it's more about Nicky'.

'If she ever found out why we fell out' 'why would that be a bad thing' 'she loves him they've always been close'.

'So he sexually abused you touched you up kissed you'.

'Then date raped you and attacked you that night he hit me when we were married he's not right'.

'Daniel doesn't respect women' 'I won't forgive him for what he did' 'he doesn't deserve to be forgiven'.

'In fact he should be in jail what if there's other victims'.

'Women ex-girlfriends' 'I have thought about that'.

'Nicky we never got on when I was a teenager and over the last few years we've gotten close'.

'What if she didn't believe me and never spoke to me again' 'surely she must have wondered'.

'Why you didn't speak for seven years' 'maybe'.

'She just kept asking us to make it up that's the only reason I did for her' 'it's your choice I couldn't do it'.

'Be in contact or even near any man who did what he did to you I know families are complicated just be careful'.

'Never let him be alone in a room with you' 'I won't'.
'Promise' 'yes' 'good I wouldn't ever want anything like
that to happen to you again' Corey knew Kitty was right.
That she shouldn't have anything to do with her brother.
Corey also vowed one day soon she'd tell Nicky
everything that had happened with her brother.
After cake and milkshakes they ventured to
Changing Seasons a seasonal shop in town.
That sold autumn & winter based items such as wreaths.
And Christmas things 'it's so windy today' the shop
assistant said as they ventured into the shop.
'I know lovely wreaths' Kitty said as they looked around.
'They are lovely we could end up bankrupt shopping here'
Kitty joked as the shop assistant smiled.
Corey spied a light up Halloween pumpkin and a witch
doll Kitty looked at carved wooden fruit in a basket.
'Mum would love this shop and Danny' Corey thought
about Kitty's brother he was great fun very camp.
'Cor' they turned around it was Nicky 'fancy seeing you
here great shop' 'I know' 'hi Kitty' 'hi Nicky'.
'Long time no see busy with the restaurant' 'always'.
'I probably spend more time on social media these days'.
'As is the nature of business I love it though and Corey is
great helping to promote the restaurant' 'I try my best'.
'More than that she's the best sister I could ever have'.

'Listen talking of family Dan's having a dinner'.
'At his house with his fiancée you'll come' 'yes'.
'I mean it's just a relaxed meal Liza will be cooking'.
'And we can all drink wine catch up on old times'.
'It's great now your back in contact Kitty you could come'.
'I would but we didn't part on good terms' 'course sorry'.
'Maybe I'll come to the restaurant sometime' 'that would
be great' 'dinner on the house' 'even better' Kitty smiled.
Corey hated the fact they had to pretend to be happy.
About the fact she was being forced to have dinner with
her brother she wished she could tell her sister the truth.
But knew it wouldn't be worth the trouble and she'd
probably never speak to her again.
Corey knew she would have to go hopefully she wouldn't
have to stay long and could make her excuses and leave.
'I'm buying this wreath' Kitty said as she went to the till.
'You'll love Liza she's a few years younger than Dan
'And since he's getting married it'll be great for you to
get to know her' 'course I can't wait to meet her'.
'I've brought pink champagne in the sale'.
'It'll be a great night I've got to get back home dinner's
next week I'll text you the details say bye Kitty bye Cor'.
Corey watched as her sister left the store 'a family meal
with him' 'I'd rather not go' 'then cancel' 'I can't'.
'She'd wonder why' 'maybe you should tell her the truth'.

'I can't' 'ok it's up to you it's your life' 'he's with his fiancée now' 'he's still a sex abuser maybe he's changed'. 'But I doubt it' 'me too I'll leave early if I can'. 'Your sister will be there so it'll probably be ok' 'agree'. 'Let's go home' Corey enjoyed shopping but it was such a cold day that they were both happy to be in from the cold. Stacey looked at the date block on top the bookcase in her living room in her London house it said October 1st. She had always loved autumn the leaves turning brown. The cooler weather but still nice enough to take walks. Stacey checked her phone her sister was coming to see her and was supposed to be coming over for 1pm. So they could have a late lunch Kim wasn't the best at time keeping even so she wondered where she was. Her phone beeped she had a text 'hey Stace sorry I'm late'. 'Looking at gifts for mum's birthday be there around 2pm'. 'Hope that's ok love Kim xxx' 'that's fine'. 'Hope you get something nice see you soon'. 'Pizza will be waiting lol'

Stacey watched Loose Women as she sipped dandelion & burdock waiting for Kim's arrival. As Kim walked through Oxford Street it was busy as it always was it was a Friday afternoon.

*She ventured towards Harrods as a child she'd rarely*
*gone due to how expensive it was.*
*Raised mostly by her Aunt Veronica money had been*
*tight growing up in Hackney.*
*Kim could only ever afford the cheapest items like*
*a teddy bear or a Christmas decoration.*
*Now as an adult she could afford anything she wanted.*
*Thanks to her girlband Crème who had been successful*
*in America she wasn't as rich as her sister.*
*But she was comfortably off with two houses.*
*One in New York and one in Essex Kim ventured*
*into the store she always felt better with someone.*
*In posh department stores as a teenager she had done*
*some shoplifting but wouldn't dare try it now.*
*Even so she felt like she was being watched she never*
*knew what to get her mother she had different tastes.*
*When it came to fashion & make-up her mother*
*was classy wore jackets and pencil skirts.*
*She wore more outrageous things although that day*
*she was dressed more conservatively than usual.*
*Wearing a dark green coat Stacey took after their mother.*
*They had similar tastes in fashion and personality wise.*
*She was the more sensible one where as she was the*
*naughty adventurous one and always had been.*
*Kim decided buying jewellery would be the best option.*

*You couldn't go wrong unless it was something*
*really tasteless she looked around 'can I help you?'.*
*A sales assistant asked 'just looking it's my mum's*
*birthday' 'what kind of things does she like?' 'earrings'.*
*'And necklaces usually silver' 'we have this four leaf*
*clover necklace' 'I think Stacey might prefer that'.*
*'My sister her dad's Irish I've seen it the perfect present'.*
*'That silver locket' 'nice isn't it it opens up you can put*
*a photo in it' 'I'll take it oh what's the chain length?'.*
*'Mum only wears twenty inch chains' 'we have different*
*lengths we could do a twenty inch' 'great and for Stacey'.*
*'I'm gonna take the other necklace it's Stacey birthday*
*soon then I won't have to worry about a present'.*
*Kim was happy she'd found her mum's present.*
*The assistant wrapped and boxed her present 'thanks'.*
*'I hope your mum and sister like the jewellery' 'me too'.*
*Kim browsed the homeware section as she noticed a*
*good looking mixed-race man older.*
*He was wearing a black polo neck jumper a flat cap.*
*Suddenly she realised who it was her old step-father.*
*Richie the man who had been a father figure to her as a*
*child age eleven she had started seeing more of her mum.*
*Who had just started going out with him later they*
*married when she turned seventeen they split.*
*And then lost touch Kim had missed him over the years.*

*And later spied on him on Facebook he had two daughters*
*they looked like her with coffee coloured skin.*
*Their mother was also mixed-race she looked like her*
*mum.*
*Kim wondered if he regretted splitting up with her.*
*She also wondered if he ever thought about her probably*
*not why would he just an ex's daughter he once knew.*
*Richie often posted photos of his wife and children*
*together out and about at events doing activities.*
*It was because her real father had never taken an*
*interest that she had been thinking about him.*
*Kim decided she would go speak to him say hello*
*before she got a chance a teenage girl appeared.*
*It was his daughter 'dad I've found something'.*
*'This soda streamer and a light up pumpkin' Kim had*
*noticed the Halloween items 'let's go check it out'.*
*She watched they looked so happy suddenly she had*
*a flashback to meeting her real dad a few years ago.*
*It hadn't gone well as he constantly talked about her*
*two sisters and brother who she had never met.*
*Then his wife had turned up angry at seeing her.*
*As she said that her children didn't know who she was.*
*And didn't want to explain her father had left a*
*voice message apologising it was too late.*
*Kim hadn't seen him since and didn't really want to.*

*Andy her mum's partner of twenty years and Stacey's*
*uncle had been more of a father figure to her*
*And had always taken an interest in her life Kim told*
*herself to forget about Richie.*
*He could never be a father to her he had his own family.*
*She left the store before he could see her she spied a taxi.*
*As she got in as she arrived at Stacey's house she felt*
*happy her sister had always been there for her.*
*Her mum Aunt Veronica she didn't need a dad.*
*She already had a family Kim told herself Stacey opened*
*the door 'sorry about being late' 'it's fine plenty of pizza'.*
*'Dandelion and burdock' 'love it you're the best'.*
*'Find anything nice?' 'a necklace a silver locket' 'great'.*
*'I hope mum likes it' 'she loves silver' 'like you I'm more*
*of a gold kinda girl' 'I'll warm up the pizza'.*
*'It only came out ten minutes ago where did you get*
*the necklace?' 'Harrods mum will be happy'.*
*'She loves that place' Kim joked 'pizza' Stacey said.*
*'Thanks' 'was town busy?' 'as always seriously I can't*
*take London shopping anymore I saw my old step-dad'.*
*'Richie' 'the guy mum was married to years ago' 'yes him'.*
*'He looked good actually' 'what did you chat about?'.*
*'Nothing he didn't know I was there' 'why?' 'he was with*
*his daughter they seemed happy after you know dad'.*

'I'm not sure I could take another rejection' 'why would he reject you?' 'his ex's child it was twenty three years ago'.
'I'm just a distant memory' 'don't say that' 'why not'.
'It's the truth' 'Kim he was your dad for a few years'.
'Exactly why would he want to know me now'.
'Me and Christian aren't together he still cares about Tally hangs out with her he's more her dad'.
'Than James ever was' 'it's different' 'how?' 'because it is' 'no it's exactly the same Christian and me were married a few years same as mum and Richie' 'she never sees him'.
'You're still good friends with Christian' 'they parted on bad terms?' 'no mum just never saw him again'.
'After all an ex is an ex she said he was nice she never really explained why they split' 'did he cheat on her?'.
'I don't know I don't think we should ask' Kim said.
'I agree but don't say your just a memory I'm sure Richie still thinks of you' 'I doubt it he only loves his daughters'.
'Which is probably how it should be I always wanted a dad and I found him and it went wrong but Richie...'.
'I always thought of as a father figure to me'.
'We haven't been in contact since I was seventeen'.
'I guess having a dad made me feel complete did meeting mum make you feel that way?' 'yes I was fourteen'.
'And before that Wendy was like a mother figure to me'.

'Even though she was my Aunt I didn't think I needed
a mother then when I became a teenager I knew'.
'That I wanted to meet my real mother I was lucky
because we got on well and she loved me'.
'And I only wish it could have been the same with
your dad' 'screw him and his wife I've got you'.
'Mum and Aunt Vee' 'and Andy' 'he's the best step-dad
ever I suppose it's cause we're coming up to Christmas'.
'I'm thinking more about family' me too I lost touch
with someone years ago as well' 'who?' Kim asked.
'My Aunt Shirley' 'who's that?' 'dad and Wendy's sister'.
'Every time she visited we had a great time she moved
to Ireland when she was twenty one she used to visit'.
'When I lived in Ireland once or twice then one day she
stopped visiting and I never saw her again I asked Wendy'.
'When Shirley would be visiting I was like eighteen
she said she was busy I said we could visit her'.
'And Wendy changed the subject I tried again a few years
later it was the same thing'.
'It's like some kind of mystery why she stopped seeing
everyone' 'maybe they had a falling out' Kim suggested.
'What about?' 'could be anything when was the last time
you saw her?' 'seventeen I was living in Blackpool'.
'Before I returned to London to live with you and mum'.
'Did you ever try and contact her on Facebook?' 'yeah'.

*'I was like early twenties I found her she had just got married why didn't she invite us dad's side of the family'.*
*'I requested her and she never accepted me as a friend'.*

## Obsession

*'Then Andy did and he got no response so she disappeared
from our family' 'you're a great person and so is Andy'.
'So it's her loss' Kim said trying to make Stacey feel better
she wondered what had happened.
To make Shirley cut them off Stacey consoled herself
with the possibility her dad and Shirley had rowed.
And never made it up she told herself to forget about
Shirley but she couldn't as she thought of the memories.
That evening Corey got ready to go to her brother's house
for a meal she'd tried to forgive him for his behaviour.
But couldn't she knew he was now engaged and had
stopped drinking she still felt uneasy being near him.
He had apologised blaming his drinking Corey didn't
know whether he was sorry or not.
But she had to act normal in front of Nicky.
One day Corey hoped she could tell her what Daniel
was really like but until then she had to hide her secret.
She had chosen a grey long sleeved top black trousers
and small silver hoop earrings making the effort.
But not going over the top she was going for the sake
of her sister not her brother it would be ok.
Corey told herself she wouldn't have to stay long hopefully
Polly didn't know she was going she had lied.*

*Saying she was seeing an old friend if Polly knew the truth*
*she wouldn't be happy Corey told herself it was a one off.*
*To keep the family happy she'd meet her brother's fiancée*
*have a few glasses of champagne then leave.*
*As she arrived for six as she rang the doorbell of her*
*sister's apartment 'hey Cor' 'hi' her sister looked cheery.*
*'Everyone's here come in' Corey pretended to be happy*
*at seeing everyone 'you look great' her brother said.*
*'You too' 'this is Liza this is my other sister' 'hi Corey'.*
*'I'm a big fan' 'thanks' 'I'll pour the champagne'.*
*Nicky said 'I'm doing broccoli in pastry and for dessert*
*black forest cake' 'sounds great' Corey said happily.*
*'It is trust me tried it out last week in the restaurant'.*
*'I love food this is so great having a sister-in-law*
*that owns a restaurant' Liza said.*
*'Me and Liza have been getting to know each other*
*the past few months' Corey felt slightly jealous.*
*She knew her sister had other friends but it sounded like*
*they were close from things she'd read on social media.*
*'I have something for you' Daniel said 'me' Corey said.*
*'As a peace offering to make it up to you us not talking*
*for years I hope you like it'.*
*'Think of it as a early Christmas present' 'you shouldn't*
*have' 'I wanted to' Daniel handed Corey a silver box.*

*With a black bow on it something told her it might*
*be expensive she opened it a silk night dress.*
*A red bra and knickers Corey was in shock it was the*
*kind of gift you'd give to a girlfriend or your wife.*
*'Cor say something' Nicky said 'I love it! I just wasn't*
*expecting anything like that thanks their lovely'.*
*'I hoped you'd like it' 'I do' 'I really like them'.*
*Nicky looked at the box 'why do you think I found*
*someone like Dan not just good looking'.*
*'But great taste in gifts for women unlike some men'.*
*Liza was clearly in love with Daniel maybe she was*
*good for him but the fact remained he abused women.*
*Corey wondered if there had been others especially since*
*he'd been violent to Kitty when they had been married.*
*When she'd told him she might not be able to have*
*children he'd smacked her across the face.*
*'I'm glad you like the lingerie hope Polly likes it'.*
*'I'm sure she will' 'I take it your still the same bra size'.*
*'Oh yes I am and I love the nightie' 'great another*
*glass of champagne' Nicky asked 'thanks'.*
*Corey knew she was acting making out everything was ok.*
*What should have been a normal family meal never*
*could be she didn't trust her brother.*
*Why couldn't he have given her perfume or a Christmas*
*decoration or any other gift.*

*Instead he'd given her Agent Provocateur lingerie.*
*That seemed to suggest one thing maybe she'd got it*
*wrong maybe it was the first gift he thought of.*
*Or maybe he had another agenda he was with Liza*
*in a relationship that everything could go back to normal.*
*But it never could she still had flashbacks.*
*To the night he'd attacked her tried to rape her.*
*If her mother hadn't come in when she did she didn't*
*know what would have happened.*
*Corey told herself she had to try and move on forget*
*the past it was harder than she thought.*
*Everyone knew what Daniel was like Polly,Stacey, Louie,*
*Kitty, Mike her mother everyone except Nicky.*
*Her own sister Corey wasn't sure she wanted to keep it a*
*secret anymore that her brother had sexually abused her.*
*That he had been obsessed with her and maybe still was.*
*But she knew it would be even worse if Nicky didn't*
*believe her and the whole family turned against her.*
*Never spoke to her again it was at times like that Corey*
*realised how dysfunctional her family had been.*
*Her alcoholic physically abusive father her distant mother*
*who always put her other kids first.*
*And made her feel like she was never good enough.*
*It was at times like that Corey was glad of being with*
*Polly and having her close circle of friends in her life.*

*To discuss her problems with Nicky served up dinner*
*the broccoli in pastry tasted delicious.*
*'Are these on the menu?' Corey asked 'I think they will be'.*
*'I wanted to test them out first before I put them on the*
*restaurant menu' 'I agree with Corey they should be'.*
*Liza said 'I'm so glad you two made it up' Nicky said.*
*'I bet you can't even remember why you fell out'.*
*'It was my fault' Daniel said 'so why did you fall out?'.*
*Corey panicked what could she say? 'Polly a row'.*
*She lied 'it's all sorted now' 'must have been serious'.*
*'Maybe it was at the time anyway I'm just glad I've*
*made it up with my sister' Daniel looked happy.*
*He was probably glad she hadn't said anything.*
*'This is great it's almost Christmas I'm hoping we could*
*all see each other Christmas Day' Nicky suggested.*
*'Course wouldn't miss it for the world we must go*
*Christmas shopping' 'of course Cor'.*
*'Maybe you could come too' Nicky said 'I'll see what*
*I'm doing' 'you have to my sister and my new best friend'.*
*'A girly day out we could have' 'I'll try and come'.*
*Corey said 'great only October but you have to plan*
*ahead' after dessert they chatted somehow she felt left out.*
*Nicky and Liza seemed to have become close in a short*
*time with lots of in jokes.*
*She had no choice but to talk to her brother.*

*Even if she didn't want to 'listen I know it's gonna take*
*you a while to forgive me but I'm sorry' Daniel said.*
*'I really do want us to start again have a normal*
*relationship' 'me too' Corey agreed.*
*'I want the family to get along' 'your not just my sister'.*
*'You were always my best friend' he hugged her*
*she didn't know what to feel was he genuine?.*
*Or lulling her into a false sense of security she*
*remembered what Kitty had said*
*That her brother didn't respect women and that he might*
*have done things to other women what if he had?.*
*Corey left early going home that evening Daniel texted*
*her to say how much he'd enjoyed the meal she replied.*
*Saying she had too what else could she do.*
*That Tuesday afternoon Corey had gone shopping with*
*Kitty she'd had a few days to think about the meal.*
*She'd had with her brother & sister as she walked through*
*the indoor market with Kitty 'so how did the dinner go?'.*
*'It was ok until…' 'until what?' 'he brought me a red bra*
*and knickers' 'no way!' 'from anyone else it would great'.*
*'He's obviously not over his obsession with you' 'I thought*
*he was he said he wanted a normal relationship'.*
*'Like how it should be brother and sister' 'it's not normal*
*sending your own sister sexy lingerie'.*
*'He said he hoped Polly would like it' 'bulls\*\*t!'.*

'He was covering himself using her as an excuse'.
'What did Nicky say?' 'not much they all said how nice it
was of him' 'if they only knew what he was really like'.
'I'm sure your mum wouldn't be happy if she knew'.
'You'd been anywhere near him' 'they asked why we fell
out' 'what did you say?'.
'That it was something to do with Polly I didn't know
what else to say' 'can I ask you a question?' 'anything'.
'Have you ever been attracted to him?' 'not really'.
'Steve's the only man I've ever really fancied he knows
about the abuse when we started going out he told me'.
'That his brother sexually abused his sister I felt like
he understood me I told him how Daniel liked me'.
'More than he should' 'you should tell Nicky the truth'.
'She'll find out one day' 'she wouldn't believe me she
would hate me she loves Daniel more than me'.
'So what was his fiancée like?' 'she was ok she and
Nicky they've become really good friends'.
'I suppose I feel a bit left out' 'you've always got me'.
'Look at that stall' Kitty said spying a cool bag area of the
market 'I'll be one second' Corey said looking at incense.
'See you in a minute' Corey smelled some scents looking
at a Turkish lamp as she did she spied a man.
Something about him seemed familiar who was he?.

*Suddenly she worked it out she felt jumpy it was Mr Cleves*
*her old History teacher the man who'd groomed Polly.*
*As a teenager given her alcohol and raped her he'd done*
*a few years in prison for his many victims all young girls.*
*From various schools but it was many years ago.*
*He was now a free man she would have loved to give him*
*a peace of her mind she felt uneasy.*
*Maybe he wouldn't recognise her 'Corey hello long time*
*no see it's been years you've hardly aged'.*
*She hated the way he was smiling at her she'd been lucky*
*not to have been one of his victims like Polly and Victoria.*
*His niece the things Victoria had told her how every*
*weekend he would come into her room rape her.*
*Or touch her where he shouldn't how she'd wanted to*
*kill herself several times as an adult because of him.*
*Now he was acting like he didn't have a care in the world.*
*'How's Polly? I heard your back together' 'you should be*
*in jail for what you did to her' 'I was in jail'.*
*'But I've been out for years life is good you know what you*
*are a pikey bitch! tried to hide the fact you were a gypsy'.*
*'At school' 'I never hid it I just didn't say anything'.*
*'Same thing' 'I know what you are' 'well I'd love to say it's*
*been great meeting you again' 'Cor coming' Kitty called.*
*'Your friend's calling you better go maybe I'll see you*
*again' Corey hoped not she ventured over to see Kitty.*

*Shaking inside 'Cor check out this bag' 'it's great'.*
*She decided to act normal and wondered whether she*
*should tell Polly and Victoria she'd seen him round town.*
*That evening Corey dropped Kitty off at Mike's as she*
*called in to see her mother on the outskirts of town.*
*She left around 8pm as she drove home.*
*As she listened to the radio after a while she became*
*aware someone was following her.*
*Corey told herself she was imagining it but there it was*
*the same car going faster behind her.*
*It meant she had to drive faster suddenly she had a*
*thought what if it was him Mr Cleves? she had to lose him.*
*Her heart was beating Corey felt scared they approached*
*the traffic lights she looked over the car was opposite her.*
*Part of her didn't want to look it was him he smiled.*
*As he drove in front of her Corey deliberately drove slow*
*so she didn't have to see him again.*
*That evening she had never been more glad to get home.*
*Next time she'd drive with someone that Friday evening*
*she went out for a takeaway.*
*She called in for some petrol before going home she saw*
*him again he was going to pay as her car arrived.*
*Corey waited until he'd driven off before getting out.*
*She'd seen him three times in one week and didn't want*
*to see him again Corey decided not to tell Polly.*

*About seeing him he was obviously dangerous.*

*Maybe she could tell Victoria the following afternoon*
*Corey met up with Mrs Rayworth at her house.*

*To many people it may have seemed odd being good*
*friends with her old headmistress from school.*

*To Corey it wasn't there was an eighteen year age gap.*

*But Corey never saw it like that they'd had chats at school*
*but Corey never imagined they'd be friends.*

*Then one day after she left school when she was at*
*College they'd chatted.*

*Mrs Rayworth had told Corey she was secretly a lesbian.*

*Who had married a man to have an easier life to her*
*surprise a year later they met again.*

*This time Corey had been escorting meeting women.*

*For sex age seventeen Mrs Rayworth or Amy which*
*was her real name had been one of her clients.*

*They became even closer Corey had never told anyone*
*not even Polly that they'd slept together.*

*They'd lost touch for years until a few years ago.*

*Now Corey visited her house regularly they chatted*
*about everything and got on well.*

*She had been the one to make Mr Cleves leave the school.*

*Get him arrested Corey knew she had to tell her that she'd*
*seen him she knocked on the door waiting for a reply.*

*'Come in' 'thanks' 'I have made fruit tarts I hope you'll
have one' 'course' 'apple juice' 'thanks'.*

*Corey took off her coat as she sat down 'any gossip?'.*
*'Yes' Corey replied 'tell me' 'I saw...him' 'him?'.*

*'Mr Cleves' 'oh my god!' 'I hadn't seen him since school'.*
*'Where did you see him?' 'the market I hate him he made
me feel jumpy' 'did he say anything to you?'.*

*'He asked how Polly was I said he should be in jail for
what he did to her he called me a pikey'.*

*'Then he followed me home tried to run me off the road'.*
*'He made me drive faster than I should then I saw him'.*
*'At the traffic lights and he was smiling I hate him and
then I saw him at the petrol station he didn't see me'.*
*'I don't know what I'll do if I see him again I haven't
told Polly because she might be upset'.*

*'If she was reminded of him' 'well if I see him in town
I'll give him a piece of my mind' 'please don't'.*

*'He's dangerous he might run you off the road too'.*

*'Ok but if he does anything like that again you must tell
the police there could have been an accident'.*

*'I'm more concerned about Victoria and Polly if they
find out he's around' 'he did his time years ago'.*

*'And at some point he was going to get out he should be on
the sex offenders register he shouldn't be around women'.*

'Like my brother' 'how are things? still in touch with him?' 'yes I went for a meal I had to meet his fiancée'.
'Nicky and Liza they've become good friends' 'what was she like?' 'nice she has no idea what he's like'.
'And I can't tell her' 'I think someone should he hit his ex-wife and what he tried to do to you'.
'He's dangerous to women men like him need to pay for their crimes and I'm betting there's other victims'.
'It's just hard because he's my brother if Nicky didn't believe me I'd be cast out of the family'.
'You've always got me Stacey Polly I know you don't want to tell anyone what he's like I always think of Victoria'.
'The things Mr Cleves did how you said every other weekend he'd come round the house'.
'Make her have sex with him a fourteen year old girl'.
'Who's mother had abandoned her father wasn't around'.
'He preyed on her he must have ruined her life I wish I'd have known why she was the way she was'.
'As a teacher I should have looked for the signs'.
'You couldn't have known none of us did and I never told anyone my dad hit me maybe I will tell my sister'.
'But it has to be the right time' 'I hope you do'.
'So what's happening in your life' 'not much' 'how are things with Elsa?' 'great we're engaged' 'that's great'.
'Do I get an invite to the wedding?' 'of course'.

## Revealing the truth

'Does Pete know?' 'yes and he's happy for me'.
'That I can finally be myself it's funny all the time we
were married he never suspected about my sexuality'.
'Probably because I don't look like the typical lesbian'.
'You know feminine I thought he'd never want to speak to
me again but it's made us closer he's seeing a woman too'.
'It's all worked out great I couldn't have come out years
ago the way things were in society it's different now'.
'Oh I forgot to tell you we're putting together a
school reunion all from years gone by'.
'Like the eighties and the nineties which of course was
when I was there all the teachers and students'.
'So will you come?' 'of course' 'Polly' 'I know she'll want
to be there and Victoria I guess I can tolerate Marion'.
'For one evening' 'I forgot about her' 'last I heard she
was trying to make it as an actress' Corey said.
'She made homophobic comments about me got me fired
from my job at the pub' 'I remember'.
'So when's it happening?' 'we're still working out the dates
it'll be great we can remember the old times' 'I can't wait'.
'I'll tell Polly about it' Corey thought a school reunion
was a great idea she was sure Polly would too.

*That afternoon Polly woke she saw her answer phone*
*beeping she had a message she listened it was Luke.*
*He wanted to talk she felt wary their last conversation*
*had ended vowing never to see each other again.*
*Which she still believed was for the best as he said*
*he hated her and would always love Sarah.*
*That she'd been a teenage slag who had deserved*
*to be taken advantage of by older men.*
*Polly wondered if he wanted something money or a new*
*apartment whatever it was she wouldn't give in to him.*
*And couldn't forgive him for his cruel words towards her*
*and Kaleigh Polly rang him back.*
*As they arranged to meet at his apartment he insisted he*
*wasn't in any trouble and wanted them to make things up.*
*She didn't trust him it was 4pm the skies were overcast*
*and Polly didn't know if she was doing the right thing.*
*Maybe Luke was really sorry for what he said.*
*Or maybe he'd finally realised he'd gone too far.*
*He answered the door as he smiled 'come in mother'.*
*Polly didn't like his tone of voice 'I thought we agreed*
*not to see each other' 'maybe I had a change of heart'.*
*Polly knew Luke too well he wanted something she had*
*a thought that maybe she could talk him round.*
*About Kaleigh convince him to stay quiet if she ever*
*found out she wanted to be the one to tell her the truth.*

*It had to be done properly 'cup of tea?' he asked.*
*'Just a cold drink' 'lemonade' 'yeah' she sat down on*
*the sofa she was curious why he'd invited her round.*
*After shutting her out of his life maybe it was about his*
*father or Kaleigh or maybe he was sorry for their row.*
*Maybe her gran or one of her Aunts had talked to him.*
*'I'll get straight to the point I'd like a bigger house'.*
*'Why?' 'because I do like really big in a nice area'.*
*'There's nothing wrong with here' 'there is it's ok'.*
*'But I want a games room big garden everything it's not*
*like you haven't got the money and I want a few million'.*
*'To keep me going' 'I'm not made of money things cost'.*
*'Exactly' 'so that's why you got me here under false*
*pretences!' 'at least I'm being honest'.*
*'I know your game! I knew you wanted something*
*from me well what if I won't buy you a house'.*
*'Then I'll tell Kaleigh the truth I might even make up*
*a few things how you're her real mother'.*
*'But you never wanted her like me' 'I did want her'.*
*'And you' 'so she doesn't know that so do we have a deal'.*
*At that moment Polly had never despised her son so much.*
*It had been a mistake meeting up with him 'no chance!'.*
*'I got you a nice apartment it's not my fault you can't keep*
*it nice if you weren't high all the time!' 'f\*\*k you!'.*

'I'll get what I want!' 'and what do you think mum will say about things' 'I don't care anymore' 'I'm going!'.
'And I know you wouldn't tell Kaleigh the truth'.
'Maybe I will maybe I won't I'll see how I feel' Polly left angry she was worried Luke would tell Kaleigh.
She had to be the one to tell her she couldn't hear it from anyone else she went to see Maggie her best friend.
Of fourteen years Maggie had moved back to the Liverpool area after many years away.
She would know what to do Polly knocked on the door hoping she would be in they chatted.
Maggie suggested she take out an injunction to stop the media reporting anything if Luke did go to the papers.
Somehow Polly felt better about things she'd told Maggie years ago about Kaleigh she had been sworn to secrecy.
And had kept her promise not to tell anyone Maggie had worked as a celebrity P.A for years.
If anyone could keep a secret she could Polly also ended up telling Harmony Kaleigh's daughter.
Although only nineteen she was wise for her age.
Polly decided she was going to tell Christian her brother had always been one of her best friends.
He was great for sharing problems with he gave great advice she knew it was now only a matter of time.

*Before Kaleigh found out the truth with Luke threatening*
*to tell her.*
*That Tuesday afternoon Polly arrived in Brighton.*
*To see her brother he'd moved there after becoming bored*
*with London and how busy it was a taxi took her.*
*To his house on the outskirts of town on the radio was*
*Charles Russell one of her favourite DJ's.*
*With a voice made for radio Stacey had got her into*
*listening to his show they listened to Chic Le Freak.*
*Before arriving Polly got out her case she was staying*
*a few days it was a cold afternoon.*
*She was wearing a Joe Brown purple coat with silver*
*buttons and matching gloves Christian opened the door.*
*'Hi' he said as they hugged 'come in' Polly followed him*
*inside 'how's things?' he asked 'great'.*
*'All the better for seeing you' 'drink?' he asked.*
*'Just a cold drink' he poured some tropical juice.*
*'I can take your case upstairs' he offered 'no it's ok'.*
*'I'll take it in a minute' Polly took off her coat.*
*'I hope you don't mind Stacey's staying she has a gig'.*
*'Two nights in Brighton' 'it's fine I was gonna tell you*
*something I can tell Stacey too' 'is it important?' 'yes'.*
*'Susie' 'Stace' 'this will be great the three of us together*
*for a few days' 'yeah' 'Polly has something to tell us'.*
*'Let me get changed and I'll tell you at tea' 'good idea'.*

'Christian's cooking pasta in a white wine sauce'.
'Sounds amazing' Polly ventured upstairs.
She'd stayed before at Christian's apartment and always had the same room it was useful.
If she had TV appearances in London 'what do you think she's gonna tell us' Stacey asked 'it sounds serious'.
'You don't think she's splitting with Corey'.
'She would have said I think' Polly changed into a T-shirt and jogging trousers as she sipped her tropical juice.
'So what do you have to tell us?' Stacey asked.
'First of all please don't be angry I told Maggie first a few years ago she was sworn to secrecy now Harmony knows'.
'And it's gonna come out anyway so I'd rather you hear it from me first' 'your not ill are you' Christian asked.
'No you know I was sexually abused in care well I was raped when I was eleven I know it sounds shocking'.
'It was anyway I got pregnant' 'I never knew'.
'Did you miscarry?' Stacey asked 'no I had the baby'.
'You gave it up for adoption' 'not exactly I wanted to'.
'But the family wanted me to keep the baby mum aunt Hilary said it wouldn't be right'.
'That no-one could find out so mum had a suggestion'.
'She said she could pretend to be the baby's mother'.
'And I would be her sister' Stacey looked confused for a moment 'Kaleigh no you're her mum!' 'yeah I am'.

*'I thought when I got older I could tell her when she turned eighteen but she got famous as a singer'.*

*'I thought it might ruin her career if she found out'.*

*'Then the years passed and then I realised it was too late'.*

*'And Kaleigh might hate me for lying to her all those years' 'it wasn't your fault you were abused'.*

*'Why didn't you tell us before?' 'I wanted to mum never wanted it to come out it was a family secret'.*

*'I was gonna do it when she turned thirty not long ago mum talked me out of it Luke found out from mum'.*

*'He says he might tell Kaleigh unless I buy him a bigger house' 'he's blackmailing you' Stacey said angry.*

*'Yeah my own son' 'I'm so glad you cut off contact with him' 'Maggie thinks I should take out an injunction'.*

*'In case he goes to the papers to stop the story coming out I know it has to but I wanted to be the one to tell her'.*

*'She'll never speak to me again' 'course she will Kaleigh loves you' 'no Stace I've lied to her all her life'.*

*'You had no choice' 'I know anyway Christmas is coming'.*

*'It'll have to be after' 'I can't believe we never knew'.*

*Christian said shocked at Polly's confession 'sorry'.*

*'That I never told you I wanted to both of you'.*

*'Surely your mum must have known the truth would come out one day' Stacey said 'she never wanted it to'.*

*'As far as she was concerned Kaleigh was her little girl'.*

'Even when she was living with Sue she was her mum'.

'When I was a teenager I knew it was for the best'.

'I didn't really see much of Kaleigh till she was twelve thirteen I always thought about her'.

'When I was living in Ireland if I'd have known I was pregnant I'm sure I would have had an abortion'.

'I was too far along' 'I can't believe you had to have a baby so young' Christian said.

'I guess everything happens for a reason now you know everything about my life'.

'It upsets me to talk about what happened in care'.

'But your my two favourite people in the world'.

'Apart from Maggie' 'Susie you should have told us years ago' 'I know Stace I always wanted to'.

'Mum made me swear never to tell anyone the truth she said that I would ruin Kaleigh's life her career'.

'That she would never speak to me again it's just as she's gotten older it's become harder to hide the truth'.

'To deal with the secrets wen I was in my early twenties'.

'I was busy with my movie career things like that'.

'And I probably couldn't have devoted my time to being a mum but I've been thinking if she had stayed with me'.

'She wouldn't have been abused by Shaun the man who was supposed to be like a step-dad to her'.

'Kaleigh could have had a normal life I know it was impossible me being a child myself I trusted him'.

'That she was better off with her aunt and husband'.

'Because they lived in a nice house were the right age'.

'To have a child that they could give her things I couldn't but she was sexually abused by him that bastard!'.

'Susie it's not your fault you were abused by older men'.

'Who preyed on you and probably others because you were a child in care'.

'You didn't know about the abuse of Kaleigh no-one did'.

'Not even your mum you were a victim' Stacey said.

'Mum always said when I was older we could tell her the truth and I never could I really wanted to so many times'.

'When I was living in L.A you in New York I wanted to tell her then and after we moved back to the UK'.

'She said no it would ruin her life that it would be selfish'.

'That I would be telling her to make myself feel better'.

'No-one should have to carry round a secret for thirty years I couldn't have kept it a secret that long' 'I know'.

'Stace me and mum don't get on and this has always made it worse' 'so many things make sense now conversations'.

'Why you and your mum don't get on' it's part of it but we never really have personality clash anyway...'.

'Now you know' 'you have to tell Kaleigh the truth'.

'I know Stace if she didn't speak me to again what would
I do I've always been her favourite sister' 'I know'.
'Gran says if I died tomorrow she wouldn't know the truth'
'exactly that's why you have to' 'mum will kill me'.
'Surely your mum must realise it's not good for anyone to
keep a secret like this' Christian said 'I'm telling Kaleigh'.
'I've decided after Christmas mum won't like it or Aunt
Hilary' 'it's your life look she might be angry for a while'.
'But I'm sure she would get used to it after a while even
if she didn't want to speak to you'.
'It would be better than living a lie' 'I guess'.
'Doesn't your mum care you were sexually abused'.
'It's never mentioned like everything else deep down
mum isn't a bad person it's jealousy if Kaleigh knew'.
'Then she wouldn't be mum's little girl anymore'.
'She'd still be her biological grandma' Stacey said.
'It wouldn't be the same she's always favoured Kaleigh
over me sometimes it's like I don't exist'.
'Or I never gave birth to her' 'you shouldn't favour
children' parents do she says she feels bad about her past'.
'Being an ex-drug addict me growing up in care'.
'I feel I have for years that she doesn't love me'.
'That she doesn't care how I feel everyone loves Kaleigh'.
'Because she's sweet' and she has special needs ADHD,
Asperger's, epilepsy all those things but she's thirty'.

'She's not a child but sometimes they want to keep her
as one I get that I do too but she's an adult'.
'Who needs to hear the truth' Stacey said 'and your own
son blackmailing you' 'nothing Luke does surprises me'.
'Did you hear about Corey seeing Daniel?' Stacey asked.
'When?' 'not long ago they had a family meal'.
'She shouldn't be anywhere near him' 'she did it to keep
Nicky happy according to Kitty'.
'Corey really didn't want to go and he brought her
Agent Provocateur lingerie' 'she never said'.
'About any meal she must have known I'd be angry'.
'Nicky has no idea about him' 'one day it'll all come out'.
'I won't be able to stop myself telling the truth'.
'Me too' Stacey agreed 'apparently Corey wasn't happy'.
'Being brought lingerie by him' 'he's scum a rapist
bastard! sorry I'm just angry not at Cor him'.
'He tried to rape her then buys her lingerie maybe it's time
Nicky did know the truth' 'I agree we were friends once'.
Stacey said 'Daniel we even sang together on tour'.
'Same he even joked about having a crush on me if only
we had known what he was really like he blackmailed me'.
'At Corey's dad's funeral' Polly confessed 'how?'.
'I was at the buffet he said he knew about Kaleigh'.
'He said one night I was drunk I don't remember'.

'Daniel says I said about Kaleigh he said if I stopped him
trying to make it up with Cor he'd tell everyone the truth'.
'More blackmail' 'you need to tell Kaleigh' Christian said.
'Then no-one can blackmail you anymore' 'I know'.
'And I need to talk to Cor as well keep him away from her'
'how are you gonna do that?' Stacey asked.
'Cutting his dick off would be a good start' they laughed.
'I wish don't worry he'll get his just desserts one day'.
Stacey said 'and not a day too soon' Polly thought about
what Christian and Stacey had said.
They knew she was right that it was time to tell Kaleigh
the truth whatever the consequences.
Polly knew she was tired of being blackmailed by her son
her mother it was time for the drama to end.
But she knew things might never be the same again.
When Polly returned to Dublin she finally told Corey the
truth about Kaleigh they also talked about Daniel.
Corey said she didn't really want to be in contact
with her brother as she couldn't trust him.
Polly also told her about their conversation at her father's
funeral somehow it felt better discussing things.
She didn't want to be blackmailed anymore.
And she also took out a temporary high court injunction
banning the papers from printing the story.
If Luke decided to contact them she felt better.

*Her son could no longer blackmail her or ruin her life.*
*That cold October morning she went to see her mother.*
*At her house on the outskirts of Liverpool there's had*
*always been a complicated relationship.*
*Polly had hated her as a child for her drug and alcohol*
*addictions that had meant she'd grown up in care.*
*Until the age of thirteen in her late teens they had become*
*reacquainted as Polly forgave her mother.*
*For things that had happened at one point they'd become*
*close at the start of her movie career in her early twenties.*
*But ever since she turned thirty their relationship had*
*started going wrong winding each other up.*
*Never agreeing on anything it was a love hate relationship*
*nowadays more hate than love.*
*Polly had come to realise they were two different people.*
*And that she would always be closer to her dad she*
*rarely saw her mum they had become estranged.*
*Over the past few years for good reason as all they did*
*was row when they saw each other.*
*And the fact her mum had told Harmony's adoptive*
*mother Vanya that Kaleigh had been raped to spite her.*
*She hadn't seen Harmony for years afterwards until*
*they saw each other at a radio station by chance.*
*When she was age fourteen her niece or biological*
*granddaughter Harmony was a product of rape.*

*As Kaleigh had been her mother changed her mind years later about seeing her now Harmony was a famous singer. She had no idea how her mother had tried to stop Kaleigh from seeing her as had her adoptive mum Vanya.*

*It was better not to tell her the truth Harmony liked her mum and she didn't really want her to see her bad side.*

*Polly knocked on the door she had decided to tell her mother she was going to tell Kaleigh after Christmas.*

*That she was her biological mother Polly knew she wouldn't like the idea in fact she'd hate it.*

*But the secrets and lies had gone on too many years. It was time to tell Kaleigh the truth 'come in cold morning' her mother wore a black polo neck jumper.*

*She had long dark brown straight hair that was slightly wavy her mum looked good for her age fifty six.*

*With an age gap of only fourteen years between them she'd been fourteen when she'd had her.*

*Despite this she'd always behaved like a mother not an older sister unlike her own relationship with Kaleigh. Where she could never be in that role 'what pleasure do I owe this visit?' she joked 'thought I'd see you'.*

*'We haven't spoken in ages' 'for good reason because we don't get on' 'we could try' her mother suggested 'I guess'. Polly agreed 'especially with Christmas coming up'.*

*'I can't wait to see you in panto' 'thanks I don't think Luke's interested not his thing' 'that's a shame'.*

*'What do you think about him taking drugs?' Polly asked. She could tell her question had thrown her mum.*

*'It's just cannabis' 'it's cocaine as well I know what I've seen in his apartment' 'I have talked to him it's his choice'. 'If we go on about it it'll push him away and I don't want to do that' 'you think it's ok he's wasting his life on drugs'. 'I don't think he's an addict maybe the computer games the drugs are just nothing' 'you were an addict once'. 'You started on weed and ecstasy look what happened to you ended up on heroin' 'I'm not happy about it'. 'He's an adult I can't tell him what to do' 'you're his second mother you looked after him'.*

*'For whatever reason he prefers you to me you could sort it' 'I don't want him on drugs anymore than you'. 'I have to be careful you know we have a close relationship' Polly couldn't believe what she was hearing. Her own mother saying it was ok for her son to take drugs 'he's a dealer' 'it's no more than his mates do'.*

*'It's just weed' 'he could go to prison' 'no-one will find out' she could see she wasn't getting through to her mum. No doubt she was afraid of ruining their close relationship the one she'd never have with Luke.*

*Because unlike her mum she actually told her son the truth*
*'it's his life don't blame me if he ends up in jail' Polly said.*
*Dropping the subject 'he won't' 'I thought you should*
*know he's been threatening me'.*
*'That he's gonna tell Kaleigh the truth if I don't buy him*
*a bigger house' 'it's just talk'.*
*'Luke even threatened to go to the newspapers'.*
*'He wouldn't!' 'I took out a high court injunction out'.*
*'Temporary as a precaution' 'he can't! it would ruin her*
*life!' 'I know that I'm not buying him another house'.*
*'The way he treats me' 'I'll chat to him make him see*
*sense' 'he should never have overheard any conversation'.*
*'I'm sorry it was years ago he always promised he*
*wouldn't say anything' 'until he saw an opportunity'.*
*'For blackmail' 'he won't say anything I promise'.*
*'I don't want to have a go' 'then don't I'll sort the Kaleigh*
*situation' 'maybe I don't want you to'.*
*'What do you mean?' 'maybe it's time to stop all the*
*secrets and lies' 'your not serious!' 'yeah I am actually'.*
*'Kaleigh will never speak to you again!' 'maybe it's a risk*
*I'm willing to take' 'it's not happening'.*
*'Under any circumstances ever!' 'don't you think it's time*
*to tell Kaleigh the truth' Polly said.*
*Hoping her mum would understand how she felt.*
*'Some things are better off untold' 'what about me!'.*

*'I can't live like this anymore!' 'you would ruin her life'.*
*'You know that!' 'this isn't about what you want'.*
*'It's about what's best for Kaleigh' 'we could tell her*
*together' 'why would I do that destroy her life'.*
*'You want that so she never speaks to either of us again!'.*
*'We could tell her after Christmas' Polly suggested.*
*'No way! put this idea out of your head it's not happening*
*do we understand each other?' 'I suppose'.*
*Her mum had never looked so angry she had mentioned*
*telling Kaleigh in the past now she was serious.*
*And her mum didn't like it if Kaleigh found out the truth*
*she wouldn't be her little girl.*
*They heard a knock at the door it was her Aunt Hilary.*
*She'd always been like a mum to Kaleigh growing up.*
*When her mum wasn't around she and mum had always*
*been close 'hey you two' Hilary said cheerily.*
*Sarah shut the door as a cold wind blew in the house.*
*'What's up?' Hilary asked you could cut the tension with*
*a knife 'Polly wants to tell Kaleigh the truth I said no'.*
*'It'll ruin her life' 'I agree besides it's too late'.*
*'We should have done it years ago' 'gran agrees I should'.*
*'We can't' 'see Hilary agrees with me your not her mum'.*
*'You never can be' Polly hated her mum couldn't she see*
*how lies tore apart families maybe she was right.*
*Maybe it was too late? she had been so sure.*

Telling herself it was the right decision her mum made
her second guess herself.
Stacey and Christian said she should tell Kaleigh the truth
they were right 'you think it's ok all these secrets'.
'That Kaleigh's life has been based on a lie!' Polly said
angry trying to make her mum and Aunt see sense.
'It's for the best things happened and your mum was
Kaleigh's mum too it's the way it's always been'.
'You know she wouldn't be able to deal with things
if you told her' 'she's an adult' Polly said.
'Her whole world would fall apart would you want
that on your conscious' her mum said angry.
'Fine! if it's what you both want!' Polly could see
it was no good reasoning with them.
Since they were determined to keep her from telling
Kaleigh the truth she hated them both.
And felt let down by her own family at least she still had
Christian and her dad she still wanted to tell Kaleigh.
That she was her mother when the time was right.
Before then she had her mum's birthday dinner to attend
she'd have to smile pretend everything was ok.
When it wasn't Polly realised she'd been estranged
from her mum for years with good reason.
That Friday evening Polly checked her appearance in the
mirror she wore a black glittery jacket white T-shirt.

*And a three-quarter length skirt a silver heart necklace.*
*If she had a choice she wouldn't be attending her mum's*
*birthday party but she had no choice.*
*As it would look bad if she didn't and she'd never*
*hear the end of it from other family members.*
*Her dad was coming he'd been seeing her mum*
*for a few years since he'd split from Wendy.*
*Her step-mother their relationship was on and off.*
*Which didn't surprise Polly herr Aunt Hilary and Sue*
*would be there and her uncle Sam.*
*Who she'd always been close to as well as her gran.*
*Stacey and Kaleigh her uncle Sam was picking her up.*
*To take her to the restaurant he also had a fractured*
*relationship with her mother so understood her.*
*Better than anyone Polly had told him about their*
*conversation he agreed it was time to tell Kaleigh.*
*She was still angry about her row with her mum.*
*The emotional blackmail she'd had to put up with for*
*years Polly heard a knock at the door she opened.*
*'You look great' Sam said 'so do you I'd probably rather*
*not be going but she is my mum I got out of it last year'.*
*'As I was ill' 'free drink' 'I hardly drink these days'.*
*Polly admitted 'me neither' 'look I hate the way they*
*spoke to you it's not right emotional blackmail'.*

'Maybe their right maybe it's too late to tell Kaleigh'.
'It's never too late' 'thanks gran said I should otherwise
I might take the secret to the grave' 'listen'.
'If anything ever happened to you I'd tell her the truth'.
'It's just one night and I'm here Stace, Kaleigh, Harmony'.
'I know' 'let's go get tipsy together' Polly loved her uncle
Sam he always understood her better than anyone.
They arrived at the restaurant just before 7pm everyone
was there her Aunt Sue sat with her gran Hilary.
With her mum and dad Stacey with Kaleigh and Harmony
and their cousin Adam Hilary's son all family together.
Somehow she only felt like half her family cared about
her feelings her mum and Hilary clocked her and Sam.
As they looked over they were sipping a coke as an
ex-alcoholic her mum hadn't touched drink for years.
So stuck to soft drinks 'we're just about to order'.
'What do you want?' her mum passed over a menu.
As Polly looked through the items she decided on fish and
chips and a chocolate brownie with ice cream for dessert.
'Let's go order drinks' Sam said as they headed to the bar.
'A coke please' 'just a coke?' Sam asked 'yeah I'll have
some alcohol later' 'coke and a pint oh my god!'.
'What is it?' Polly asked 'my ex-boyfriend' they looked
over a blonde man with another man sat chatting.

'We only split two weeks ago' 'don't worry the best thing you can do is show him what he's missing'.

'Get another man' 'no enjoy life show him you don't need him' 'thanks maybe this night won't be so bad'.

'Now you're here' Sam said Polly smiled they returned to the table 'we thought we'll open presents'.

'While waiting for the food twenty minute wait'.

Hilary suggested 'good idea' Sam agreed Polly watched as her mum opened presents from Hilary and Sue.

She seemed to like them she hoped her mum would like hers she'd put a lot of thought into it.

Polly had wanted to get an earrings and necklace set.

Silver which her mum liked with butterflies on she'd talked about it before but they had sold out.

Instead she got one with moons and stars on her mum liked cosmic things Sam gave her a new phone.

It was her turn as she handed over the carefully wrapped present 'I hope you like it' 'I'm sure I will' she opened it 'It's great I love cosmic jewellery' Polly was happy her mum liked it they looked up as Luke arrived.

Polly had almost forgotten he was coming.

His dark presence threatened to ruin the evening.

No doubt her mum would be thrilled by his arrival.

'Luke where have you been?' 'sorry I'm late'.

'You never need to say sorry to me' he smiled.

*He thought her mum was great he didn't even*
*acknowledge her presence which didn't surprise her.*
*It was as though she didn't exist somehow she didn't care*
*anymore for years she'd put up with his behaviour.*
*Told him the truth her mum thought he could do no wrong*
*'we're just doing presents I ordered you fish and chips'.*
*'Is that ok?' 'great' he smiled he handed over her mum's*
*present she took off the badly wrapped wrapping paper.*
*Polly suspected it wouldn't be anything special.*
*'Oh my god! it's the jewellery set I wanted' 'you like it?'.*
*'I love it!' Polly couldn't believe it the same jewellery set.*
*That she'd shown to Luke in a magazine with one of the*
*Sunday papers she'd told him she was ordering it.*
*Then told him when they were out of stock she didn't know*
*where he'd got it from of course her mum was delighted.*
*Her present now meant nothing 'it's lovely' Hilary said.*
*'I know come here' Sarah said as she hugged Luke.*
*They were more like mother and son than grandma*
*and grandson Kaleigh handed over her present.*
*Polly had no idea what she'd got for their mum.*
*She opened it 'my favourite perfume thanks darling'.*
*Thier mother hugged Kaleigh 'you two are the best'.*
*'When it comes to picking out presents I love you so much'*
*Polly couldn't help but feel jealous.*

*Sometimes she felt as if she seemed to mean nothing*
*to her mother Polly knew they didn't get on.*
*But she hated always being treated second best.*
*'You're the best mum in the world' Kaleigh said.*
*'And you are the best daughter in the world me and*
*you nothing will ever separate us' Polly felt angry.*
*It was her mum who had stopped Kaleigh seeing Harmony*
*when she was a child even getting rid of the one photo.*
*That she had of her daughter luckily they'd been able to*
*meet in real life years later Polly didn't blame her sister.*
*Kaleigh was a sweet person at that moment Polly*
*felt unloved unwanted the food arrived.*
*Something to take her mind off things her fish and chips*
*were good Stacey glanced over Polly didn't seem herself.*
*She'd already said that she didn't really want to attend*
*Sarah's birthday party it was no surprise after her row.*
*With her mum she still thought Kaleigh deserved to know*
*Polly was her mum she sipped her coke.*
*Wanting the evening to be over with 'how's Marley?'.*
*Her mum asked Luke Polly assumed it was his dog 'fine'.*
*'I got him some clothes the other day' 'you've got a pet?'.*
*'No as if! my son' Polly paused for a moment wondering*
*if she'd heard him right 'you never told me'.*
*'It wasn't planned' 'I'm a grandma' 'yeah wouldn't be*
*the first time' Luke said looking over at Harmony.*

*Polly knew one comment and Kaleigh would know*
*everything she tried to gauge his mood.*
*He seemed to be more upbeat than usual Polly told*
*herself she had nothing to worry about.*
*Luke got out his phone showing them the baby dressed*
*in a blue baby suit 'he's gorgeous' Sarah said.*
*As Polly looked over she felt angry her mother must have*
*known and not told her could she sink any lower?.*
*At that moment she hated her family except her dad and*
*Christian at least her half-sister Emily wasn't there.*
*Then it would have been world war three Polly got up.*
*'Where are you going?' her mum asked 'drink at the bar'.*
*'Will you get me a lemonade?' 'I'll see what I can do'.*
*'I'll get it' Luke said Sarah smiled Polly decided to talk*
*to Luke alone 'why didn't you tell me I had a grandson'.*
*'It's no big deal!' 'I think it is!' 'why it wasn't planned'.*
*'Marley's great chill out' 'I suppose mum knew!'.*
*'Only after she gave birth I didn't know she was pregnant*
*my ex' 'how do you think that makes me feel!'.*
*'Not bothering to tell me!' 'f**k you!' 'no f**k you!'.*
*'And your pathetic blackmail attempts which won't work'.*
*'As I have a high court injunction against the papers'.*
*'It'll come out and when it does Kaleigh will never speak*
*to you again!' 'we'll see about that!' 'I could tell her now'.*

'If you want' 'you wouldn't!' 'I might do if you don't stay
away!' 'you're not my son' 'good your not my mum'.
'And you never will be!' 'fine by me!' Polly was angry.
They returned to the table 'what was that all about?'.
Sarah asked Luke 'mum being a bitch as usual'.
'What did she say?' 'the truth' what!' Polly said.
Overhearing their conversation 'what the f**k would you
know! you think it's ok I don't know I have a grandson!'.
'Polly calm down!' 'no mum he told you I don't actually
care about your pathetic relationship!'.
'You're welcome to him! but to not be told I'm
a grandmother by both of you! as if it's ok'.
'Polly don't make a scene!' Hilary said trying to calm her
down 'oh I could really make a scene! if you want me to!'.
'We all came to have a nice lunch to celebrate your mum's
birthday' 'she's not my mother anymore!'.
'And your not my son drug dealing cocaine taking scum!'.
'Who tries to blackmail me and threatens to sell stories
to the newspapers!' 'Polly stop now!' 'no mum'.
'I've only just begun!' 'if you don't stop you can leave!'.
'What are you worried about the truth coming out!'.
'Are you drunk?' 'I've had one drink that's all!'.
'This isn't the time or the place' 'you dare say anymore!'.
Hilary said angry 'Stacey knows Christian even Harmony
so your threats mean nothing to me!'.

'I want you to leave before you say something you regret!'
Sarah said angry 'fine I'm going!' 'Susie don't go'.
Stacey said getting up from the table 'I'm going to the
toilets then I'm going home'.
'Because only dad Christian and Stacey are my family'.
'The rest of you can go f**k yourselves!' Polly went to
the toilet close to tears 'how can she behave like that'.
Hilary said 'you're unbelievable all of you! you don't care
how Polly feels your emotional blackmail threats'.
'You've treated her like nothing for years always making
her feel second best!' 'Stacey!' 'it's the truth!'.
'Where are you going?' 'to see Polly' 'no I'll see her'.
'I'll sort this out once and for all!' Sarah followed Polly
to the ladies toilets 'you're here good we can chat'.
'What do you think your playing at!' 'scared I was gonna
reveal your little secret!' 'why didn't you then?' 'because'.
'I care about Kaleigh' 'then you need to stop all this and
face facts you'll never be her mother even if you want to'.
'You know it's a joke! Sue raised her not me or you I love
Kaleigh and she may be my sister but she's my daughter'.
'And one day I'll tell her the truth!' 'no you won't!'.
'Even if she never speaks me to again at least our
relationship won't be based on a lie!'.
Polly couldn't stop crying 'you will never tell her the
truth! because if you do I'll never speak to you again!'.

'Or the family!' 'I don't care! if you loved me you'd
let me tell her the truth!' 'the truth hurts people'.
'Some things are meant to be kept secret because it's
for the best' 'who for? you kept it a secret for years'.
'Because it was the right thing to do now it's not'
'It is as far as I'm concerned you want her to know her
father was a rapist and not Simon' 'no course not'.
'Then you stay quiet I've got nothing left to say'
Her mother left as she cried a woman came in as Polly
tried to compose herself going into a cubicle to cry.
As she grabbed some tissue she heard a knock at the door.
'Stace' 'no it's Kaleigh' 'how did you know I was here?'.
'I just did assumed it was you' 'I had a row with mum'.
'I hate my family' 'do you hate me?' 'I could never hate
you I don't want you seeing me like this'.
'It's not your fault mum was out of order' 'we don't get on
and we never will!' 'please come out mum's gone'.
'To slag me off to everyone!' 'please Susie I want to make
it ok again' 'no-one can make it ok!'.
'I should never have come out tonight! we don't get along'.
'All we do is row' Polly opened the door still crying.
Kaleigh hugged her 'mum shouldn't have said what she
did' 'I thought you and her were the best of friends'.
'She's my mum but I don't always agree with her'.
'Nothing I ever do or say is good enough' 'it is'.

Kaleigh offered her a tissue 'you always make me
feel good when I feel like I'm nothing'.
'You make me feel like I can do things we could call a taxi
go home' Kaleigh suggested 'mum wouldn't like it'.
'If you left early' 'I want to and Stacey and Christian'.
'If your sure' 'I am I'll go get the others' 'meet you
in the foyer' Polly tried to wipe away her tears.
All she wanted to do was go home never see her mum
Aunt Hilary or her son again.
They weren't her family anymore Polly called a taxi as
she waited Stacey, Christian and Kaleigh appeared.
'Are you ok?' Stacey asked 'I'll be alright is dad ok about
me going?' 'he's concerned about you' 'I'll phone him'.
'I've called a taxi' 'let's go' they got into the taxi Polly was
glad to be going home 'she was a bitch' 'Hilary or mum'.
'Both' Stacey replied she could see how upset Polly was.
And she'd obviously been crying 'can I ask what your
mum said' 'same old rubbish' they arrived home.
Kaleigh went to the toilet 'tell us what your mum said?'.
Stacey asked 'that the family will never speak to me'.
'If I tell Kaleigh the truth that it's for the best Kaleigh
came in heard me crying she didn't know about our row'.
'She didn't overhear your conversation?' Stacey asked.
'No there was nothing to suggest she had she came in
afterwards maybe I'll just forget the whole thing'.

*'You can't they can't emotionally blackmail you'.*

*'Stace I'm tired of fighting anyway I'm done with them'.*

*'Luke and mum are welcome to each other screw the both of them I want to be happy' 'I understand Susie'.*

*'I'm sure if Corey had been here she wouldn't have been happy about it' 'it's probably best she wasn't here'.*

*'I'm not attending any of mum's birthday parties ever again' 'me too' Stacey agreed Christian hugged Polly.*

*Which instantly made her feel better the following morning Kaleigh woke she'd slept badly.*

*Tossing and turning still unable to process the news that her sister was really her mother.*

*Why had she never realised how could she not have known Polly had always been very protective and loving.*

*Towards her she had always assumed it was just her personality she tried to act normal as she ate breakfast.*

*But Kaleigh knew she was quieter than normal she had pretended she hadn't heard Polly's row with her mum.*

*Kaleigh decided to talk to her mum first get some answers she told Stacey she needed to see her mum.*

*That afternoon they went to see her in Liverpool.*

*Her mum answered the door happy to see her 'Kales'.*

*'Come in' 'listen I'm sorry about last night everything went too far you know Polly drama queen'.*

*'Is it true Luke does drugs?' 'it's just sometimes'.*

*'It's not like he's an addict' 'Polly says he's always stoned'.*
*'With cocaine lying around the apartment' 'Stacey look*
*I'm not denying he does drugs'.*
*'But it doesn't have to be a big deal' what about his son?'*
*'her mother looks after him most of the time it's fine'.*
*'Mum I need to talk to you alone?' Kaleigh asked.*
*'What about?' 'private stuff' 'I'll wait here' Stacey said.*
*As they went to the kitchen she wondered what Kaleigh*
*wanted to talk to Sarah about 'so what's the problem?'.*
*Sarah asked 'I know' 'know what?' 'the truth that Polly's*
*my real mum' 'how?' 'I overheard you in the toilets'.*
*'When you were rowing' 'I had no idea you were there'.*
*'It doesn't matter I'm your mum always will be just forget*
*what you heard' 'how can I Polly's my mum!'.*
*'She never raised you Sue and I did Polly's your sister'.*
*'It's the way it is' 'I heard the things you said to her'.*
*'What things?' 'that you'd cut her out of the family'.*
*'That you didn't want her to tell me the truth' 'I protected*
*you for a reason' 'I don't need protecting! I'm thirty'.*
*'I'm not a kid anymore and I know Simon's not my dad'.*
*'maybe not biologically but he cares about you and Polly'.*
*'You grew up as sisters and that's it' 'she's still my*
*real mum!' 'I'm your mum!' 'no your my grandma!'.*
*'I'm whatever you want me to be I never wanted you to*
*find out and not like this' 'I'm glad I did' 'why?'.*

'It's ruined everything!' 'I don't like being lied to!'.
'We had no choice Polly got pregnant as a child she
was eleven it would have been a scandal in the papers'.
'And everyone would have known we decided I should
raise you as my own then things went wrong'.
'I was still doing drugs so Sue brought you up it worked
out ok and with Polly's modelling career taking off'.
'She couldn't have looked after you not the way I could'.
'It was an arrangement it's the way things were'.
'Why couldn't you have told the truth!' 'look I'm your
mum Polly's your sister' 'but she's not is she!'.
'She gave birth to me' 'I know this is a lot to take in for
you' 'what happened? who's idea was it?'.
'There was no other option an eleven year old bringing up
a kid' 'she was raped like me' 'yes' 'by her foster dad'.
'That's it isn't it when Polly talked about being
gang raped at eleven she said it was her foster dad'.
'Foster brother and another man' 'I'm sorry the truth
had to come out like this' 'I bet she wanted an abortion'.
'To get rid of me' 'she didn't find out till she was
five months gone it was too late' 'then she was raped'.
'At thirteen by her uncle like what Shaun did to me'.
'Kaleigh Simon is your dad he loves you and you don't
have to think about those men what happened?'.

*'How can you say that! which one is my father?'.*
*'I don't know and don't think about those people ever
again this is why I never wanted you find out just forget'.*
*'That you know the truth' 'how can I' 'this is Polly's fault'.*
*'Rowing if she'd have been more careful' 'no this is your
fault! trying to keep it a secret'.*
*'There's nothing more to say' 'nothing has to change'.*
*'Don't you get it this changes everything'.*
*'Polly's my real mum!' 'so what! just move on'.*
*'You want me to pretend I don't know the truth!' 'yes'.*
*'That is a good idea Polly doesn't even have to know
that you know' 'more lies!' 'it's for the best!'.*
*'What would you know! if you hadn't been on drugs'.*
*'Shaun would never have been my step-uncle and raped
me!' 'I'm sorry drugs ruined my life'.*
*'Everything I've ever done is because I love you'.*
*'And you never wanted me to meet Harmony'.*
*'Everything's fine now isn't it this conversation is over
with!' 'I'm sending Polly a Mother's Day card next year'.*
*'Like f**k you are! now we'll pretend everything is
normal I'm not having Stacey find out the truth'.*
*'Is everything ok?' Stacey asked 'fine' Sarah said Stacey
could tell it wasn't Kaleigh didn't look happy.*
*'Why don't you tell Stacey the truth about my life!'.*
*'What do you mean?' 'Polly's my real mum' 'I know'.*

Stacey confessed 'how?' 'she told me' 'so everyone knew
except me!' 'I only found out like a week ago'.
'And Christian please don't be angry' 'I'm not besides
it's mum's fault! you said if Polly told anyone the truth'.
'That you'd cut her off from the family'.
'Everything I've ever done is to protect you'.
'So you could have a normal family' 'what's normal about
lying to me about who my mother is!' 'she was too young'.
'And I don't regret anything your still my little girl!'
'actually Kaleigh's right' Stacey said.
'You'll always be the only mum she's ever known'.
'But Polly is her biological mother and you thought
she'd never find out that you could make threats to Polly'.
'Emotionally blackmail her but you can't anymore'.
'Stacey stay out of this it doesn't concern you!'.
'Polly told me you told her not to say anything
because it would be selfish she wanted to tell you'.
'When she turned thirty but she was stopped by you'.
'And Hilary' 'it was for Kaleigh's own good!' 'and Luke'.
'He blackmailed Polly he said if she didn't him a bigger
house he'd tell the papers about you' 'it was just talk'.
'He wouldn't have!' 'yes he would! Polly even had to take
out a high court injunction' 'just forget everything!'.
'Polly doesn't have to know' 'what?' 'that Kaleigh knows'.
'This is ridiculous!' 'she's not your mum I am!'.

*'I always have been and it's the end of this conversation!'*
*Kaleigh knew there was no point trying to talk to her mum.*
*She needed to talk to Polly about what had happened.*
*That Monday afternoon Polly woke the row with her mum*
*and son was still playing on her mind.*
*She had decided to see a solicitor about changing*
*her will she wanted Luke to get nothing from her.*
*As he had always been ungrateful about her buying*
*him designer clothes sending him to a good school.*
*Buying his apartment now she wanted to show him*
*he couldn't walk all over her anymore.*
*He would get nothing from her or her mum except for*
*some jewellery.*
*She wanted to leave everything to her other kids.*
*Kaleigh, Susan, Marie and Louie as well as her*
*Harmony her brother uncle Sam and her friends.*
*Polly thought about things Kaleigh the secret she was*
*tired of keeping secrets destroyed lives tore families apart.*
*After the solicitor had come round she received a*
*phone call from her mum.*
*That she wanted to come round to her house and that*
*it was important she was dreading her visit.*
*Any time spent in her mum's company always ended*
*in a row her mum seemed to hate her so much.*

Polly quickly got changed  it was a rainy day as she saw
her come up the path 'what's this about?' Polly asked.
'Something important listen there's no way to say this
Kaleigh knows the truth I wasn't gonna let on she knew'.
'When?' 'that row we had she was in the toilet cubicle'.
'Before we came in' Polly couldn't believe it 'I didn't want
her to find out like that I wanted to tell her properly'.
'You didn't' 'if you hadn't been having a go at me'.
'It wouldn't have happened and she wouldn't know the
truth!' 'me if you hadn't been such a bitch!'.
'Kaleigh would have found out eventually' 'no'.
'She wouldn't! I protected her her whole life'.
'Against finding out the truth that her dad was a rapist'.
'So she never had to worry about anything and she
could have the perfect family' 'how was it perfect!'.
'You and Aunt Charlotte drug addicts Shaun abusing
Kaleigh our family is f***d up'.
'And you know it always has been!' 'no-one's family is
perfect!' 'you made everything more screwed up!'.
'How you'd disown me from the family well I don't want to
be part of this family anymore with it's lies and secrets!'.
'Keep your voice down! do you want people finding
out the truth!' 'they will anyway!' 'no why should they'.
'This doesn't have to go outside the family' 'so we all
pretend nothing's happened and Kaleigh's still my sister'.

'Yeah we do! you grew up as sisters and you always will be!' 'I'm her real mum!'.

'You think she wants you as her real mum after finding out the truth that she wants anything to do with you'.

'You lied to her too this was your idea! you're her grandmother' 'I'm her mum whatever you think!'.

'Kaleigh will never think of you as her mum'.

'And she knows you were raped so that family image even if it was never real is ruined I'm blaming you!'.

'If you hadn't started that row at dinner' 'if you stopped defending Luke and saw him for what he is!'.

'I know he's not perfect but he's my grandson who I love'.

'Not like me f**k you! I'm glad Kaleigh knows!'.

'She wants nothing to do with you!' 'I hate you!'.

'I hate you too!' 'I'm going!' Polly had heard enough.

'Stay away from me!' Polly saw a waiting car as her mum got in it relieved to be away from the drama.

She didn't want anymore rows but now according to her mum Kaleigh hated her at least she knew the truth.

Polly decided she would go and see her even if Kaleigh hated her she would put her side of the story.

She decided she'd wait a week or two let things calm down before there were anymore rows.

Polly worried she wouldn't get her own happy ending.

*How could she have thought telling Kaleigh would be*
*a good idea no more secrets but it didn't feel that way.*
*Not if she hated her at least her mum Hilary and Luke*
*couldn't emotionally blackmail her anymore.*
*No more guilt no more pretending to be her sister.*
*Maybe her mum was right maybe she always would be*
*Kaleigh's sister maybe she'd never accept her as her mum.*
*That Friday afternoon Corey watched a Michael Jackson*
*DVD of his music videos it included Gone Too Soon.*
*About a boy who had died of HIV Corey wasn't an*
*emotional person but she had tears in her eyes.*
*Suddenly she realised Louie was coming back soon.*
*He'd gone to get a few things at the local shop he hadn't*
*taken his recent HIV diagnosis well.*
*And seeing her crying over a video about someone*
*who had died of the condition wasn't a good idea.*
*She turned off the DVD as she ventured upstairs putting*
*on a dance cd to lift her mood as she re-did her make-up.*
*Her eyes looked red never mind she thought it was the*
*31st October Halloween.*
*When Corey was younger she had enjoyed it now she was*
*older she couldn't be bothered Susan loved it though.*
*As a teenager she insisted on going to a party every year*
*Corey looked at the clock on the wall it was almost 5pm.*

## Love triangle

'I thought you weren't coming' 'just getting the Lambrusco for the night' 'is that pizza I smell?' 'yes the best'.

'I'll put the wine in the fridge for later' 'I have cloudy lemonade' 'fantastic! I'll pour' Louie got out the ice.

As he poured the drinks 'to us darling' 'to us'.

'So how's Polly?' 'great she's coming back soon things back home...you know' 'I can't believe she never told us'.

'About Kaleigh' 'I know' 'I knew she was protective of her I thought it was just her being a big sister' Corey said.

'Imagine being forced to keep a secret like that all your life like something off Jerry Springer'.

'My sister is my daughter' 'I know I had no idea'.

'Her son sounds awful blackmailing her and her mum and Aunt over this' 'Polly's been really upset'.

'At least Kaleigh knows the truth' 'Polly hasn't seen her in weeks apparently she's got texts and voicemails'.

'But she's afraid to listen or read them Polly's convinced Kaleigh will hate her' 'not if she explains'.

'She's never been allowed to tell her the truth'.

'And the fact she was raped as a child I think that's why no-one ever wanted it to come out' 'a secret like that'.

'Had to come out at some point even if Kaleigh does hate her she won't be living a lie anymore' Louie said.

'How's Lance?' Corey asked 'I wouldn't know'.
'Your splitting up?' 'more like on a break I don't want
to get a divorce but it's hard when you know...'.
'He's been cheating on me I didn't want us to be like
all those other gay couples sleeping around'.
'I wanted things to be different more romantic now
I'm HIV positive because of the bastard on medication'.
'For the rest of my life' 'have you talked to him?'.
'He says there's nothing to talk about' 'he slept with other
people gave you HIV' 'I have no proof but I got tested'.
'Before we got married I'm starting to think marriage
is a joke' 'really' 'no I want to believe in marriage'.
'Have what you and Polly have' 'we did split up for
a few years' 'I know but no-one cheated did they'.
'It was just pure love until you grew apart I think it's great
your back together' 'me too' 'think you'll get engaged'.
'Maybe' 'if you do let me know' Corey served the pizza.
As Louie poured them lemonade with ice 'so have you
seen the bastard lately?' Louie asked.
Referring to her brother 'no' 'good how he has the nerve
to walk around after what he did to you'.
'Blaming it on alcohol hope he gets caught one day' 'me
too' 'what did you do with that lingerie he brought you?'.
'I haven't done anything I can't get rid of it in case Nicky
asks to see it she's good friends with his fiancée Liza'.

'If only they knew the truth' 'do you think there are others? victims that he might have raped'.
'Anything's possible maybe it was just me that he was obsessed with Kitty says it's not normal'.
'Sending me sexy lingerie' 'course it's not I'll look out for you if he ever tries anything' 'thanks' 'anytime'
'Still haven't told your sister who you are' 'Victoria no'. 'we're both busy I will one day when the time is right'.
'I wish I still had my sister' At 7pm they watched Emmerdale as planned followed by a music documentary.
Later they began drinking Lambrusco as they watched Graham Norton they didn't get many trick or treaters.
Which Louie was glad about 'f**k Halloween' Louie said.
Sipping his wine 'it's not that bad' 'oh it is'.
'It's just tradition all hallows eve' Corey said trying to win him over 'so you don't like my light up pumpkin'.
Corey asked 'I do actually sounds like a chat up line'.
'I am tipsy' 'well darling so are you still bi? or was Steve a one off?' Louie asked 'my preference is women'.
'But I find some men attractive' 'do tell apart from Steve'.
Steve had been Corey's ex-husband and the only man she'd ever loved they'd been married a few years.
But were now divorced 'there was one man before I got back with Polly' 'who?' 'you can't tell anyone' 'I promise'.

*'My lips are sealed' 'it was a fling well short relationship*
*I really liked him it was Christian' 'not Polly's brother'.*
*'Yes' 'he is gorgeous' 'please don't tell Polly she wouldn't*
*be happy I was seeing him for a while'.*
*'But once I got back with Polly I ended it' 'I'm so jealous'.*
*'I always fancied him had no chance even though he's bi'.*
*'Why?' 'I'm too much of a queen anyway I won't tell*
*anyone so any other secret relationships'.*
*'You've never told me about' 'there was one' 'I want all*
*the gossip especially as we're tipsy' 'Kaleigh'.*
*'When I split from Polly when I moved to L.A'.*
*'She's sweet if I was straight I would be attracted to her'.*
*'When has that ever stopped anyone you know I was*
*a bit jealous when you married Steve' 'really why?'.*
*'I don't know I like him but I always fancied you' 'me'.*
*'Yes look I know I'm a massive queen but like I've said*
*before I've occasionally liked women'.*
*'Well I think your attractive too' 'me' Louie said surprised*
*'well what are we going to do about our attraction'.*
*'For each other' 'nothing you love Polly' 'I do but one kiss*
*wouldn't hurt' 'no it wouldn't' as Corey kissed Louie.*
*She was drunk but she enjoyed it he was a good kisser.*
*And her best friend as Corey woke the next morning*
*she looked at the time it was 11am.*
*As she remembered she'd gotten drunk the night before.*

*And she'd kissed Louie as long as Polly never found out.*
*Corey climbed out of bed looking at herself in the mirror.*
*She brushed her hair 'ragdoll' 'Louie' 'I've made you*
*boiled eggs with soldiers and orange juice with bits'.*
*'Thanks' Corey ventured downstairs eating breakfast.*
*She loved Louie he was so thoughtful who else would*
*make her breakfast 'sorry about our kiss' 'I liked it'.*
*'But don't tell Polly' Corey asked 'not a word or*
*we'd both be in trouble besides it was the wine'.*
*'We did have a fun night' Corey agreed as her phone*
*beeped she had a text from Violet her oldest friend.*
*Who was twenty years older than her now over sixty.*
*She looked a decade younger thanks to botox and*
*chemical peels Violet wanted to meet in town 'it's Violet'.*
*'She wants to meet up' 'sounds great' 'today I've said*
*you're with me that we can meet at Annie's' 'good idea'.*
*'I'd better start getting ready' Corey chose something*
*to wear put on some make-up.*
*Choosing some silver leaf earrings she was ready to go.*
*They met at 12.30pm as Corey and Louie waited Violet*
*arrived wearing a dark purple coat.*
*Her hair dyed a shade of strawberry blonde she always*
*looked great 'darling you look great' Violet said.*
*As she hugged Corey 'thanks I love the coat' Corey said.*

'Christian Dior in the sale' 'Louie hello' 'darling'.
'You look fantastic!' he said complimenting Violet.
'As do you' 'so what's your secret?' Louie asked 'botox'.
'Man's greatest invention' they laughed 'I try and dress
well if you dress like your sixty you'll look sixty'.
'How's Jason?' Corey asked 'great' 'how old is he?'.
Louie asked 'thirty three what about Angelica?'.
Violet asked 'she's twenty eight I feel so old now'.
'Time flies so fast dosen't it' Violet said looking sad.
She and her son Jason had been estranged for
many years but now had a good relationship.
'Let's go eat something' they went inside Annie's.
'Busy today' Violet said looking around they sat down.
'I'm having a milkshake' 'me too' Corey agreed.
'Chocolate Louie?' 'same strawberry and a chocolate
brownie' 'I'll have the same as Louie' 'right darlings'.
'I'll be back' 'I love her' Louie said 'I know it's like
everything's ok when Violet's around' Corey said.
'Everything is ok when Violet's around' Louie joked.
Violet returned as she took off her coat 'so what's Angelica
doing these days?' Violet asked 'just painting really'.
'And selling jewellery online' Louie informed Violet.
'I love her work' 'how's Christy?' Corey asked 'ok'.
'I believe why did no-one tell me as many gay marriages
end in divorce as straight ones luckily we're still friends'.

'I'm hoping Miss Right is out there somewhere'.
'How's things going with you and Polly?' 'great'.
'Good to hear it darling at least one of us can have
a successful love life' Violet joked 'I hope so'.
'Still in touch with Steve?' 'yes still good friends'.
'So no more men then' 'I don't think so' Louie smiled.
'Am I missing something?' Violet asked curiously.
'We had a drunken kiss last night' 'really' 'just don't tell
Polly' 'not a word' 'we were drunk on Lambrusco'.

## After the storm

'How drunk?' 'a few glasses' Louie said 'there's nothing
wrong with having a bit of fun' 'no sex' 'no'.
'It would be a step too far' 'tell Violet about Christian?'.
'She knows' 'he is gorgeous' 'I suppose I'd have turned
for him myself' Violet said before sipping her milkshake.
'I chose Polly and I think it was the right decision'.
'How is she?' 'good considering recent events' 'they
sound terrible her family imagine being blackmailed'.
'Over your own daughter and her son' 'he's a nightmare'
Louie informed Violet 'Sarah thinks it's ok he deals drugs'.
Corey said 'it wouldn't be ok if it affects lives'.
'He thinks he's helping the community because it's
cannabis' 'even so'.
'I'm not saying I haven't taken drugs in the past'.
Violet confessed 'but I've never dealt drugs'.
'He sounds awful the things he says about Polly'.
'He's horrible' Louie said 'she's cut contact with him'.
Corey said 'Polly says she's had enough of all the drama'.
'Sometimes it's the only way Polly is a good person'.
'And she dosen't deserve to be treated like that' Violet said.
'Luke even condones the fact his father slept with her'.
'She was underage thirteen he says she must have been
asking for it' 'bastard! at least she has her girls'.

*Violet said 'I need your advice' Corey said 'anything'.*
*'You know I once went with Kaleigh' 'yes' 'and Christian'.*
*'Not that long ago should I tell her I don't want their*
*to be any secrets between us should I tell her or not?'.*
*'That you went with her brother how would she take it?'.*
*'I don't know I mean what do you think?' 'don't tell her'.*
*'What about Kaleigh?' 'maybe Kaleigh was years ago'.*
*'And she's with Stacey now it wouldn't be an issue'.*
*'But Christian wasn't that long ago and it might be*
*more of a bigger deal' 'your right'.*
*'What about your headmistress?' 'Mrs Rayworth' 'yes'.*
*'Did you ever tell her?' 'no' 'how come?' Louie asked.*
*'I never got round to it and I was worried what people*
*would think if they ever found out'.*
*'That she was my teacher' 'didn't you help her to come*
*out?' Louie asked 'yes'.*
*'I mean she was with her husband for years but she could*
*never tell him they were good friends she loved him'.*
*'But she always liked women we slept together a few times*
*but I had a girlfriend so it never became serious'.*
*'Isn't that everyone's fantasy going with your teacher'.*
*Louie said 'maybe' 'I never told anyone'.*
*'Apart from you two not even Stacey or Kitty' 'it's ok'.*
*'Listen you had a fun life and you were a great escort'.*
*Violet said 'I wasn't as good as you' 'I was older'.*

*'I had more experience' 'did you sleep together?' 'once'.*
*'Didn't we Cor but we got on so well we decided we'd*
*be better off as friends which worked out well'.*
*'Violet took me to Paris my first time out of Ireland'.*
*'You two have had quite the life' 'we have and it's not over*
*yet' Violet said Corey thought about what Violet had said.*
*She was right there was no need to tell Polly about*
*Christian after all it was in the past.*
*It was a frosty November 3rd as Polly cooked herself*
*a tomato & basil pasta ready meal.*
*As she poured herself some cloudy lemonade with ice.*
*Food and drink always lifted her spirits especially after*
*recent events her mum who seemed to create drama.*
*In her life her son who she hated and her Aunt Hilary.*
*Who always sided with her mum no matter what and*
*her ex-wife Margie trying to get back with her.*
*At least she had Corey Polly heard her phone beep 'Susie'.*
*'I need to see you Kaleigh xxx' Polly hadn't seen Kaleigh*
*for a week hadn't heard anything assumed she hated her.*
*The fact she wanted to see her made her feel better.*
*According to her mum Kaleigh wanted nothing to do*
*with her maybe she hadn't been telling the truth.*
*She had to see Kaleigh even if she did hate her Polly*
*knew she had to put her side of the story she replied.*
*Kaleigh was coming over she was worried.*

*What if she'd come to have it out with her she would*
*explain she'd wanted to tell her the truth.*
*But was never allowed half an hour later Kaleigh arrived.*
*They didn't live too far from each other she and Stacey*
*lived on the Wirral as did she.*
*Polly watched as the taxi arrived Kaleigh stepped out.*
*As she rang the doorbell she was wearing a white winter*
*coat with fake fur trim Polly opened 'I like the coat'.*
*'Thanks why didn't you reply to my other texts?'.*
*Kaleigh asked 'I thought you hated me that's what mum*
*said' 'it's not true'. 'lemonade' Polly offered 'yeah ok'.*
*Kaleigh took off her coat as Polly brought her some.*
*'What do you know?' Polly asked 'everything that Simon's*
*not my dad that mum's my gran and you were abused'.*
*'Age eleven and you had me that you couldn't have*
*an abortion cause you were too far gone' 'yeah'.*
*'That mum tried to protect me that she stopped you telling*
*the truth about me and Luke threatened to tell the papers'.*
*'Unless you brought him a bigger house' 'and Daniel*
*threatened me' 'Corey's brother'.*
*'If I stopped him making it up with Cor mum said*
*you'd never speak to me again if you knew the truth'.*
*'It's not your fault they wouldn't let you tell me the truth'.*

*'It was like too many years passed Aunt Hilary said*
*it was too late gran said I should tell you I couldn't'.*
*'I wasn't allowed they said I'd ruin your life'.*
*'You wouldn't have' 'I might I had to keep it a secret'.*
*'I knew you'd only ever think of me as your sister'.*
*'Not your mum I was worried if you found out dad*
*wasn't your real dad I wish he was' 'me too'.*
*'I feel like it's my fault that you were abused by Shaun'.*
*'If they'd have let me look after you but I was too young'.*
*Polly cried 'it's ok' Polly reached for a tissue Kaleigh*
*hugged her and it felt so good to know she didn't hate her.*
*Like her mum had said 'I love you so much' Polly said.*
*'Love you too' Kaleigh said 'I don't mind if you think*
*of me as your sister or mother whatever you want'.*
*'I just always wanted to be there for you' 'you are'.*
*'You've always been there for me' 'I always will be*
*it was the best thing to do at the time'.*
*'But I couldn't live a lie anymore I'm proud of you all*
*the things you've achieved' Polly said 'you're the best'.*
*'You always make me feel good about myself like I can*
*do anything' 'you can' Polly assured Kaleigh.*
*As Polly looked out the window it had begun to snow.*
*Somehow she felt everything was going to be ok Kaleigh*
*loved her she felt relived happy.*
*That everything would be ok.*

*That afternoon Corey walked through the streets*
*of Dublin it was a sunny day everything was going well.*
*The restaurant was doing good business her new*
*solo album was coming out soon.*
*And Christmas was just around the corner Corey had gone*
*to see a new exhibition at the art gallery she'd had lunch.*
*At her favourite café a cheese & tomato toastie followed*
*by a chocolate brownie and a bottle of Pepsi.*
*It was now 2pm as she made her way to the restaurant to*
*see Nicky it wasn't too busy as it was quiet after lunch.*
*Nicky wore a pastel pink apron with blue handwriting on.*
*As she wiped down tables 'hi Cor I have something*
*important to tell you' 'the business isn't in trouble'.*
*'No this is something worse wait here' Corey sat down*
*at a table as her sister took off her apron.*
*She hoped nothing bad had happened 'what's wrong?'.*
*'It's Daniel' 'the wedding's not off is it?' 'no everything's*
*fine with the wedding' 'then what is it?' 'this girl'.*
*'An ex-girlfriend is accusing him of... raping her'.*
*Corey couldn't believe it she'd always wondered if*
*her brother had sexually assaulted other girls.*
*Now she had proof 'it's unbelievable! how can she!'.*
*'And why wait so many years?' 'it was years ago?' 'yeah'.*
*'Seventeen years ago it's a joke!' 'how come she waited*
*so long' 'because she's a liar that's why'.*

'Of course Daniel's upset dosen't understand why'.
'He's being accused of rape I feel so sorry for him you
know Dan he's always treated women with respect'.
'He would never do that to a woman' what could Corey
say Nicky was convinced of his innocence.
Nothing would change her mind 'I've told him to stay
strong that we've got his back'.
'That he'll be proved innocent there's gonna be a trial
can you believe it' 'when?' 'after Christmas poor Dan'.
'Imagine the kind of Christmas he'll be having I've told
him she's got no case that she's a liar and a fantasist'.
'Come on if I was raped why wait so long there's two
of them' 'two girls' 'friends obviously ex's'.
'Trying to bring him down Dan would never abuse
a woman' Corey thought of Kitty how he'd hit her.
When they were married when she said she might
not be able to have kids if only Nicky knew.
What her brother was really like 'I was thinking maybe
you could see about getting a good lawyer for him'.
'I'm not sure I know nothing about legal stuff' Corey lied.
She was always interested in different laws.
'You had a good lawyer years ago'.
'When you got joint custody of Douglas and Polly'.
'She's worth millions she could help us then those girls
wouldn't stand a chance with a good lawyer'.

*The last thing Corey wanted was for her brother*
*to be proved innocent when he wasn't.*
*'The trial's at the end of January please say you'll b*
*e a character witness' 'maybe' 'that's a yes then'.*
*'All you have to do is say what a great person he is'.*
*'How he'd never do something like this I'll be one too'.*
*'And Liza we're going to build a strong case so those girls*
*don't stand a chance I can't see my brother in jail'.*
*'For something he didn't do say you'll help me' 'ok'.*
*'You'll talk to Polly' 'I'll try' considering Daniel*
*had blackmailed her over Kaleigh.*
*Corey knew there was no chance that Polly would*
*ever help Nicky and she didn't want to either.*
*'There's something else one of them is Amy your ex'.*
*'What?' 'yes her the one that dumped you and broke your*
*heart' 'it can't be her' Corey said surprised 'it is her'.*
*'I'm sorry anyway sounds like you had a lucky escape*
*all those years ago if that's the kind of person she is'.*
*Luckily Corey hadn't told Nicky they were back in contact.*
*She needed to talk to Amy find out the details.*
*Suddenly Corey remembered Amy telling her about a*
*boyfriend she'd dated who wasn't nice to her.*
*It had to be her brother 'anyway let's forget about her'.*
*'She'll be shown up for who she is in court' Corey*
*hadn't seen her sister that angry for a long time.*

'I'm sure the truth will come out' Corey said.
What else could she say she'd always known the day
would come when Nicky would have to find out.
The fact their brother had sexually assaulted women.
'We have to support him Cor make everything ok get him
through this' Corey didn't know what to say.
If only Nicky knew what Daniel was really like.
'Anyway customers' Nicky said as a couple came
through the door 'well bye' Corey left still thinking.
About what her sister had said about her brother.

## Family connected

*Corey decided to look around the shops for an hour going
into Debenhams as she glanced at the jewellery section.
Before looking at some evening dresses as Corey looked
over at a blonde girl she realised she recognised her.
It was Victoria's sister Katie she'd only met her twice.
As she'd never much taken to her finding her a bit
stuck up thinking she was better than anyone else.
But she had to respect the fact she was Victoria's sister.
She was two years younger they'd reunited a few years
ago 'so what do you think about that hat?' Katie said.
To her friends 'great' 'your mam would love it' 'I know
she would' 'what's Victoria getting her?' 'I don't know'.
'She always tries to out do me with mam's birthday and
Christmas presents I'll always be her favourite'.
'Because we grew up together but I'm closer to Nina'.
'My other sister Victoria's ok but sometimes I wish
it was just the three of us you know like before'.
'She came back into our lives anyway I'm sure Christmas
will be ok' Corey couldn't believe what she'd heard.
She had been under the illusion that Victoria and Katie
were close due to all the photos on Facebook and Twitter.
When all the time Katie didn't really care for her
the way Victoria thought she did.*

*What would Victoria think if she knew the truth.*
*About their relationship Corey decided to go and see*
*Victoria she knew Thursday was her day off.*
*As she rang the buzzer on her apartment a voice answered*
*'it's me Corey' 'come on up' Corey opened the door.*
*As she went up some stairs Victoria opened she was*
*wearing a Star Wars T-shirt dressed unusually casual.*
*And some black jogging trousers and some silver star*
*earrings.*
*Even dressed down Victoria always dressed well fashion*
*was her life always had been 'how's things?' she asked.*
*'Grand' Corey said as she made her way inside.*
*'Drink?' 'what do you have?' 'Del Monte apple juice'*
*'love some' Corey sat down on Victoria's designer sofa.*
*She noticed the Christmas tree was up silver with*
*pink twinkly lights.*
*As well as some other upmarket Christmas decorations.*
*Gold fircones and autumn leaves in a silver vase.*
*'Like the Christmas decorations' 'thanks some of it's*
*Gisella Graham' 'Polly loves her stuff we have a wreath'.*
*'I can't really have a wreath since I live in an apartment'.*
*Victoria handed her the glass of apple juice as she sat*
*down 'so any gossip?' Victoria asked.*
*'My brother's being accused of rape by two girls'.*
*'Not before time' 'Nicky doesn't see it like that'.*

'She even wants me to get him a good lawyer she thinks
he's innocent' 'you're not going to' 'I don't want to'.
'Apparently it was seventeen years ago they even
want me to be a character witness' 'you can't'.
'Not after what he did' 'I don't want to but I can't get
out of it Nicky wouldn't believe me' 'it's terrible'.
'And after he brought you that sexy lingerie I know
what it's like to be abused by a man uncle Richard'.
'I've never seen him not for years apparently I heard
he has a girlfriend blonde in her late thirties'.
'I wonder if she knows what he's like' 'I doubt it no man
would go anywhere near him if they knew the truth'.
'There's something I should tell you I meant to before
I just didn't know if I'd upset you' 'tell me' 'I saw him'.
'It was a month ago' 'where?' 'in the indoor market
he tried to be nice I said he should still be in prison'.
'For what he did he had a go at me called me
a pikey bitch I was shaking inside'.
'Then he tried to run me off the road it was dark
he passed me at the traffic lights' 'I can't believe it'.
'And then I saw him at the petrol station he didn't see me'.
'I told Amy I mean Mrs Rayworth sorry I never told you'.
'It's fine don't worry as long as I don't have to see him'.
'He's dangerous' 'I know if he ever comes near me again'.

'I'll get a restraining order' 'good idea' Victoria poured some more apple juice 'I have something else to say'.
'More bad news' 'kind of I know it's not my business'.
'But I overheard a conversation your sister Katie in Debenhams I wasn't spying I was just nearby'.
'She was with two friends' 'tell me what about?' 'you'.
'What were they saying?' 'she was buying a hat for your mam I'm guessing for Christmas'.
'Anyway she said how she would always be your mam's favourite and she was closer to her other half-sister Nina'.
'That she wished it was how it was before you came back into their lives' 'your lying!' 'sorry it's the truth'.
'I couldn't not tell you that your whole relationship is based on a lie' 'bulls**t! is this your autism thing'.
'How you hate being lied to!' 'no it's the truth!'.
'You must have heard wrong!' 'I didn't hear wrong!'.
'I know what I heard! don't you remember how they treated you that time when you were fifteen'.
'And you were upset and she tried to ignore you at your mam's wedding' 'oh thanks for bringing that up!'.
'Your mother abandoned you like my mother did she picked Katie over you like my mam did'.
'Picking Nicky and Daniel over me I was never the favourite' 'your life was different!' 'how?'.

'Your dad didn't care like mine remember when you
were crying and it was raining' 'that was years ago!'.
'This is rubbish! you know nothing about my life!'.
'I know more than you think!' 'no you don't your dad was
an alcoholic but at least he was around mine wasn't'.
'Too busy screwing younger girls half his age and uncle
Richard he raped me not once or twice every other week'.
'He made me have sex with him my own uncle said it
would give me an advantage over other girls'.
'Because I'd be experienced that's why I couldn't have
boyfriends I didn't have one till I was seventeen'.
'And even then I didn't want to have sex they all went
on about it how great it would be it wasn't'.
'It was torture for me you were lucky being a lesbian'.
'I wished I was at the time so I wouldn't have to let a man
touch me I felt like there was something wrong with me'.
'And my housekeeper Mrs Harvey she turned a blind eye'.
'She even had a crush on him let him abuse me and she
and Mrs O'Donnell controlled me'.
'Never let me have friends round except Marion you
could Stacey Polly everyone except me look at Victoria'.
'Living in a castle with money they controlled everything'.
'What I ate what I was allowed to watch on TV I couldn't
have a normal life like you going out to clubs'.

'Meeting people' 'you think my life was normal my dad going on holiday leaving me alone! a fourteen year old'.
'Beating me so hard I wanted to die being an escort girl at seventeen because my father stopped me working'.
'As a waitress' 'you met your real mother Carol who loved you and your step-dad I never had a mother or a dad'.
'I never had any real friends! not one's that actually cared about me I would go to work then come home alone'.
'I even wanted to kill myself because no-one would have cared if I died that's why I went to Canada and America',
'For a few years maybe Katie is the favourite maybe my mother isn't perfect but I'm not alone anymore'.
'For the first time in my life I feel loved even Sapphire isn't enough for my mother'.
'She brought Katie's daughter a better birthday present'.
'But their my family' 'but they don't treat you like they should' 'same as your sister'.
'Who doesn't know your brother abused you but their still your family' 'no it's different' 'how is it different?'.
'Your brother date tried to rape you then date raped you'.
'Touched you up your sister treated you like s**t growing up because of your sexuality'.
'You run a restaurant together so I'd say it's all the same'.
'I was trying to look out for you!' 'I don't need you looking out for me your not my family! your just a friend'.

'Who feels sorry for me like everyone else does!' 'if that
was the case then why am I still here after so many years'.
'I don't know and I don't care!' 'what if I told you…'.
'I'm not interested in anything you have to say
please go!' 'why are you being like this!' 'like what!'.
'Telling the truth!' 'fine if you want me to go' 'I do!'.
'If you push people away you won't have anyone left'.
'Nothing new there!' Corey left the apartment she now
knew why Victoria put up with her sister.
Who didn't really love her it was so she didn't feel
so alone they made her feel loved and wanted.
To Victoria being part of an imperfect family was
better than not being part of one at all.
How Corey wished she could have told her she was
her sister that evening she told Polly everything.
That Daniel was being put on trial for rape her row
with Victoria and that she had seen Mr Cleves in town.
No more secrets the following day they decided to go
and see Amy at her flat Corey needed to speak to her.
About Daniel they knocked on the door Amy opened.
'Is this about your brother?' 'yes' 'if you've come to
have a go there's no point I know I'm telling the truth'.
'And that's all I have to say I'm sorry if you don't
believe me' 'I do believe you he abused me too'.
'Why do you think we never spoke for seven years'.

*Amy looked surprised 'come in' 'I'm sorry I just*
*assumed...' 'Daniel's been abusing Cor for years'.*
*'That's why she broke off contact' Polly explained.*
*'I had no idea' Amy said as they talked in the living room.*
*'I couldn't tell anyone' 'until finally she told us me'.*
*'And Stacey Kitty everyone except Nicky she wouldn't*
*believe me Daniel was always her favourite'.*
*'We get on well now but for years we didn't I was worried*
*it would ruin our relationship now I don't care'.*
*'How did he abuse you?' 'Dan always touched me up tried*
*to kiss me then like seven years ago he date raped me'.*
*'I thought maybe I'd imagined it but I didn't he was*
*on top of me I was dazed I think he drugged me'.*
*'And then one night he tried to rape me he was angry'.*
*'If my mam hadn't have come to visit me when she did'.*
*'I couldn't tell anyone but all my closet friends know'.*
*'And he brought Cor lingerie recently' 'he tried to make*
*out he wanted a normal relationship but he was lying'.*
*'He's obsessed with her always has been' 'I wish I knew*
*before I assumed you'd hate me if you found out'.*
*'About what he did to me' Amy confessed 'I was twenty six*
*we dated for six months at first he seemed ok'.*
*'I said I didn't want to go out with him anymore he was*
*jealous possessive one night he asked to chat I said ok'.*
*'He locked the bedroom and he raped me'.*

'I blamed myself that it was my fault for agreeing to talk to him putting myself in that situation' 'it wasn't your fault'.
'It's just what he's like' Polly said trying to make Amy feel better 'who's the other girl accusing him of rape?'.
Corey asked 'a friend one day we swapped stories'.
'Turns out he did the same to her they dated a few months'.
'He locked her in the bedroom I couldn't believe it'.
'I always thought I was the only one' 'me too'.
Corey confessed 'I'm so glad you came round'.
'I don't feel so alone now what did your sister say?'.
'She thinks he's innocent that the girls accusing him are liars and fantasist's Nicky wants me to get a lawyer'.
'For him even be a character witness' 'what did you say?'
'not much I don't want to I can't lie in court for him'.
'What are you gonna tell your sister?' 'I don't know'.
'The truth' 'what if she hates you' 'what if he does it to more women' 'Cor you know we'll support you'.
'Whatever you decide' Polly said 'thanks' 'I agree with Polly I waited so long to tell the truth'.
'About what happened I didn't have the strength before'.
'I saw him at a club not long ago I was shaking anxious'.
'I heard him in a club saying he could have any girl he wanted it made me so angry he was making comments'.
'About the size of women's chests I knew then what I had to do I knew it might not even go to trial but I had to try'.

'Your so brave' Polly said 'thanks it didn't feel like it
at the time' 'just to try and get justice is a big thing'.
'Thanks Polly I feel better now' that late afternoon
Corey and Polly returned to their house.
As they tried to make sense of things somehow Corey
had always wondered if there were other victims.
And now she had proof that evening they sat down to
watch Emmerdale as they heard a knock at the door.
Corey opened it was Nicky 'hi sorry to disturb you'.
'It's fine I need to talk to you about Daniel I know
the trial's not till January but I'm doing all I can'.
'To make him feel better build a stronger case for the
defence I need to get hold of the best lawyer we can'.
'I said I know nothing about legal things' 'I don't care'.
'I just need addresses phone numbers' 'I don't know'.
'Polly you must know some good lawyers' 'yeah I do'.
'If you can help me out I would be so grateful' 'I can't'.
'Why? do you want Daniel to go to jail' 'how do you know
the girls are lying' 'what? you've known Daniel for years'.
'They are lying I understand anyone would have doubts'.
'But you know Dan he could never rape a woman'.
'Are you so sure?' 'why are you being like this?'.
'I'll tell you why he threatened me at the wake at Corey's
dad's funeral he said if I kept out of his relationship'.

'With Corey he wouldn't tell anyone about Kaleigh
being my daughter not my sister'.
'Why didn't you keep out of their relationship maybe
you're the reason they didn't speak for seven years!'.
'I'll tell you the reason he tried to rape Corey he was
drunk and if Carol hadn't come back in the time'.
'He would have!' 'Dan doesn't drink anymore' 'oh so that
makes it ok!' 'your lying!' 'Dan would never do that!'.
'Tell her Cor' 'it's true I never wanted you find out'.
'Because I knew you wouldn't believe me' 'this is some
made up fantasy! you're a forty two year old woman!'.
'Your telling me you waited till now to tell everyone
he abused you Polly's put you up to this'.
'Because she had a falling out with Dan!' 'it's true'.
'I can't support him in court I'll be supporting Amy!'.
'The bitch that dumped you years ago' 'we're friends now'
'well she's got you as a friend has she!'.
'Something about this does not add up!' 'I'm telling the
truth so is Amy' 'when your ready to admit your lying'.
'About everything then maybe I'll speak to you until then
I want nothing to do with you!' 'Nicky!'.
'No your no longer my sister! unless it's to do with the
restaurant I don't want to hear from you!'.
'I can only think what Dan will think about this!'.

*'His own sister supporting the women accusing him of*
*rape you've made it clear where your family loyalties lie'.*
*'Have a good Christmas Dan won't' 'no more than he*
*deserves!' Polly said angry at Nicky 'screw both of you!'.*
*Nicky slammed the door shut 'don't worry Cor we're*
*doing the right thing' 'she hates me'.*
*'Think of the women you'll be helping he's a sex abuser'.*
*'Who should have been locked up years ago' 'I know'.*
*'Your right she didn't even hear us out' 'she'll come round*
*when she hears all the evidence against him'.*
*'Christmas will be ruined' 'no it won't I'll make sure*
*it's not darling' the next day Corey woke early.*
*As she hadn't been able to sleep thinking about things.*
*Corey knew she needed to get out of the house she left*
*a note for Polly who was a late sleeper.*
*And never rose before 12pm unless it was for work.*
*It was a cold day she selected an emerald green winter*
*coat some snowflake earrings she'd brought recently.*
*To get her in the mood for Christmas as she walked*
*through town she saw a man busking with a guitar.*
*Playing Christmas carols Corey made her way to*
*Changing Seasons.*
*When she'd last visited it had been before Halloween.*
*Now it would be Christmas soon even if her sister hated*
*her Polly loved her and her mother and step-dad.*

*As she entered the shop Christmas Carols were playing.*
*Corey couldn't decide what she wanted to buy or even*
*look at there were so many things.*
*Different colour schemes she and Polly had decided on*
*classic red and green Corey spied some green baubles.*
*She decided she'd get them to replace the old ones as well*
*as a red nutcracker she loved shopping for Christmas.*
*More than the day itself Polly had always preferred*
*Christmas Eve and New Year's Eve as did she 'Corey'.*
*A voice called she turned around a pretty woman with*
*red hair stared back at her.*
*Suddenly she realised it was her dad's ex-girlfriend Cora.*
*'Hi' Corey said surprised to see her 'Corey you look*
*great' so do you' 'I haven't seen you in years' 'I'm sorry'.*
*'About the time dad pushed you into the Christmas tree'.*
*'Don't be it wasn't your fault he was an alcoholic'.*
*'I thought I could change him one day I realised*
*I couldn't' 'no-one could he died recently' 'I'm sorry'.*
*'I think his liver probably packed up we were estranged*
*for years and Dan' 'how is he?' 'fine he's going on trial'.*
*'For rape Nicky's not speaking to me because she thinks*
*he's innocent' 'and you don't' 'he did it to me'.*
*'I could never tell anyone and he raped my ex-girlfriend'.*
*'Nicky wanted me to be a character witness I couldn't do*
*it lie' 'and you shouldn't have to'.*

*'Anyway Christmas is ruined Nicky won't speak to me'.*
*'She wouldn't even give me a chance to explain' 'listen'.*
*'How about we have a chat there's a café over there'.*
*'I can only stay half an hour lunch break' Corey was*
*happy to see Cora again after so many years.*
*She had been the closest thing to a mother that she'd had*
*as a teenager they ordered a black forest hot chocolate.*
*And a slice of carrot cake 'I love the snowflake earrings'.*
*Cora said 'thanks what do you do for a job?' Corey asked.*
*'I work in an art gallery I love it what about you?'.*
*'I have a new solo album coming out after Christmas'.*
*'I can't wait to hear it listen I know how sexual abuse*
*tears families apart my sister our dad you know...'.*
*'My younger sister never believed her they said she*
*was lying I knew she wasn't I saw her crying'.*
*'The pain she went through' 'I kept it a secret for years'.*
*'Because he was my brother I just wanted a*
*normal relationship we did a long time ago'.*
*'And then he became obsessed with me' 'I'm sorry'.*
*'You've done nothing wrong' 'it feels like it' 'I always say*
*the truth comes out in the end' 'what if it doesn't'.*
*'What if Nicky never speaks to me again' 'then it's her*
*loss the bravest thing anyone can do is stand up'.*
*'In a witness box be cross examined by some horrible*
*defence lawyer accusing you of lying'.*

'Yes there are people who lie make up stories but I know your telling the truth' 'what happened to your father?'.
'He got away with it but he died only a year later people get their comeuppance in the end if they do bad things'.
'I promise things will be ok Christmas doesn't have to be ruined still with Polly?' 'yes' 'she's a great girl'.
'Can I ask you something?' 'anything' 'I had this falling out with my friend we've been friends since school'.
'She's not always the easiest person I mean she's nice but things happened to her her mam left when she was eight'.
'She had two kids with this other man then her father wasn't around she was brought up by the housekeeper'.
'Then her uncle abused her and she was like a bitch at school we never knew why'.
'And she told me about the abuse just me no-one else till years later I always thought there was a reason why'.
'She told me anyway her sister didn't treat her well'.
'Like she always goes on about being their mother's favourite and I can relate to that'.
'Because my mam always hated me preferred Nicky and Dan this one time I was at her mam's wedding'.
'We were fifteen I started playing in bands and she was crying because they ignored her'.
'Somehow I felt we connected we had this row the other day Victoria she said she'd always been lonely'.

'Throughout her life that she wanted to kill herself'.
'I never realised I heard this conversation her sister
said how she preferred her other sister'.
'That things were better before Victoria was reunited
with them I told her I thought I would be helping'.
'She got angry first she said I was lying then she said
that she knew she wasn't her mother's favourite'.
'But that being with them was better than being alone'.
'But I hate the way they treat her like second best'.
'Her mam's ok sometimes but not her sister she said
I was only her friend because I felt sorry for her'.
'But it's not true what should I say to make it ok?'.
'I wish I never heard the conversation' 'we've all made
mistakes whatever even if her family don't treat her well'.
'All you can do is be there as a friend she'll come round'.
'What if she doesn't' 'it sounds like she has issues'.
'Nothing to do with you the fact she told you about
the abuse over anyone else show's she trusts you'.
'All friendships have their up's and downs' 'I know'.
'There's something else I found out a few months ago'.
'Victoria she's my sister but she doesn't know dad has
two other kids one son he died of a drugs overdose'.
'And Victoria my aunt told me she started saying these
things like her mam worked in a wedding shop'.
'And her dad was a politician I knew it was her'.

'And I've never told her I spoke to her mam April'.
'She owns the wedding shop in town we both agreed not
to tell her yet apparently she had a fling with my dad'.
'Same time as dad was seeing mam she said she thought
I was happy with Dan and my dad'.
'Victoria's mother went with this other man she said she
never wanted to rock the boat so Victoria never knew'.
'That my dad is her dad and I only found out a
few months ago' 'that is a family secret'.
'I think you should make it up with her then tell
her the truth' 'I can't not till things have settled'.
'Maybe in the new year' 'ok but do it listen life's too short'.
'And family becomes more important the older you get'.
'I know' 'listen I have to go because I have an
art exhibition but it's been great seeing you'.
'I'll give you my business card then we can follow each
other on Twitter' 'ok' Cora gave her a hug 'bye Corey'.
'Bye' Corey thought about what Cora had said she knew
she had to tell Victoria the truth one day soon.
And she hated the fact they had fallen out with each other.
Corey left the shopping centre as she ventured into
St Ann's church with it's beautiful stein glass windows.
She always loved churches and her faith was important
to her she ventured inside she sat down thinking.
If only god had all the answers she'd be ok.

*Corey saw some people walking around she unzipped her jacket as she looked at the windows.*

*And she had always wanted to do a stein glass making course she loved them with their different designs.*

*And colours Corey spied a girl with dark brown hair silver hoop earrings wearing a navy coat.*

*She realised it was Victoria 'Corey' 'hi' 'I'm sorry'.*

*'For the horrible things I said' 'it's ok' 'I never meant them I was angry at everything' 'I shouldn't have told you'.*

*'About the conversation' 'no it was only the truth'.*

*'It wasn't my business' Victoria sat down beside her.*

*'Your life was hard too being beaten by your dad'.*

*'Having to deal with an alcoholic' 'I had no idea you thought about killing yourself'.*

*'You always seemed so confident' 'it was an act I hated my life it wasn't until I had Sapphire I finally felt ok'.*

*'And I'm sorry what I said about your brother and sister'.*

*'It's true your right I run a restaurant with my sister'.*

*'Who I could never tell the truth to about Daniel'.*

*'Now I have Nikcy hates me but at least I don't have to pretend everything is ok when it's not'.*

*'I'm glad that you told the truth about him' 'me too'.*

*'You were right about my family everything you said'.*

*'They don't care about me like I want them too'.*

*'I'm sure they do' 'no Corey I went to this family party'.*

'The other day it was like I wasn't there I felt invisible'.
'Me my mother and Katie all of them my Aunts they barely
spoke to me I hate them all' 'you know I'm here for you'.
'I'm sorry I had a go at you your one of my closest friends
and I don't have that many' 'I don't either'.
'A lot of people in showbiz are fake their only friends
with you if you're flavour of the month'.
'So do you come here often?' Corey asked 'sometimes'.
'When I have the time to come here I find churches
calming if I'm having a bad day' Victoria said 'me too'.
'Want to come round this weekend?' Corey asked.
'I'd love to' 'do you like pasta?' 'love it' 'Polly does this
great pasta dish' 'I can't wait'.
Corey was glad she'd made it up with Victoria.
She hated falling out with people she hoped one day
they could be sisters as well as close friends.
That Saturday night Victoria came round at 6pm as
planned Corey wanted to make sure Victoria was ok.
After the problems with her family it was good they
could be there for each other they listened to music.
As they chatted Polly cooked pasta in white wine sauce.
They sat down to eat they had been friends for so many
years that the conversation always flowed easily.
Polly poured coke with ice 'this pasta looks amazing'.

*Victoria said happy 'it is' Corey said 'my most popular dish' Polly said 'food makes everything ok again'.*

*Corey said 'almost everything' Polly agreed.*

*'I wish your brother never did those things to you'.*

*Victoria said sadly 'he's gonna get what's coming to him'.*

*'We've waited years haven't we Cor he always thought he could do what he wanted to women'.*

*'His ex Amy even saw him bragging in a club how he could get any woman' Polly said 'he sounds awful'.*

*Victoria said 'I never fancied him' 'he used to fancy Polly'.*

*'He always flirted with her' Corey said 'we were good friends once until I found out what he was like'.*

*'I'm worried what will happen at the trial' 'don't worry Cor we'll support you' 'Polly's right'.*

*That evening they watched Strictly Come Dancing as they ate Maltesers and drank Coca Cola.*

*At 8.30pm they heard a knock at the door Corey checked her appearance before answering.*

*As she stood there in shock it was Daniel she felt anxious immediately her happy mood turned sour.*

*The last time she'd seen him had been at the family meal.*

*When he gave her the lingerie he occasionally texted her. He'd given no warning he was coming to the house.*

'Can I come in?' 'ok' she didn't want him anywhere the house but if she said no it would make things worse.
'Party night with your friends going about your life as normal' 'I can't because your ex-girlfriend and her mate'.
'Are accusing me of rape!' 'I didn't know Amy had gone out with you until recently' 'no but your supporting her'.
'In court unbelievable are you forgetting what she did!'.
'How she treated you! she cheated on you with another man you even threw her out the flat you shared'.
'Now she's your best mate!' 'it's not like that!' 'then how is it?' 'I saw her two months ago at a speech I was doing'.
'For a charity and Amy was there and then I met her again at the train station we got on well we became friends'.
'Amy's a liar!' 'I don't think so' 'she is! you don't seriously believe her over me your own brother!' 'she wouldn't lie'.
'Why didn't she come forward seventeen years ago when the rape supposedly took place' 'maybe she was scared'.
'Cor you don't have to answer him we all know what you did and what your doing now!' Polly said angry.
'Your trying to make out your innocent!' 'I am' 'remember when you tried to rape Corey and she was so scared'.
'Carol had to calm her down or when you date raped her'.
'We know what you did to her and Amy so don't bother coming round here playing the innocent!'.

*'This is all your fault!' 'mine how?' 'you must of put her up to it one minute she's prepared to support the defence'. 'Now she's on the prosecution's side Amy's side'.*

*'Polly didn't do anything! I never said I'd support you'. 'It was Nicky asking for a lawyer I won't do it I won't lie in court knowing what you are!' 'what's that?'.*

*'A sex abuser!' 'you bitch!' Daniel pinned Corey against the curtain a reminder of how threatening and violent. Her brother could be 'leave her alone before I call the police!' Polly said 'ok here's one last chance'.*

*'To put things right you either support me in court'. 'Or what?' 'I'll turn Douglas against you he'll never want to speak to you ever again!' 'you wouldn't do that!' 'I will'. 'She doesn't need your threats!' Polly said 'when you change your mind let me know'.*

*'She won't change her mind' Daniel left Corey knew why she'd been estranged from her brother for so many years. He was a nasty piece of work just like their father.*

*'Cor are you ok?' 'I can't have Douglas hate me'.*

*'You can't let Dan get away with it he's dangerous violent'. 'And a sex predator' 'I know he is' 'you need to talk to Douglas explain what happened'.*

*'If he chooses not to believe you there's nothing you can do but at least talk to him about things' 'I will'.*

'I'll make him believe me' 'explain that you're not doing
this to get revenge just justice for what's right'.
'To stop him doing it to other women' 'Polly's right'.
'We'll both support you in court' Victoria said Corey was
grateful she'd show her brother he couldn't control her.
Like in the past the following afternoon Corey decided
to go see Douglas she was worried.
That her brother would turn her own son against her.
He was that cruel she had to talk to Douglas first he
was dancing at a Christmas event at a local church.
He'd been doing Irish dancing since he was a teenager.
He usually told her when he had an event on he hadn't
this time a bad sign Nicky had probably told him.
About  Daniel they would probably have blamed Amy.
And now Polly Corey knew she had to explain everything.
Douglas was now twenty nine she hoped he could make
his mind up about things that he might believe her.
But as Daniel had helped raise him she knew how close
he was to his uncle which made things harder.
As Corey ventured out alone this was something she had to
do by herself her mother Carol drove them to the church.
As they sat watching the show Corey wondered what
Douglas's reaction might be.
If he knew she would be attending they sat somewhere
in the middle as the show started people sang carols.

*As musicians played instruments the harp and flute.*
*Douglas danced well over the years he'd developed*
*into a confident dancer he was also a good singer.*
*Inheriting her singing talent he'd joined a boy band.*
*For years they'd had some hits in the Irish charts he was*
*now a solo singer an hour later the show was over.*
*As people collected charity tins Corey made her way to the*
*back as she asked someone if she could talk to her son.*
*'Wait here' she was told he appeared 'you came then'.*
*He sounded angry at her 'course I always come to*
*see you in your shows' 'you've got a nerve!'.*
*'After what you've done!' 'please can we chat let me*
*explain' 'fine! I'll see you in a minute' 'he hates me'.*
*Corey said sadly 'it's only natural for him to believe*
*Daniel but he must listen to you' 'what if he doesn't?'.*
*'We'll make him see sense' Carol assured her.*
*Corey wasn't so sure at least her mother was there for*
*moral support Douglas returned wearing a grey sweater.*
*As he put on a matching coat 'I'll be outside you were*
*great' Carol said 'thanks' Douglas replied.*
*He didn't look happy how was she going to make him*
*see she was telling the truth about Daniel.*
*Corey remembered what Polly had said that there was*
*nothing she could do if he chose to believe Daniel.*
*She just had to put her side of the story 'I'm sorry'.*

'That things have to be like this' Corey said 'your sorry'.
'Really this is a joke! my uncle your brother could go to
jail because of this her lies Amy and the other girl'.
'How can you make up things accuse him of rape!'.
'Daniel would never rape a girl what kind of woman
waits seventeen years to accuse someone'.
'And you making out your own brother sexually abused
you! 'don't you see this is what he's doing trying to do'.
'Poison you against me!' 'you had dinner with him'.
'Not long ago with Nicky and his fiancée you didn't have
a problem then if he did what you said he did'.
'You wouldn't have you wouldn't be anywhere near him'.
'Polly put you up to this Nicky said because they had a
falling out just admit it you were planning to support him'.
'Now your taking their side I thought we were family!'.
'We are!' 'family don't stab each other in the back'.
'He was always your best friend your doing this to us!'
'For the record I couldn't stand to be anywhere near him'.
'But I knew how people would react if they knew the truth'
'you know the truth about what really happened'.
'That he isn't capable of what your saying I'm ashamed'.
'To call you my mother I hope the truth comes out in
court!' Douglas was angry Corey understood why.
But it hurt that everyone assumed she was lying.

*Even her own son that everyone thought Daniel was wonderful a great person Corey watched.*

*As Douglas walked away rejoining his friends he got into a car she got into her waiting car with Carol.*

*'How did it go?' 'he hates me' 'listen I'll talk to him for you' 'he wouldn't listen he didn't even hear me out'.*

*'Or give me a chance Dougie just assumed I was lying'.*

*'And Daniel was innocent' 'Daniel is persuasive but let's see how convincing he is in court cross examined'.*

*'By a jury he's bound to get found out soon I'll talk to Douglas I'll make him listen to me'.*

*'And if he still doesn't believe me it's his choice' 'thanks'.*

*'I promise I'll be there for you everything will work out'.*

*It was a frosty December afternoon Kim and Stacey were getting ready to go to Hyde Park's Winter Wonderland.*

*The UK's biggest annual Christmas event with Christmas markets ice skating, Paddington On Ice, a comedy club.*

*A bar and even ice sculpting the whole family was coming.*

*Their mum Aunt Veronica their children Shandy twelve.*

*And Tahilia who was nineteen Stacey had gone through a phase of hating Christmas finding it over commercialised.*

*But now loved it and had started adding different decorations every year Polly couldn't come.*

*Due to appearing in panto for two months till the end of January a taxi arrived to pick up Kim and Shandy.*

As they climbed inside 'love the coat' Stacey said her
sister wore a silver coat with white fur trim.
And a silver hairband her hair dyed with golden blonde
streaks her sister didn't do understated.
Stacey wore a Joe Brown long berry coloured coat and
beret they looked around as they wondered where to go.
Their mum suggested the Christmas markets as they
looked at wood sculptures,candy canes and paintings.
And Christmas lamps they brought a few gifts as they
walked round with paper bags.
There was a lovely atmosphere after they decided to watch
Paddington On Ice Stacey had always loved ice skating.
'I can't remember the last time I saw an ice show'.
'Me neither Stace' Kim replied 'I know it's for kids but
I don't care' 'agree I'm Peter Pan I never grew up'.
Stacey joked 'have you seen Stacey's Disney collection'.
Marcee joked to their Aunt Veronica 'not for a while'.
'In my defence I only collect top quality items I'll tell you
why I love Disney because there's always a happy ending'.
'Except the Fox & the Hound and I love the characters
especially Frozen' 'me too Elsa and Anna's relationship'.
'Is like me and Stace' Kim joked Kim looked over as she
spied a mixed-race man with his daughter.
Suddenly she did a double take 'oh my god!' 'what is it?'.
Veronica asked 'nothing' 'what's up?' Stacey asked.

'It's Richie' 'are you sure?' 'yes look over there don't tell mum besides he's with his teenage daughter'.

'Maybe it's fate you were meant to see him again'.

'Not like this besides we don't know why mum split from him' 'he looks happy' 'I know' 'think he'll recognise you'.

'Course' 'I mean you haven't seen him since you were seventeen and you dyed your hair blonde recently'.

'Maybe not I wanted to see him again not like this'.

'See who again?' Marcee asked 'no-one just an ex'.

'You just seen an ex-boyfriend?' 'something like that'.

'Don't worry safety in numbers' 'I guess' the show started Kim couldn't completely relax.

Richie didn't seem to have recognised her chatting to his daughter after forty five minutes there was an interval.

'I'm staying here' Veronica said 'well me and Stace are gonna go get some hot chocolates' 'sounds tempting'.

'But I can't be bothered to queue' Marcee said.

'Maybe after the show' Kim said as they made their way to a kiosk 'how about I just queue' Kim suggested.

'Ok I'll wait here' Kim browsed the flavours black forest mint and chocolate orange on the board.

She just hoped the queue would go down quick Kim turned around looking at a man 'long queue' he said.

She smiled as she realised it was Richie it was him.

'Yeah living in London' 'I live in Hampshire'.

'Couldn't move back but love to visit' he clearly didn't
recognise her he'd aged well Kim thought.
She'd last seen him age seventeen he'd been in his
mid-thirties he must have been now around sixty.
But looked a decade younger Kim knew she had to
tell him who she was she might never see him again.
Stacey was right it was fate they were meant to see each
other again she was sure her mum had loved him.
To stay with him for so many years 'Richie it's me Kim'.
'You might not remember me' 'not Marcee's Kim' 'yeah'.
'I didn't recognise you' 'I just dyed my hair blonde'.
'How old are you now?' 'forty one' 'you look much
younger' 'thanks so do you' 'I can't believe I've seen you'.
'After so many years how's your mum?' 'great'.
'She's been with Andy for years her husband my step-dad'.
'That's great I've been with my wife for years what about
you?' 'I'm single I was with someone for years'.
'I dated some other people but it didn't work out I've got
a daughter Shandy she's twelve' 'does she look like you?'.
'Kind of' Kim realised she'd reached the front of the queue
'what can I get you?' 'chocolate orange hot chocolate'.
'Coming up' 'and one black forest one mint' 'will you be
able to carry all those?' Richie asked 'Stace is over there'.
Kim beckoned her over 'I've ordered three'.
'One of each flavour Stace this is Richie' 'hi' Stacey said.

*'I'm a big fan' 'thanks' 'well I'd best be going nice*
*seeing you again and you Stacey' 'was that him?' 'yeah'.*
*'My old step-dad' 'he seems nice' 'yeah he was'.*
*'Let's wait here one minute' they waited as Richie left the*
*café he greeted his wife and daughter a younger child.*
*Was with them possibly his granddaughter.*
*'Let's go told you it was a bad idea me seeing him again'.*
*Kim said disappointed 'he didn't even ask for my number'.*
*'Or even social media' 'I would have when Polly split from*
*Corey she always thought of Douglas as her step-son'.*
*'How could I have thought I meant something to him'.*
*'I mean nothing just like my real dad' 'Kim it's ok' 'no'.*
*'I always wanted a dad so much I did once Andy's*
*the only father figure who cares about me'.*
*'Please don't say anything to mum' 'I won't let's go back'.*
*They made their way back to the ice rink area 'you two*
*took a while it's about to start' 'sorry mum queue'.*
*'Got you a mint hot chocolate' 'lovely me and Vee*
*can share it' Stacey felt sorry for Kim.*
*Not having the father figure she'd always wanted.*
*They watched the show Kim smiled and clapped but*
*Stacey could see how upset she was she glanced over.*
*Richie never glanced back focused on his daughter.*
*As she promised she didn't say anything to her mum.*
*The next day they went round to visit Louie at his flat.*

*Stacey knew he'd cheer Kim up after the night before.*
*It was 2pm as they arrived knocking on the door.*
*'Stace Kim come in I'm just about to put up the*
*Christmas tree fake of course' 'if you need any help?'.*
*'That would be great I have boxes of baubles'.*
*'I'm thinking snowflake for the top of the tree the star*
*kept falling down last year and candy canes'.*
*They hung their coats up as they stepped inside the living*
*room they were glad to be out of the cold 'how's Rod?'.*
*Stacey asked 'my brother he's fine' 'found a job yet?'.*
*'He did not one completely legal he got involved in*
*one of those winter wonderland's'.*
*'You know the ones you hear about on the news for*
*taking money from people for rubbish attractions'.*
*'We went to Hyde Park's Winter Wonderland last night'*
*Stacey said 'I really don't want to see him back inside'.*
*'Anyway he's been writing an adult panto' 'sounds like*
*fun' 'oh it will be I'm playing Prince Charming'.*
*'In that case I have to see it' 'thanks Stace it's at the*
*start of February for two weeks' 'we'll come see it'.*
*'Won't we Kim' 'course' 'thanks we're also looking at*
*buying a building for Rod for a restaurant'.*
*'Since that whole fiasco of him getting fired for having*
*a criminal record'.*
*'He decided that he should open his own restaurant'.*

'Great idea' 'I think so no boss to answer to we're
thinking start small maybe a café we're looking around'.
'How is ragdoll?' 'Corey ok I guess considering Polly
says Daniel came to the house threatening her'.
'She needs to make sure the doors are locked
and that bastard can't get in'.
'He was hoping she'd support him in court but she just
couldn't bring herself to do it' 'I don't blame her'.
'So now she's on the prosecutions side with Amy
and the other girl' 'good on her it must be hard'.
'I always got a dark vibe off Daniel never knew why
he always seemed possessive I don't know what it was'.
'Well it's all going to come out at the trial I'm gonna
go support her I don't care what I'm doing'.
'If I have to take a week off' Stacey said 'I'm the same'.
'I just hope it's all worth it' 'what do you mean?'.
'He got away with it this long being a sex predator'.
'And sometimes these cases collapse hopefully he'll
get what's coming to him if he calls round again'.
'Make sure she records him any conversations'.
'Good idea I'll tell her' Stacey said the girls began
helping Louie put baubles on the tree as they chatted.
'So how's your love life still with Lance?' Stacey asked.
'Still separated looks like divorce is on the horizon'.

'Can't you sort things out' 'no he's been posting photos
of his new boyfriend on social media' 'sorry'.
'It's for the best shows what he thinks of me'.
'You'll find someone soon' 'I don't actually know
if I want to now I'm a bit older in my forties'.
'I quite like it being single not having to text someone all
the time I can go out when I want no-one to answer to'.
'I'm thinking he did me a favour I hang out with Rod'.
'And my friends life is ok actually except having HIV'.
'But as long as I take my drugs in fact I think I'm over men
at the moment looking at my copy of Attitude magazine'.
'Is enough for me and Christmas is coming' 'we can't wait
Kim's single too so don't worry'.
'You're welcome to come round for Christmas' 'thankyou'.
'For the offrer but I'll be having it with Rod and my
favourite Aunt' 'we'll be in Essex this year with mum'.
'Andy Aunt Veronica and the kids' 'how are they?' 'great'.
'Loving the polar bear' Stacey said spying a giant statue
in the corner of the living room 'thanks'.
'I am going to try and be Mr Christmas this year except
none of those annoying Christmas lights outside'.
'Just one snowflake in the window but inside will be
a different story' 'same as us' Kim said.
'Put it this way we keep the Christmas shops in business'
Stacey joked 'that's the spirit' Louie agreed.

*As Douglas walked through Grafton Street with his sister*
*Nicky and Daniel's fiancée Liza.*
*He somehow felt left out they laughed as they shopped.*
*Since meeting several months ago they had become*
*the best of friends he found Liza a bit annoying.*
*But since his uncle was marrying her he tolerated her.*
*She was also one of those girls who's life revolved*
*around clothes and make-up.*
*Liza also thought she was more attractive than she was.*
*Squeezing herself into dresses that were too small.*
*Wearing too much fake tan and dying her hair a*
*gothic very dark brown almost black and gossiping.*
*About boring subjects he didn't get what his brother*
*saw in her or even Nicky who was much more intelligent.*
*And naturally pretty with blonde hair and natural*
*make-up he also missed Corey a lot.*
*Growing up she'd been his sister until he found out*
*age thirteen she was his mother.*
*Secretly brought up by their mother Marie she had*
*died several years ago and they'd never gotten on.*
*Or his step-father Clive Daniel had always been a father*
*figure to him there was only twelve years between them.*
*Which meant he was also like an older brother that's*
*why he couldn't believe he would hurt Corey.*
*Especially since they were brother and sister.*

*When he'd found out they had assured him Daniel's*
*accusers were lying and wanted to cause trouble.*
*Now he wasn't so sure what if there was the smallest*
*chance they were telling the truth.*
*He hated himself for feeling that way 'Nicky' he asked.*
*'Yes' 'what's gonna happen to Daniel?' 'he's gonna get off*
*you know he is' 'what if he doesn't' 'he will their lying!'.*
*'Their pathetic case will collapse especially in court'.*
*'But what if it doesn't' 'they are lying!' 'even Corey'.*
*'Yes I don't know what she's playing at Polly had some*
*bust up with Daniel and she got caught in the crossfire'.*
*'What kind of row?' 'I don't know she even claims Dan*
*tried to rape Corey while drunk unbelievable!'.*
*'They've been best friends all their life and now she's*
*mates with Amy clearly Amy is using Cor'.*
*'Just for her case hopefully she'll see sense until she does*
*I want nothing to do with her and neither should you'.*
*'What about the fact they didn't speak for seven years her*
*and Daniel please tell me you're not doubting him'.*
*'Your own brother' 'I was just saying I want to believe he's*
*innocent' 'he is and it will be proved in a court of law'.*
*'Have you ever witnessed him abusing a woman?' 'no'.*
*'Well then come on' Douglas still had doubts and he didn't*
*know why Corey wouldn't lie about something like this.*
*Would she? maybe he should have talked to her properly.*

Just then he received a text it was from Carol 'just wanted to say hi I know things are awkward at the moment'.
'Between everyone but your still my grandson and I wanted to wish you seasons greetings xxx'.

Suddenly he had an idea maybe he could talk to Carol.
Then he could make up his mind about things he wouldn't tell Nicky or Daniel they wouldn't be happy he replied.
'Hi sorry if I was off with you the other day can I come round?'.

It was a cold December 12th as Douglas made his way through the snow it was only a light covering but even so.
It felt Christmassy as he reached the red door of Carol's house on the outskirts of Dublin.
There hung a pretty wreath he knocked on the door.
As she opened 'hi' she smiled 'come in' 'thanks'.
'Would you like a cup of tea?' 'please' 'coming right up'.
'Shortbread biscuits' 'please' Douglas looked around.
At the photos of family Carol with John her two sons and Corey suddenly he realised his family was split in two.
Would Corey do that unless she had good reason?.
Or had Amy asked her to lie in the trial? he had to know the truth Corey was close to Carol 'I need to talk to you'.
'Is it about Daniel?' 'I wondered if you knew anything'.
'Yes I know a lot things that happened years ago'.
'It's up to you who you believe Corey's not doing this for revenge it's because she couldn't lie for Daniel'.

'And she always knew this day would come she hid
the truth for years about Daniel'.
'Because she knew she wouldn't be believed'.
'Did he sexually abuse her?' 'yes emotional abuse too'.
'He's always been controlling there's been so many
incidents' 'what kind of incidents?'.
'Remember Kitty's wedding' 'yes' 'Daniel got angry'.
'Steve was there he was jealous because he always wanted
Corey to himself he has inappropriate feelings for her'.
'When she married Steve in Vegas he made her get it
annulled and say that she was drunk'.
'He couldn't bare the thought of her being with another
man because he'd always been the only man in her life'.
'Corey always thought it was her fault if he came on
to her that she'd done something to encourage him'.
'When they started going out Daniel threatened to tell
him she had autism or was a gypsy but he didn't care'.
'They'd started going out she said she couldn't see him'.
'Till Daniel had gone back to Ireland because he was
jealous anyway after she married Steve he was angry'.
'Daniel smacked her in the face she covered up her
bruises with make-up'.
'She even lied said a man broke into her house then
Daniel said he wanted to apologise cook her a meal'.

'That's when...' 'what happened?' Douglas could see
Carol looked upset 'tell me what happened'.
'It was that night Dan cooked her a meal I came round'.
'You were there she seemed ok but when I returned
Corey was upset shaking not herself'.
'I knew something had happened so she came back
to mine and told me he read some texts from Steve'.
'That they loved each other wanted to be together'.
'She said he tried to rape her that if I hadn't come round
I would never have left her for ten minutes'.
'To pick up Connor if I knew' suddenly Douglas
remembered that evening 'I remember that night'.
'I knew something was going on they had a row Dan said
he needed to talk to her alone upstairs he looked angry'.
'Corey told me to watch the saucepan cause it was
bubbling I heard shouting I didn't know what it was'.
'Then she told him to get out by tomorrow I don't
remember the rest Corey doesn't get angry very often'.
'It's ok Dougie' 'why didn't I ever realise I remember'.
'When I visited Corey in L.A Daniel hated Steve I didn't
get why he seemed ok'.
'Daniel said he wasn't good enough for Corey called him
an American bastard' 'don't worry you weren't to know'.
'Corey made us promise not to tell anyone she said Nicky
and the rest of her family wouldn't believe her'.

'Who's us?' 'me Polly, Stacey, Louie, Mike and Kitty'.
'You mean you all knew and never said' 'we couldn't
he touched her up at a family meal'.
'Corey said he said he fancied her since he was seventeen'
'I can't believe she never told me I'm her son'.
'It's hard being a woman sometimes when it's your word
against someone else and this is hard for Corey it's incest'.
'You should also know that she thinks he date raped her'.
'When? 'not long after the other incident at a club'.
'I don't know why she agreed to go with him she'd
just secretly married Steve'.
'I suppose she thought she would be safe and she
went with her friend Julie and Colin'.
'She asked him to watch her drink Daniel anyway
one minute she felt fine the next she was ill'.
'And she only had two beers Corey wasn't intoxicated'.
'He took her home anyway she woke later then she had
a flashback Daniel was on top of her it wasn't clear'.
'She can't prove it but she thinks it happened I'm sorry'.
'I had to tell you all this especially just before Christmas'.
'I didn't want you thinking Corey lied she's not a liar'.
'And she wouldn't not about this I witnessed his behaviour
so did Kitty he hit her when they were married'.
'When he found out she might not be able to have kids'.
'I know you love him and he's your uncle'.

*'But he's not the person you think he is' 'I'm glad you told me the truth' Douglas stayed for a while at Carol's.*

*Before leaving a while later as she gave him her Christmas present suddenly it didn't feel like Christmas.*

*He'd been convinced of Daniel's innocence now he wasn't Carol wouldn't lie and neither would Corey.*

*Suddenly things made sense especially the night Carol had come round after they cooked a meal.*

*How he hated himself for not knowing what was going on.*

*Why had he never realised it before his own mother could have been raped and it would have been his fault.*

*As December 24th came round suddenly Douglas didn't feel like celebrating Christmas anymore.*

*With Daniel, Nicky and Liza and he didn't have a girlfriend his last relationship had been a year ago.*

*He wished he could have been celebrating with Corey and Polly they would be seeing Carol and John.*

*Corey's half-brothers Grahame & Connor.*

*Instead he was having Christmas Day with people he didn't want to be with his dad Colin had invited him over.*

*A few weeks before he'd said he'd see him Boxing Day.*

*How he wished he'd taken him up on his offer it was too late as Douglas woke that Christmas morning.*

*He didn't feel like celebrating no girlfriend estranged from his mother and having to be around Liza.*

*Who he couldn't stand Daniel had never been good*
*at picking women.*
*His ex-wife Lizzie had been even more annoying.*
*Somehow he'd get through Christmas Day at least Nicky*
*was a good chef her husband Ryan would be coming.*
*And her two sons Nicky woke him at 11am as he had never*
*been a morning person he reluctantly got dressed.*
*Selecting a dark green long sleeved top and grey jogging*
*bottoms as Nicky greeted him.*
*She threw him a packet of crisps 'keep you going till*
*dinner ready soon we can open presents'.*
*'Merry Christmas' Daniel said 'you too' Douglas knew*
*he'd have to pretend everything was ok when it wasn't.*
*They were his family what choice did he have?.*
*'Shall we open presents?' Daniel suggested they went over*
*to the tree all lit up a classic red and green theme.*
*With a gold star 'these are from me' Daniel handed over*
*his presents as Douglas opened them.*
*It was some computer games and cuff links 'thanks'.*
*Suddenly he felt uneasy being in the company of someone*
*he knew was a rapist Douglas handed over his presents.*
*Some shirts and dragon ornaments which Daniel collected*
*'look at you two all cosy in Christmas Day it'll be great'.*
*Half an hour later dinner was ready as Ryan and Nicky's*
*two sons arrived Jamie twenty and Reagan thirty.*

*They all ate round the table like one perfect family.*
*Only it wasn't he wished he could spend it with*
*his parents his grandmother Nicky's dinner was great.*
*Which somehow made things better but it still wasn't*
*his dream Christmas 'enjoying dinner?' Nicky asked.*
*'Yes lovely' Douglas replied 'you seem quiet'.*
*'Just thinking' 'about Corey' 'maybe' 'well it's her own*
*fault and she's with Carol probably I'm guessing'.*
*'And unlike Dan she doesn't have a false rape charge*
*hanging over her' 'I don't hate her'.*
*'I just don't get why she lied' Daniel said 'cause of Amy'.*
*'Using her to win her trial and her friend we're not*
*discussing this on Christmas Day'.*
*'Daniel will be vindicated in a court of law!'.*
*'And those three will be shown up for the liar's they are!'.*
*Nicky said angry how Douglas wished he could have said*
*what Carol told him but it would create a row.*
*'Anyway let's enjoy Christmas Day forget about Corey'.*
*'She is your sister' 'yes but we're not blood related'.*
*'I want nothing to do with her after what she said and*
*neither should you unless your on her side' 'course not'.*
*'But she is my mam' 'if you want to see Corey it's your*
*choice but we won't be happy about it'.*
*'How would you feel if someone accused you of something*
*you hadn't done some girl you slept with years ago'.*

'Maybe now you get what it's like for Dan and the trial will be so stressful' 'I'll be ok' 'I know you will'.

'We'll help you get through it' Nicky said as she hugged Daniel Douglas felt trapped.

Knowing he might not be innocent later that afternoon Douglas faked being happy.

When he didn't want to be there he texted Corey Happy Christmas he received a reply.
'Hope your having a great Christmas see you soon xxx'.

That evening everyone watched TV drank wine the next day Douglas went to see Colin.

A few days later he decided to see Corey he missed her. And had to make sure she was ok he had also felt bad since their row outside the church he knocked on the door. Polly answered 'is Corey in?' 'one minute Cor Dougie's here' she shouted upstairs she came downstairs.

'Hi' she said thanks for the text I thought you hated me'.

'I'm sorry for having a go at you not hearing you out'.

'Giving you a chance to explain' 'it's ok I don't mind'.

'That you believe Dan but I want you to know I'm telling you the truth and Amy' 'I know you are'.

'But you didn't believe me before' 'I talked to Carol'.

'She told me everything that he hit you tried to rape you'.

'Because he was jealous of Steve that he made you get your wedding annulled in Las Vegas'.

*'And that night we had dinner when you rowed and you
chatted upstairs why didn't you say he tried to rape you'.
'Because I knew no-one would believe me he found texts
from Steve saying he loved me and he got angry'.
'And forced me on the bed' 'it's ok' Douglas gave her
a hug 'I believe you and I'll be on your side'.
'You don't have to I'll understand if you don't want to'.
'I want to I can't support him knowing what he's done'.
'I don't want him to hurt other women that's why
I'm doing this' 'I know' 'they hate me'.
'Nicky and Daniel' Corey said upset 'I don't hate you'.
'It's ok I'll be with you in court' 'you'd do that for me'.
'Your my mother I wish I could have had Christmas
with you I hate Liza she's so plastic' Corey smiled.
'She's not you I hate her I don't know what Dan see's in
her and Nicky their two best friends now' 'I know'.
'We used to be close' Corey said 'you've got me I promise'.
'Thanks you know you might have to give evidence'.
'They'll want to know about that night' 'I don't mind'.
'Really' 'no anything to support you' Corey was happy.
Her son was now supporting her she felt better she hoped
her brother would get justice for what he'd done.
He was a danger to women.*

## Fighting the pain

It was a cold January 28th and the first day of Daniel's
trial Corey didn't have to give evidence.
Until the following week Douglas had told Daniel
he wouldn't be a character witness for him.
And would be supporting Corey she was grateful.
She knew how angry Nicky would be and Daniel as she
made her way to court she saw Amy 'hi Cor you ok?'.
'Yes' 'I'm nervous but I have to do this' 'I know'.
'Good luck I'm not giving evidence till next week'.
'I'm at the end of the week' Amy said 'see you later'.
Somehow seeing Amy calmed her nerves they made
their way into court suddenly it all felt real.
The last time she'd been in a courtroom was age
twenty seven when she got joint custody of Douglas.
Corey looked around Polly was with her having finished
Panto they watched as the judge walked through the court.
Along with the barristers 'all rise the prosecution
will go first' Corey had hired her solicitor Greg.
Who had helped her many years ago she knew he was
good at his job Amy had also hired him on Corey's advice.
'The defendant is charged with two counts of rape'.
'And one attempted rape on three women the victims
claim they were locked in a bedroom'.

'Where the defendant raped them a third victim also says he attempted to force himself on her'.

'Over the next few days we will hear evidence from the three victims as well as character witnesses'.

'And other witnesses who know what really happened'. 'I am satisfied with the opening statement over to the prosecution' 'I call the defendant to the stand'.

'Please give your full name' the judge asked.

Corey watched as her brother stood she couldn't read his expressions but she knew he must have been nervous.

'Daniel Steven O'Hanlon' 'do you swear to tell the truth'. 'And nothing but the truth?' 'I do' 'we can now start the trial' Greg stood up ready to begin questioning Daniel.

'I'm going to start with the first victim Martine Mulley'. 'She was an ex-girlfriend of yours?' 'yes' 'how long were you together?' 'around a year'.

'How old were you when you were dating?' 'nineteen'. 'Twenty' 'how did you meet?' 'in a bar' 'what kind of bar?' 'just a regular pub bar I chatted her up'.

'Then we swapped numbers started dating' 'you were together a year means this was a serious relationship'. 'Yes it was' 'did you ever talk about anything more serious like getting engaged?' 'yes we were young'.

'Would you say you treated her with respect?' 'yes'.

'I brought her flowers opened doors' 'did you ever have any fall outs?' 'occasionally like all couples do'.

'But I liked her we were in love' 'on September 26th 2005'.

'It's alleged you raped Miss Mulley that you locked her in her bedroom while her parents were out on a fishing trip'.

'Is it true?' 'no' 'that afternoon she says you pressured her for sex when she didn't feel like it' 'no'.

'I'd never pressure any woman for sex it's not who I am'.

Corey couldn't believe what she was hearing 'she said she wouldn't have sex without a condom'.

'But you said you wanted it anyway when she said no you locked the bedroom door and raped her on the bed'.

'After the relationship ended' 'no that never happened'.

'The door didn't even have a lock on and even if it did how would I know where the key was it wasn't my house'.

'So you deny the charge' 'of course I never raped her'.

'I now want to move on to your next victim Amy O'Dowd'.

'You were also in a relationship' 'yes' 'you were twenty six at the time' 'yes around that age'.

'I'll ask you how you met' 'at a club I liked her she saw me she started chatting me up we agreed to see each other'.

'So we did' 'miss O'Dowd says you dated for six months'.

'Around that' 'what kind of relationship was it?' 'great'.

'She was great she had class we liked each other'.

'Did you love each other?' 'I've had a few serious
relationships in my life' 'she alleges you were possessive'.
'Controlling checking her phone who she talked to in the
pub is that true?' 'no I've never controlled any woman'.
Corey knew her brother was lying and only hoped the jury
would see through his lies 'it's not me what she said'.
'Miss O'Dowd says she tried to end the relationship'.
'But you didn't want to' 'it came to a natural end'.
'We both agreed' 'before it ended she alleges you
came home drunk one night to the flat you shared'.
'And you demanded sex she said no you locked the
bedroom door and raped her' 'no I never raped her'.
'Or Martine' 'I now want to ask about your third alleged
victim your sister Corey O'Hanlon'.
'Tell me what would you say your relationship was like?'.
'Close we were always close we grew up with an alcoholic
father he was violent so it was always me and her'.
'Looking out for each other' 'did you ever fancy or have
feelings for your sister growing up?' 'never'.
'What about when you became adults' 'no she's my sister'.
'I care about her not like that' 'is it true you shared a flat'.
'For two years you were sixteen she was seventeen' 'yes'.
'Is it true you once said 'if you were with another man
I'd be jealous they'd be taking my sister away from me'.

'Maybe it was a joke that's all' 'did you begin to have feelings for her when she was around eighteen'.
'That you tried to kiss her?' 'no it's a lie I never did that'.
'I never would' 'is it true you tried to kiss Corey again'.
'Age twenty seven after you split from your first wife?'.
'It was a peck on the lips that's all nothing else'.
'And what about on Corey's twenty ninth birthday'.
'You had cocktails at a club McCoy's you again kissed her inappropriately' 'it never happened!'.
'I do not fancy my sister never have done!'.
'Are you sure?' 'I've only ever kissed her on the cheek'.
Or a peck on the lips I've never put my tongue down her throat we don't have that kind of relationship'.
'Let's talk about Steve Corey's ex-husband after she split from Polly Patterson she began dating Steve'.
'And from what I've heard you didn't like it because you were always the only man in her life'.
'Due to the fact she was a lesbian' 'I didn't like Steve'.
'Because I felt he was using her' 'in what way?'.
'For career reasons he hadn't had a hit film in years'.
'Until he did that movie I Love New York with her I just didn't like him I thought she deserved better'.
'Is that because you had inappropriate feelings for Corey?' 'no because he was using her for his career'.

'That's all he was a womanizer I was looking out for her'.
Corey couldn't believe what she was hearing there were
men who'd dated far more women than Steve.
She knew her brother was trying to find a way out.
Of the accusations 'you also saw Steve one Christmas'.
'Corey was thirty four at the time you were staying in
New York you said some things to him'.
'That she would be a notch on his bedpost' 'well it's true'.
'That's what he's like' 'is it true when Corey married Steve
in Las Vegas you weren't happy'.
'And made her annul her marriage?' 'I suggested she
should and Kitty her bandmate'.
'Because we felt she rushed into it and she'd been
drinking the night before' 'not because you were jealous'.
'That she'd married Steve' 'no' 'is it true you smacked
Corey in the face and she had to cover up her bruises'.
'With make-up because you were jealous of her
relationship with Steve?' 'no I'd never hit my sister'.
'I love Corey she's my best friend I'd never let her come to
any harm anything I said about Steve was to protect her'.
'Not because I had inappropriate feelings' 'is it true
you got so angry that you attempted to rape Corey'.
'In April 2018 in her own bedroom? that you found texts'.
'From Steve saying how much he loved your sister'.

'When she said she wanted a normal relationship you
pinned her down on the bed so you could rape her' 'no'.
'None of this is true it's all lies!' 'that if her mother Carol
hadn't called round you would have raped her'.
'You saw Corey in a club with Colin her son's father'.
'And Steve his friend Kieran Corey had secretly married
Steve this time in Ireland which she kept secret worried'.
'As to what you would say or do she even lied saying
she kissed a girl' 'she kept it secret'.
'Because she was a lesbian Steve was the only man
she'd dated as an adult she was worried'.
'What her lesbian friends or fans would think it had
nothing to do with me' 'and finally for my last question'.
'Is it true you attempted to date rape her at a club Jamie's
you spiked her drink'.
'When her friend Julie Hutchings went to the toilet'.
'Not long after she felt ill disorientated you took her
home offered her a glass of water took off her clothes'.
'And raped her using a date rape drug in May 2018' 'no'.
'Why would I do that to my sister' 'because having failed
in your attempt to rape her you now knew the only way'.
'Was by date rape' 'Corey had been drinking several
pints of beer she felt ill and I took her home'
'Because she's my sister and I care about her
do you know how upsetting this is'.

*'To be accused of raping my own sister!' 'I just want*
*the facts' 'the facts are I never did any those things'.*
*'That I'm being accused of doing' 'no further questions'.*
*'The court will return tomorrow court adjourned'.*
*'That bastard makes me angry!' Polly said to Corey.*
*'I know he's done nothing but lie hopefully he'll finally*
*admit the truth' 'I doubt it' 'we can but hope'.*
*Corey hoped Daniel would be made to pay for his crimes.*
*The following day the court returned for the defence's*
*turn as Daniel returned to the dock 'this is day two'.*
*'Of this trial we will now hear from the defence'.*
*'Thankyou Daniel O'Hanlon is accused of these crimes'.*
*'Which are not true I will now question the accused*
*on the three counts Martine Mulley tell me about her'.*
*'Was she your first serious girlfriend?' 'yes I had some*
*flings but she was the girl I wanted to marry'.*
*'I'm from gypsy culture and we don't play around'.*
*'This was a loving relationship in which you even*
*talked about getting married' 'yes we would have…'.*
*'Why didn't you?' 'she cheated on me' 'how far into*
*the relationship before you found out?'.*
*'About two months before things changed she went quiet'.*
*'I thought it was me that I'd done something'.*
*'How did you find out?' 'a friend told me and I found*
*texts on her phone' 'how did you split up?'.*

'I told her one day I'd found out she was cheating that
I didn't want us to be together if I didn't trust her'.
'Now about the day of the alleged rape her parents went
out on a fishing trip was this a regular occurrence?'.
'Sometimes they liked outdoor sports like absailing'.
'Walking that kind of thing we only went with them
occasionally'. Martine said she felt pressured for sex'.
'And that she wouldn't have sex without a condom'.
'Is this true?' 'no she said we didn't need to worry about
protection that she didn't care if she got pregnant'.
'Because she wanted to be a young mother' 'what
did you say?' 'I wanted to wait a while a few years'.
'Till I was at least twenty one I was the one who suggested
wearing a condom we had before but then she stopped'.
'Wanting to wear protection so we did' 'your accused
of locking the door and raping her'.
'After the relationship ended tell the court what
happened?' 'I never raped her as for locking the door'.
'The door never had a lock on just a handle' 'so you could
not have locked the door?' 'no and it wasn't my house'.
'Why would I rape someone i someone else's house
someone I loved for a year' 'ok let's move on'.
'To Amy O'Dowd you dated in your mid-twenties after
meeting at a club it's said you were possessive'.

'No Amy was in a controlling relationship before me'.
'With an older man that's the last thing I wanted to be'.
'We had a great relationship I loved her' 'tell me did
you come home drunk one night to the flat you shared'.
'Demanding sex?' 'no I'd never behave like that'.
'We hardly ever had sex but I didn't care I loved her'.
'I was a gentlemen' 'you hardly had sex?' 'no she didn't
like having sex I later found out she was a lesbian'.
'And our relationship was a cover but I had no idea
at the time I loved her she was special'.
'So how many times did you have sex?' 'twice'.
Corey couldn't believe her brothers lies and how clever
he was being waiting to be questioned by the defence.
To create a story for each victim she wondered what
he'd say about her 'finally your sister Corey O'Hanlon'.
'Did you ever have a relationship that was more than
friends?' 'no I loved her as a sister no more'.
'Did you have a problem with her ex-husband Steve?'.
'No only because I felt he was using her' 'so you were
never jealous?' 'no' 'what about kissing your sister'.
'Your accused several times most notably outside a Dublin
pub and on her twenty ninth birthday' 'she kissed me'.
'I was shocked it happened after I split from my first wife
Lizzie I never told anyone because I felt uncomfortable'.

'I thought it was my fault that I'd done something
to encourage her to have feelings for me'.
'Corey always said I'd always been the only man in her
life I had no idea she fancied me maybe it's her autism'.
'I don't know' 'in what way?' 'some people with autism
can get obsessed with people'.
'One day Corey confessed she had feelings for me
she shouldn't she always hated my ex-wife'.
'And I never knew why until years later one day when
Corey lived in L.A she kissed me on the lips again'.
'I was shocked I kissed her back I knew it was wrong'.
'I hoped if I did it would stop her feelings for me'.
'Now tell me about the supposed night of the rape on
your sister she said you found texts on her mobile'.
'From her ex-husband' 'I read them I asked her how
serious the relationship was? it was general chat' 'right'.
'She says you pinned her down on the bed' 'no she came
on to me she said she wanted sex I said no'.
'That it was wrong that she was confused she wouldn't
take no for an answer we ended up on the bed'.
'Nothing happened Carol her mam came to the house'.
'I had a go at Corey because it was wrong she said
no-one would have to find out about what happened'.
'That we could have a secret relationship' Corey couldn't
believe how her brother had twisted things.

*Now people would think she came on to him how could he do this to her? 'let's move on'.*

*'To the night of the attempted date rape in May 2018'.*
*'You went to a club with your sister and her friend'.*
*'It's said you spiked her drink took her home and raped her is this true?' 'no I never touched her drink'.*
*'I took her home because she was drunk she was ill'.*
*'I wanted to make sure she was ok' 'so you never date raped your sister' 'no and I never would'.*
*'No further questions' 'the court will return tomorrow'.*
*'Where we will hear the victim's accounts' Corey looked over at her sister who looked angry at her.*
*'Cor are you ok?' Polly asked 'no he lied he said I came on to him and it's not true and now they'll believe him!'.*
*'We still have the victims to be questioned' Greg said.*
*'There's no way he'll be able to be seen as innocent after Martine and Amy speak in court don't worry Cor'.*
*'He's trying to be clever get away with it' 'Polly's right'.*
*'Don't worry we've got this' 'thanks Greg' Corey said.*
*That Wednesday everyone returned to court for the third day of the trial.*
*Amy and Martine would be giving evidence.*
*Hopefully this time her brother would have no chance of being believed after their speeches Greg spoke.*

As they stood up 'may I present to the court the first victim Miss Martine Mulley'.

After saying her name she was ready to give evidence.

'I'd like to ask you about your relationship with Daniel'.

'You dated for around a year' 'yes' 'and during that time would you say the relationship was serious?' 'yes'.

'We talked about getting engaged' 'how was Daniel when you were going out?' 'he was lovely we got on well'.

'I loved him' 'so no cause for concern over his behaviour?' 'no' 'let's move on to the alleged rape'.

'It's said your parents were out that afternoon on a fishing trip' 'yes they were' 'what were you and Daniel doing?'.

'That afternoon if you can remember?' 'we played scrabble we used to play a lot and watch telly'.

'And that afternoon we were kissing he suggested we go into the bedroom to have sex' 'what did you say?'.

'That we should use a condom because I didn't want to get pregnant' 'what happened next?' 'he said it didn't matter'.

'If I got pregnant' 'is it true he locked you in the bedroom?' 'yes' 'did you know he was?'.

'He said one minute I have to do something he locked the door and he pinned me down on the bed'.

'And no-one was in I had to…lie there after the rape'.

'Did you tell anyone?' 'no I thought no-one would believe me' 'Daniel says you cheated with another man'.

'Which led to the end of the relationship was this before or after the rape?' 'I'm not sure it was a long time ago'. 'I can't remember' 'why did your relationship end?'. 'Aside from what happened?' 'because towards the end we fell out of love I knew he was from a gypsy culture'. 'And my parents weren't happy about it they were middle class and I felt we were too young'. 'To be in a serious relationship and I started to like this other guy' 'ok no more questions'.

The defence lawyer stood up 'I'd now like to question Miss Mulley' 'go ahead' the judge said 'first of all'. 'We've established this was a serious loving relationship'. 'Daniel treated you with love' and kindness most of the time' 'yes he was a great boyfriend'. 'That this rape would have been out of character' 'yes'. 'Let's talk about that afternoon you say he locked you in the bedroom saying he had something to do'. 'Did you not consider running out at that point?' 'no'. 'I assumed he was maybe going to the toilet by the time I realised it was too late' 'let's talk about these locks'. 'On the door did the door have a key?' 'I think so'. 'How long did you live in the house?' 'all my life'. 'And you don't remember what locks the door had'. 'I hardly went in that room it was my parents bedroom'. 'Mr O'Hanlon claims the door had a handle'.

'I don't remember but he shut the door and raped me'.
'That I do remember!' 'I put it to you about what really
happened did you not accuse Daniel of rape'.
'Because two months before the relationship ended you
cheated with another man and wanted out'.
'Of the relationship' 'no' 'because Daniel was from
a culture different to yours'.
'And you knew your parents wouldn't approve' 'no'.
'I know what he did' 'he says you didn't want to wear
protection because you were happy to be a young mum'.
'That when he suggested wearing a condom you said no'
'we sometimes had sex without but I started to worry'.
'About getting pregnant so I suggested it and he got angry
at me' 'which led to the alleged rape' 'yes'.
'I have one more question tell me how you know
Amy O'Dowd?' 'Amy I worked with her in a café'.
'I'd left College we became friends' 'your still good
friends?' 'we've known each other over twenty years'.
'She dated Daniel as well did you ever talk about him?'.
'No she just said she was seeing a guy I saw him once'.
'At a club we didn't speak for a while because I suffered
anxiety over seeing him then when she said they split'.
'I knew I could see her again' 'and you never discussed
Daniel' 'no never' 'no further questions'.
'You may leave the stand' the judge said.

*As Martine got up it was now Amy's turn Corey hoped*
*she'd do well on the stand Greg spoke.*

*'I now present the second victim Miss Amy O'Dowd'.*
*Amy looked nervous 'I now need to ask you some*
*questions about what happened'.*

*'You met Daniel in a club?' 'yes' 'and you chatted him up'.*
*'Then began a relationship' 'yes' 'how was the*
*relationship?' 'at first it was great'.*

*'Then later around three months in he became possessive'.*
*'And controlling' 'in what way?' 'he got angry at me'.*
*'If I chatted to another man he banged down his fist'.*
*'He checked my phone didn't want me wearing anything*
*too sexy or revealing'.*

*'You eventually decided after six months to end the*
*relationship' 'yes I did' 'but he didn't want to' 'no'.*
*'Tell me about the night of the rape he came home*
*one night drunk did he drink a lot?' 'quite a bit'.*
*'Not like an alcoholic but more than he should' 'is it true*
*he demanded sex?' 'yes I said no' 'what happened?'.*
*'When you said no?' 'he got angry really angry'.*
*'I was scared he locked the bedroom door' 'just to be clear*
*was this a lock or a handle?' 'a handle he shut the door'.*
*'Then...put himself on top of me he said we were having*
*sex whether he wanted it or not' Amy was clearly upset.*
*Corey thought as her voice quivered 'I'm sorry'.*

'To have to put you through this' 'it's ok' 'after he raped
you did you tell anyone?' 'a friend' 'which friend?'.
Amy paused for a while 'Martine I didn't say it was Daniel
this was like a year later I just said an ex raped me'.
'No further questions' 'now for the defence questioning'
the judge spoke 'this won't take long'.
'This like the relationship with Miss Mulley was serious'.
'Mr O'Hanlon says the relationship was good and
that he wasn't controlling towards you'.
'Due to the fact you had come out of a controlling
relationship' 'not at first later he was'.
'Let's talk about your relationship with Daniel'.
'He says you hardly ever had sex that he was a gentlemen
towards you is that true?' 'it was more kissing'.
'And cuddling some relationships are' 'that's true'.
'But in this case things are different he alleges
you used him as a cover up for your true sexuality'.
'No I knew I was a gay but I still liked him' 'liked'.
'Not loved' 'you can still be gay or lesbian and have
strong feelings for the opposite sex'.
'Clearly you rarely had sex did it make you
uncomfortable? having sex with a man?' 'yes I guess'.
'What has it got to do with anything my sexuality'.
'He raped me!' 'let's move on I have nearly finished my
questioning I'd like to ask you about Corey O'Hanlon'.

'Daniel's sister you once had a relationship' 'we dated for two years at College' 'why did this relationship end?'.

'I kissed a man I wasn't comfortable with my sexuality'. 'And my parents wouldn't accept it' 'so this relationship ended badly?' 'yes at the time'.

'Is it true Corey threw you out of the flat you shared'. 'That she put your possessions in a black bag' 'yes'. 'She never spoke to you again' 'no I felt bad about how things ended' 'you never spoke to Corey until recently'.

'I saw her last September we spoke and finally sorted things' 'so you hadn't spoken to her for twenty four years'.

'No we met at a charity do in Dublin' 'how were things?'. 'Frosty at first but we're both adults now and then we met again at the train station Corey was having her car fixed'. 'We chatted it was fine' 'you then became friends again' 'yes Corey invited me round her house'.

'With my other half Melanie it was all good' 'so you met someone you hadn't seen for twenty four years'.

'Who you parted on bad terms with who you admit had a frosty relationship with then became the best of friends'.

'Like I said we sorted things out' 'did you not befriend Corey with the intention of getting back at Daniel'.

'By falsely accusing him of rape' 'no I didn't even know Corey was Daniel's sister' 'are you telling the truth?'.

'This is despite the fact she's famous that her brother
even played as part of her group' 'I didn't know'.
'Tell me did you ever try and befriend Corey on
social media prior to meeting her again?' 'no'.
'I would follow her but I was afraid to befriend her'.
'In case she wasn't happy after what happened'.
'What about Martine your friend of twenty years'.
'Did you ever wonder why she wasn't around?'.
'When you dated Daniel' 'I assumed she was busy'.
'Sometimes in friendships you have periods when
your not so close' 'this was a twenty year friendship'.
'You never told her about Daniel' 'like I said I did'.
'A year later when I was ready to talk about what
happened I couldn't tell anyone even Martine'.
'When did she tell you?' 'about a year ago then
I understood why she kept her distance'.
'Did she know who Daniel was?' 'I don't know'.
'Not everyone keeps tabs on a famous person's brother
or sister' 'yes but Daniel was in Corey's band'.
'Only later Martine never knew Corey' 'ok no further
questions' 'you are free to go' Amy looked angry.
Corey thought 'court adjourned' 'what a day thank god it
wasn't you up there' Polly said they went over to see Amy.
'Are you ok?' Polly asked 'I don't know did I come off
as angry?' 'I'd be the same'.

'I tried to be as truthful as possible' 'that defence lawyer
is a bastard' Corey said trying to make Amy feel better.
'I agree but remember he's paid to defend your brother'.
Greg said joining them Corey had no idea how things
would turn out the next day was a Thursday.
It was Corey's turn in the dock she knew she had to
get it right she could do this she told herself.
'We will now hear from the defendant's sister'.
'Would you please give your full name?'.
'Corine Carol Ann-Marie O'Hanlon' Greg stood up.
Somehow it made Corey feel ok as she knew him well.
And that he was good at his job and would hopefully
make Daniel confess the truth.
'I'd like to ask about your relationship with your brother'.
'You grew up together with your father as your mother
left when you were seven it was an abusive atmosphere'.
'He was an alcoholic and emotionally abusive' 'yes'.
'Because of this it made you have a close relationship'.
'How would you describe your relationship as children
and teenagers?' 'we had a great relationship'.
'He was my best friend' 'you were so close you even
shared a flat together' 'yes after we left school'.
'Is it true he tried to kiss you when you were eighteen?'.
'Yes' 'on the lips' 'yes I thought I imagined it but I didn't'.
'How did you respond?' 'I tried not to I was with Amy'.

*'At the time' 'it made you uncomfortable' 'yes' 'he kissed*
*you again after he split from his wife Lizzie' 'yes'.*
*'What happened?' 'I was shocked I didn't know what*
*to do then it happened again when I lived in L.A'.*
*'By now he had feelings for you' 'yes' 'when you moved*
*to L.A age twenty nine you split from Polly'.*
*'Then started a relationship with Steve this was the only*
*man as an adult you'd dated'.*
*'How did your brother respond?' 'he was angry'.*
*'He really hated Steve' 'is it true you couldn't see*
*each other till he went back to Ireland' 'yes'.*
*'You later told Steve about the abuse from your brother?'.*
*'Yes his sister had been abused by his brother I told him*
*about Daniel trying to kiss me'.*
*'He told me abuse was abuse even if it was kissing'.*
*'Aside from kissing did he make it clear he fancied you*
*as more than his sister' 'yes' 'how?'.*
*'He brought me a black and silver dress a size too small'.*
*'Because he never liked me putting on weight he said*
*I looked better slimmer'.*
*'One time I was in the swimming pool in L.A and*
*I was wearing my swimming costume'.*
*'He said I'd put on too much weight then he kissed me'.*

'Then apologised' 'so this jealousy of Steve was driven by his inappropriate feelings for you' 'yes'.

'Daniel said he was a womanizer using you for career reasons' 'no Steve isn't like that'.

'Is it true your brother made you get your wedding in Las Vegas annulled?' 'yes he was jealous and angry'.

'I had no choice' 'he was so angry he later smacked you in the face' 'yes I couldn't tell anyone'.

'Let's talk about the night you were raped Daniel cooked you a meal to apologise' 'yes I didn't want to see him'.

'But I didn't want Douglas to find out' 'your son' 'yes'.

'He always looked up to Daniel I never wanted him to find out what he was really like' 'that night'.

'Your brother got angry at you he found texts between you and Steve saying you loved each other' 'yes'.

'Dan said that I never took up his advances I said I wanted a normal relationship'.

'He made it clear he wanted to sleep with me but I didn't'.

'Your brother tried to rape you that night' 'he shut the door pinned me down on the bed'.

'Put his hand over my mouth so I couldn't shout for help'.

'Then your mother Carol arrived what happened next?'.

'He left me alone opened the door acted like everything was normal I went to the bathroom applied some lipstick'.

*'I didn't want Douglas or my mam to know what happened*
*I was shaking trying not to cry my mam came'.*
*'And then she had to pick up my half-brother Connor*
*from somewhere then she returned ten minutes later'.*
*'She knew something was wrong I drank wine so I didn't*
*have to feel anything then my mam took me to her house'.*
*'Is it true not long after he asked for your forgiveness'.*
*'He turned up he asked me for one last kiss' 'what*
*happened?' 'when he tried to kiss me I told Stacey'.*
*'Who's my best friend and Polly the truth about him'.*
*'Did Daniel know the other people knew the truth*
*about his behaviour?' 'we had this family meal'.*
*'It was my mam Kitty Daniel some other people'.*
*'He tried to touch me up under the table my mam knew'.*
*'That he was upsetting me we chatted outside he said*
*he fancied me since I was seventeen'.*
*'He said he would tell everyone about me and Steve'.*
*'If I told anyone about him' 'finally I'd like to talk about*
*the night you were date raped you went to a club'.*
*'With your friend Julie and your brother how did you feel*
*that night?' 'ok' 'how much alcohol did you drink?'.*
*'Around two pints of beer that's all not enough to be drunk*
*or intoxicated' 'no just tipsy I also had some crisps'.*
*'How did it feel being around your brother?' 'difficult'.*
*'I suppose I wanted to prove to myself I could carry on'.*

'After he attacked me by having a night out' 'you went to
the ladies toilets' 'yes Julie said she'd watch my drink'.
'And when you returned and sipped your drink how
did you feel?' 'not myself I didn't understand'.
'Because I hadn't had that much to drink I felt dizzy'.
'Your brother took you home?' 'yes' 'what do you
remember of that night?' 'not much'.
'I must have passed out it was two in the afternoon'.
'When I woke up Daniel said I'd been drunk but
I wasn't only tipsy' 'do you think he was lying to you?'.
'Now when I look back' 'when did you realise you'd
been date raped?' 'I had a flashback that night'.
'I was sure Daniel was on top of me' 'how sure?'.
'Pretty sure I mean my memory was hazy but I know what
I remember' 'did you tell anyone what happened?' 'no'.
'Because I had no proof and because he was my brother'.
'I understand I have no further questions'.
'Over to the defence' the judge said Corey was worried
she hated Daniel's defence lawyer.
She was worried he would try and trip her up deliberately
Corey told herself to be strong.
Answer any questions to the best of her ability.
As she looked up Victoria sat down with Polly she had
said she would come but thought she might be busy.

*Or not want to she was grateful and felt better.*
*With her friends there 'Corey it's established you had*
*a great relationship with your brother as children'.*
*'And teenagers and you shared a flat for two years'.*
*'Without any problems you say this relationship changed'.*
*'Age eighteen when he kissed you on the lips' 'yes'.*
*'Are you sure the kiss was more than a peck on the lips'.*
*'Yes' 'could it not have been a friendly kiss' 'no I know*
*how he kissed me''what about the other kiss'.*
*'Age twenty seven outside the pub in Dublin' 'it was*
*the same he kissed me' 'how did you respond?'.*
*'I kissed him back it was a friendly kiss' 'what about*
*in L.A Daniel alleges you kissed him' 'he kissed me'.*
*'What did you do?' 'I kissed him back I thought if*
*I did he'd stop having feelings for me'.*
*'Were you starting to get feelings for him?' 'no'.*
*'I was with Steve' 'and you later split after a few months'.*
*'I still loved him' 'this is someone who you claim you*
*felt uncomfortable with his advances yet kissed him'.*
*'Let's talk about your sexuality you came out as a lesbian'.*
*'Age fourteen then not long before you turned thirty*
*you started seeing Steve your ex-husband'.*
*'It was a one night stand I was with Polly we've all*
*made mistakes then after we split we started dating'.*

'Would you describe yourself as bi-sexual?' 'I saw myself as a lesbian who happened to fall for a man'.

'But at this point you had feelings for men and women?'.

'Yes' 'so you could have feelings for Daniel' 'not in that way I wanted us to have a normal relationship'.

'But it wasn't is it true you were jealous of your brother's first wife Lizzie?' 'I hated her'.

'Because I thought he could do better' 'you hated her'. 'So much you even stood up in the church'.

'And told him not to marry her this jealousy went beyond her not being good enough for Daniel'.

'You had feelings for your own brother' 'no he had feelings for me I thought it was my fault he fancied me'.

'That I'd done something to encourage him' 'but you did'. 'You kissed him three times and the occasion of your twenty ninth birthday party' 'it was to stop him'.

'Most women would have said no or spoken to him'.

'Maybe I should have I couldn't have anyone finding out'.

'That you liked him in a way you shouldn't that you had illicit kisses with your own brother'.

'No it wasn't like that!' 'how was it then?' 'even our dad knew he fancied me he said when I visited him in prison'. 'That Dan fancied me I tried to deny it' 'did you fancy him?' 'no he's my brother'.

'Let's talk about your ex-husband Steve'.

'Daniel says he was just looking out for you by making it clear he didn't want him around' 'no he was jealous'.
'Because he fancied me and I'd never been with a man'.
'Not since I was a teenager' 'he says he was a womanizer'.
'And he was protecting you' 'Steve is a great person'.
'I didn't need protecting' 'it's claimed you couldn't date him until your brother went back to Ireland'.
'This is despite the fact your were a woman of thirty years of age' 'yes'.
'In May 2014 you attended your mother's funeral'.
'Together and in October of that year you also attended the wedding of Polly Patterson's parents in Blackpool'.
'At the Tiffany's hotel with your brother' 'yes' 'and that Christmas you even went to New York staying with Polly'.
'Yes we did' 'this is despite as you say your brother making unwelcome advances'.
'May the court ask themselves this why would you hang out with your brother as if nothing ever happened'.
'I was worried that no-one would believe me'.
'In February the following year you attended your brother's wedding to bandmate Kitty'.
'Also one of your closest friends in Edinburgh now let's move on to your Las Vegas wedding to Steve'.
'You claim Daniel made you annul the wedding but isn't it true you made the decision yourself with Kitty's help'.

*'Because you were worried as to what your lesbian fanbase would think that you married a man'.*

*'And because it was a quick decision' 'I did but he encouraged me' 'he forced you' 'no but he wanted me to'.*

*'You also claim Daniel smacked you in the face after finding out you'd married Steve yes there are no photos'.*

*'To prove it' 'I know what he did my mam saw the bruise'.*

*'And Polly and her ex-wife Margie' 'you even said you'd been broken in to did you not invent this story' 'no'.*

*'Why would I!' 'then changed your story worried you would be caught out lying' 'no I didn't'.*

*'Let's talk about the night of the attempted rape you say your brother cooked a meal to apologise at your house'.*

*'Yes' 'you say he took you upstairs under false pretences'.*

*'Then tried to rape you is it not true that you were the one who came on to him' 'no it was him' 'are you sure?' 'yes'.*

*'He tried to rape me' 'he later turned up at your house for one last kiss which you agreed to'.*

*'I thought he'd leave me alone' 'let me get this straight'.*

*'He tried to rape you then you still kissed him afterwards'.*

*'Most women wouldn't do that would they?' 'no'.*

*'They wouldn't come anywhere near a man who'd done that now on to the alleged date rape'.*

*'Which by your own admission you have no proof of'.*

*'You again went out with your brother despite him
apparently abusing you this time to a nightclub'.*
*'With your friend Julie and Colin another good friend'.*
*'And father of your son Douglas you ask your friend
to look after your drink'.*
*'You say after you come back from the toilets you feel ill
dizzy' 'yes I did' 'you admit you'd been drinking beer'.*
*'Two pints maybe three' 'maybe' 'is it not possible you had
alcohol poisoning' 'I don't think so' 'but it's possible?'.*
*'Maybe your brother took you home you don't remember
much is that because you were drunk?' 'no'.*
*'Because I believe something was put in my drink'.*
*'You believe but you don't know that flashback you had'.*
*'Is it not possible you were so drunk you forgot where
you were or what you were doing' 'I don't know'.*
*'Your brother said he took you home because you were ill
is it not possible he was looking after you' 'maybe'.*
*'But knowing the feelings he had for me' 'or the feelings
you had for him' 'I have one last thing I need to know'.*
*'Did you know Martine Mulley?' 'no' 'never even though
she dated your brother' 'no I was living in London'.*
*'I was eighteen and a half we didn't see each other for
a while so I never knew who he was dating at the time'.*
*'What about years later' 'I don't know her' 'so you'd have
no reason to cross paths' 'no'.*

'Tell me about Amy O'Dowd we know you dated for
two years were you in love?' 'yes we were in love'.
'The relationship ended because she cheated on you' 'yes'.
'With a man' 'you got so angry you threw her out of your
flat you shared along with her belongings' 'yes'.
'Did you ever see her again until last September?' 'no'.
'So in twenty four years you never saw her or ever
contacted her?' 'no I wondered about her sometimes'.
'Looked on Facebook but we never spoke I never
messaged her we parted on bad terms'.
'And you got reacquainted at a charity event' 'yes'.
'And things were frosty' 'I was shocked to see her'.
'Then you saw her again at the train station' 'yes'.
'I was having my car fixed we just had a brief chat'.
'Then I saw her at my...friend's wedding shop'.
Corey had almost said sister 'this has become quite
a habit you seeing each other'.
'Despite the fact you didn't talk for so many years'.
'She came round it was me her and her wife Melanie and
Polly' 'did Amy ever tell you Daniel had raped her?' 'no'.
'She never mentioned it' 'I think I know everything I need
to know no further questions your honour'
Corey felt defeated Daniel's lawyer had twisted everything
she'd said she felt like she wanted to cry.
But didn't want to give anyone the satisfaction.

'Cor are you ok?' Polly asked 'no I want to go home'.
'He's a bastard! they both are' Polly said trying to make
Corey feel better 'it's not true! I never came on to Daniel'.
'He came on to me!' 'we know that' Greg said.
'Remember we still have witness statements to come'.
Corey hoped her brother would be found guilty the
following week the trial continued.
Steve had agreed to fly over from the States.
Corey was grateful to him 'today we will hear from
the prosecution witnesses'.
'First we will hear from Steve Green' 'you may begin'.
The judge said as they waited 'Mr Green tell me
about your relationship with Corey how you met'.
'We met on a movie we did I Love New York we got on
well then a few years later when Corey moved to L.A'.
'After she and Polly split we got together' 'you started
going out' 'yes' 'how was Corey's brother to you?'.
'Not nice' 'in what way?' 'he seemed off with me'.
'He thought that I was a threat he said he wanted
to chat with me alone so we did' 'what did he say?'.
'That I was using Corey that she was his best friend'.
'And he wanted no-one to come between them'.
'He even said she was of gypsy heritage and
high functioning autism but I didn't care'.
'I loved Corey from the first moment we met'.

'But whenever Daniel was around she didn't seem herself'
'tell me about this text Daniel sent to Corey'.
'Did he say the words 'are you still going out with that
American bastard?' 'yes she showed me his text'.
'It made you angry' 'I didn't understand why he was
so controlling possessive over her'.
'Is it true she told you she was abused by her brother?'.
'Yes we'd been dating a few months I told her about my
sister Eve who was abused by my brother'.
'What did Corey say?' 'that since she was eighteen he
would try and kiss her touch her where he shouldn't'.
'Corey said she felt it was her fault that maybe she'd
done something to make him fancy her'.
'I said it wasn't her fault she even made me promise
not to tell anyone' 'tell me about this Vegas wedding'.
'Did Daniel make her annul your wedding or did she want
to?' 'it was all him' 'how did he react when he found out?'.
'That you'd gotten married?' 'he went mad they tried to
make out Corey was drunk she'd had a few drinks'.
'But she wasn't intoxicated she knew what she was doing
we both did' 'is it true you later got married in secret?'.
'In Ireland because of Daniel?' 'yes to avoid all the drama
Corey even lied to him after the wedding'.
'Telling him she was looking for a girl and that she only
saw me as a friend' 'this was because Daniel was jealous'.

'Possessive' 'yes' 'finally how would you describe
Daniel?' 'as cruel obsessive controlling'.
'Especially over Corey' 'no further questions' Corey was
happy Steve had done well telling the truth about Daniel.
'I will now call two further witnesses first Douglas
O'Hanlon' Corey watched as Douglas took to the stand.
Hoping things would go well the defence lawyer went first
'I would like to first ask you about your relationship with
Daniel have you always been close?' 'yes all our lives'.
'He got joint custody of me when I was thirteen with
Corey so he helped bring me up' 'like a father'.
'Or older brother type figure?' 'yes' 'what about Corey?'.
'The same she's a great person kind and funny'.
'And what kind of a relationship did they have?' 'they
always seemed close they always got on really well'.
'So no falling outs' 'no only when he married Lizzie'.
'His ex-wife but after they divorced everything went back
to normal' 'let's talk about that night of the alleged rape'.
'When you had a meal with your uncle and mother'.
'How did your mother seem?' 'Corey seemed fine'.
'So not upset or on edge' 'no' 'so she went upstairs with
your uncle' 'yes she asked me to watch the pan of water'.
'So it didn't bubble over' 'when you were downstairs'.
'In the kitchen did you hear any noise from upstairs?' 'no'.
'And when she came downstairs how did she seem?' 'fine'.

'So everything was normal' 'yes' 'she even drank wine afterwards' 'no further questions'.

'Over to the prosecution' 'Douglas tell me your grandmother Carol arrived at the house then left'. 'To pick up her son she returned ten minutes later is this correct?' 'yes' 'when she returned how did Corey seem?'. 'Ok but she said she didn't want Daniel laying the table'. 'Why not?' 'I don't know she seemed off with him' 'She said she was going to Carol's house Daniel apologised because they'd had a row'. 'All I remember is she said she wanted him gone by the following afternoon'.

'You don't know what the row was about?' 'no'. 'That's all I know' 'thankyou no further questions'.

'That concludes todays proceedings' Corey felt better as if the trial was finally going her way.

Both Steve and Daniel had done well Greg came over to her looking happy 'Steve and Douglas were both great'. 'I know they did really well do you think it'll go our away?' 'hopefully it'll be in the bag'.

'Your brother is dangerous and deserves to be locked up for crimes against women' Corey knew Greg was right. She remembered why she was there to help other women the following day was the final day of evidence. Her mother and Nicky would be giving evidence.

*Before the verdict would be announced the next day.*

*Corey watched as her mother went to the stand hopefully she'd do well Greg questioned her first.*

*'So tell me what were your impressions of Daniel?'.*

*'Over the years' 'well I always liked him he seemed kind'.*

*'And he loved Corey until I found out what he was really like' 'so that night he tried to attack Corey'.*

*'You turned up at the house what was the atmosphere like?' 'at first it was fine'.*

*'I remembered I had to pick up Connor my son I returned ten minutes later' 'how did Corey seem?' 'not herself'.*

*'She drank wine we both did Corey said she wanted to come home with me after we stepped outside'.*

*'It was clear she'd had a row with Daniel and was upset'.*

*'Corey said she couldn't be alone in the house with him'.*

*'And started to cry she told me he had feelings for her'.*

*'That he shouldn't and that he'd tried to rape her'.*

*'And he'd hit her before when he found out she was seeing Steve that when she was nineteen when she came home'.*

*'To visit Dublin she was living in London at the time he kissed her then two years later'.*

*'And he put his hands round her waist basically unwanted advances from him' 'ok thankyou that's all'.*

*'Over to the defence' 'Mrs O'Kelly tell me a few things'.*

*'You turn up at the house the atmosphere seems fine'.*

'No sign of any problems' 'yes that's right' 'you later
say your daughter didn't seem herself'.
'Despite this you drive to pick up your son leaving for
ten minutes despite Corey being upset not herself'.
'She seemed fine when I left her' 'ok so even if your
account is true'.
'You and Corey despite her just being attacked by her
brother decides to start drinking wine both of you'.
'Enjoying the meal that's been cooked as if you don't have
a care in the world' 'it wasn't like that' 'how was it?'.
'I didn't know what happened till we left the house if
I did I would have marched her straight out of there'.
'Ok so say the attack did happen' 'it did I know how she
was when she was at my house'.
'You say Corey said she was kissed when she was nineteen
by Daniel'.
'How come Miss O'Hanlon has stated she was eighteen'.
'Strange how she can remember the exact age she was'.
'Yet your account is different' 'it doesn't matter he kissed
her on the lips when she didn't want him to'.
'No further questions' Corey was happy her mum had
stuck up for her after the final witness was called.
Her sister Nicky she was dreading it what she might say.
Especially when it seemed the case was going her way.
'I call to the stand Nicky Hagan' Nicky stood.

*The defence went first as the last witness she would be important as to whether Daniel was found guilty.*

*'Mrs Hagan Corey is your step-sister and Daniel is your brother'.*

*'First tell me about your relationship with Corey'.*

*'We were close as children when she was seven she went to live with her dad and Daniel'.*

*'So we didn't see each other for a few years'.*

*'Except at family occasions but when Corey was in her early twenties we began hanging out together'.*

*'And we got close quickly and from then on we were the best of friends despite me being four years older'.*

*'I always thought she was great we're close we even own a restaurant together we text all the time'.*

*'So for twenty years you've been very close' 'yes'.*

*'And Daniel' 'the same he's a great person we're all close'.*

*'We all get on well as a family' 'so this revelation did it come as a shock?' 'yes I couldn't believe it was true'.*

*'In all our conversations Corey had never suggested anything that Daniel would ever be capable of this'.*

*'What kind of person is Daniel?' 'he is the most kind caring person you could wish to meet he loves his family'.*

*'And he respects women opens doors always sticks up for anyone he loves' 'what about the claims'.*

'That he kissed your sister and made inappropriate advances towards her' 'it's not true'.

'In all our conversations over the years me and Cor'. 'She's never mentioned anything her and Dan were always close the best of friends all of their lives'.

'And Dan wasn't jealous of Steve he was looking out for Cor possibly because she has autism'.

'And because he cares about her as his sister'.

'He didn't want someone who was a known womanizer'. 'And who's career wasn't doing well prior to working with her trying to use her for sex or his career'.

'Tell me about Corey's friendship with Amy her ex'. 'Who she got back in contact with recently do you know her?' 'not really but I heard all about her when they split'.

'I just found it odd she'd choose to see her again'.

'After all these years' 'so they weren't friends' 'no'.

'All of a sudden she turned up everywhere I couldn't help thinking that she was using Cor to help her'.

'And her friend Martine against Dan why didn't she contact her years ago on social media'.

'So you believe she preyed on Corey to help her in this case' 'yes I do she had no interest in Corey before'.

'If Dan did what they said he did why did Corey come round to our house for a family meal before Christmas'.

'With Dan's fiancée she even hugged him if a man had done that to me I'd want him nowhere near me' 'I agree'. 'I will now let the prosecution ask any final questions'. 'Mrs Hagan you say you always had a close relationship with your sister why would she make this up?'. 'Like I said she was encouraged by them' 'Mrs O'Dowd'. 'And Mrs Mulley' 'yes' 'is there not a chance she could be telling the truth'. 'Not many people would put themselves through this'. 'Cor's a good person they used her to get back at Daniel'. 'You believe that?' 'yes I do what other explanation could there be'. 'Did you ever witness any inappropriate behaviour'. 'From your brother towards your sister?' 'no never'. 'They didn't speak for seven years why was that?' 'I don't know Dan had been drinking heavily around that time'. 'They stopped speaking he later quit drinking she never said why it could be any number of reasons'. 'Families often have feuds about all kinds of things' 'ok'. 'Just say they didn't fall out about the alleged sexual abuse explain why he brought her lingerie at the meal'. 'Before Christmas?' 'it was a gift he never brought her that before he's brought her clothes before'. 'Nothing out of the ordinary fleeces, T-shirts, dresses'. 'And she's brought him stuff over the years'.

'Corey says she felt uncomfortable about the gift he gave
her Agent Provocateur lingerie' 'no she didn't'.
'She was happy she thanked him with a smile on her face'.
'It was all good it meant nothing he has a fiancée Liza'.
'Who he loves' 'ok no more questions' 'if we are all done'.
'This is the end of all questioning from both sides'.
The judge said Corey was relieved she felt angry at
her sister the trial had been going her way.
If only she'd known all the occasions she'd abused her.
She wouldn't have said what she did but Nicky didn't.
She only saw the good side of Daniel the one he wanted
people to see not the dark abusive possessive side of him.
The real person he kept hidden 'thank god it's over'.
Polly said to Corey 'I know' 'I can't believe what Nicky
said she should be ashamed of herself'.
'She doesn't know what Dan's like she doesn't want to
believe the truth' 'well we all know what he's like'.
'If only Kitty had been here she would have told them
what he's like when he hit her when they were married'.
Corey agreed she'd been too ill to come to give evidence.
In the trial finally it was time for the closing speeches.
From both sides of the case Greg went first 'ladies and
gentlemen of the jury we have concluded our trial'.
'Heard all the witness testimonies evidence there can
only be one outcome from this case'.

'Daniel O'Hanlon raped Martine Mulley when he was only nineteen after she refused to wear protection'.

'When having sex he was also likely jealous due to the fact he discovered she was interested in another man'.

'Then he locked the door of the bedroom and forced himself upon her'.

'He had demonstrated controlling behaviour'.

'Throughout most of their relationship the same behaviour he would with his own sister despite her sexuality'.

'I believe he did rape Miss O'Dowd after returning home to the flat they shared drunk and aggressive'.

'Shutting the door as he did with Miss Mulley forcing himself upon her and his third victim his own sister'.

'Who he sexually and emotionally abused for many years displaying inappropriate feelings towards her'.

'Becoming jealous when she started a relationship with another man even becoming violent'.

'When Daniel discovered texts from Mr Green he took out his jealousy on his own sister attempting to rape her'.

'When he was unable to do what he wanted he then date raped her by spiking her drink taking her home'.

'Then undressing her and raping her Daniel O'Hanlon is a dangerous sexual predator'.

'Who I believe needs locking up for his crimes against women I urge the jury to look at the evidence'.

'And do the right thing' 'thankyou now for the defence'.
'Closing speech' Corey was happy with Greg's speech.
He was a good lawyer who'd done all he could 'from the
evidence we have heard it is clear this case is flawed'.
'In so many ways from all three victims I'll explain why'.
'Daniel and Martine Mulley enjoyed a loving
relationship'.
'The truth is Miss Mulley was not bothered about using
contraception during their relationship'.
'And it was Daniel who suggested using a condom'.
'When having sex Miss Mulley also claims she cannot
remember what lock was on the door'.
'This is despite the fact she had lived in that house
all her life and would have known'.
'Whether the door had a lock on yet cannot tell us if it
was a handle or a lock as the rape did not happen'.
'On to the second alleged victim Amy O'Dowd the
relationship was not controlling as has been suggested'.
'Mr O'Hanlon has himself stated due to the fact she
had previously been in a controlling relationship'.
'That he wanted to make sure he was not controlling'.
'The relationship also came to a mutual end agreed by
both parties'.
'As for the suggestion that Daniel forced her for sex'.

*'This is not true as pointed out she did not enjoy having sex with a man due to the fact she is a lesbian'.*

*'They only had sex twice in six months'.*

*'Ask yourselves there are not many men who would agree to a relationship like this Daniel was a gentlemen'.*

*'He respected Mrs O'Dowd despite the lack of a sex life'.*

*'So why would he turn on her demanding sex she also claims the bedroom door was locked'.*

*'Yet under questioning revealed it was shut and had a handle not a lock the same as Miss Mulley's testimony'.*

*'Now these two women have been friends for twenty years'.*

*'Yet despite this we are to believe she never knew the truth about Daniel not once did Miss O'Dowd confess'.*

*'What happened except a year after the incident when she referred to the alleged rape as an ex-boyfriend'.*

*'And are we to believe that his own sister did not know about Miss Mulley despite the fact they shared a flat'.*

*'For two years and were very close finally let's talk about Miss O'Hanlon this alleged incest abuse'.*

*'That Daniel is accused of is not true in fact it was Corey who wanted to be with Daniel kissing him several times'.*

*'Most notably after he split with his wife Lizzie'.*

*'Who Corey made it clear she could not stand due to her jealousy of them being together'.*

*'She was the one who asked for sex not her brother'.*

'She alleged he kissed her age eighteen and twenty one'.
'And at her twenty ninth birthday party ask yourself
why an adult would agree to that'.
'If Daniel was emotionally abusive it's because Miss
O'Hanlon has always had feelings for her brother'.
'Not as it's been suggested the other way around'.
'She didn't mind these kisses in fact she encouraged them'.
'As for her ex-husband Steve Green Daniel was looking
out for his sister as a known womanizer'.
'Daniel was also concerned he was using her to further
his acting career which hadn't been doing so well'.
'Until he met her the actions were of a concerned brother'.
'Not a sexual predator as in fact despite claiming he
was abusive she continued to hang out with him'.
'In May 2014 they attended their mother's funeral'.
'In October the same year they also attended Polly
Patterson's parents wedding in Blackpool'.
'And even went to New York for Christmas staying
with Polly at her apartment for a family holiday'.
'With her son and his nephew and the following year
Corey attended her brother's wedding in Edinburgh'.
'Ask yourself if Daniel was abusive as she claims why
did she continue to spend so much time with him'.
'Why would any woman if he'd done what she claims'.

'Now the night of the alleged rape despite her son being downstairs and calling for her when her mother arrived'.

'He heard no noise and no shouting her mother arrived at the house then left for ten minutes'.

'When she returned despite claiming her daughter did not seem herself began to drink wine with their meal'.

'Ask yourself this if you'd just been raped you'd be in a state crying angry upset not drinking wine'.

'Acting as if nothing had ever happened after the rape Miss O'Hanlon admits she saw Daniel again'.

'And they had one last kiss why would she want to go anywhere near her alleged rapist'.

'She also then decided to go clubbing with him with other friends where she drank pints of beer'.

'Miss O'Hanlon claims it was two or three possibly more'.

'The truth is she admits she does not know if she was date raped in fact it was her imagination'.

'In fact it's just as likely to have been alcohol poisoning'.

'Which is why she fell ill as for the alleged flashback'.

'It's also as likely to have been caused by too much alcohol the rape did not happen'.

'Miss O'Hanlon even had a family meal just this Christmas gone with her alleged rapist'.

'This alleged abuse did not happen and finally her relationship with the two other alleged victims'.

'Most notably Miss O'Dowd someone she had not seen for twenty four years did not even contact on social media'.
'Who she admits when she saw her at a charity event last September things were frosty between them'.
'Due to what happened in their relationship many years ago Miss O'Dowd befriended Corey'.
'With the intention of using her against Daniel to pursue a false conviction'.
'Miss O'Hanlon also admits she never mentioned the rape at any time during their conversations'.
'You see this case is full of holes and lies Daniel O'Hanlon is an innocent man'.
'Targeted by two ex-girlfriends assisted by his sister'.
'He should not go to jail for a crime he did not commit'.
'That is all your honour' 'thankyou court adjourned for today' 'how could he lie!' Corey said to Polly angry.
'I've never had any drinking problem ever!' 'I know Cor'.
'He twisted everything he said I came on to Daniel'.
'Why would I how can they make things up that aren't true!' 'they'll do anything to win the case'.
'This is all Nicky's fault with that glowing testimony about Daniel if she knew what he was really like!' 'Polly's right'.
Greg said 'but remember we still have a chance'.
'You did well on the stand and Steve and Douglas but your sister didn't help' 'I'll never speak to her again!'.

Corey said angry 'it'll be ok' Polly said trying to make
things better the next day they returned for the verdict.
Corey was dreading it she hoped Daniel would be found
guilty 'all rise do the jury have their verdict' 'we do'.
'How do you find the defendant on the first charge of
rape?' 'not guilty'
'How do you find the defendant on the second charge
of rape?' 'not guilty'.
'How do you find the defendant on the third charge of
attempted rape?' 'not guilty' 'the defendant is not guilty'.
'Of all three charges the trial is over you may leave the
courtroom' Polly looked over as Daniel hugged his lawyer.
Who smiled she was in shock and felt angry as she left her
seat 'you bastard! you know what you did!' 'I did nothing!
I'm an innocent man' 'like f** you are! we all know what
you did me Carol, Mike, Kitty!' 'calm down!'.
'You're a rapist that's what you are!' 'I never raped
anyone in my life!' 'you tell yourself that!'.
'Polly how dare you! accuse Daniel of things he hasn't
done he's just been through hell!' Nicky said.
As she hugged him 'more like he put his victims through
hell!' 'he never did anything! you helped them Corey'.
'And the other two trying to ruin Daniel's life!'.
'He ruined Corey's life there were so many incidents
you ignored!' 'I don't know what you're talking about!'.

'You were never there for her! you Marie and you're joke
of a family!' 'family she even convinced Douglas'.
'To help the defence without knowing all the facts!'.
'Carol informed him' 'she knows nothing and neither
do you! this could destroy someone'.
'Being accused of something they haven't done how would
you feel! if it happened to you now if you don't mind'.
'We're going home where I'm going to help my brother
rebuild his life' 'hopefully Corey can rebuild hers'.
'I can't help it if Corey has feelings for Dan I should have
realised years ago I could have got her counselling'.
'He needs counselling!' 'no Polly face facts Corey has
serious issues' 'your whole family has'.
'Like yours is perfect! why would Cor destroy her career
over this' 'like I said she was roped in by the other two'.
'Hopefully one day she'll see sense and apologise'.
'For what she did and maybe Dan and me will forgive her
but it's highly unlikely' 'f**k you and him!' Polly left.
As she spied Greg 'where's Corey?' 'I don't know I'm
so sorry' 'no you were amazing you do believe Corey'.
'Of course I would never doubt her' 'if only Kitty had
been here it would have been a different outcome'.
'She knows what Daniel's like he hit her when they were
married she saw what he was like around Steve' 'I know'.

'All we can do is hope in future maybe another victim comes forward until then there's nothing I can do'.

Iif Corey needs to talk she knows where I am' Greg said.

'Hi' it was Mike 'I feel so down right now like he's got away with it' 'we all know what he's like'.

'He just had a good lawyer and the fact the first victim did badly on the stand he'll get his comeuppance' 'I doubt it'.

'He will I'll make sure of it' they spied Corey outside.

Looking sad 'hey we all know what he did' Mike said.

'I'm trying not to cry' 'then don't he's not worth it'.

'The worst part is he might attack other women in future'.

Polly said 'I'll sort it I promise' Mike said 'what do you mean?' Corey asked 'I'm a gypsy'.

'We don't play by the rules' 'your not going to do anything stupid like shoot him I don't wanna see you in jail'.

'Who said anything about weapons' 'I don't care what happens to him' Polly said 'no-one does except Nicky'.

'Deluded if she knew what he was like' 'like I said an eye for an eye he's not safe around women'.

'Corey's my cousin one of my best friends he pulled the wool over the jury but no-one else'.

That afternoon as Corey sat in the living room of her house she felt down after the court case.

She'd put herself through things emotionally she'd never told anyone only for her brother to escape jail.

*Possibly attack more women in future Corey*
*wondered where it had gone wrong.*
*She should never have mentioned the kissing she told*
*herself now even Douglas would probably doubt her.*
*Polly poured her a glass of lemonade 'Cor what happened*
*isn't fair in fact it's wrong I am so angry'.*
*'He had a good defence lawyer who twisted everything'.*
*'I meant to tell Amy to lie say she was bi-sexual'.*
*'And I forgot' 'don't worry I doubt it would have been*
*a different outcome we should have won the case'.*
*'Steve said what he was like and Carol' 'maybe they*
*assumed they were lying' 'no Cor'.*
*'This is all down to Nicky if she hadn't said those things'.*
*'And the gifts I mean what person buys their sister sexy*
*lingerie I know Christian wouldn't unless I asked'.*
*'Or we were in a store together' 'there's nothing we can*
*do you did your best' 'what if Dougie believes them'.*
*'He was on your side' 'they'll convince him that*
*I'm not telling the truth they did before the trial'.*
*'Well he can believe what he likes we know your telling*
*the truth and one day like Mike said'.*
*'He'll get what he deserves' 'I hope so I hope Amy's ok'.*
*'You should call her swap stories' that afternoon Corey*
*called Amy they chatted about the trial.*

*Where it went wrong somehow it felt better talking to Amy
Polly came into the living room 'Cor'.*

*'What's this text about?' 'what text?' 'sent yesterday',*

*'Do you know Corey was seeing your brother?'.*

*'Who's it from?' 'no number' 'it might be Dan'.*

*'Because you rowed with him after the trial' 'you were
seeing Christian?' suddenly Polly felt a pang of jealousy.*

*She assumed Steve was the only man Corey had been with
'it was before we got back together it was a summer fling'.*

*'That's all we were both single' 'did you sleep together?'.*

*'Not much it was just kissing hanging out together'.*

*'Why did you never say?' 'I didn't know how you'd react'.*

*'Like I said it wasn't a proper relationship it was a while
ago I love you' 'I know I just wish you'd told me'.*

*'I'm sorry are you angry?' 'no it's fine' 'it's just Dan'.*

*'Trying to get a reaction split us up' 'I know well he won't'
Polly kissed Corey they were in love.*

*For the next few days everything was ok as they tried
to forget about the trial move on with their lives.*

*That cold February afternoon Corey received a
phone call from Colin asking about Daniel.*

*He'd apparently taken an ecstasy overdose Corey knew
he occasionally took the drug she didn't know what to feel.*

*As he'd turned out exactly like her father controlling
angry emotionally abusive.*

*Any love she'd had for him disappeared years ago.*
*Along with her father in some ways it was better he*
*hadn't gone to jail however awful his crimes.*
*He was still her brother she felt sad for the good times*
*they'd shared she realised Nicky would blame her.*
*For his death even Douglas they'd say he'd turned to*
*drugs because of the stress of the trial.*
*Even though he'd been using for years that afternoon*
*Corey felt in a daze she tidied the house swept the floor.*
*Did the dishes somehow it made her focus helped her get*
*through the day that evening she chatted with Polly.*
*Despite hating Daniel as much as she did she said that it*
*was ok if she needed to cry after all he'd been her brother.*
*Corey didn't know what she'd do without Polly the*
*following afternoon they heard a knock at the door.*
*As she opened it was Nicky 'I hope your proud of yourself!*
*our brother is dead because of you!' 'no'.*
*'He's been doing ecstasy for years' 'you know that for a*
*fact do you!' 'yes I would never wish anyone dead'.*
*'Then you shouldn't have gone to court!' 'I just didn't*
*want him to attack any more women'.*
*'Why don't you just admit you made up all those lies!'.*
*'I didn't I was telling the truth!' 'Cor's right just because*
*Daniel had a good defence lawyer'.*
*'Doesn't mean he was telling the truth'.*

'We all know what he did!' 'who's we?' 'Mike Kitty he hit her when they were married Stace Louie everyone'.
'Mike heard the way he talks about women he was a violent sexual predator! who should have been locked up!'
'Dan never raped those women Corey lied'
'And so did the others!' 'why would any of them put themselves through a trial if they were lying'.
'Especially Corey who is a celebrity I'll tell you why because they wanted to stop him abusing other women!'.
'This is all rubbish! Dan never abused you you came on to him he told me like the defence said'.
'If he really did those things why would you continue to hang out with him because you're a liar my own sister!'.
'I'm not a liar!' 'oh yes you are! you came round for dinner before Christmas with your so called rapist!'.
'The judge saw through your lies!' 'I came round for dinner because I had to' 'oh so I forced you!'.
'You went on and on about me coming round I didn't want to I didn't want to be anywhere near him'.
'You made me make it up with Dan and I didn't want to'.
'I knew if I told you the truth you wouldn't believe me!'.
'Guess what I still don't believe you I never thought I'd see the day when my own sister lied about being raped'.
'To support some ex who dumped you where's Amy now then?' 'I phoned her yesterday' 'swapping stories'.

'I'm surprised she still has a need for you now the trial is over' 'she's my friend' 'she's scum she's nothing!'.
'And you are nothing to me anymore! and another thing you won't be welcome at the funeral!' 'she will be'.
'She's coming!' Polly said 'not if I can help it!'.
'Cor has every right to mourn the person he was before he changed he was her brother even if he was flawed'.
'I remember when we were teenagers we never got on'.
'Then in your early twenties we made it up and you know what it was the biggest mistake I ever made!'.
'I wish we never had a relationship! Daniel was my brother one of my best friends' Nicky said angry.
'He was my best friend too!' 'you screwed him over'.
'Mam would be turning in her grave!' 'you know what your mum was a vile nasty homophobic woman!'.
'Who blamed me for our daughter having autism'.
'Claiming I was a bad luck charm all she did was try and split me and Cor up and she never succeeded!'.
'And all you and Marie did was treat Corey like s**t!'.
'Making her feel she was never good enough well guess what you're the ones who weren't good enough!'
'I've got nothing left to say to either of you!'.
Nicky shut the door angry Corey knew that was the end of their relationship she felt sad 'sorry Cor'.

*'I had to say what I've always felt that you were treated second best' 'I know I'm just glad the trial's over'.*

*That February afternoon was a damp rainy day Nicky was getting ready to go round to her brother's flat. Douglas would be coming with her she felt sad Daniel was too young to die at forty two she felt angry at Corey. How could she let herself be used by two girls who wanted revenge on her brother.*

*Nicky felt like she'd lost both her brother and her sister. Why had Corey taken part in the trial? why hadn't she supported her own brother?.*

*She told herself Amy must have convinced her to support her she couldn't work out why they wanted revenge.*

*On Daniel and why they'd left it so long to go to the police she'd never wavered in her belief of her brother.*

*He'd assured her he was telling the truth and she believed him Nicky grabbed her umbrella.*

*As she drove to pick up Douglas as they made their way there Nicky had a second key to the flat as she walked in. It was reasonably tidy the living room had a plasma TV. A sound system some books they had decided they would make a note of what they wanted.*

*Then come back the next day the rest would go to charity.*

*'I can't believe he's gone' Nicky said sadly 'me either'.*

*'That we'll never speak to him again' Douglas said.*

*'Let's go upstairs check out the more important things'.*
*Nicky suggested they went upstairs to the bedroom.*
*It was average sized a double bed and a side table*
*with aftershave on a table with dragon ornaments.*
*Daniel had always liked fantasy a collection of fantasy*
*themed novels were on the bookcase.*
*Along with boxsets of Father Ted and Only Fools &*
*Horses there was a large cd collection.*
*Opposite the bed was a large wardrobe with mirrors.*
*'I'll check the drawers' Nicky rummaged around as she*
*looked for anything important she found some photos.*
*Of the family 'he's gone and mam they'll be no-one left*
*soon' 'it's ok you've got me we'll get through this'.*
*Nicky found a shoebox as she opened it she saw it was*
*more photos 'he should have put all these in an album'.*
*'Or on disc' 'maybe their copies if not we can put them in*
*an album' Nicky opened the box as she sat on the floor.*
*'It's Cor their all Corey' there were photos of her and*
*Daniel as teenagers and by herself in her twenties.*
*And thirties at weddings and parties' 'what a bitch!'.*
*'What she did to Daniel!' 'maybe she was telling the truth'*
*'come off it! she lied they all did he was found innocent'.*
*'In a court of law how can you doubt him' 'I guess'.*
*Douglas still wasn't a hundred per cent convinced either*
*way but he didn't want to upset Nicky.*

*He still tried to go over the night Daniel attacked Corey.*
*But couldn't come to a conclusion 'he loved her so much*
*Dougie he wouldn't have kept these photos otherwise'.*
*'I'm gonna check the attic wait here I'm getting the*
*step ladder' Nicky returned 'hold it steady'.*
*'There might not be anything but we'll see' Nicky went up.*
*'I'm here ok give me five minutes don't leave this room'.*
*'Ok I won't' Douglas looked around looking in the*
*wardrobe as he found a box inside he put it on the bed.*
*Douglas opened it there were three big books one labelled*
*'The Art of S & M' 'The Art of Good Sex'.*
*And 'The Karma Sutra' Daniel must have really liked sex.*
*He told himself as he flicked through curious about the*
*books as he found a note Corey's name.*
*And three page numbers from the 'Art Of S & M' as he*
*flicked to the pages he wondered what he would find.*
*One diagram showed someone being tied to a bed.*
*Another to a chair another how to pin someone down on*
*the bed he looked again at the piece of paper.*
*There were other girls names along with page numbers.*
*Douglas felt uneasy Daniel wasn't who he thought he was.*
*Didn't this prove he was guilty how could he have ever*
*doubted Corey's innocence in the trial.*
*'Everything ok up there?' Douglas asked 'fine just two*
*more boxes' 'I have to tell you I've found something'.*

'Really important' Douglas said 'one minute' as he looked around the room but only found computer games. And clothes 'I've found everything we want in the bedroom' Nicky had gone quiet.

'Are you ready to come down?' 'yes I need to give you these boxes' Douglas took them one by one.

As Nicky came down from the attic 'you need to look at this' Douglas said as he showed Nicky the books.

'This piece of paper look at this page and he's written girls names still think they were lying in the trial'.

'Look at these photos in this box' Nicky said as she opened it 'their all Corey with dividers with him at weddings'.

'And then this' Nicky pulled out some CD-R's in cases.

'What's on them?' Douglas asked curious 'their labelled'.

'Top secret I found this the beginners guide to voyeurism'.

Douglas looked through the photo box he pulled out a photo it showed Daniel kissing Corey on the cheek.

'How could I have ever doubted her' Nicky said.

'Carol told me what he was like how Corey had been upset after Daniel attacked her I even supported her'.

'On the defence in court then after you made me believe she was lying Dan was always jealous of Steve angry'.

'You made me doubt her' 'I was convinced she was lying'.

'Well she's not she needed us especially after he was found innocent and if the police had searched this house'.

*'They would have found out he's not you let her down'.*
*'We both did' 'I'm sorry I loved him he was my only
brother I wanted him to be innocent he was so convincing'.*
*'And the fact Corey saw him even after the alleged abuse'.*
*'It wasn't alleged it happened and you know it'.*
*'Why do you think they didn't speak for seven years'.*
*'Dan told me it was his drinking I believed him'.*
*'And the sexy lingerie he brought for Corey he pinned her
down on the bed I was downstairs I remember now'.*
*'I heard raised voices he was upstairs trying to have sex
with his own sister he spiked her drink'.*
*'So he could date rape her Corey was telling the truth'.*
*'Even worse he tried to make out in court she came on
to him that she fancied him'.*
*'When it was the other way around that lawyer twisted
everything that she said in court'.*
*'And because of your statement saying what a great person
he was he got off and how he always brought her gifts'.*
*'He lied to both of us he wasn't the person we thought he
was look at this and at the back of this book'.*
*A print out sheet fell out 'all about the drug GHB'.*
*'A date rape drug if these things don't prove what he was
nothing will' Nicky began to cry 'sorry'.*
*'But this is what he was a sick person obsessed with doing
things to women that he shouldn't' 'I know your right'.*

*'Everything is right I'll tidy up and we'll go downstairs'*
*after they tidied up Nicky went downstairs.*
*As they made tea wishing they could unsee the things*
*they'd just found 'I let Corey down my own sister'.*
*'We were so close I've ruined everything' 'no it wasn't*
*your fault' 'it was I didn't even listen to Corey'.*
*'Give her a chance I believed him' 'like you said he*
*convinced us both' 'I miss Corey I miss hanging out'.*
*Nicky confessed 'if you weren't so obsessed with Liza'.*
*'I thought you liked her' 'she's ok she's not Corey'.*
*'What can I do to make it right' 'give her some space'.*
*'For a while then apologise we need to tell her what*
*we've found' 'I hate what we've found'.*
*'Maybe we were meant to at least we know those women*
*were telling the truth' 'I've just had a flashback'.*
*Nicky said 'remember when I relaunched the restaurant'.*
*'When we were in trouble Corey left early one minute*
*everything was fine it was after Dan turned up'.*
*'She went back to her apartment I asked her if she was*
*having relationship problems she said no'.*
*'I knew she was upset about something Cor said she*
*couldn't say what I knew something was wrong'.*
*'Oh my god Dan brought her a dress why didn't I suspect'.*
*'And when we had that meal before Christmas he brought*
*her that lingerie you know what he said'.*

'That it was an early Christmas present Cor didn't seem
that happy I didn't know why she did say thanks'.
'That she loved it but she didn't seem herself quieter
than usual she said the other week'.
'She never wanted to go for the meal didn't want to be
anywhere near him that I made her make it up with him'.
'And the funeral they didn't speak for years if only I knew
why Dougie why didn't I ever ask I mean properly'.
'I jumped to conclusions about everything I don't know
what I can say to make things better'.
'How about we come back with a van take what we want
get rid of the rest then put the flat on sale'.
'I think it's a good idea' Nicky agreed 'do you think Cor
will forgive me?' Nicky asked 'I hope she will'.
'Maybe we can all be a family again' 'I'd really like that'.
A week later Nicky decided to see Corey she couldn't wait
any longer she had to see her sister.
Apologise for everything that had happened to her.
Tell her what she'd found hopefully Corey would forgive
her she also knew there was a chance she wouldn't.
But she had to try and make it up with her.
Nicky knocked on the door as she waited hoping she'd
be in it was 2pm in the afternoon.
Hopefully it would be a good time Corey opened.

*She was wearing a grey fleece four leaf clover silver*
*earrings she looked nice 'Cor look I'm sorry'.*
*'About everything what I said can we talk?' 'maybe'.*
*Nicky knew Corey didn't look happy 'can I come in?'.*
*'I guess' 'you look good considering the stress from the*
*trial' 'what do you care!' 'please don't be like that'.*
*'I am your sister' 'no you said you wanted nothing to do*
*with me! when I tried to tell you what happened'.*
*'You said it was a made up fantasy' 'I'm sorry ok'.*
*'You tried to say Polly put me up to it!' 'I thought she did'.*
*'Well she didn't! you said that I was no longer your sister'*
*'that was before I assumed he was innocent'.*
*'Before the trial Dan came to my house threatened me'.*
*'Did you put him up to it?' 'no not really I suggested he*
*could talk to you' 'your unbelievable!'.*
*'You even tried to turn my own son against me!'.*
*'You never talked to me you never listened to me gave me*
*a chance to explain you said you wanted to help him'.*
*'Rebuild his life after the trial what about mine you said*
*you didn't want to forgive me'.*
*'Well I don't want to forgive you! you said I was a liar'.*
*'That you wanted nothing to do with me all my life you*
*made me feel like I wasn't part of the family'.*
*'Because Dan was the favourite you and mam hated me'.*

'Well now you got your wish because guess what I don't need you anymore I've got Polly, Carol and John'.

'My half-brothers they don't judge me like you and mam did all my life!' 'please let me explain!' 'why'.

'So you can say what a great person Daniel was well he wasn't maybe when we were teenagers but not later on'.

'I don't care if you believe me I know the truth what he did to me he got off because he had a good lawyer'.

'We went to his flat me and Dougie we found things sex books about tying women to chairs on beds S & M'.

'Girls names written on page numbers then photos of you'.

'With dividers he was obsessed with you wasn't he'.

'I wonder why he chose you over me I'm only four years older than you' 'how can you say that!'.

'It's just an observation I know he date raped you'.

'Dougie found a print out about GHB the date rape drug'.

'You never believed me you all tried to make out I was drunk or I imagined it well I didn't' 'I know that now'.

'It's just all this is hard to take in' 'I'll make it easy for you I don't want to see you anymore'.

'Families support each other they don't accuse each other of lying I don't want you as my family!'.

'Don't be like this! I'm trying to apologise for everything'.

'Well your too late!' 'I'm your sister I don't care I may have autism but I can make decisions for myself'.

'Especially now I'm older Carol or Polly would never judge me or uncle Tommy' 'listen we can sort things out'.
'Put the past behind us' 'I don't want to! I want you to go!' 'you don't mean that!' 'I do I don't want to see you again'.
'I want to move on with my life' 'fine well the funeral's on March 3rd at St Michael's church at 11am'.
'You don't have to speak to me I think you should come say goodbye whatever his faults'.
'I don't think deep down Dan was a bad person anyway'.
'I'll go now if you change your mind about us speaking'.
'You know where I am' Nicky shut the door Corey watched from her window as she walked down the road.
Corey couldn't believe the things Nicky had said.
It sounded like her sister still couldn't come to terms with what her brother had done.
That Wednesday afternoon Polly called a taxi she was going shopping to meet Victoria.
They hadn't had the chance to catch up for a while.
Apart from supporting Corey during the court case.
Polly met Victoria at the indoor shopping centre.
'Love the coat' Polly said 'thanks Julian McDonald'.
'Autumn collection from last year' 'emerald green Cor suits that colour' 'it's a great colour how is she?' 'ok'.
'Nicky came round last week after all the things she said to Cor accusing her of being a liar imagining things'.

'Even trying to turn Douglas against her now she says she believes her apparently they found sex books in his flat'.
'With dark things in page numbers with girls written down' 'what kind of dark things?' 'S & M bondage'.
'Including how to pin someone down and there was a print out about the date rape drug GHB'.
'And photos of Corey' 'what kind of photos?' 'I don't know anyway Corey told her where to go'.
'All Nicky did was make out I'd put her up to it due to a falling out with Daniel she never believed Corey'
'Never gave her the time of day and do you know what she said when she came round' 'tell me'.
'She asked why he'd chosen Corey over her' 'oh my god!'.
'What a bitch!' 'I know she talked about Daniel's funeral'.
'And said that he wasn't a bad person how can she say that after what he did to Cor'.
'If she'd been sexually assaulted she wouldn't be saying those things' Victoria said.
'Her family's always been a joke they've never been there for her at least Carol came into her life and John'.
'Mine are pretty rubbish too I hated Christmas my mother and Katie acting like they didn't want me there'.
'You should have stayed with me and Cor' 'oh I will next year' 'I promise one day you'll have the perfect family'.
'Maybe not perfect but people who care about you'.

'I hope so least I have Sapphire I just need to find love again' 'I'll help you' 'thanks no internet dating' 'ok'.

'Maybe I could find a celeb to set you up with' 'sounds interesting I guess anything's worth a try your so lucky'.

'You and Corey' 'well we tried to get back together years ago it didn't work this time it's for keeps'.

'I don't think I'd have it in me to find Mrs Right'.

'Now I'm in my forties' 'I just want to meet someone nice'.

'I'm not that bothered about getting married' 'takes too much organising anyway' Polly joked.

'What about you and Cor?' 'I'm sure she's gonna propose soon' 'really' 'I mean she's dropped hints'.

'About us getting engaged not that I'm expecting anything' 'where would you get married?' 'probably here in Dublin'.

'We got married in London last time we were so young'.

'Early twenties I'm pretty sure if we'd been a few years older we'd never have split anyway I'm so happy'.

'That we got back together' 'so am I you two belong together like Ant and Dec Edina and Patsy'.

'I must watch my Ab Fab boxset' 'we can watch it together' Polly suggested.

After eating at a café they went shopping two hours later they finished as they met in Debenhams.

As they browsed Phase Eight 'look at these dresses'.

*Victoria said 'I know amazing!' 'look I've forgotten I need*
*to buy this pyjama set and clock upstairs'.*
*'It's Matthew Williamson I love his stuff so tropical'.*
*'I'll be back soon' Victoria said 'I'll hold your bags'.*
*'You're the best' Victoria made her way upstairs to the*
*second floor as Polly looked at the jewellery.*
*Nearby she spied a couple in the clothing section the*
*woman was around forty the man older.*
*'I can't believe I'm going to be Mrs Cleves I just love*
*the ring you brought me' 'only the best for you'*
*Polly recognised the voice she felt anxious it was the man*
*who'd abused her as a teenager Victoria's uncle.*
*And their History teacher who'd brought her lingerie.*
*Gave her alcohol so he could groom her he'd raped her.*
*Age fifteen she'd blocked it out he'd even gone to jail for*
*a few years for abusing teenage girls.*
*Polly never dreamed she'd come face to face with him*
*again she hid out of view 'and I'm buying you this dress'.*
*'I will see you later at home business meeting'.*
*'Bye darling' she kissed him on the cheek Polly watched.*
*As he paid quickly no-one was at the tills he walked out*
*the store she spied his fiancee looking around.*
*Polly knew she could have walked away but something*
*told her she had to tell her what he was really like.*

*She'd want to know she told herself as she approached his*
*fiancé Polly told herself she knew what she was doing.*
*'Hi' 'hello' his fiancée wore a navy jacket and skirt.*
*She had curly golden blonde shoulder length hair she*
*was stylish attractive too good for him 'listen'.*
*'You don't know me but I once knew your fiance I don't*
*think you should be marrying him' 'why not?' 'well...'.*
*'Oh I know who you are one of his ex-girlfriends jealous*
*are we that he's marrying me' 'no'.*
*'Then why else would you be asking me not to marry*
*the man I love!' 'because he's not a nice man'.*
*'He can't stay faithful and he's got a dark past'.*
*'We've all got a past' 'you'll thank me for it' 'I don't know*
*who you are but how dare you!'.*
*'Tell me who I can and can't marry if you'll excuse me!'.*
*'I'm going home to see my fiancé jealousy isn't a nice trait*
*in people!' 'I'm not jealous!' 'stay away from me!'.*
*Polly watched as his fiancé walked away she could have*
*told him the whole story but it wasn't the right time.*
*Or place 'what happened with that woman?'.*
*Victoria asked 'not much I saw him your uncle'.*
*'Uncle Richard?' 'with her his fiancé' 'oh my god!'.*
*'I haven't seen the bastard for years I always wondered*
*what I would do if I ever saw him' 'he didn't see me'.*
*'He paid for a dress for her then left she was alone'.*

*'I know I shouldn't have but I had to tell her what he was like' 'what did she say?' 'she thought I was jealous'.*

*'An ex-girlfriend I said he was a womanizer and that he has a dark past she didn't want to listen to me'.*

*'Did I do the right thing?' 'yes I'd want to know if I was marrying a...' 'I didn't say that he'd abused girls'.*

*'I couldn't' 'don't worry you tried your best it's her fault'.*

*'If she wants to marry someone like that knowing uncle Richard he'll probably charm her into not believing you'.*

*'If I'd have known what he was like as a teenager I wouldn't have gone anywhere near him'.*

*'None of you couldn't have known' 'I always wondered what the girls at school saw in him' 'he was charming'.*

*'He paid me attention made me feel it was ok to be me'.*

*'When I always felt I was from the wrong side of the tracks that I wasn't educated or rich he knew what to say to me'.*

*'So I would be friends with him then go out with him'.*

*'How could I if dad had known what was going on'.*

*'I know he would have come to the school if anything like that happened to my daughters' 'I feel the same'.*

*'I hate him so much I've tried to let go of the hate but I can't he ruined my teenage years my life'.*

*'Relationships with men I thought all men wanted to use me for sex' Victoria confessed 'me too'.*

## Moving On

'Let's forget about him' Polly suggested 'agreed let's go
home' that late afternoon they returned home.
Trying to make sense of things that had happened.
'I hope I never see that bastard again' Victoria said angry.
'Me too what do you say I make that pasta dish you like'.
'I'd love that the one with white wine sauce' 'yes that's
the one it shouldn't take too long'.
'What do you say we go out for dinner Friday if your
not doing anything' 'I'd love to' Victoria said.
'We could go to Rusty's there's twenty per cent off all
meals on Friday's' 'sounds like a great idea'.
'I haven't been out for ages I mean I've been busy
working' 'then it's time we went out forget about him'.
'I probably need counselling what happened but I prefer
to just forget if I can' 'same here' Polly agreed.
'Now I look back that I was failed by the people who
were supposed to be looking after me Mrs Harvey'.
'Mrs O'Donnell I mean why did they never wonder why
he spent so much time in my bedroom'.
'Why did they never care about me like they should have
done' 'because their scum their as bad as him'.
'They were paid to look out for you since your parents
weren't around remember all those women he attracts'.

'Most of them are unaware of his past he spins them a load of lies just like he did with all the other girls he abused'.

'One day his dark web will catch him out' 'your right'.

'Listen we can't change the past what happened'.

'But we can help other girls not to be in the situation we were in' Polly said.

Trying to make Victoria feel better 'how?' 'well you know I work with the NSPCC but I was thinking'.

'Of maybe writing a blog so other girls aren't victims' Polly said 'I think it's a great idea'.

'We could also talk about abuse in families' 'I'm just glad Sapphire will never have to be in the position'.

'That I was in' the following Friday evening Polly and Victoria went to Rusty's they had booked a table for two. Polly always went under her original name of Susan O'Malley because it attracted less attention as a celebrity. And as she got older she didn't want to be bothered so much with unwanted attention.

Even though she didn't mind signing autographs or having selfies taken the booking man looked up.

As she entered with Victoria already she could tell he knew who she was 'table for two Susan O'Malley'.

'Come this way' he showed her to the table she'd asked for one at the back of the restaurant.

'Is this a romantic meal?' 'just a general meal we love
Friday's' Polly replied 'can I get you any drinks?'.
'I'll have a vodka and tonic and a coke' 'coming up here
are the menu's I'll be back when you've decided'.
'What you want' 'thanks' 'he thinks we're together'.
Victoria said 'I know two girls can't even have a meal
together without people thinking we're…' 'lesbians'.
'How old were you when you knew?' Victoria asked
'nineteen twenty I mean before that I thought I was bi'.
'I mean I loved Andy we were married five years but Cor'.
'It was magic I've dated other women over the years'.
'But they all went wrong eventually do you think it was
me or them?' 'them I mean that vile woman Margie'.
'Cheated on you with' 'she was awful' 'agreed'.
'And then that actress Jeanie used you for the lifestyle'.
'Then Natalie' 'less said the better if I hadn't got back
with Cor I think I'd have stayed single'.
'When she does propose I want an invite to the wedding'.
'Of course you can be bridemaid along with Stace and
Kaleigh let's choose our food 'I'm having vegetable soup'.
'For starter then main course fish and chips then dessert
black cherry sundae with a flake' 'I'm having the same'.
The waiter returned as they placed their orders they
looked around the restaurant Polly saw a familiar face.

It was Mrs Rayworth 'hi' 'who is it?' Victoria turned
around 'let's go say hi' Polly suggested 'hello you two'.
'Taking advantage of the twenty per cent off of Friday's'.
'Yes Polly we are as a matter of fact this is Elsa my
partner' 'hello Polly' 'I'm a big fan of yours'.
'Amy's told me all about you' 'all good of course'.
'How are you Victoria?' 'I'm great Mrs...' 'call me Amy'.
'We're not in school now' 'sorry I forgot'.
'Are you still in that designer clothes shop?' 'yes I am'.
'That's great' 'and I sell things online' 'how's your
daughter?' 'Sapphire' 'she's great'.
'Starting secondary school next year' 'time flies'.
'I know it does' 'will you be having anymore children?'.
'I doubt it I'm in my forties now I quite like having just
the one child' 'Corey showed me a photo on Facebook'.
'Are you married or seeing anyone?' 'no I'm single'.
'I haven't had a boyfriend in ages I heard your engaged'.
'Yes Victoria oh will you come to the Angelsfields
school reunion it's at the end of the year'.
'We decided it was too much of a rush to do it before
Christmas' 'of course I'll be there me Polly, Corey'.
'And Stacey' 'that's great you remember Georgina' 'yes'.
'I saw her in town recently she's coming' 'is she still..'.
'You know' 'fat' 'big' 'yes but not as a big as she was'.

'More of a size twenty than a twenty four in her defence
she did have twins a few years ago' 'I can't imagine'.
'I mean it was hard enough having one child'.
'Georgina said she had IVF most people who get IVF
end up having twins' 'remind me never to have IVF'.
'If I want another child' Victoria joked 'I think now it
wasn't a bad thing I didn't have kids' Amy said.
'I would never have gone to all the countries I did'.
'What was the best you went to?' Polly asked 'we went to
Greece recently' 'I love Greece me and Victoria went'.
'On holiday there when we were seventeen' 'I remember
Corey telling me about it' 'oh our foods here chat later'.
They returned to their table as they ate their vegetable
soup 'this looks great' Victoria said.
'I am considering becoming vegetarian like Corey'.
Victoria said 'I was when I was married to Cor then
I ate chicken for a while now I'm mostly vegetarian'.
'And there are loads of great meat substitutes around'.
'Well if I do maybe you and Corey can give me some
advice on dishes' 'we will nice seeing Mrs Rayworth Amy'.
'It's so hard for me to call her Amy' Victoria said,
'I know I'm glad she found love it must have been hard
being in the closet for so many years'.
'In fact it must have been impossible' Polly said 'I know'.
'I never realised how hard it can be for people'.

'To come out' Victoria said 'I'm just glad it's easier than years ago how good is this soup' 'amazing!'.
Victoria sipped her coke 'I am having a great night'.
'Me too' Polly agreed before they knew it their fish and chips arrived Polly cut into the fish to cool it down.
As she put on vinegar 'the batter is incredible' Polly said after she sprinkled her chips with salt.
'Don't you have high blood pressure' Victoria asked,
'Yes but you only live once' 'the chips are really good'.
Victoria said as she enjoyed her meal after they ordered more drinks as they waited for their black forest sundae.
As it arrived 'oh my god! it looks amazing!' Victoria said.
She looked at the cherry and toffee sauce vanilla and cherry ice-cream with two chocolate flakes on top.
With sprinkles 'I never order a dessert when I go out'.
'Now I wish I did' 'how can you not you know I'm queen of yo-yo dieting I'm in between at the moment'.
'Not at my biggest or my smallest I agree this dessert looks amazing' Polly said they each took a spoon as they ate.
'Bit of advice take it slowly you'll think half way I can't finish it then you take a minute finish the rest'.
'And the sauce is always at the bottom of the glass'.
Victoria did what Polly said as they finished their black forest sundae 'I can't eat anymore I'm stuffed'.

*'You'll be ok in a minute I'll be one minute and I'll be back' Polly said 'your dessert looks amazing' Amy said.*

*As she came over to see Victoria 'oh it is you need to have one' 'which one is it?' 'the black forest sundae'.*

*'Make sure you share though' 'we'll ask for two spoons'.*

*Victoria thought about how many calories were in her meal she'd just eaten but didn't care.*

*She wished she could be like Polly and not care about her weight she checked her appearance in her pocket mirror.*

*As she reapplied her lipstick and powder Polly soon returned as she sat down 'nice toilets'.*

*'I like being part of a pretend lesbian couple'.*

*Victoria joked 'let's do it again' 'definitely' Polly looked around the restaurant she couldn't believe it.*

*As she saw Mr Cleves and his fiancée they were laughing.*

*Without a care in the world only two tables away 'it's him' Polly said 'oh my god! it's uncle Richard we need to get out of here' Victoria could feel her heart beating fast.*

*As she came face to face with the man who'd abused her as a teenager who'd ruined her life.*

*Affected her relationships she tried to remember the last time she'd seen him she'd been around eighteen.*

*Outside College he'd been walking around for her whole adult life she'd tried to forget about him.*

*Try and block out everything that had happened.*

Now in one second it all came back to her every time he'd visited the house.

Forced her to have sex with him she felt shaky 'f**k him'.

'We'll go when we're ready' Polly said 'if she knew what he was like' 'she didn't believe you'.

'I didn't tell her everything' 'let's just go she'll find out for herself' 'how?' they turned around.

Mr Cleves and his fiancé they'd seen them it was too late to just walk out the restaurant 'it's you again is it!'.

His fiancé looked angry 'that's the same girl I was telling you about who was trying to tell me not to marry you'.

'She said you had a dark past I told her where to go'.

'A dark past Polly why don't you tell everyone about your dark past how you slept your way around the school'.

'Men women there was no-one she wouldn't go with'.

'You were always a stupid tart throwing yourself at anyone who would have you'.

'You thought you could interfere in my relationship'.

'And get away with it!' inside Polly was shaking but she knew she couldn't not say anything.

She owed it to herself and Victoria 'why don't you tell your fiancé what you did to me!' 'I did nothing! you chased me'.

'You were obsessed with me you even wrote me love letters postcards I could have had you done for stalking!'.

'I don't know what I ever saw in you still we've all
fallen for people we shouldn't as teenagers'.
'One word desperate!' 'Richard she was just a kid'.
'Is that what you think it was me coming on to him!'.
'Course it was! he told me everything how you begged
to go to his country club his house'.
'How you phoned him after he left the school where
you worked how you were a teenage alcoholic'.
'You clearly had issues but you need to leave me alone'.
'I'm happy with my fiancé' 'you don't know him do you'.
'I know all I need to know' 'how would you feel if you
knew he'd groomed me gave me alcohol' 'she's lying!'.
'Of course she is' 'I'm not lying! yes I had sex as a
teenager yes I was bi-sexual but you took advantage'.
'You got me drunk twice then you raped me in my room'.
'When I was fifteen because you knew I'd grown up in
care'.
'Because at an all-girls school you'd never be suspected
because you knew I only saw my parents on weekends'.
'Like all the other girls' 'how can you lie! she's got serious
issues she always fancied me'.
'She was a screwed up teenager' 'that you took advantage
of and your own niece! who you abused for years!'.
'He even went to jail for abusing teenage girls!'.

'Shame they couldn't have locked you up and thrown away the key! you're a sex offender a danger to society!'.

'Polly's screwed up she's lying! you're gonna regret this!'.

'Maybe I was screwed up once but I'm not now!'.

'You're drinks sir' the waiter said as he put his tray down.

'Thankyou' Richard picked up his drink as he threw it at Polly she threw one back 'you bitch!' 'he's not worth it!'.

Amy said as she joined them 'whole gang's here I see'.

'Almost like a school reunion' 'you're a pathetic excuse for a man! you stay away from Polly and Victoria!'.

'If they stay away from me!' the whole restaurant watched as Polly paid for their meal before leaving.

'I can't believe he was there tonight of all nights!'.

Victoria said angry they hailed a taxi it had begun to rain heavily they got inside the taxi 'where to?'.

'Sixteen Cherry Tree Lane' 'you live where Mary Poppins lives' Victoria joked 'it's the name of the street'.

'Corey's house' 'I never realised' 'I'm sorry about tonight'.

'I shouldn't have said anything I guess all the anger came out the way he called me a stupid tart'.

'I never begged to go to any country club he invited me'.

'One weekend it sounded so posh a country club exclusive for people with money well I never had much growing up'.

'And even though dad and Wendy worked as hairdressers we were just a working class family'.

'He was a teacher with a middle class lifestyle I thought he liked me how stupid was I' 'he charmed everyone'.
'All the girls' 'he used me I was an easy target just a kid desperate for love from anyone'.
'Since I never had it as a child she tried to make out because I drank a lot that I imagined it all made it up'.
'You didn't none of us did' Victoria said trying to make Polly feel better 'that night he raped me'.
'I must have made it so easy for him all he had to do was give me alcohol tell me he fancied me'.
'Polly you were a teenager he took advantage of you'.
'He abused you and me' 'I know and I know he couldn't stay in jail forever sometimes I have flashbacks'.
'To that night it was the autumn fate I remember I drank Hooch before that night something didn't feel right'.
'When I said we didn't have to have sex he got angry'.
'I knew I had no choice so I asked if we could use protection he said it was fine that I wouldn't get pregnant'.
'Then he climbed on top of me I kept saying I didn't want to have sex I was half drunk he forced himself on me'.
'I knew it was all my fault he took the key out the door it was planned' Polly's voice began to quiver.
'After he said he could get a hundred girls like me'.
'That I was a slag and it was true' 'no Polly he's a horrible person' 'he opened the door called me a little tart'.

'I was in shock shaking I had a panic attack that turned into an asthma attack I wanted to die then'.

'Because nothing felt as bad as I did in that moment'.

'What about me then I should have helped you listened to you when I found you I didn't know what to do'.

'It's ok you found a teacher they took me to first aid'.

'It wasn't enough the morning after we had breakfast we chatted you said you felt used by him'.

'That you invited him up to your room I should have known' 'you couldn't have'.

'And I should have warned you what he was like'.

'But we didn't get on' 'I wouldn't have listened I couldn't tell anyone what happened'.

'I was worried they'd blame me I know now it wasn't all my fault then I got pregnant this woman gave me a pill'.

'To get rid of it what a situation I got myself into' 'it was all him ok you shouldn't have invited him to your room'.

'But you never stood a chance none of us did I hate him so much your so brave' Victoria said 'me' 'yes'.

'What you said in the restaurant' 'I thought…you'd be angry at me' 'no now his fiancé knows what he's like'.

'I couldn't have done what you did stood up to him like that at least not without alcohol'.

'Polly your stronger than I ever could be' 'we both are'.

*'Because neither of us will let anyone treat us like that again' 'here we are sixteen Cherry Tree Lane'.*

*The taxi driver said 'thanks' Polly said as they arrived home somehow Polly felt better.*

*She'd said everything she ever wanted to say she only hoped she'd never see him again.*

*Polly also hoped she'd given Victoria a bit more strength.*

*As Polly looked outside it was a rainy March day.*

*She had eaten lunch that afternoon she was expecting a visit from her Aunt Sue.*

*She had some important information that she had to tell her Polly wondered what it was.*

*Knowing her luck it would probably be something to do with her mum they still weren't talking.*

*Even worse Mother's Day would be coming up soon.*

*For the past few years Polly had begun to dread it now she was also estranged from Wendy her step-mum.*

*The person who'd been there for her as a teenager.*

*When her mum wasn't they'd drifted apart after she'd fallen out with her half-sister Emily.*

*Around twelve years ago in her eyes Emily was perfect.*

*And she could do no wrong the truth was she was nasty.*

*Vindictive and had done everything she could to ruin her relationship with their father.*

*Who could see through her fake perfect daughter act.*

*Polly had tried to look out for her despite the fact she could never stand her by trying to give her advice. Trying to stop her taking drugs sleeping around as a teenager when her dad and Wendy had been desperate. She'd let her stay at her house when she lived in L.A. It had been a disaster ending with Polly taking her stash of cocaine away before boarding a flight back to the UK. She had gotten no thanks from Wendy despite the fact she could have ended up in jail.*

*Over the years Emily's behaviour had gotten worse. Once a talented dancer she now spent her time as a Vlogger on YouTube in beauty salons and clubbing. Even doing topless modelling never holding down any job. For long as it could never be guaranteed she would turn up as she didn't have her work ethic.*

*Wendy had even said that if only Polly had helped Emily when she was younger. Then she might have the career she had the truth was she had little talent Emily could sing ok. But when Polly had arranged a visit from a top vocal coach she hadn't turned up.*

*And she had no interest in acting you could never say anything against Emily. According to Wendy she should have been more supportive of her sister Polly had enough over the years.*

*They now only spoke if they had to at family occasions.*
*Even then the conversation was limited Polly felt sad as*
*she had been so close to Wendy as a teenager and Stacey.*
*Who was also estranged from her all because of Emily.*
*Polly never thought it would happen but at least she had*
*her gran and Aunt Sue as a child she'd been angry at Sue.*
*For looking after Kaleigh not her now years later she*
*understood how hard it could be looking after a child.*
*And being married to someone as nasty and abusive*
*as Shaun was to her Polly saw a blue car drive up.*
*Near her house her aunt got out she opened the door.*
*'Hi Polly' 'come in cup of tea' 'I'd love one' Sue took off*
*her coat 'wet outside' 'yes' 'I made orange biscuits'.*
*'Yesterday' 'that sounds good' Sue seemed quieter than*
*usual Polly wondered if everything was ok Polly made tea.*
*As they sat down on the sofa Dickinson's Real Deal was*
*on TV 'been up to anything?' 'Polly I have some news'.*
*'It sounds serious' 'it is' 'bad news' 'in usual*
*circumstances but I think it's good news for me for us'.*
*'It's Shaun he's died' 'how?' 'heart attack no surprise'.*
*'He was a heavy drinker smoker loved his food too much'.*
*'Well I'm not sad after what he did to Kaleigh'.*
*'Neither am I Polly he ruined my life'.*
*'He hit me he controlled everything when I was with him it*
*was always rows it was always him telling me what to do'.*

*'Worried if I didn't he'd hit me or do something to*
*humiliate me I thought if I was the perfect wife'.*
*'Shaun would be nice to me it never happened'.*
*'Everyone hated him even his own mother and brother*
*didn't want to know so I'm not sad either I'm happy'.*
*'Because now I never have to worry about seeing him*
*around town I'm free and so is Kaleigh' 'well I'm happy'.*
*'I have some pink gin in the fridge shall we celebrate*
*his death I mean it's un Christian but in his case'.*
*Sue thought about it for a moment 'I think I'll have*
*a glass' 'I'll get the ice out' Polly was happy.*
*The man who'd abused Kaleigh was gone he could*
*never hurt her ever again Polly served the drinks.*
*'Let's have a cheers' 'ok' Sue agreed as she picked up her*
*glass 'Shaun you can never hurt anyone again' Polly said.*
*'Your turn' 'ok Shaun I'm finally free of you' they sipped*
*their drinks 'that felt good thanks Polly'.*
*'I know how many lives he ruined Kaleigh will be happy'.*
*'Does she know?' 'she's just found out' 'are you going*
*to the funeral?' 'I'd rather not but I want to make sure'.*
*'The bastard's dead Candice dosen't want to either but*
*he's her son so she and Charlie will be there reluctantly'.*
*'Dean dosen't want me to go but I need closure'.*
*'Then I can forget all about him' 'think you and Dean*
*will get engaged?' 'yes what about you and Corey?'.*

'I think so we've talked about it getting married again'.
'You should you know life's too short' 'yeah we should'.
'I'm thinking if we do I'll wear a dress this time as I wore
a jacket and skirt last time' 'if was nice though' 'ivory'.
'Cor wore pink I haven't looked through the photos
for a while I'm lucky I had three good marriages'.
'Until Margie cheated on me' 'she wasn't worth it'.
'She said recently she wanted to try again' 'I hope you
told her where to go' 'course'.
'No way would I get back with her I love Cor the love
of my life' 'good when you do get married let me know'.
'Course we will' they watched telly 'look Dinky cars'.
'I didn't know they were worth that much Shaun has lots
of them' Sue said they looked at each other for a moment.
'What are you waiting for you could flog the lot in fact
other things of his' 'you're right that bastard'.
'All the things he put me through let's do it make some
money he never remarried dated some girls'.
'I know where he lives' 'he's dead now we could break in'.
'Just make out you left some stuff at his house you are
his ex-wife' 'what if he had a serious girlfriend'.
'So what if he did listen Mag's is an expert on things
like this she'll help you if not I'm sure Steven will'.
'You're right you know I'd even go to jail if it meant
getting my own back' 'Shaun he can never hurt you again'.

'I know I'm happy' 'we can all move on now forget about the past' Polly said 'agree here's to new beginnings'.
They sipped their pink gin happy that things could be ok.
That evening Corey returned home she'd been out for the day with Stacey visiting art galleries and museums 'hi'.
'Good day out' 'the best' 'that's good' 'did Sue come round?' 'yes she had some good news'.
'What kind of news?' 'Shaun the bastard he's finally gone' 'gone as in dead?' 'yes heart attack'.
'No more that he deserves' 'wow!' 'Kaleigh knows he can't hurt anyone me and Sue had some pink gin to celebrate'.
'Is it wrong?' 'not with him the things he did to people'.
'Apparently Candice dosen't want to go to the funeral'.
'His own mother and Sue's only going for closure'.
'Are you going?' 'I might for Sue but then Dean's going'.
'I don't know how I'd feel if one of Shaun's mates stands up in church'.
'Asking people to forgive him for all he's done'.
'Saying what a wonderful person he is' 'it was like that with dad really hard after the way he was towards us'.
'Still your father whatever he did could never be as evil as Shaun was he controlled Sue all through their marriage'.
'He was horrible to Kaleigh emotionally abusing her calling her thick because she has ADHD'.

*'Even abusing his own son his whole family and all
the other girls anyway one less bastard in the world'.
'I'm glad you had a great day I'll have to come'.
'I just fancied a chill out day' 'I understand I thought
we could go to that new restaurant you wanted'.
'This Friday' Corey suggested 'I'd love to'.
'I thought we could dress up have a romantic meal'.
'That would be great' Polly smiled she knew it meant
one thing the possibility of a proposal.
She knew they'd been married before but it had been
years ago now they were older.
Ever since she'd gotten back with Corey it had been great.
Polly couldn't wait for them to get engaged she could plan
her outfit in advance she decided it would be red.
As they were going to a Chinese restaurant she owned
one or two red jackets and a matching skirt.
That Friday evening she got ready to go out she chose
a red jacket black skirt gold cross earrings.
And a red rose necklace Corey wore a black glittery jacket
Polly was excited they arrived for 6.30pm that evening.
They had booked a table in advance 'this is nice'.
Corey said looking around at the Chinese décor red
lanterns with gold writing on hanging from the ceiling.
On all the tables was a red candle they looked at the
menu's 'what do you fancy?' Corey asked.*

'Definitely egg fried rice' 'me too I'm having vegetable spring rolls' Corey said 'I'll have the same'.
A waiter came to the table as they ordered 'foods sorted'.
'Polly said 'Victoria told me about Mr Cleves that you saw him shopping with his fiancé' 'yeah then he left'.
'I tried to warn her off she wouldn't listen then me and Vicky saw him at Rusty's he saw us'.
'She said you gave him a peace of your mind'.
'I wasn't going to but I had to I hoped she'd listen to me'.
'His fiancée I don't think she did unless she googled him'.
'What did you say to him?' 'everything I needed to'.
'I never thought I'd see him and I never wanted to'.
'But there in that moment I told him what he was in front of his fiancé the whole restaurant even Mrs Rayworth'.
'Amy was there he even threw a drink at me I threw one back he was angry really angry at me'.
'Because I'd exposed him for what he was I'm scared'.
'In case I see him again I guess I'll have to stay out of Dublin for a while' 'you'll be fine'.
'As long as you make sure you don't go out on your own' 'Have someone with you even if your just shopping'.
'Even so it's for the best' the food arrived 'looks great'.
They helped themselves to rice 'there's something I should tell you' Corey said 'nothing serious' 'no'.

*'I used to sleep with her' 'not Mrs Rayworth' 'it was years ago she was one of my clients we were mates'.*

*'When I was seventeen she told me she was a lesbian'.*

*'That she loved her husband but she could never be out'.*

*'Live a normal life then a while later I was escorting'.*

*'She was there at the hotel I met people at she didn't use her real name she was surprised it was me she'd booked'.*

*'But it was fine' 'you slept with our headmistress' 'yes'.*

*'Maybe it was a big deal at the time but it's not now'.*

*'I never told anyone I told Violet and Louie a while back'.*

*'So how was it?' 'the sex' 'yes' 'ok it was years ago'.*

*'Twenty five years ago now' 'and she still looks good for her age' Polly said 'your ok about it?' 'why wouldn't I be'.*

*'It was years ago you were giving her a service especially since she couldn't be out about her sexuality'.*

*'I guess I was not just her all the women I went with'.*

*'I guess some people have to spend their lives in the closet due to circumstances' Polly said 'we were lucky'.*

*'We were out at a young age' 'there's something else I want to tell you especially as I want to be honest with you'.*

*'About everything' 'sounds serious' 'I guess it's a secret'.*

*'Sounds curious' 'remember when we split up after moving to L.A' 'yes' 'I was like twenty nine thirty'.*

*'You went with Jeanie and I also had a girlfriend' 'who?'.*

'Kaleigh' Corey waited to see what Polly's reaction would be to her revelation 'not my sister Kaleigh' 'yes'.
'Did anyone else know?' 'Stacey Louie we kept it quiet'.
'Kaleigh couldn't be out about her sexuality when someone from the record company found out'.
'We had to end it and I knew I was too old for her'.
'That's why I was surprised years later when she got together with Stacey I should have told you before'.
'I just never knew how you'd react' 'it's fine it was years ago there's no-one else you dated I should know about'.
'No I just wanted there to be no secrets between us'.
'I don't think there is although knowing both our families there might be' Corey joked.
'These spring rolls are amazing' 'I know' Corey agreed.
As they ate their food Polly was shocked at Corey's revelations but tried not to show it.
'Don't they usually give us fortune cookies while we're waiting' Polly said 'maybe they forgot' Corey said.
'Dessert after?' Polly asked 'of course' 'Banana fritter with ice-cream' Polly said 'yes definitely' Corey agreed.
'So how's Dougie?' 'fine at least we're speaking even if me and Nicky aren't' 'I wouldn't'.
'There are some things you just can't forgive if it wasn't for her speech in court he'd have been found guilty'.
'I'm still angry about it anyway I was in town a night out'.

*'Anyway we saw Dougie with his mate only you wouldn't
have known it was him' 'what do you mean?'.
'He was dressed in drag for a party he said as
Alice In Wonderland blue tunic blonde hair'.
'I saw his mate again he said Dougie wants to get a
sex change' 'what! oh no Cor why?' 'I don't know'.
'I asked Dougie about dressing as a woman he said
he just does it occasionally'.
'I thought I knew everything about him how could I not
know this' 'it's ok' 'I mean is it a terrible thing to say'.
'I don't know if I could accept him as someone else'.
'Listen you've got to make sure he gets counselling'.
'Before anything why did no-one say before' 'I don't know
why he didn't tell me is it my fault because of everything'.
'That was going on the trial' 'no you need to sit down
and talk to him everything will be ok whatever happens'.
'I guess' 'how is everything?' the waiter asked 'great'.
'Can we have two banana fritters' 'coming up' 'Cor
I want you to know we can get through anything'.
The banana fritters soon arrived 'somehow this makes
everything ok' 'I know Cor my two biggest vices'.
'Shopping and food' after they finished eating Polly
went to the toilet Corey checked her appearance.
In her compact mirror before going over to where
the staff were as she took her two fortune cookies.*

Larger than usual one had been specially made.
Polly returned 'oh look they brought the fortune cookies'.
'They forgot' Polly noticed it was bigger than a normal
size she had a suspicion a ring was inside.
She didn't say anything 'be careful when you eat them'.
Corey said 'I will' Polly took a small bite enough to open
the rest of the cookie a ring fell out 'oh my god!'.
'Is this an engagement ring?' 'yes' 'let me put it on' 'ok'.
'Will you marry me?' 'yes you know I will!' 'I wanted to
find a different way to propose' 'I love it!'.
Polly hugged Corey as people cheered she was beyond
happy she was getting married again.
To the love of her life that evening she announced her
engagement on Twitter.
Polly knew everyone would be happy for her and couldn't
wait to start planning the wedding.
A few days later Polly found an envelope in the post she
wondered who it was from it was a Mother's Day card.
She'd already received one from her two daughters
Susan and Marie she really hoped it wasn't from Luke.
She was done with their relationship and had no desire to
give him any money Polly reluctantly opened the card.
It read 'To Polly I know we're sisters but your also
my mum love Kaleigh xxx' she couldn't believe it.

*She wanted to cry for so many years she'd dreamed*
*about the possibility of being her mum.*
*But never believed it would happen everything would be*
*ok despite what her mum had said Kaleigh loved her.*
*And the card proved it everything was going ok in her life.*
*Nothing could stop her happiness she was engaged to*
*Corey Kaleigh loved her.*
*And her mum and son were out of her life no more*
*negativity Polly told herself.*
*That Tuesday lunchtime Stacey ate her favourite pizza*
*cheese and tomato as she watched Loose Women.*
*Sipping her favourite cloudy lemonade as she looked over.*
*At the sealed cardboard box in her lounge Stacey was*
*excited she was launching her own brand of cherryade.*
*And limeade she'd been wanting to do it for years many*
*celebrities had put their name to fizzy drinks.*
*But not many had ever been involved with making them.*
*Stacey couldn't wait to see what they tasted like her*
*manager Steve had helped her.*
*By putting her in touch with drinks manufacturers now the*
*product was finally here it was a good day she decided.*
*Stacey heard a knock at the door she looked out the*
*window she saw a red car that she didn't recognise.*
*As she opened she immediately recognised the face*
*of the woman in front of her 'Aunt Shirley!' 'Stacey!'.*

*They hugged she hadn't seen her aunt since she was*
*seventeen and never thought she would again.*
*'You look great Stacey' 'so do you you haven't aged*
*since I last saw you' Stacey said 'and you'.*
*'I want that fountain of youth you seem to be drinking'.*
*Shirley joked 'come in drink?' 'love one what do you*
*have?' everything the bar is always stocked'.*
*'Lemonade, coke,orange juice' 'I'll have some lemonade'.*
*'Ice' 'yes' Stacey poured her aunt a drink 'thanks'.*
*'So are you here on holiday?' 'yes I'm seeing Andy'.*
*'Uncle Andy' 'yes we've been in touch a lot lately' 'great'.*
*'What about Wendy and dad' 'I'd like to see your dad'.*
*'I haven't seen Wendy for years' 'how come?' 'it's a*
*long story I had an affair with someone close to her'.*
*'I shouldn't have but you know in life we all do things*
*we shouldn't have done make mistakes anyway'.*
*'She never forgave me' 'that's why you cut yourself off*
*from the family' 'yes the affair was years before'.*
*'When she found out that was it we never spoke again'.*
*'I thought you all would hate me too but then Andy*
*told me he missed me that he was never angry at me'.*
*'That it was between Wendy and me I never knew that'.*
*'I know you got married' Stacey said 'yes years ago'.*
*'And a second time they never worked out'.*
*'I was always in love with the idea of getting married'.*

'Finding Mr Right but it never worked out I see your
happy with Kaleigh' 'yes we've been together for years'.
'I never want to be with anyone else Wendy never
approved of me dating women'.
'She said after I dated Corey years ago that it was
a phase and I should go back to men' 'she's your aunt'.
'She should have supported you' 'we don't talk much now'.
'Wendy's not the same person she was Polly dosen't
either' 'how's Polly?' 'great she's just got engaged'.
'To Corey they'll be getting remarried soon' 'it's great'.
'That your all happy' 'most of us' 'you must meet my kids'.
'Their older now' 'how old?' 'Tally's eighteen'.
'The twins are thirteen Crystal and Connor' 'very Irish'.
'Connor' 'I know' 'I like it are you still on good terms
with their father?' 'Christian yes he's a great person'.
'If his mother hadn't been such a bitch we might have
stayed together' 'I know the feeling'.
'That's why my second marriage ended but then I might
not have got together with Kaleigh'.
'I guess everything happens for a reason can I ask
who you had that affair with was it someone random'.
'Adrian' 'Wendy's husband' 'yes it was towards the
end of their marriage'.
'She blamed me for the marriage breaking up according
to him they would have split up anyway'.

'Course I don't know the truth we've never spoken since'.
'We all make mistakes' Stacey said trying to make
Shirley feel better 'thanks it was awful'.
'Wendy found us in bed together like one of those
moments from a soap opera you say those words'.
'It's not what it looks like or I can explain it's obvious
what we were up to if I could go back in time'.
'But I can't you know' 'did you really like him?' 'yes'.
'Adrian he was so lovely I can see why she married him'.
'We became good friends he was someone I could talk to'.
'I even fell in love with him he said they were having
problems it started with a kiss then became more'.
'How long did it last?' 'six months I know I should regret
it because it ruined my relationship with Wendy'.
'Even your dad hated me but I was in love or lust'.
'That's the thing with married men he said that he was
thinking of leaving her I believed him'.
'You know married men they always say they'll leave their
wives he did actually but someone else came on the scene'.
'And it wasn't me so I was left without a boyfriend and my
family' 'I'm sorry I used to like Adrian growing up'.
'I thought he was my dad because he had curly dark hair
and everyone else in the family was Irish looking'.
'I haven't seen him since I was twelve I've looked for him
on Facebook too many Adrian's with the same name'.

*'I have no idea about him' Shirley said 'and Simon'.*
*'I heard they split' 'a few years back they were together almost twenty years I don't know if she's seeing anyone'.*
*'He's with Polly's mum Sarah on and off' 'well it's been good catching up' 'where are you staying?' 'with a friend'.*
*'She lives in Liverpool actually' 'I've been here a while now in The Wirral and Polly we visit each other'.*
*'Do you think you'll come back to the UK?' 'I might do'.*
*'But I'm only over the sea' 'how did you know my address?' 'Andy gave it to me I hope that's ok' 'of course'.*
*Stacey had enjoyed seeing her aunt Shirley she finally knew why she'd been estranged for so many years.*
*She didn't blame her aunt for having an affair after all everyone made mistakes.*
*Even part of her had been in love with Adrian he'd been like a second father to her before Wendy married Simon.*
*Shirley looked over at the parcel on the floor curious.*
*'Something good' she asked 'Cherry and Limeade my new business venture' 'your own recipe' 'yes'*
*'I've been involved at every stage if I open will you try some?' 'love to' Stacey got a pair of scissors.*
*As she cut open the box she was impressed with the packaging she went to the kitchen getting out two glasses.*
*As she poured them a drink a glass of cherryade it tasted great just as she wanted 'well what do you think?'.*

'Lovely' Shirley said 'you're not just saying that'.
'It tastes really nice' somehow Stacey had a feeling
she was going to enjoy getting to know her aunt.
That afternoon Victoria walked through town trying to
select a present for her sister it was Katie's birthday.
She would be turning forty a big party was planned
in a week's time all the family would be there.
Their mother Katie and Nina's dad her aunts and uncles.
They would all be happy somehow she wouldn't be.
She'd been close to her sisters but recently Victoria
couldn't help feeling they didn't want her around anymore.
The way she was left out of certain things her mother
had left her age eight she hadn't seen her again.
Until she was twenty nine a whole lifetime it felt.
Victoria wanted to believe her mother had missed her.
Regretted leaving her now she wasn't so sure Katie
was always the favourite she understood.
As she'd been two years younger but they were adults.
Women in their forties she was fed up of always feeling
second best not good enough for her family.
For years she pretended it didn't bother her that it
was better than not having any family at all.
As it had been growing up now she realised she'd had
enough Corey was right she didn't have a father.
Her mother preferred her sisters she had Sapphire.

*Maybe she could meet someone join a dating agency.*
*Have her own family maybe that would be better*
*than years of heartbreak and pain.*
*As Victoria looked in the mirror at her blue and green*
*tartan dress with a big blue bow at the back.*
*It looked perfect it was her favourite dress she had many.*
*But this one was special it was for Christmas it had been*
*brought for her two years ago at the time it was too big.*
*Now age eight it fitted perfectly Victoria lived in*
*a big house not quite a mansion but not far off.*
*With a massive garden just outside Dublin she knew*
*her father was rich she didn't know what he did.*
*Just that he wore suits and was very well off.*
*It was Christmas Day she had opened her stocking earlier*
*'Victoria' her mother called Christmas dinner was ready.*
*'Coming mammy' she walked quickly as Victoria looked*
*out through the glass doors in the living room.*
*Looking at the snow outside her sister Katie was sat*
*round the tree with their parents.*
*She wore a pink princess style dress she was slightly*
*jealous of Katie she had blonde hair.*
*Which she wished she had instead of dark brown.*
*And was spoiled a lot by their parents Victoria knew*
*her parents loved her especially her father.*
*She was a real daddy's girl 'let's open presents'.*

'Before dinner' her mother suggested Victoria smiled she
was excited to see what she had for Christmas 'mine first'.
Her mother said Victoria looked at the slim box
wrapped in green paper with a bow.
Her mother was always good at wrapping presents she
opened it a porcelain doll with a tartan dress 'I love it!'.
'I'm glad' 'now open mine' her dad said it was a bigger
box wrapped in gold she undid the wrapping excited.
At what the present would be 'tap dancing shoes'.
'Just for you' 'thankyou daddy' her father smiled happy.
At how happy she was 'I know you wanted to learn
tap dancing for ages now you can do classes'.
'Without borrowing shoes you'll have your own' Victoria
couldn't wait they were black with silver on the bottom.
'Now for Katie's second present' her mother said as they
watched her first present had been a Tiny Tears doll.
Katie ripped off the packaging as she opened the box.
'Tap shoes for me as well' 'yes you can both learn'.
Victoria suddenly felt jealous of her sister Katie's were
white her's were black yes they were tap shoes.
But it wasn't the same she'd also always wanted a
Tiny Tears her mother said they were childish.
That they'd sold out in the shops 'we can arrange
tap classes first week of January' her father said happy
Victoria decided not to say anything.

*Or else she wouldn't be able to do tap classes.*
*Somehow Victoria knew her mother's favourite was Katie.*
*Was it because she was younger or had blonde hair?.*
*Victoria tried to please her mother it was never enough.*
*Her dad however gave her lots of attention one day*
*things changed it was the end of January.*
*Victoria was outside in the garden playing in the snow.*
*Her mother had been quiet all day she called as she took*
*off her wellies and gloves 'I've got something to tell you'.*
*'What is it?' 'you'll be moving to another house'.*
*'I like this house' 'this one will be nice the reason is*
*I've wanted to tell you for a while'.*
*'It was never the right time me and your dad we're*
*splitting up getting a divorce but it'll be ok'.*
*'You can still come and visit me nothing much has to*
*change' 'but why?' 'sometimes things happen in life'.*
*'Adults fall out of love and when that happens they can't*
*stay together anymore' Victoria felt sad.*
*As she didn't want to move house she didn't want her*
*parents to split up why couldn't they stay together?.*
*As Victoria snapped out of her flashback she chose*
*a Ruby Shoo bag for Katie she returned home.*
*Later that afternoon as Victoria thought about her mother*
*and their relationship how she'd loved her idolised her.*
*A fashion designer with her perfect English accent.*

*She'd moved to Ireland age nineteen when her father*
*took a job in Dublin her mother stayed in the UK.*
*Victoria had never heard from her mother as a teenager.*
*Despite asking to see her it was as if she didn't exist.*
*Her step-dad would turn up occasionally at the house.*
*To talk to her dad about childcare arrangements for Katie.*
*No sign of her mother she'd vanished until age fifteen*
*when it was announced she was marrying Katie's father.*
*She hadn't even got a proper invite it had been suggested*
*by her housekeeper Mrs Harvey that she should go.*
*Her mother had looked beautiful in a carriage as it*
*went past before the wedding service.*
*Victoria had been sat at the back of the church.*
*Watching as her sister and two other people had been*
*bridesmaids.*
*When she'd met her sister for the first time in years.*
*It was strange as she made out she didn't remember her.*
*Victoria had then taken out her anger on her mother.*
*For not being there for abandoning her all those*
*years ago she'd wanted to go home.*
*Mrs Harvey had made her stay for a while so she could*
*enjoy the buffet of sandwiches Victoria had stood outside.*
*As she overheard a row between her mum and sister.*
*Katie had said she was the favourite that they could forget*
*about her that's all they'd ever done.*

*Made it obvious they didn't want her around she'd cried
that day and she rarely cried as it poured down with rain.
Corey had comforted her made everything ok.
Like her her mother had left age seven and her sister
Nicky had always been the favourite.
Why had she never realised how much they had in
common Victoria had seen her mother again.
When she was eighteen she'd read about her shop on the
internet 'Wedding Dreams' she'd planned to talk to her.
Apologise for their row she'd looked in the window.
At the beautiful dresses entered the shop only to see her
favourite aunt with her mum and Katie laughing.
And chatting she left never thinking she'd see her again.
One day age twenty seven she'd logged into Facebook.
To find a message from her mother asking if they wanted
to meet up put the past behind them she'd been excited.
To meet her mother after all those years she'd stood her
up then arranged another meeting two years later.
When she'd arrived she'd been disappointed to see Katie
was with her.
Victoria had wanted to chat to her mother alone and
she'd never forgiven Katie for the way she had acted.
At their mother's wedding despite this Katie had soon
made it clear she wanted them to have a relationship.
So she'd forgiven her they became close.*

*Shopping going out and rebuilding their relationship.*
*Victoria had also found out she had another younger*
*sister Nina for a few years everything was great.*
*Recently she'd begun to realise how close Katie and Nina*
*were with in jokes and mutual friends.*
*Victoria had begun to feel like she was on the outside.*
*Maybe she had been and never realised it maybe she*
*always would be.*
*She knew she couldn't pretend everything was ok anymore.*
*And deserved better a week later Victoria got ready for*
*Katie's birthday party she didn't really want to go.*
*But knew she had to she hoped Katie would like the bag.*
*That she'd brought Victoria had selected her outfit.*
*A black Phase Eight dress black high heels and a*
*diamante cross necklace and cross earrings.*
*As she waited for her taxi to arrive it was raining.*
*Luckily she had with her an umbrella in her designer*
*evening bag it would be a good party she told herself.*
*She would have a good time chat to her mum maybe her*
*aunts and uncles might be there.*
*Deep down Victoria knew she didn't want to be there.*
*As she thought about things what Corey had said the time.*
*She'd overheard the conversation when Katie had said it*
*would be better the three of them before they met her*
*If they really loved her they wouldn't treat her like that.*

*Corey was right Victoria arrived at her sister's house.*
*She could hear loud talking as she walked up the path.*
*'We are gonna have a great night' 'come in' the door shut.*
*Victoria arrived at the front door she knocked 'Victoria'.*
*Her sister Nina greeted her 'hi' 'hi come in drink'.*
*'There's loads of punch' 'I'll have some' as Victoria*
*looked around the living room was full of people.*
*Some sounded drunk already at least in a nightclub*
*she could have gone off had a dance somewhere.*
*No chance at a house party 'Vicky' Katie saw her.*
*She was dressed as if she was attending a wedding*
*wearing a white satin dress.*
*That her large bust threatened to come out of at any*
*moment Katie had always struggled with her weight.*
*Since she'd known her as an adult her mum never said*
*anything about Katie's apperance.*
*However she would always comment if she'd gained*
*a few pounds Victoria knew Katie was the favourite.*
*And she always would be somehow she'd get through*
*the party she told herself it was only a few hours.*
*Then she could make her excuses and leave.*
*'Happy Birthday' 'thanks' 'you look good on it'.*
*'Well you should know being two years older' 'yeah'.*
*Victoria felt annoyed at her comment she knew she looked*
*younger than her age that she could pass for twenty five.*

Katie however looked her age 'I've got your present'.
'Thanks' she put it in a corner of the room not even
looking at it Nina sat down 'my present!'.
Katie sounded excited 'can't wait to open it' Katie ripped
off the wrapping like an excited child 'oh my god!'.
'It's Marc Jacobs' it was a designer bag Victoria knew
hers was nicer.
But Katie clearly didn't want to open her present.
'I love it!' their mother appeared wearing a similar dress
to Victoria's 'hi' she said acknowledging Victoria.
'Look Nina got me a Marc Jacobs bag' 'it's lovely'.
'This is great all my girls together' she hugged Katie.
As Nina sat close Victoria had never felt so unloved.
She hated her so called family 'oh Vicky let me show you
what mam brought me' Katie showed her a photo.
Of a designer car 'isn't it amazing' 'yeah' 'and a gold
plated phone case' Victoria pretended to be happy.
How could she be if ever she'd doubted how much her
mum loved her 'music time' Nina put on a cd.
Of dance music 'love the dress' her mum said 'thanks'.
'See you later' Victoria was annoyed a quick comment
about her dress and that was it she watched.
As they all chatted as if she wasn't there she decided
to find someone to chat to Victoria looked around.

*A fat man arrived at the house she suddenly realised it was her father she hadn't seen him since she was fifteen. He hadn't aged well Victoria wondered if he'd be happy to see her 'dad hi so glad you could make it'.*

*'Party's in full swing' Katie said why had no-one told her that her dad would be there Victoria glanced over.*

*'Victoria hi you look great' 'and you' she lied her father looked terrible*

*'I hear you work in the fashion business'.*

*'Yes I work in a shop and I sell online' 'that's good'.*

*'What about you?' 'I sell properties these days'.*

*'Are you and mam back together?' 'no I'm a regular visitor that's old news I've been married for years'.*

*'That's great' 'what about you?' 'I'm single I have a daughter Sapphire she's ten' 'April told me'.*

*Victoria was about to get out her phone to show him a photo 'I'll go get a drink catch you all later'.*

*Victoria put her phone away what kind of man wouldn't want to see a photo of his granddaughter.*

*So her father had been around for ages and no-one bothered to tell her not that it mattered anymore.*

*He'd always been a terrible father after half an hour her father had only glanced in her direction.*

*Everyone was talking to someone Victoria wanted to leave she wished she'd asked Polly to come or Corey.*

*Just as she was about to leave she spied a man with red hair it was uncle Patrick.*

*She hadn't seen him in ages he lived in the UK and only visited occasionally 'Victoria' 'hi' 'you look nice'.*

*'Thanks' 'I haven't seen you in ages' 'I follow you on Twitter' 'I know I follow you too'.*

*'It's great that everyone gets along so well now since you were estranged from your mother'.*

*'When you were younger' 'yeah' 'I thought it was a shame what happened when families split up' 'yeah'.*

*'They never told me my father was back on the scene'.*

*'He didn't even ask to see a photo of Sapphire'.*

*'Between you and me I never liked him not a nice man'.*

*'I've done my research on him as a politician and the fact he never stayed around'.*

*'I thought I'd never see him again I dreamed if we met that he'd say I'm sorry I abandoned you'.*

*'But he only asked me about my career what I was up to'.*

*'He's not worth bothering about' 'I know but it still hurts sometimes I wish you were my father'.*

*'I would have made a terrible dad that's why I never had kids' 'I'm sticking with one hard work' 'I can imagine'.*

*'I love her though' 'she's pretty like her mother'.*

*'She's the best the only member of this family apart from you I can rely on' 'listen try the punch' 'I will back soon'.*

*Victoria made her way to the toilet after she flushed she heard voices talking 'where's Victoria?' 'I've got no idea'. 'She's just here to make up the numbers' 'Katie that's mean' 'but true' Victoria opened the door.*

*Just in time to see Katie and a friend walking upstairs. How she hated them she decided she was going to leave the party early as she came down the stairs.*

*She spied her father talking to her uncle Richard. How could they invite him after what he'd done after being in jail for abusing teenage girls.*

*After he'd destroyed her teenage years her life. 'How could you invite him!' 'we've all done things we regret made mistakes' 'your my father!'.*

*'And you can't even defend me!' 'Victoria it's in the past'. 'I have to live with what he did to me!' 'and you tell Polly if I see her she's in serious trouble!'.*

*'Because of her my fiancée left me pathetic tart she is!'. 'Polly's more of a person than you'll ever be she told the truth that your nothing but a sexual predator!'.*

*'You keep your voice down!' 'or what? I'm not scared of you anymore!' 'you will be!' 'I'm going anyway!' 'good'. 'Oh and he's not your father never was' 'what!'.*

*'Your dad he's Katie's father not yours!' 'your lying!'. 'It's true I'm sorry I was only ever your step-dad'. 'So all my life I thought you were my father'.*

'No wonder you never cared about me I should have known! thank god we're not related and him!'.
'This is the best news I've had in ages so who is my father?' 'he's dead' Richard said smirking.
'F**k you! and this family' Victoria spied her present. Near the door she grabbed it as she left she dialled the taxi number grabbing her umbrella as it rained.
It had been the worst night ever Victoria vowed not to have anything to do with her family again.
Except her uncle Patrick she was still in shock at hearing the news that her father wasn't her real dad.
She should have known when he'd been younger he'd had dark hair like her there had never been any suspicion.
It all made sense why he never cared about her because he wasn't blood related.
Then she remembered he had loved her once as a child. But later he couldn't be bothered anymore with a string of girlfriends he didn't love her.
Maybe he'd seen her as an inconvenience to palm off to housekeepers and servants anyone except him.
Maybe he turned a blind eye to the abuse she'd suffered from her uncle and she hated her mother and sisters.
They were welcome to each other Victoria knew there was no place for her in the family.
That evening she arrived home it was raining heavily.

*As she got changed watched telly then allowed herself*
*to cry she'd never felt so alone.*
*Victoria looked over at the bag she'd brought her sister.*
*Unwanted like her she decided she'd give it to Polly.*
*It was her birthday in August she would be more grateful*
*than her sister that night she hardly got any sleep.*
*As she woke the next morning she made herself a*
*cup of tea with her new silver tea service.*
*Polly had brought her for Christmas she'd been meaning*
*to get one for years tea always tasted better in a teapot.*
*Victoria ate shortbread as she looked out at the view*
*from her apartment she had everything she wanted.*
*Somewhere to live a daughter a good career but she didn't*
*have what she really wanted a proper family.*
*Now she knew how Corey felt it was after lunch*
*she heard her apartment buzzer.*
*Victoria wondered who it could be Polly was in the UK.*
*She opened it was her mother 'can I come in?' 'course'.*
*'Tea' 'please' Victoria boiled the kettle 'I like the*
*tea service' 'it was from Polly at Christmas'*
*'It must be your English heritage' 'you sound off with me'.*
*'Why did you leave the party early?' 'why do you think'.*
*'I have a few reasons tell me why you invited him to the*
*party?' 'him' 'Richard if I'd have known he was coming'.*
*'I never would have come' 'I didn't know'.*

'He came with your father' 'he's not my father' 'what?'.
'They told me dad and Richard they said my real father's
dead tell me their lying... no then it doesn't matter'.
'He never cared about me anyway except for the time he
brought me that doll for my eighth birthday'.
'When we were a perfect family not for long' 'we fell out
of love' 'why didn't you tell me from the start'.
'He was my step-dad I wouldn't have minded'.
'You were a child and he loved you even though you
weren't his and your real dad didn't want you'.
'You went to live with him Katie stayed with me it was the
way things were' 'he brought me those black tap shoes'.
'Remember' 'yes' 'and guess what you got Katie white
ones better ones that's the way it always was'.
'And the Tiny Tears you knew I wanted one I don't mind
you having a favourite child most parents do'.
'But did you have to be so blatant about it and you
brought her that car gold plated everything'.
'She's not as well off as me and you' 'well maybe if she
spent less money on botox, sunbeds and holidays'.
'And another thing you promised me you'd come back
for me you never did an eight year old'.
'Wondering where her mother was I bet when I moved
to Canada for three years you were happy'.
'You didn't have to think about me for a while' 'no'.

'I thought about you all the time I didn't even know you'd gone till he told me' 'why didn't you fly out?'.

'I would if Sapphire's dad took her to another country'.

'Couldn't be bothered' 'things were difficult your dad and me were separated not together anymore'.

'I remember one day it was after I started secondary school I realised you'd never come back'.

'You waited till I was twenty seven to make contact'.

'He was abusive to me your father he hit me that's why I had to leave him' 'then why is he back in your life?'.

'A regular visitor to your house which no-one told me about!' 'it's Katie who wanted to see him'.

'We don't talk much I understand why your angry' 'angry'.

'You have no idea what it's like for me! I missed you for years do you know what it was like for me'.

'All the other girls at school with their perfect families'.

'Even Polly had a step-mum and dad who loved her'.

'I had no-one! my own father or the man I thought was my dad only turned up to one parent's evening'.

'The rest he couldn't be bothered all the other girls parents did and uncle Richard abused me for years'.

'No-one cared not even the two people who looked after me who weren't my parents' 'I always thought about you'.

'It wasn't enough! you stood me up when you contacted me when I went to meet you' 'I was scared'.

'That's why I cancelled I did meet you' 'I was twenty nine'.
'I'm sorry it took me so many years ok' 'when I met you
after all those years I was excited happy I had questions'.
'Then when we met Katie was there' 'I thought you wanted
to meet her she's your sister' 'I did'.
'But I wanted to see you first hug you tell you I loved you'.
'And Nina I could never have you to myself I was never
enough!' 'you are! it was complicated'.
'And why do you hate Katie out of jealousy' 'no'.
'Because of the things she's said' 'what things?'.
'She said it was better if it was just the three of you'.
'Before I came back into your lives' 'she wouldn't'.
'She did! Corey overheard her in Debenhams and she
wouldn't lie and it's not her fault she wanted me to know'.
'The truth because it's like that with her family her mam
always put her brother and sister first'.
'She never felt good enough like me and Katie at the party
I overheard her'.
'Say she only invited me to make up the numbers Nina
and her I know they grew up together'.
'But for once it would be good to be included not left out
of everything' 'is that how you feel?' 'all the time'.
'I never wanted you to feel that way' 'I do in fact I want
nothing to do with you!' 'you don't mean that!' 'yes'.

'All of you! except uncle Patrick you know what Polly, Stacey and Corey are more family than you'll ever be!'.

'Don't say that!' 'it's true they care about me'.

'They always make sure I'm ok and their there to pick up the pieces everytime you or Katie upset me'.

'Make me feel like I'm invisible that I don't exist to you'.

'Like I'm not good enough and it's a good job my dad's dead because he probably wouldn't want to know me'.

'Please don't get upset!' 'I am upset!' 'your dad was an alcoholic who beat his own kids'.

'I wouldn't have wanted someone like that raising you'.

'I have other siblings well don't worry if they turn out like Katie I'll be doing myself a favour' 'you have a sister'.

'Your brother died' 'how old?' 'same age' 'does she know about me?' 'yes she's known a while it's Corey' 'what?'.

'Corey she's your half-sister' 'why didn't she tell me'.

'She was worried how you'd react she only found out before Christmas' 'I don't understand'.

'How can we be related?' 'I had a fling with her dad'.

'Terry I was twenty he was seeing Corey's mother at the same time he chose her and I married your dad'.

'And you were with me and your dad and Katie'.

'She was with her dad and brother and I thought everything was fine as they were'.

'And then when I divorced your dad it would have complicated things I never told you I'm sorry'.
'Why didn't Corey tell me as soon as she found out'.
'She was worried you wouldn't accept her as your sister'.
'Why couldn't you have been straight with me from the start about my father the fact I have another sister'.
'That no-one told me about!' 'it was for the best!'.
'For you what about me!' 'I'm sorry!' 'this is why I want nothing to do with any of you' 'please Victoria!' 'no'.
'I'm doing you a favour you Katie and Nina can have your perfect family you don't have to worry about me'.
'Ever again go off into the sunset enjoy your life together!'
'I love you!' 'if you did you wouldn't treat me the way you do I never had a mother or a father'.
'From the time I was eight years old not parents that cared so I'll be fine without you' 'please don't do this!'.
'I have no choice because I'm tired of being hurt by you'.
'And Katie I'm not putting up with it anymore!'.
'Sapphire's my family we'll have each other' 'I won't let you do this!' 'I am because I have to' 'I love you!'.
'You don't love me and you never have! 'I'm sorry I upset you I never meant to' 'please go!'.
Victoria watched as her mother left after she cried for an hour upset angry in despair.

## Spring wedding

*That afternoon she decided to look at some old photos.*
*Victoria had to see if she and Corey resembled each other.*
*She found a box of photos some school trips*
*official photos and others from recent events.*
*As she realised there was a resemblance they had similar*
*lips and facial expressions she wanted to tell Corey.*
*But decided to wait a while she needed to get herself*
*together after what had happened with her mother.*
*A few days later Victoria picked up the mail as she*
*read through the usual bills and junk mail.*
*She spied a white satin envelope it looked interesting.*
*It was a wedding invitation 'Kitty Johnson &*
*Michael O'Kelly invite you to their wedding April 23rd'.*
*'At St Michael's Church RSVP' she'd heard they were*
*getting married Corey's bandmate and close friend.*
*She didn't know Kitty that well but whenever they*
*hung out they got on well.*
*And it would give her a chance to talk to Corey*
*especially if they ended up sat on the same table.*
*Victoria knew she'd have to plan her wedding outfit.*
*She only had a few weeks Victoria texted Polly that*
*evening who told her the wedding was eighties themed.*
*But guests could wear what they wanted it sounded fun.*

*Just what she needed after recent events she had several*
*unread texts on her phone from her mother.*
*And even her sisters she had decided not to read them.*
*As she didn't want to be around negative people anymore.*
*No more feeling left out or second best she decided.*
*The next day Victoria ventured into town as she looked*
*for an outfit to buy for the wedding.*
*As she tried to resist the temptation to visit*
*Wedding Dreams but she couldn't as she walked past.*
*A satin white wedding dress that was in the window.*
*She looked over at some women talking it was Katie*
*and Nina 'I'm engaged! I'm getting married' Katie said.*
*'When?' 'I don't know I'm planning it now mam's so*
*happy for me' somehow Victoria didn't feel angry.*
*She felt relieved knowing she'd made the right decision*
*to break off contact with the three of them.*
*And their happy gang made her feel angry they were*
*welcome to each other Victoria quickly walked away.*
*Before they saw her she found an outfit in a department*
*store an emerald green dress and matching shoes.*
*Shopping always made her feel better that everything*
*was ok in the world at least for a moment.*
*A few days later she found herself on social media.*
*Spying on Katie on her Facebook account as she looked*
*through her photos she had posted.*

*Victoria realised all the photos of her had been deleted.*
*The one's with Nina and her mother remained she even*
*found one with her father.*
*Or the man she'd assumed was her father how she hated*
*them all now she knew her own family didn't care.*
*Sapphire was the only good thing in her life*
*Before Victoria knew it April 23rd had arrived that*
*morning at 10.30am Polly arrived in a taxi with Stacey.*
*To take her to the wedding 'you look great' Stacey said.*
*As Victoria sat beside them 'so do you' Polly was wearing*
*a crème jacket and skirt Stacey a berry coloured dress.*
*And jacket 'should be a good wedding eighties themed'.*
*Polly said she looked happy Victoria thought she knew*
*she'd started planning her wedding to Corey.*
*Victoria also thought about her sister's engagement*
*she decided if she was invited she wouldn't go.*
*As far as she was concerned she didn't have a family.*
*They arrived at the church the wedding was at 11am.*
*Corey was going to be bridesmaid along with Kitty's*
*friend and sister Darcy they took their seats in the church.*
*In the middle of the room 'guess what? Danny's also*
*going to be a bridesmaid' Stacey informed them 'Danny?'.*
*'Kitty's brother in drag she told me on Facebook'.*
*Stacey said 'sounds fun' Polly tried not to think about*
*Douglas the fact that he had been her step-son.*

For many years and even after she and Corey had split she'd still spoken to him regularly on the phone.
And social media it made her sad still somehow she'd support him in his decision to be a woman.
She just hoped Corey was ok about it deep down Polly knew she wasn't why was life so complicated?.
They spied him in the front row with Corey's uncle Tommy.
'Nice church' 'I know love the white flowers' Polly agreed.
'Can't wait to see the bridesmaids' 'me either their wearing mint green' Stacey informed Victoria.
Who was curious to see Corey and Kitty's drag queen brother 'hello you gorgeous girls' it was Louie 'hi'.
Polly said excited to see him 'can't wait to see the bride'.
'She's wearing white and Mike's wearing a dark green suit' Stacey informed him 'sounds great'.
'I brought Angelica with me' 'love the outfit' Stacey said.
Angelica was wearing a black and white jacket and skirt.
With a big hat 'thanks' 'oh Violet's coming as well she said she's running late' 'the more the merrier' Polly said.
As they watched people arriving 'see you later'.
They moved back to the opposite side of the room just before 11am the church doors opened.
As the bride made her entrance everyone looked the bridesmaids made their way down the aisle.

*Victoria looked over a big girl who she assumed*
*was Kitty's sister walked through the church.*
*Followed by Corey she looked pretty Victoria thought.*
*Her hair was dyed copper red cut short but feminine*
*she looked good in mint green they looked over.*
*As Kitty's brother made his entrance towering above*
*the others in high heels and perfect make-up.*
*Somehow he looked just as good in his own way.*
*Some members of the congregation gave him funny looks.*
*Others were curious finally the service began.*
*'We are gathered here in the sight of god to join this*
*woman and this man in holy matrimony'.*
*The church doors opened it was Violet she sat beside*
*Louie she looked great wearing a peach dress.*
*And matching hat the service didn't last long as they*
*left the church to Wet Wet Wet Angel Eyes.*
*Everyone watched Kitty and Mike leave the church.*
*'She looked great' Stacey said and they all agreed.*
*Suddenly Victoria felt sad what if she never got married.*
*To someone she loved she'd always had problems*
*forming relationships she'd been marred once.*
*It had only lated six months she was forty two now.*
*What if it was too late and she couldn't meet someone?.*
*Even worse her annoying less attractive sister Katie*
*was engaged to someone.*

*She hadn't thought that coming to a wedding would*
*make her feel bad about herself she got into a car.*
*With Polly and Stacey to go to the hotel a short distance*
*away 'nice service' Victoria said making conversation.*
*Not wanting anyone to know she felt bad 'I agree'.*
*Stacey said 'I hope the food's good' Polly said.*
*'I Googled it on Trip Advisor says the food's really good'.*
*Stacey replied 'then we'll all have a great night'.*
*'I wonder how Corey is after finding out Dougie wants*
*a sex change' Stacey said 'you are joking!' Victoria said.*
*Shocked 'no Corey's not happy she feels like it's her fault'.*
*'The stress of the trial' Polly explained 'it's not her fault '.*
*'She had no idea he liked to dress as a woman'.*
*Stacey said 'so he's...you know' 'transitioning I don't know*
*when or why' Polly said 'he's dressed normally'.*
*'He looks nice in his blue suit' Polly said 'we should*
*say hi later on' Victoria suggested.*
*'We will act as if everything's normal' Stacey said.*
*They soon arrived at the hotel for the meal it was beautiful*
*with lots of white flowers and white table cloths.*
*They looked at the seating plan 'we're together'.*
*Polly said noticing their names they sat down at the*
*opposite table Louie was sat with Violet and Angelica.*
*'That was good of Kitty to put us all together' Polly said.*
*Dougie and Tommy sat down 'hello girls' 'hi Tommy'.*

'How are you?' Polly asked 'I'm grand you all look
really great' 'as do you in your suit'.
'I brought a new suit for the occasion and Dougie'.
'I guess you won't be wearing suits from now on'.
Polly said as Douglas sat down 'what do you mean?'.
'I mean when you transition become a woman'.
'Who said that?' Tommy asked 'your mate said you're
having a sex change' Tommy spat out his lemonade.
As he started laughing 'I'm not having a sex change'.
'I just like to dress as a woman sometimes for fun'.
'I'm a transvestite not a tran-sexual' 'if it's Harry he
always plays jokes on people looks like you've been had'.
Tommy said as they all laughed 'you promise' Polly asked.
'Course if I was I would have done it years ago'.
'I'm twenty nine' 'Cor will be relieved'.
'And me it's not that we wouldn't be supportive'.
'But we thought you were becoming someone else'.
'That's the biggest laugh I've had in ages' Tommy said.
'You want the truth I'm a drag queen it's for fun then after
I take off the clothes and make-up I just want to be me'.
'Wear T-shirts and jeans I've got no interest to have
a sex change' 'well that's cleared everything up'.
'Champagne' Polly asked 'yes' someone came over
as they poured champagne in everyone's glasses.

'Corey's over there don't say a word Corey' she came over
as Tommy called 'you look great' he said 'thanks'.
'I agree mint green is a great colour on you' Polly said.
'We were just discussing Douglas's sex change operation'
Tommy said as they tried not to laugh 'so when it is?'.
They burst out laughing 'what's so funny?' 'I'm not
having one I just do drag Harry was joking'.
'What you mean…' 'I'm not becoming a woman'.
'You mean it?' 'yes I mean it' Douglas took off his jacket.
As he hugged Corey she'd never felt so relieved.
'Cor champagne' Polly asked 'yes please I'm on Kitty's
table but I'll come over later mam's here as well'.
'We'll see her later' Corey sipped her champagne.
As she returned to her table Victoria wanted to talk to her.
It would have to wait until later 'can't wait to see Carol'.
'Not seen her in a while' Polly said 'Corey's mam'.
Victoria asked 'yeah' she realised if she and Corey
were half-sisters Douglas was her nephew.
And Corey's daughters were her nieces her dad's side
of the family were her family too.
'I have something to tell you' Victoria said 'I found out
a few weeks ago Corey's my half-sister' 'what really?'.
Tommy asked surprised 'Corey's dad was my biological
father' 'Terry' 'I didn't know'.
'I found out at my sister's birthday party I saw my dad'.

*'The person I thought was my dad you'll never guess*
*who showed up my uncle Richard we got into a row'.*
*'I asked why he was friends with him then he said that*
*it didn't matter because he wasn't my real dad'.*
*'That's how I found out' 'I knew a while ago' Polly*
*confessed 'Cor found out from her Aunt Matilda'.*
*'Terry's sister she saw how close you were to Katie'.*
*'She was worried you wouldn't accept her as your sister'.*
*'I would have I'm not close to my other sisters I want*
*nothing to do with them they treat me like I don't exist'.*
*'So I don't want to see them again' 'that's so sad'.*
*Stacey said 'I know but it's for the best I think that way*
*they can't hurt me anymore' 'sorry' Polly said.*
*'I'll be ok you know I never met them till I was twenty nine*
*so I'm sure I can manage without them'*
*'It's always the three of them against me so a few weeks*
*ago I had enough' 'I think you should tell Cor'.*
*'You know after all you've been friends since you were*
*teenagers' 'what about Nicky'.*
*'They were always really close' 'their estranged' 'I know'.*
*'But what if they made it up would she accept me as her*
*other sister' 'Cor's been wanting to tell you for ages'.*
*'Polly's right if your Corey's sister then your our family*
*too' Douglas said 'I'll do it later after the speeches'.*
*'Welcome to the family' Tommy said 'thanks'.*

*Victoria was touched she remembered the first time*
*she met her mother and sister it felt awkward.*
*As she'd been scared of saying the wrong thing.*
*Of not being accepted yet here was two people she didn't*
*know that well saying she was part of the family.*
*What did she have to lose by talking to Corey.*
*Their lives were similar Corey's mother who had always*
*made her feel not good enough growing up.*
*Who had put her brother and sister first just as her*
*own mother had done.*
*And had left her as a young child to live with another man.*
*Victoria thought about their lives how similar they were.*
*The waiter took their food orders as they returned with*
*their dishes Victoria had chosen pasta.*
*As she was on a vegetarian diet 'love this pasta' she said.*
*'It's amazing' Stacey agreed 'what are you gonna say to*
*Corey?' 'I don't know I'll think of something'.*
*'I'm sure she'll be happy you know' Polly said 'it would be*
*nice to have a sister I get on with' they ate their desserts.*
*Chocolate brownies with ice-cream before the speeches*
*started Kitty stood up first 'I was married before'.*
*'Years ago and it didn't work out I didn't know if I would*
*get married again but I found my life partner Mike'.*
*'And we have our son Thomas and everything's great'.*

*'I believe in true love sometimes we have to date people*
*who aren't always right for us'.*
*'So we know when we do meet the one we're really happy*
*to be surrounded by all of you our friends and family'.*
*'And we're glad the weather stayed nice and very soon*
*the disco will start eighties music of course'.*
*Everyone clapped as Mike did his speech 'I'm married'.*
*'To a woman I love who is kind caring'.*
*'We were friends for years but now we're husband*
*and wife I love her and I want to give a shout out'.*
*'To my brother Jake and my mam and my aunt Carol'.*
*'Uncle Pete and Corey your all great love you all'.*
*The speeches went on for half an hour after they went*
*to the ladies to touch up their make-up.*
*Victoria thought she looked nice in her emerald dress.*
*And her newly dyed mahogany red hair worn up as she*
*finished applying powder she spied a familiar face.*
*Her sister Katie with her friend 'Victoria what are you*
*doing here?' 'I was invited' 'how do you know them?'.*
*'Corey their her bandmates didn't mam tell you she's*
*my half-sister' 'course we've known for ages'.*
*'Oh really why dosen't that surprise me' 'it's no big deal'.*
*'I thought you would be happy to be related to Corey a*
*pop singer' 'I am' 'then what's the problem?' 'you'.*

'And everyone else keeping it a secret' 'we knew how much you loved dad we didn't want to hurt you' 'I'm forty two'.
'Your telling me you waited till now to tell me'.
'It's just the way things are' 'mam's upset you haven't called her for ages' 'well maybe it's your fault'.
'Mine how?' 'you never wanted us to have a relationship'.
'I remember the wedding when I was fifteen you said you didn't want me there' 'I didn't we were young kids'.
'Separated' 'as if! remember the Christmas when I was eight you were six when we got given tap shoes'.
'I don't remember' 'liar!' 'and you getting given an expensive car for your fortieth' 'jealous!'.
'I could get a car if I wanted' 'why don't you then!'.
'You didn't even tell me my dad was still around I haven't seen him since I was fifteen' Corey could hear rowing.
As she emerged from her cubicle washing her hands.
'So it never came up in conversation!' 'well it was fine for you seeing him all the time I never saw my mother'.
'Or my father!' 'that's not my fault! you can't blame things going wrong in your life on me or mam'.
'If she'd been around I wouldn't have been raped by him! uncle Richard' 'please don't bring that up'.
'Neither of us knew about that' 'no-one knew about that for years! except Corey I was what fourteen'.

'When I told you then later Polly for ages I could never tell mam or anyone what he did to me'.

'Because I knew I wouldn't be believed' 'that's no reason to cut mam off! or me'.

'Oh because now your playing the caring sister I heard what you said at your birthday party'.

'That I was just there to make up the numbers at your party!' it was a joke!' 'it was hurtful!'.

'And it proves you don't care! and why should you as mam's favourite who bankrolls your sunbed addiction!'.

'Your just jealous always have been why do you think mam never came back for you as a kid!'.

'Because your hard work! a stuck up bitch we were better off without you!' 'you always wanted mam to yourself'.

'Now you have her! oh and your nothing but a bitch!'.

'If mam heard how you speak to me we don't want you around!' 'yeah that's clear!'.

'Since you deleted all my photos on Facebook like I don't exist' 'why do you have to be so mean to Victoria'.

'I heard what you said in Debenhams how things would be better without Victoria in your lives'.

'You don't deserve her as a sister!' 'Corey stay out of this!'.

'You pikey bitch!' 'I'd rather hang out with a gypsy girl than you anyday screw you! and mam and Nina'.

'I want nothing to do with you!' 'good! I may be a bitch'.
'But I'm engaged who wants to marry a stuck up bitch like you!' 'why are you here anyway! free food and music'.
'Wedding crashers!' Katie left with her friends as Victoria wondered why she'd ever had anything to do with her. If she'd ever doubted her decision to cut off contact from her family now she knew she'd made the right decision.
'Are you ok?' Polly asked 'I'll be ok I won't let her get to me it's what she wants I'll have some champagne'.
They followed Victoria was angry upset she really hoped she didn't see her sister again 'I can't believe she's here'.
Victoria said 'well I'm pretty sure Kitty and Mike don't know her' Corey said trying to make her feel better.
'I can't stand her I can't believe we were close once'.
Corey had always assumed Victoria and her sister were close now she had fallen out with her family.
'Your estranged from your sisters' Corey asked 'yes'.
'And my mother I couldn't take it anymore being treated like nothing so it's better I have nothing to do with them'.
'I have Sapphire' 'and us' 'Cor's right sometimes it's better to have friends than family'.
'I don't speak to mum much after the whole Kaleigh situation or Luke but I have dad and gran aunt Sue'.
Polly said 'thanks at least I'm not the only one who has problems with her family' 'let's forget about her'.

*'She's not worth it' 'hopefully we won't see her again'.*
*Stacey said 'maybe if I know Katie she'll be throwing*
*some serious shapes on the dancefloor'.*
*'She won't be throwing any shapes if I see her'.*
*Polly joked 'come on' Victoria hoped she didn't see her*
*sister again she had visions of having a cat fight.*
*With Katie then someone filming it just her sister's trashy*
*style they danced to the music as Kitty came to see them.*
*'Hi love the dress' Victoria said 'thanks glad you could*
*all make it Cor's chatting to Colin and Dougie'.*
*'Did you hear he's not having a sex change after all'.*
*Polly said 'a joke from his mate Harry' 'Cor just told me'.*
*'Do love a bit of drag though' 'your brother was great'.*
*'He's here Danny' 'hi girls' Danny was now dressed*
*normally in T-shirt and jeans.*
*'I wouldn't have recognised you' Victoria said.*
*'I only dress in drag at night or at pride events' 'is Carol*
*around?' Polly asked 'yeah she's somewhere with John'.*
*Victoria realised she wasn't going to get a chance to chat*
*to Corey at the wedding.*
*Their conversation would have to wait 'who's that girl?'.*
*Kitty asked as they looked over Katie was grinding up and*
*down on the dancefloor 'sadly it's my sister' Victoria said.*
*'Your sister' 'yes wedding crasher and not the first time*
*class free zone whenever she's around'.*

'If there was a pole in the middle of the dancefloor
it would be even worse' 'nasty piece of work'.
Polly told Kitty 'Cor had a run in with her earlier'.
'I should have checked my guestlist' 'she still would have
found a way in I'm staying over this side of the floor'.
'You should see me in drag doing a slut drop'.
Danny joked 'I'd love to Stace is queen of the slut drop'.
Polly joked as Stacey arrived 'did I hear my name
being mentioned?' 'all good' Polly assured her.
'Cocktails are great' Stacey said clutching a blue drink.
'I'd love to try one' Victoria said 'I can get you one'.
'It's ok the bar's only over there back soon' 'is she ok?'.
'Victoria seems quiet since the row' Stacey noticed.
'As long as Katie keeps her distance we should be ok'
Polly said watching Katie dance to the music.
Victoria approached the bar as she decided what cocktail
to order 'hi what would you like?' the waitress asked.
'What do you recommend?' 'a Margarita is good'.
'I'll have one' 'what are you ordering?' Corey asked.
'You've changed' Victoria said instead of her bridesmaids
dress she was now wearing a 1920's style black top.
And skirt 'I've ordered a Margarita' 'I love cocktails'.
'You should try the Ocean Breeze as well' 'I will another
time I thought Kitty looked nice in her dress' 'me too'.
'And it was three hundred off Ebay' Corey informed her.

'Just goes to show you don't have to spend thousands on designer dresses no offence'.

'Well I doubt I'll be visiting Wedding Dreams again'.

'So your really having nothing to do with your sisters'.

'Or my mother Katie's fortieth birthday party it was a disaster I should never have gone' 'what happened?'.

I gave her a present a designer handbag she tossed it to one side as if I didn't exist'.

'And then when Nina gave her a present she was so excited they were all drunk there were loads of people'.

'I hate house parties all the noise then we sat down on the sofa mam Nina Katie chatting like I was invisible'.

'Like I wasn't there Katie showed off this car our mother had brought her then my dad turned up' 'your dad' 'yes'.

'I hadn't seen him in years since I was fifteen I thought he'd be pleased to see me he wasn't'.

'Then Katie and her friend were slagging me off in the toilets' 'that's mean'.

'Then just as I was about to leave the worst party ever uncle Richard turned up he's dad's brother'.

'He wouldn't even defend me when I asked why he'd been invited then uncle Richard he was angry at Polly'.

'For what she said his fiancée left him I was angry'.

'I called him a sexual predator everyone was looking'.

'Then just as I was about to walk out the door he told me'.

'That my dad was just my step-dad now it makes sense'.
'Why he never cared about me at least me and uncle
Richard aren't related' 'what did you mother say?'.
'She came round to see me the next day asked why
I left the party early I had a go at her'.
'About Katie being the favourite how for Christmas
when we were children she brought her a Tiny Tears'.
'I was never allowed one and white tap shoes me
black ones I know it sounds pathetic'.
'But I always wanted white ones' 'it's like dad stopping me
playing with dolls' Corey said 'you know how I feel'.
'And she promised me she'd come back for me she never
did I was only eight I didn't see her for years anyway'.
'I told her I was fed up of feeling left out at least I saw
my uncle Patrick he's British he's really nice'.
'Mam's brother I might see him' 'you should my family
always made me feel like I wasn't good enough'.
'Mam and Nicky' 'you're the only person who knows how
I feel and Katie shouldn't have called you a pikey bitch'.
'I've been called it before' 'she doesn't know you'.
'Anyway she's still around at the disco I'm trying to keep
my distance' 'she doesn't seem very nice' 'she's not'.
'Still I won't have to see her anymore pretend to be nice'.
'For the sake of our mother' 'I always thought you were
close all those photos on Facebook' 'we were for a while'.

'Until I realised that she secretly hated me screw her all
of them except uncle Patrick I don't need them anymore'.
'I'm starting my life again no more negative people'.
'Let's have a cheers' Corey suggested 'ok cheers to a
fresh start where's Douglas and Tommy?' Victoria asked.
'Over there' they looked over Douglas was chatting up
a girl 'so he's a transvestite not a trans-sexual' 'yes'.
'Is he a professional drag queen or just for fun?'.
'He does bits and pieces Dougie says he'd like to turn
professional but there's a lot of work involved'.
'The right wigs make-up he says if your not up to it
you get the piss taken out of you by bitchy queens'.
'Well if he puts his mind to it he could be successful'.
'What's his drag name?' 'Miss Angel' 'sounds cool'.
'He could always go on Drag Race UK' 'that's a great
idea' 'oh look who it is!' Katie said drunk.
'Who?' Victoria said 'my joke of a sister!' 'you're the
joke! why don't you go home you weren't even invited!'.
'You'll be crashing funerals next' Victoria said 'me and
mam are better off without you!' 'go f**k yourself!'.
'I never want to see you again!' 'that makes two of us'.
'I'm getting married soon' 'so what!' 'so you won't be
invited you won't be part of our family anymore'.
'Not that you ever were!' Corey threw her drink over Katie
she looked surprised 'pikey!' 'bitch!' Corey said angry.

*Katie looked as if she was about to swing for Corey.*
*That was all she needed 'what's going on?' Kitty asked.*
*'That bitch ruining my dress!' 'Corey is one of my*
*best friends I never invited you to my wedding'.*
*'And I want you to go!' 'you can't make me!'.*
*'I could call security or the police you've already taken up*
*half the disco with your drunken antics!' 'who are you!'.*
*'The disco police!' 'just go now! unless you want trouble!'.*
*'This wedding's rubbish anyway!' 'so rubbish that you've*
*been here for hours' 'f\*\*k all of you!' Katie said angry.*
*'So glad she's finally going can't believe she's my sister'.*
*Victoria said angry 'like you said you won't have to see*
*her anymore' Corey said 'I know it'll be great'.*
*They looked over it was Violet 'hi you two'.*
*'Have I missed anything?' 'yes bust up with my sister'.*
*'Is that the overweight blonde girl grinding and doing*
*stupid dance moves' 'unfortunately'.*
*'I love your peach outfit' 'at my age you've been to so*
*many weddings it's hard to come up with a new outfit'.*
*'Each time' 'well you look great' 'I'll have to visit your*
*clothes shop' Violet said 'please' 'I've seen some outfits'.*
*'On your Twitter page' 'it's good to find someone*
*interested in my shop' 'retail can be hard nowadays'.*
*'That's why I'm always promoting on Instagram'.*

Victoria said 'same with my jewellery' 'listen I'm gonna go now past my bedtime I know it's only ten but anyway'.
'I'll see you round' 'bye Violet' 'bye you two you both look great oh Louie's over on the dancefloor'.
'Chatting up a good looking guy bye girls' 'I love her'.
Victoria said 'she's great I feel like we've known each other a lifetime' 'I might go soon I'm tired'.
'Are you sure?' Corey asked 'yeah listen do you want to come round the apartment later this week?'.
Victoria asked 'yes' 'I have something to need to talk to you about? did Kitty throw the bouquet earlier?' 'yes'.
'I missed it' 'that's a shame' 'weddings cost money think of the money I'll save' Victoria joked.
Trying to hide the fact one day that she wanted to get married but probably never would 'who caught it?'.
'Polly' 'that's great see it's fate your getting married'.
'I guess your right she seemed happy to catch it' 'so have you decided where your getting married?' 'not yet'.
'Polly's planning it all' 'sounds fun if I didn't sell things I'd have loved to have been a wedding planner'.
'Have you picked out a wedding dress yet?' 'not yet'.
'Well let me know when you do' 'course you can be bridesmaid and Stacey' 'I'd love that'.
'I'm going now have fun say goodnight to everyone for me' Victoria said 'I will night'.

*Victoria made her way upstairs to her hotel room as she*
*changed into her bed clothes taking off her make-up.*
*She'd had a good time despite Katie being there.*
*She watched telly as she decided what she was going*
*to tell Corey she knew she was her sister.*
*And had done for a while Corey had no idea she knew.*
*Victoria felt happy she had another sister someone*
*who was nice and kind who wouldn't slag her off.*
*Put her against her own mother make her feel unwanted.*
*And unloved like she didn't matter she thought about*
*Corey's family her father was dead.*
*Victoria knew he wouldn't have been any better than*
*her own father as he had beaten his own family.*
*A violent alcoholic and Corey's brother Daniel*
*who'd emotionally and sexually abused her.*
*But she did have a nephew Douglas two nieces Corey's*
*daughters family she never knew she had.*
*Things would be ok Victoria told herself the next morning*
*she woke early before going to have a cooked breakfast.*
*In the hotel she sat down as she ordered before getting*
*some orange juice 'Victoria' 'hi' it was Carol.*
*Corey's mother 'is Corey around?' 'no she's got an early*
*morning TV appearance to do are you with anyone?'.*
*Carol asked 'no just me' 'you can't sit alone come sit with*
*us' 'ok' Victoria sat down with Carol's husband John.*

And their son 'hi Victoria great wedding wasn't it'.
John said 'really nice I loved the dress' 'Kitty and Mike
have been together for years'.
'It was great to see them finally get married' Carol said.
'She always seems really nice' Victoria said 'any plans
for you to get married?' 'John' 'I'm only asking'.
'An attractive young girl' 'I'm forty two now'.
'You don't look it' 'or Corey' Carol said 'I don't smoke'.
'And I've always moisturised' 'Carol doesn't look her age
either' 'can I ask are you both gypsies?' 'Carol is I'm not'.
'Her parents are eastern european' 'so Corey's a hundred
per cent gypsy' 'yes her dad was an Irish traveller'.
'I think it's interesting' 'what about your background?'.
'I'm half-English' 'really?' Carol asked 'my mother
she came to Ireland at nineteen her dad had a job here'.
'Then later she moved back to the UK when I was eighteen
then she returned ten years later if you know her shop'.
'Wedding Dreams' 'Corey told me all about it I'm sorry'.
'About what happened with your sisters' 'it's ok'.
'Everything happens for a reason I'll be ok 'you're a nice
girl you don't deserve things like that to happen to you'.
'Thanks' as their cooked breakfast arrived Victoria
wondered if they knew she was Corey's sister.
She would most likely have discussed it with Carol.
But she was worried to say anything just in case.

*She liked Carol and John they had become Corey's*
*parents after she met Carol age twenty three.*
*Her biological mother her other mother Marie*
*had been a nasty piece of work.*
*John had become Corey's step-father her own father*
*Terry not caring about his own daughter.*
*Only trying to get money out of her physically abusing her.*
*If Corey had ended up with another family one who loved*
*her maybe she could too.*
*Anyone was better than her own parents who'd done*
*a rubbish job inviting her uncle Richard to the house.*
*Not telling her that her father was around after assuming*
*he'd disappeared all her life was the final straw.*
*She didn't care if she never saw her mother or half-sisters*
*ever again they had never behaved like family.*
*That Thursday afternoon it was raining as she looked*
*outside she was expecting Corey at 1pm.*
*Outside she spied a rainbow coloured umbrella outside*
*it was Corey Victoria had planned what she might say.*
*But decided just to speak from the heart if things didn't*
*go ok with Corey then she may as well be an orphan.*
*Victoria opened the door 'come in' 'heavy rain'.*
*'Love the umbrella' 'thanks' 'I have your favourite drink*
*Lilt' 'I haven't had one for ages' 'good neither have I'.*
*Victoria pressed her ice machine as it filled her glass.*

*Before pouring the Lilt 'I need an ice machine'.*
*'It's the best I should have got one years ago'.*
*'Polly's always wanted a Slush Puppy machine'.*
*'I'd love to work in a bar and make cocktails'.*
*'I've starting learning' Corey said 'the cocktails*
*were great at the hotel' 'they were amazing'.*
*Corey sipped her drink 'so what did you want to talk*
*to me about?'.*
*'You know what bitches my mother and sisters are'.*
*'How I've cut off contact with them' 'yes' 'and you've*
*stopped seeing Nicky your sister do you regret it?'.*
*'Since she's the only sister you've ever known' 'no'.*
*'She hurt me the way she stuck up for Daniel in court'.*
*'Accused me of being a liar for years she treated me*
*like second best as a teenager her and mam'.*
*'And then I thought we were getting on well and I can't*
*forgive her for the way she treated me' 'then you agree'.*
*'I've done the right thing too' 'yes I hate the way your*
*family treat you we both have screwed up families'.*
*'Until they treat us with the respect we deserve'.*
*Corey suggested 'how would you feel if I said you had*
*another sister?' Victoria asked Corey looked confused.*
*For a moment 'how did you find out?' Corey asked.*
*'When my mother came round after the bust up with Katie*
*at her party I was angry'.*

'No-one had told me about dad still being around she told
me I had a half-sister that she had a fling with your dad'.
'When she was twenty that she was seeing your dad at the
same time that you had your family your dad and brother'.
'And I had mine at least for a short time and that's why
she never told me' 'she said the same thing to me'.
'When did you find out? 'not long after my dad's funeral'.
'My Aunt Matilda we had a row at the funeral she said
I had a brother and a sister my dad's kids'.
'I heard rumours she confirmed it one day I went round
to see her I didn't want to I always hated her'.
'But she was the only person who knew about everything'.
'Apparently our half-brother was a drug addict who died
age twenty eight'.
'And she said dad never had anything to do with you or
your mam'.
'She said your mother was called April Hutchings that she
married a politician that she ran a designer dress shop'.
'And I knew straight away it was you I went to see your
mam not long after at her shop'.
'She just said my dad didn't mean that much to her that
she was angry he ignored his daughter'.
'I used to see her at the primary school I went to she was
like an assistant teacher I never knew she was your mam'.

*'I wish she told us before' 'you wouldn't have wanted to*
*grow up with my dad' 'I know I felt so alone as a child'.*
*'I may as well have been an only child then as an adult*
*I find out I have two other sisters Katie'.*
*'Who doesn't care about me or want me in her life' 'I do'.*
*'I grew up with a brother and Nicky she always acted like*
*she never wanted me around she never accepted me'.*
*'My sexuality we just never got on until I was in my*
*mid-twenties she got pregnant at sixteen'.*
*'And mam said nothing yet I had to give my baby up*
*for adoption'.*
*'Nicky and mam made me feel like I was never*
*good enough' 'like my mother and Katie'.*
*'How do you feel about me being your sister?' 'good'.*
*'I thought you'd hate me being your sister' 'no I love it'.*
*'Finally a sister I get along with' 'I looked through old*
*school photos when I found out you were my sister'.*
*'Just to see if we looked alike' Corey confessed 'I did*
*the same thing I wanted to tell you at the wedding'.*
*'That I knew you were my sister it wasn't the right time'.*
*'You should have said I would have liked another sister'.*
*'Now you have one' Victoria hugged Corey it felt so good.*
*As Corey woke that morning she should have been happy.*
*It was a Friday Victoria had found out she was her sister.*

*Everything was great there was something*
*playing on her mind as it had been for weeks.*
*The fact that she was engaged to be married to Polly.*
*And they were getting married soon she'd believed it*
*was the right thing to do.*
*Everyone talked about how happy they were that they*
*were getting remarried but something didn't feel right.*
*When they'd first got back together they'd fallen deeply*
*in love again and believed this time it was forever.*
*But Corey wasn't so sure she was questioning if she still*
*loved Polly lately she felt as if they were two friends.*
*Spending time together they were still close.*
*But Corey wasn't sure she wanted to marry Polly.*
*She hadn't told anyone how she felt they would only*
*tell her that they were meant to be together.*
*But hadn't they got divorced the first time for a reason?.*
*Wouldn't they be better off as just friends she'd chosen*
*Polly over Christian when they got together.*
*Had she made the wrong decision? she knew he was*
*dating someone else now they'd both agreed to call it off.*
*A summer romance even though they'd both had strong*
*feelings for each other.*
*Corey had fallen back in love with Polly made a*
*commitment to stay together they'd chosen a venue.*
*And Polly was busy planning a summer wedding*

*choosing a wedding dress writing a guest list.*
*Things were moving too fast it was her own fault.*
*She'd proposed it had seemed a good idea the next step*
*in their relationships but now she wished she hadn't.*
*All Polly seemed to be talking about lately was the*
*wedding Corey didn't know if she still loved her.*
*Or even wanted to be with her anymore if she called off*
*the wedding everyone would hate her especially Polly.*
*Even when they'd split the first time they'd remained*
*civil to each other.*
*If they did break up she wanted them to stay friends.*
*If possible Corey decided to go see Carol she always*
*gave good advice she'd know what to do.*
*That afternoon she went to her house as she knocked on*
*the door Carol answered 'hi darling how are you?' 'ok'.*
*'Come in tea and shortbread' 'I'd love some' Corey*
*hung up her coat as she sat on the sofa.*
*'Still planning the wedding?' 'Polly's doing most of it'.*
*'I guess it must be easier having one person do*
*most of the arrangements have you chosen a dress?'.*
*'I've just been looking' 'don't wait too long June'.*
*'Your get married' 'probably' 'you don't sound too*
*enthusiastic' 'I guess I'm not'.*
*'What would you say if I said I had second thoughts'.*

*'I'll make tea and you can tell me about it' Carol brought
in the tea from an old fashioned tea pot.*
*With a small milk jug and shortbread 'I thought you were
happy' 'we are I just don't know if I love her enough'.*
*'Everyone gets second thoughts' 'no this isn't that I think
we'd be better off as friends I mean I care about her'.*
*'And when we kiss and cuddle it's great I don't think
I want to get married'.*
*'Can't you just stay as a couple then' 'Polly's a great
person but I don't think I love her anymore'.*
*'I can't tell her and if I called off this wedding she'd hate
me forever' 'no she wouldn't' 'yes she would'.*
*'She thinks we're happy together but I have these feelings'.*
*'I mean I could marry her then in like a year we could
split' 'no Corey that's a really bad idea'.*
*'If your having doubts or don't want to marry her then
don't' 'I feel like a bad person' 'your not a bad person'.*
*'You can't help your feelings and it's better to pull out
now than at the wedding' 'what if she hated me'.*
*'She probably would for a while but then after a while'.*
*'She'd realise it's for the best how long have you felt like
this?' 'since after I proposed at first I didn't know why'.*
*'Now I do I feel like part of me wanted what we had years
ago we've been close in love but the last few weeks'.*
*'It's like what we had is gone she still loves me'.*

'But I don't love her I want to it's like when we're together it's two best mates' 'you need to tell Polly the truth'.
'Else you'll make yourself and her unhappy is there anyone else you've got feelings for?' 'no'.
'What about Christian' 'he's seeing someone else' 'if he was single' 'maybe I think this is about me' 'I understand'.
'You know I'll support you whatever you decide to do'.
'Thanks' 'how's Victoria?' 'great' 'you know you need to tell her the truth' 'I have'.
'She asked me round her apartment said she had something to tell me she and her mam were rowing'.
'A few weeks ago and she told her she had a sister'.
'She found out dad was her dad' 'that's great news'.
'I know she's really happy about it says it's great to have a sister she gets on with' 'you'll have to invite her round'.
'Now she's part of the family have a meal' 'I think she'd like that' 'you arrange a date'.
'Dougie can come too everyone' Corey thought about what her mother had said she was right.
She'd have to tell Polly the truth soon else it wouldn't be fair maybe she'd be ok about it.
That afternoon Polly felt excited she had just received the delivery of her wedding dress.
Wrapped in protective plastic as she opened it carefully.
It was beautiful ivory with beading around the neckline.

*Butterflies on the dress she'd spent ages picking it out.*
*Going to various shops it had cost £1,300 she could have*
*spent more but she didn't want to spend too much money.*
*For the sake of it she liked the dress and hoped Corey*
*would too.*
*Polly had spent weeks planning the wedding wanting it*
*to be perfect she couldn't wait for their summer wedding.*
*They'd get married outside drink fruit cordial have people*
*play Irish music violins and flutes.*
*She had also booked a venue on the Irish coast by the sea.*
*Polly put her dress away she wanted it to be a surprise*
*for Corey when they got married.*
*Later that day Corey got home she'd been out to see*
*a friend 'your back'.*
*'I thought for main course at the wedding quiche we could*
*do two one for vegetarians and one for everyone else'.*
*'And new potatoes with parsley and I'm thinking mint*
*ice-cream for dessert' 'you've got it planned out'.*
*'So what do you think?' 'sounds good' Polly noticed Corey*
*didn't seem herself maybe she was having an off day.*
*'Cor is everything ok you seem really quiet'.*
*'I've got something to tell you' 'sounds serious'.*
*'I can't wait any longer I have to do it now' 'we can't*
*get married' 'why?' 'it's not the right time'.*

'What do you mean?' 'it's not' 'then I'm sure we could
rearrange the date' 'we can't' 'why not?' 'because'.
'I can't marry you' 'you don't love me' 'you're a
great person but things have been moving too fast'.
'It's ok we can just stay engaged for a while postpone the
wedding for later in the year if that's what you want'.
'No I don't want us to get married' 'why?' 'it's not you'.
'It's me I don't think we're right together we're better off
as friends' 'and you waited till now to tell me'.
'When we're getting married' 'isn't it better I tell you now'.
'Than the day of our wedding' 'how can you! do this!'.
'I've booked a venue brought a wedding dress I wondered
why you hadn't chosen a dress yet'.
'Or taken much interest in the wedding now I know why'.
'So you were planning to do this all along!' 'no Polly!'.
'I hate that I have to do this' 'then don't!' 'it's not fair'.
'On either of us' 'it's not fair on me! I love you!'.
'Why am I not good enough!' 'you are!' 'I thought it
was forever' 'so did I' 'so what's changed between us?'.
'I have I will always love and care about you'.
'Not enough to marry me!' 'I still want us to be friends'.
'Nothing has to change' 'you've just broken my heart!'.
'I never meant to I've been waiting weeks to tell you
how I feel I didn't want to hurt you!' 'you have!'.

*'Why did you even propose to me?' 'I felt it was the right thing to do' 'so I mean nothing to you!' 'course you do'. 'When we got back together it was magical it has been'. 'Then what changed?' 'the last few weeks I realised I loved you as a friend' 'that's great! just friends'. 'We were supposed to be getting married!' 'I know'. 'Why couldn't you have told me before how you felt!'. 'It was never the right time I never want to hurt you'. 'I just couldn't walk down the aisle get married knowing I didn't love you anymore the way I was supposed to'. 'Thanks! I should be grateful you didn't dump me on our wedding day!' 'Polly please!' 'no Cor'. 'I'm packing my things and going back to The Wirral'. 'It doesn't have to be like this we can still be friends'. 'With someone who just broke my heart! your as bad as Margie is there someone else then your seeing?'. 'Because I'm trying to think why you would do this to me'. 'To us what we have is special' 'I'm not seeing anyone'. 'I promise!' 'I'll start packing now!' 'you don't have to go'. 'We can talk about this!' 'there's nothing to talk about!'. 'I'm sorry' 'so am I that I ever got back with you!'. 'If I'd have known you were gonna split up with me'. 'You'll always be the love of my life' 'not anymore!'. 'I'm packing and tomorrow I'm leaving so you can enjoy your life without me!'.*

*'What can I say to make it better' 'nothing it's over!'.*
*That evening Polly had never felt so low the love of her*
*life was leaving her their wedding was off.*
*She didn't even know if she could get her money back*
*on the wedding venue the dress was beautiful.*
*Maybe she could keep it use it for a photoshoot or give*
*it to someone else how could she not have realised.*
*How Corey felt she'd been quiet lately she had assumed it*
*was just because she was busy now Polly knew why.*
*She'd been working out a way to tell her it was over.*
*Their dream wedding was off their relationship was over.*
*How would she ever get over this? she wondered if there*
*was someone else as far as she knew there wasn't.*
*That's what made it even harder her life was ruined.*
*How could she ever trust another woman again?.*
*She would stay single then no-one could ever hurt her.*
*She'd been let down in most of her relationships.*
*At least Corey had left her before they got married.*

## Finding happiness

*It didn't hurt any less the next day Polly flew home*
*to the UK as she went to her house in The Wirral.*
*After she changed her clothes took off her make-up.*
*She cried on the bed for an hour wanting the pain to go*
*away but it didn't Polly wondered if anyone else knew.*
*What Corey was planning Carol must have known.*
*Polly didn't know how she would get through life.*
*For the next few weeks she decided to make an*
*announcement on Twitter that the wedding was off.*
*She didn't say Corey had dumped her for whatever*
*reason she decided to protect Corey.*
*As she didn't want their split to affect her career*
*one day she would tell the truth about what happened.*
*It was a sunny April afternoon Polly had decided to go*
*into town a visit to Chester shopping.*
*It would take her mind off things she decided she had been*
*thinking about her split from Corey non-stop for days.*
*Wondering what it was that had made her decide*
*they would be better off as friends.*
*Polly had been the perfect girlfriend always making*
*the best of herself supporting Corey through her trial.*
*With Daniel keeping a tidy house it hadn't been enough.*
*She tried to work out why things had ended.*

*She'd been so happy finally she thought her life was*
*sorted in a happy relationship.*
*Only to find Corey had no intention of marrying her.*
*Polly kept wondering if there was someone else that*
*she didn't know about Carol would know.*
*Polly knew it still wouldn't make Corey come back to her.*
*She felt she could never trust another woman again.*
*Was she better off staying single? maybe Corey had done*
*her a favour as she was three times divorced.*
*She couldn't face another one again Polly looked around*
*the shops alone all she wanted was to feel ok again.*
*Shopping was one of her biggest vices it gave her a buzz.*
*Made her feel like everything was ok again she went into*
*HMV as she browsed the cd's 'Polly' she looked up.*
*At a dark haired woman she was young in her twenties.*
*Polly guessed 'I'm Demi Luke's ex-girlfriend' 'hi' now*
*she was curious at meeting the mother of her grandson.*
*Then she had a thought what if he had asked her to*
*track her down to get money from her or the house.*
*He was after as a celebrity you had to be on your guard.*
*Especially with her son they were estranged for a reason.*
*Polly knew she couldn't trust him anymore all he cared*
*about was drugs and getting money from her.*
*Making out he'd had a hard life when nothing could be*
*further from the truth he'd had everything he ever wanted.*

*More opportunities than many other people if Luke*
*wanted to portray her as a bad mother.*
*There was nothing she could do about it 'are you still*
*together with Luke?' 'no we split ages ago'.*
*'I didn't even tell him I was pregnant' 'how come?'.*
*'I realised after a while we weren't right together'.*
*'And I found out he was a heavy drug user I did drugs*
*years ago but I've been clean for a while'.*
*'And I didn't want to go back there after I had the baby'.*
*'I told him he asked to get back together I said no'.*
*'Good on you' 'really your not angry at me' 'no'.*
*'I'm estranged from him for good reason'.*
*'Your better off keeping the baby away not completely'.*
*'But put it this way I wouldn't trust Luke to look after*
*anything except himself' 'thanks for telling me'.*
*'I'm a fan of yours' 'thanks' 'I have a photo of the baby'.*
*Demi took out her phone 'this is Marley'.*
*'He's seven months' Polly looked at the photo*
*of her grandson 'he's gorgeous' 'I know he's great'.*
*'The best thing that ever happened to me a least I got*
*something good out of the relationship' 'anyway'.*
*'Anytime you wanna visit' 'really that would be great'.*
*'I'll give you my number' Polly got out her phone as she*
*saved Demi's number 'where is he today?' 'with my mum'.*
*'She's the best anyway it was great meeting you' 'and you'.*

Polly said as Demi walked away she felt happy she never thought she'd get to meet her grandson she liked Demi. She was different from Luke's usual type of bimbo girlfriend Polly wondered if her mum saw Marley. That afternoon she felt happy having seen a photo of the baby and couldn't wait to meet him.

When Polly arrived home at 5pm she listened to her voicemail she had a message from her dad. Reminding her Emily's birthday dinner was next week. How could she forget like her mother's birthday she had no desire to attend but felt she had to. Her relationship with her sister was non-existent. And had been for many years if she even spent five minutes in her sister's company it would end in a row. Polly wasn't looking forward to seeing Wendy. Their relationship was non-existent she thought everything Emily did was great.

And everything she did was wrong instead of admitting that Emily wasn't a nice person. At least her dad could see through her which Wendy hated. She tried to see her dad away from Wendy's house in Essex which wasn't hard as they had been separated. For several years and he spent a lot of time up north. With her mum that way she could avoid a row with Emily. The following Friday night it was her birthday dinner.

*Polly had no choice but to attend at least Stacey would*
*be with her.*
*She never knew if her sister would say something nasty.*
*As she was unpredictable they were going to the Toby Inn.*
*Emily was bringing her two best friends along how she*
*had any friends was a miracle as she was so vile.*
*Polly thought hopefully she wouldn't stay long.*
*It couldn't be any worse than her mum's birthday dinner.*
*She'd brought Emily a perfume gift set reduced from*
*£30 to £10 in Debenhams it would do the trick.*
*If she had a choice she wouldn't have got her anything.*
*But it wouldn't have gone down well with Wendy Polly*
*chose a black blazer silver top silver heart earrings.*
*As she wanted to look smart but not over the top*
*after all she didn't really want to be there.*
*She was staying at Stacey's London house which she used*
*for work commitments they arrived by a black taxi.*
*As they entered the restaurant entrance Wendy saw them.*
*'Hi you two' she said 'hi' Stacey said faking a smile*
*she felt exactly as she did about Emily 'come in'.*
*'Can I get you a drink?' Wendy asked she seemed in*
*a good mood 'just a coke' Stacey said.*
*She rarely drank alcohol 'I'll have a vodka and tonic'.*
*Polly said 'tables over there' Wendy said as they saw*
*Emily chatting with her friends Wendy ordered the drinks.*

'Have presents been opened?' Stacey asked 'some'.
'I got Emily the most gorgeous Phase Eight dress
she's wanted it for ages and one from Quiz'.
'And your dad got her a necklace' 'where is he?'.
Polly asked 'over there I'm surprised your mum's not
here'.
'From what I hear their relationship's on and off'.
'Oh right' 'what about you seeing anyone?' Polly asked.
'Not at the moment I'm single you won't mind if I make
a move on your dad we've been talking again' 'no'.
'I'm not speaking to mum much these days we're
estranged' 'I'm sorry' 'it's for the best'.
'You both look great see you in a minute' Wendy rejoined
their table 'she seems happier than usual' Polly said.
Sipping her drink 'I know' 'I never thought she and
your dad would get back together' 'me either'.
'But he and mum are always on and off maybe
it's for the best' 'I guess'.
'I think Sarah and your dad make a good couple shame
it couldn't work' 'if he wants to get back with Wendy'.
'It's up to him but I don't want a relationship with her
too much water under the bridge' 'same here'.
'She's my aunt but she can be a bitch I think I prefer aunt
Shirley these days you must meet her' Stacey said.

'I'd love to' 'Wendy would hate it if she knew I was in contact with her' 'best not say anything' 'not a word'.
'Let's go over' Polly said 'hi' 'hi' Emily said giving Polly a dirty look 'I've got your present' 'thanks' she opened it. As everyone watched 'perfume set just what I've always wanted' Emily said sarcastically Wendy gave Polly a look. 'I'm sure I'll find a use for it look what Rihanna gave me'. 'Nintendo Switch' Emily said happy she clearly hated her present but somehow Polly didn't care 'let's order dinner'. 'What about starters?' Stacey asked 'we already had them but if you want to order one' Wendy said 'it's fine'.
Stacey picked up a menu she ordered a vegetable lasagne. Polly ordered beer battered fish & chips they watched as the others chatted 'I thought they said get here for seven'. 'How can they have ordered already' 'I know Stace'. 'Looks like we're not being made to feel welcome'. 'Hi Susie' her dad said 'enjoying the evening' 'trying to make sure it doesn't descend into world war three'. 'Me and Emily' 'your doing a good job so far' 'I didn't know you and Wendy were getting back together'. 'We're not' 'she wants to make a move on you she said'. 'Well I'm not interested we were together twenty years'. 'I did love her but the last five years weren't great'. 'Then you should tell her' 'I will I can't believe you and Corey have split' 'I know I'll get over it somehow'.

'Dad come sit with me' 'you better go Emily's calling you'.
'Speak later' Polly watched as her dad sat down.
'She's so childish for her age' Stacey said 'I know'.
'Thirty more like a sixteen year old I do think she's jealous of my close relationship with dad'.
'Always vying for his attention' 'let her carry on'.
'She can't come between you' 'I know' their dinner arrived Polly noticed her dad looked distracted.
Wendy seemed happy chatting with Emily Polly decided to order some more drinks 'dad want another' 'I'm fine'.
'Can't you see he's already got one' Emily said Polly wanted to say something back but didn't.
As she tried to stay calm she went to the bar 'pink gin'.
'Coming up' Wendy approached her 'hi why did you get Emily such as a cheap perfume set' 'it wasn't cheap'.
'It was thirty pounds' 'you're a multi-millionaire you could get her something better' 'I could'.
'If she was a bit nicer to me!' 'if you made more of an effort you could be closer' 'I don't want to be closer'.
'This is close enough' 'why did you come?' 'because'.
'It's her thirtieth birthday and to please dad'.
'Oh and he's told me he's not interested in dating you'.
'And no I don't know if he's seeing anyone' Polly returned to the table with Stacey.
Somehow she didn't think she'd be staying much longer.

'Thanks Susie' 'I had a row with Wendy' 'how come?'.
'She hates my present thinks I should have spent more
a lot more I said dad wasn't interested in dating her'.
'Wendy's not happy I won't be staying much longer'.
'Don't worry she probably hates my present too and why
should we spend anymore than the bitch deserves'.
'Agreed' Polly sipped her pink gin trying to avoid Wendy's
gaze at that moment the lights dimmed.
As a waiter brought the cake it was blue with lots of
candles Emily blew them out they began to sing.
Happy Birthday Polly sang happy birthday you slag
Stacey smiled no more than Emily deserved.
Somehow Stacey knew a big row was about to happen.
They clapped as Polly sat down 'don't order dessert'.
Stacey said Polly looked at Wendy she didn't look happy.
As she came over to where they were sitting 'if you've got
something to say then say it Polly!'.
'I heard what you said!' 'no more than the truth!'.
'You want the truth why did you even come tonight'.
'Tell me that!' 'I told you why' 'you're a disgrace!'.
'Coming here to insult your own sister!'.
'What's going on?' Simon asked 'tell your dad what you
said' 'I'm not a child!' 'then don't behave like one!'.
'I called her a slag!' 'she sang happy birthday you slag'.

'She is a slag and a bitch!' Stacey said sticking up for Polly.

'Why did either of you come to make trouble' 'Wendy'.

'Why don't you realise what she is your perfect daughter'.

'Emily is a homophobic racist evil bitch!' Stacey said,

'We know what you are go on tell everyone what you did with my husband!' 'ok I slept with Simon'.

'It was a one off mistake we all make mistakes'.

'Like aunt Shirley going off with Adrian you casting her out from the family'.

'Maybe if you weren't such a bitch your husbands wouldn't cheat on you!' 'come on let's calm down'.

Simon said 'you both should know better especially you!'.

'Polly that awful present you brought!' 'Wendy said angry.

'Then give it to charity! if you don't like it' 'you were a nice person once' 'no Wendy I am a nice person!'.

'You were once you were my surrogate mum growing up'.

'Who I loved more than anything when my own mum wasn't around same with Stacey'.

'Now your nothing but a bitch! sticking up for her!'.

'Emily's my daughter!' 'she's a nasty piece of work!'.

'Who makes my son look like an angel! can't you see what she's like me and Stace want nothing to do with her'.

'It Should tell you something!' 'let me say something'.

'Mum is a great person your just jealous!'.

'Of our close relationship and Stacey you couldn't even look after your own kids so your ex-husband had to do it!'.
'Emily' Simon said angry 'it's the truth and Polly Corey dosen't want to marry you anymore does she!'.
'What has that got to do with you nothing!' 'you do know dad's probably not even your own father'.
Polly looked confused for a moment 'your lying!'.
'It's the truth! I overheard a conversation a few weeks ago yeah that's right your mum went with another man'.
Polly threw a drink at Emily as it soaked her dress.
'You walk out of here your not welcome in this family!'.
Wendy said angry at Polly 'good I hate this family!'.
'Stace and Kaleigh are my family I don't need anyone else!' Stacey followed Polly as they walked out 'Susie'.
'I want to go to your house' 'I'll phone a taxi' they stood in the entrance of the restaurant as they waited.
Polly knew it was a mistake coming out 'I can't believe she said that we should never have come' 'we had no choice'.
'I'm sorry I slept with your dad it was years ago I should never have done it' 'it's ok we all make mistakes'.
'He was married it was wrong it was a one off' 'I won't ever have anything to do with Wendy or Emily again'.
'Me either' it had begun to rain 'Susie don't go not like this!' it was her dad 'I have to'.
'So how long have you known you might not be my dad?'

*'I only just found out' 'yeah right! please tell me the truth'.*
*'I bet you were all gossiping about me behind my back!'.*
*'No Susie it's the truth!' 'what other secrets haven't you*
*told me about you and mum' 'nothing else'.*
*'I would have expected it from mum not telling me*
*but never from you' 'Susie I promise!'.*
*'I only found out a few weeks ago I was as shocked as*
*you it doesn't matter I'm your dad' 'of course it matters!'.*
*'That you might not be my real dad' 'why I love you'.*
*'And so does your mum' 'if she loved me she would have*
*told me the truth years ago!' 'she didn't want to hurt you'.*
*'Or me that's why she kept it a secret from both of us'.*
*'I suppose Christian might not be my brother' 'we can get*
*a DNA test' 'what if I don't want to' 'you don't have to'.*
*'We can just carry on as normal' 'you should have told me*
*as soon as you found out!' 'I'm sorry!' 'taxi's here'.*
*'Enjoy the rest of Emily's birthday!' 'well I won't without*
*you here' as the taxi arrived Polly felt sad.*
*As she tried to take in the fact that her dad might not be*
*her dad they got in.*
*As she tried to forget how awful her night had been.*
*'Susie maybe you were a bit harsh on your dad it wasn't*
*his fault that he didn't know' 'he still should have told me'.*
*'Straight away as soon as he found out' 'maybe'.*

'He's probably getting over being told you might not be his real daughter' 'Emily will love this won't she'.
'Like your dad said you don't have to get a DNA test'.
'I'm not dad is the only dad I've ever known I'm not having her win Emily' 'I hate her so much'.
'At least that's one good thing she might not be your real sister' Polly smiled they arrived home.
'I wish I'd never gone out' Polly said 'me too'.
'Let's get changed we can watch some music documentaries on BBC four chill out forget about tonight'.
Polly knew however hard she tried she couldn't forget the life changing news she'd received.
She didn't know who she should be angry at.
Her mum for keeping it a secret for her whole life.
Her dad for not telling her straight away or Emily for telling her in front of her family.
There was only one person who could tell her what she needed to know her mum.
Even though they were estranged she needed to talk to her.
Find out why she'd never told her that her dad might not be her real father Polly needed answers.
And her mum was the only one who could give her the information she needed to know the truth.
It had been months since she'd seen her last October.
She had vowed she would never speak to her again.

After her mum had tried to stop her telling Kaleigh
the truth that she was her real mother.
Did she really want to have a relationship with her
mother? after everything that had happened in he life.
That evening she texted her mum saying they needed to
talk they arranged to meet at her house in Liverpool.
The next day Polly hoped she'd get some answers.
She really didn't want anymore rows she rang the doorbell
as she waited her mum opened the door 'Susie you came'.
'Course' 'I'm sorry about everything I was out of order'.
'Yeah you were' 'the whole Kaleigh thing'.
'Why did you lie to me? you said Kaleigh wouldn't want
anything to do with me she sent me a Mother's Day card'.
'If she hated me she wouldn't have done that'.
'I was jealous' 'so you finally admit it then' 'I wanted her'.
'For myself I was worried she wouldn't love me anymore'.
'That I wouldn't be her mum if it's any constellation
she hates me now you got what you wanted'.
'All I wanted was to tell her the truth for us all to be a
family like we used to instead of all the lies and threats'.
'That if I told her who I was I'd ruin her life I understood
when she was younger'.
'She's old enough to know who she is who I am all of us
the truth' 'I want us to be a family all of us me you'.
'Kaleigh Luke' Sarah said 'mum I'm not interested'.

'I want nothing to do with Luke if that makes me
a bad person then so be it'.
'Just when I thought all the secrets and lies are over'.
'I find out dad might not be my real dad' 'he told me what
happened what Emily said she had no right to tell you'.
'If she hadn't overheard what you said' 'I had no idea
anyone was listening to our conversation' 'well she was'.
'Her of all people why did you never tell me?' 'drink 7up'.
Polly sat down on the sofa her mum poured her a drink.
'I was trying to protect you and your dad I know how
close you've always been to your dad'.
'Whatever you think of me everything I've ever done
has been for this family for all of us'.
'Like not telling me about my grandson' 'that's different'.
'I don't want you getting hurt I've read stories of things
that went wrong people who met their real parents'.
'And they weren't accepted by them the person who
might be your dad might accept you with open arms'.
'Or he might reject you he has a family I'd hate for things
to go wrong' 'who is the other man you slept with?'.
'He was a mate we were teenagers we used to hang out
at a youth club in Liverpool we were the same age'.
'We were more mates than anything else I was seeing
your dad you know we were teenage sweethearts'.
'One time we had a row I was upset'.

'So a few days later I slept with him even though
he was good looking I regretted it afterwards'.
'Because I loved your dad' 'what happened?' 'me and
your dad made it up we tried sex me and my friend'.
'It was in a room on a pool table' 'very romantic'.
'A while after I found out I was pregnant I didn't know
who's baby it was and I wanted it to be your dad's'.
'It would have been easier because...' 'because what?'.
'We were a couple and he was black' 'what?' 'mixed-race'.
'He was black but light skinned' 'my father was could be
mixed-race' 'it was back in the early eighties'.
'Things were different then no-one cares now but
back then it was a bigger deal to go with someone black'.
'Your gran might not have approved I had this neighbour
she was a few years older she had a baby'.
'With a mixed-race guy and it looked white'.
'She told me she lied to her mum about who the father
was so I thought I'd do the same'.
'I thought I'd wait and see what you looked like'.
'And I waited a few months and you looked white had
red hair so I never told anyone'.
'About the possibility your dad might be black'.
'We were mates imagine telling a fifteen your old lad
he's gonna be a father' 'dad took it well'.

'Your dad was a one off the other lad I didn't know
so well he came round the house once'.
'The rest of the time we just hung out together'.
'At the youth club I never told him he might be the father'.
'I just told everyone it was your dad's your dad was
always interested in you even after you were born'.
'Most lad's wouldn't be I saw no reason to rock the boat'.
'When there was a fifty per cent chance he could be
your dad' 'but you weren't straight either'.
'He always loved you he was a good dad the years
went by everything was fine as it was'.
'I thought about telling the truth but I read the other lad
he had a son and he was married you were in care'.
'I thought it was better to leave things as they were
especially if he turned out not to be your father'.
'And your dad loved you so much' 'why didn't you tell me
years ago' 'I couldn't even your gran doesn't know'.
'The longer things went on the harder it was to tell
the truth so I never did' 'who do you think my dad is?'.
'When I was younger I was convinced it was your dad'.
'Now I'm not so sure no-one on my side of the family has
curly hair and maybe you have his facial expressions'.
'But I'm not sure' 'what does he do for a living?'.
'He's done a few different things in his career'.
'Presented TV shows he's a successful DJ'.

'How successful?' 'a household name I'm not telling you
who he is I don't want you getting hurt' 'he's got a family'.
'Maybe your right' 'listen your dad loves you nothing
has to change he will always love you' 'I know'.
'What made you tell dad the truth?' 'I couldn't live with it
anymore and I felt it was the right time you know'.
'That enough years had passed' 'you should have been
more understanding what it was like for me'.
'With Kaleigh' 'I was' 'no you weren't' 'some things are
better off kept secret what if I had told the other man'.
'Years later when he was married with a child what good
would that have done he remarried a second time'.
'With a daughter I read an interview with him if I'd have
turned up or messaged him what would he have thought'.
'He might not have been interested maybe he would'.
'But I wasn't prepared to find out' 'so I have two
half-siblings who I'll never meet'.
'Because I'm the product of a fling! a love child'.
'Unwanted by my real dad!' 'we don't know that'.
'But it's better things stay as they are just forget about
what Emily said' 'how can I' 'why not Susie'.
'Your dad will always be your dad no-one will ever take
his place' 'I know that I wish I never found out the truth'.
'Well so do I if I see Emily I'll have some things
to say to her' 'I said everything I needed to say'.

'I even poured a drink over her there's no good you
saying anything I had a row with Wendy and Stacey'.
'I wouldn't be surprised if someone heard our
conversation and it gets in the papers'.
'Your not the first person to find out your dad might not
be your dad I hope he is we could get a DNA test'.
'I don't want to' 'you don't wanna know the truth'.
'Maybe in future not right now' 'if you change your mind'.
'I just need to think about things' 'I understand'.
'Why couldn't you have told me when I was a child'.
'What difference would it have made your life wouldn't
have been any different Simon loves you'.
'And he's as angry at me as you ever more so'.
'Somewhere out there I have a biological father
who probably doesn't want to know me'.
'Let's forget about everything try and carry on'.
A week later Polly decided to get a DNA test she couldn't
stop thinking about everything that had happened.
Whether her dad was her biological father she knew it
didn't matter that he would always love her.
But she needed to know the truth Stacey had also decided
to get one done she never knew.
If her dad or Andy was her dad it wasn't such as big deal
for Stacey as she had known.

*For several years her mum had dated both men.*
*At the same time and they were twin brothers.*
*For Polly it was if the results came back that Simon*
*wasn't her dad she knew she would be devastated.*
*And Christian wouldn't be her real brother anymore.*
*That lunchtime Polly looked at the date block in her*
*kitchen it was May 15th late Springtime.*
*Outside it looked as though it might rain she was about*
*to find out if her dad was her biological father.*
*Stacey was coming over so they could open their DNA*
*results together.*
*Polly hoped her dad was her real father but she knew*
*there was a chance he might not be.*
*She had never suspected anything throughout her life.*
*He had naturally strawberry blonde hair that he dyed*
*blonde she had red hair they were both fair haired.*
*Both loved the cinema the theatre & reading.*
*Her mum had dark hair for that reason everyone said she*
*looked more like her dad Stacey knocked on the door.*
*As she opened 'hi I've got my results I haven't opened*
*them yet' Stacey said 'me neither'.*
*'I just keep looking at the envelope' Polly confessed.*
*'Drink of juice' 'good idea' Polly poured them*
*orange juice with bits that they both loved to drink.*
*Stacey hung up her coat they sat on the sofa.*

'Shall we do it?' Polly said worrying what the results
might be 'I'll go first' Stacey offered.
'Dad was always my dad growing up and Andy's
always been my uncle and also a father figure'.
'So whatever happens' Stacey opened the envelope.
As she read the letter carefully 'it says dad is 99,9
per cent not my father Andy is I'm ok with that'.
'I've always felt like I have two dads I'm happy'.
'At least I know the truth' 'ok I'll go next' Polly
looked at the envelope she didn't want to open it.
As she knew the results would change her life.
'I can't do it' Polly felt her voice quivering 'it's ok Susie'.
'You don't have to' 'but I won't know the truth I want to'.
'But I can't open the letter' 'don't worry listen why don't
you keep the letter somewhere safe until your ready'.
'Stace what if I'm not' 'you will be one day even if it's
in a few weeks or months' 'it's not just dad'.
'Christian won't be my half-brother anymore and he's
one of my best friends he's always been there for me'.
'He still is your brother even if your not biologically
related he's still your step-brother' 'I know'.
'I wish mum had told me years ago'.
'Ever since I found out I've found it hard to deal with'.
'Splitting with Cor now this' 'you know I'm here for you'.

*'What do you think? I mean no-one else in my family*
*has curly hair my mum dad gran my aunt's'.*
*'My Welsh granddad I've been thinking about that'.*
*'It would be rare for someone who had a mixed-race*
*parent not to have curly hair but not impossible'.*
*'If you took from your mum's genes' 'I don't know'.*
*'It doesn't matter your dad will always be your dad'.*
*'Christian will always be your brother' 'thanks Stace'.*
*'I know your right' 'course I am Susie'.*
*A few days later Stacey returned to Essex to see her*
*mum & sister she couldn't stop thinking about Polly.*
*And she hoped she'd be ok about everything.*
*She and Kim decided to take a walk at the local park.*
*It was a lovely day 'so how's Polly?' Kim asked.*
*'I don't know I think she's really upset about everything'.*
*'Finding out her dad isn't her real dad she hasn't been*
*herself' 't least her dad loves her'.*
*'Even if their not biologically related my dad and even*
*Richie don't want anything to do with me'.*
*'Their not worth it' 'it still hurts being rejected'.*
*'It's their loss maybe Richie wanted to talk to you'.*
*'But because he was with his daughter & granddaughter*
*he couldn't we were on an interval'.*
*'With the ice-skating show' 'I guess but why couldn't he*
*have asked for my number or social media' 'oh my god!'.*

*'Now's your chance' they looked over at a man in a
grey coat with his teenage daughter 'it's him isn't it?'.
Stacey asked 'yes' he looked over at them 'hi Kim' 'hi'.
'You look nice like the coat' Kim was wearing a
silver jacket 'you too' she smiled.
'Well nice seeing you again' 'I'm on social media'.
'I don't think that would be appropriate' Richie replied.
As he walked away Stacey felt sorry for Kim.
'Who was that dad?' his daughter asked 'no-one'.
'Just someone I used to know' 'bastard!' Stacey said.
'It's ok' Kim replied 'no it's not!' Stacey walked up to
Richie 'how can you behave like that' 'like what?'.
'You were Kim's step-dad from the age of eleven
till she was seventeen' 'it was a long time ago'.
'We've all moved on' 'moved on how can you reject your
own daughter!' 'she's not my daughter never was'.
'Your scum!' 'he's not worth it Stace!' 'look I was with
your mum for a few years yes I cared about you Kim'.
'But I have my own family now grandchildren' 'you were
the only father I knew my own dad didn't want me!'.
'That's not my fault' 'f**k you for years I idolised you'.
'I loved you I wish I didn't' 'Kim I think you need
counselling me and your mum split up years ago'.
'I know that I thought you might actually have feelings'.
'Or be interested in my life' 'I am' 'no your not!'.*

'It's best I go' Richie said as he walked away Kim
watched as the man she'd loved as a child rejected her.
As had her own father Kim sat down on a park bench.
She cried 'he's not worth it' Stacey said as she comforted
her sister what could she say to make things better.
'I know I'm in my forties now and I shouldn't care'.
'But I do I always wanted a dad I never had one he was
the only dad I knew growing up and he doesn't want me'.
'You don't need him a real man wouldn't behave like that'.
'He doesn't love me how can he bring up a child then
reject them' 'I'm sure mum wouldn't be happy'.
'If she heard how he behaved' it had begun to rain.
'Let's go home forget about him if he wants to behave like
that it's his loss' Stacey handed Kim a packet of tissues.
As they walked home Stacey also decided she should tell
their mum what had happened.
And ask why she and Richie had split then Kim could
move on with her life.
Forget about a man who never loved her and never would.
Stacey had always known her sister was affected by not
having a dad growing up but she never knew how much.
Until now they returned home that late afternoon.
'How was your walk?' Marcee asked 'fine great'.
'To have some fresh air' Stacey said trying to put a
positive spin on things 'I'm going upstairs for a bit'.

'Is everything ok?' Marcee asked Stacey as they watched Kim go upstairs 'no Kim's upset we saw Richie' 'who?'.
'Your ex we saw him at Christmas at the winter wonderland at Hyde Park we didn't wanna say'.
'Because we didn't know why you split' 'he was there'.
'I never saw him' 'we both did when we went to get hot chocolate before that Kim saw him shopping in Harrods'.
'With his daughter before Christmas but she didn't speak to him then she did at the ice-skating'.
'Why didn't she say?' 'we didn't want to upset you in case you split on bad terms anyway Kim was upset'.
'That he wasn't interested he didn't even ask for her social media she idolised him as a child she said'.
'I mean he was her step-father from eleven till seventeen'.
'Anyway we saw him in the park today we went to say hello anyway he said he'd moved on'.
'That she was never his daughter that he has his own family'.
'He told his daughter Kim was just someone he used to know I had a go at him I know maybe I shouldn't'.
'Kim was upset for years she dreamed of seeing him again and when she did he rejected her' 'I left him for a reason'.
'Why?' 'he was controlling who I saw when I went out'.
'But because I loved him I wanted to please him everyone said how lucky I was to be dating him'.

'Because he was good looking a lawyer but he tore me down in the end'.

'I spent the whole time never feeling good enough'.

'Twice he hit me he liked to drink he got aggressive'.

'One day I had enough so I left him we rarely rowed'.

'Because I never answered back when he made me unhappy I never told Kim what he was like'.

'I guess this whole things my fault but I never thought she'd see him again or try to track him down.

'I would have given him a piece of my mind'.

## Family matters

'Don't worry I did maybe we should leave her for a while'.
'Andy will be back soon we can have tea later'.
Somehow Stacey felt better about things.
Now she knew Richie wasn't the perfect dad Kim had
dreamed about all her life Andy soon returned home.
As Stacey and Marcee told him everything he decided
he would talk to Kim as he went to see her 'hi' he said.
As Kim sat on a wooden storage box in the corridor.
'Mints Harrod's' he offered 'thanks' 'is everything ok?'.
'No but I'll be alright' 'your mum and Stacey told me'.
'What happened' 'I hate him and my real dad'.
'Richie's not worth it' 'maybe I'm not worth it' 'Kim the
man is scum he was very controlling towards your mum'.
'From what I've heard he even hit her twice not a
nice man' 'I had no idea I always thought he was perfect'.
'I always thought even when my real dad rejected me
that I could always go looking for him one day'.
'And when I found him he wasn't interested he was my
step-dad for six years eleven to seventeen'.
'Like the most important years in a child's life'.
'I loved him how could I have wasted so many years
caring about someone who didn't care about me'.
'We've all done it pined for a lost love or old friend'.

'Sometimes it works out other times it doesn't and
you wish you never bothered searching'.
'I once tracked down an old friend from school'.
'I was excited at meeting him then when I did'.
'I realised we had nothing in common but then after
I saw another guy from school we never chatted much'.
'Then that night it was like I'd known him forever'.
'So we stayed in touch but not the other person'.
'Your not to blame what man would reject his own
daughter' 'but I wasn't his biological daughter'.
'So he helped bring you up as his own you were a family'.
'I always wanted a dad so much' 'if it's any consolation'.
'My dad was a bastard he beat us sexually abused Paul
and Wendy I never loved him I never think about him'.
'I always wanted another dad' 'I think I'll stop looking'.
Kim said sadly 'well you've got your mum and me'.
'I know and you're the best step-dad ever' 'thanks'.
'Let's have dinner' they went downstairs Kim realised
Andy was right that she should let go of the past.
That she had a great family a mum and step-dad.
Victoria looked at her phone she decided to go on
Facebook she hated herself for doing it.
As she looked at Katie's account she had posted photos.
She'd been on holiday for a week in Spain with her fiancée
who looked younger he had blonde hair matching tans.

*Not that you could tell as Katie always made her skin look darker with fake tan & bronzer.*

*In contrast Nina looked more natural with dark brown hair and light olive skin.*

*Katie had posted photos of possible wedding dresses.*

*Victoria wondered if she'd be able to use her mother's wedding shop since she only stocked up to a sixteen.*

*Katie made out she was a size sixteen when in reality she was more of an eighteen to twenty.*

*Victoria couldn't stand her with her photos of nights out drunk with a bottle of champagne in her hand.*

*Any little event had to be uploaded to Facebook prior to their estrangement she had noticed posts.*

*Only to be shared with other people Victoria wondered what these posts were or even if they were about her.*

*She reminded herself she was better off without her sisters and mother but it didn't hurt any less.*

*Not being part of her mother's life anymore.*

*Not that she had ever felt like she was maybe for a short time she had Corey now and her daughter.*

*That afternoon she ate her favourite pizza.*

*As she sipped Cherry Coke with ice she heard the buzzer go for her apartment she had to get herself a cosy house.*

*Somewhere she decided on the coast of Ireland Corey had mentioned the same thing.*

*Maybe they could even live together now she had split*
*from Polly Victoria checked her appearance in the mirror.*
*As she went to answer the door she opened it was Nina.*
*She was surprised she assumed she wouldn't hear from*
*her family again 'hi' Nina said 'come in' Victoria said.*
*She was curious as to why she'd come to visit Nina would*
*have a go at her for not replying to any of her texts.*
*'Drink' Victoria asked 'please' she poured Nina a drink.*
*'I never realised how nice your apartment is' Nina said.*
*As she looked around 'I'm thinking of selling it' 'why?'.*
*'Because I'm fed up with the city I'm thinking of moving'.*
*'To the seaside' Victoria noticed Nina seemed quieter*
*than usual 'I'm surprised you came to see me'.*
*'I wanted to but I also have some news'.*
*'What kind of news?' 'your dad died the other day'.*
*'Not only that but uncle Richard' 'how?' 'dad was a*
*heart attack Richard he fell out a boat hit his head'.*
*Victoria couldn't believe it finally he'd gotten what*
*he deserved for all his years of pain 'I'm not sad'.*
*'About uncle Richard he abused me for years and dad*
*I hadn't seen him since I was fifteen until Katie's party'.*
*'And even then he didn't care about me but I'm sorry*
*for you and Katie since he was your father'.*
*'He was never my father' 'he was your step-dad'.*
*'I always hated him I tolerated him because of Katie'.*

'I never knew that' 'you do now' 'is Katie upset?' 'yes'.
'I just try and say the right things' 'when's the funeral?'.
'They don't know yet their organising it right now'.
'What about uncle Richard is anyone upset about him?'.
'Because I'm not' 'I missed you how come you never
replied to my texts?'.
'Because I don't want to see our mother or Katie
or anyone I cut myself off from everyone'.
'Because I was sick of being left out being treated
second best' 'Victoria your not ok'.
'And because I thought you wouldn't want anything to do
with me' 'I do why would you think that?' 'because'.
'It's how things are you Katie and mam me on the outside'.
'I know I didn't grow up with her you and Katie but for
once I didn't want to be not included'.
'Is that how you feel?' 'yes I thought you Katie and our
mother could spend the rest of your lives together'.
'Happy without me because I wasn't needed anymore'.
'I didn't feel part of anything like the black sheep of the
family the one who isn't married'.
'The one with the mixed-race daughter' 'but your not the
black sheep' 'I am you and her Katie with your in jokes'.
'Talking about men all the time nights out together on
Facebook see you don't need me anymore'.
'Just let me know when the funeral is for dad and I'll go'.

*'Don't be like this!' 'I have to because it's better than being hurt by people my own family'.*

*'I have to protect myself' 'from us' 'from being made to feel worthless!' 'please don't say that'.*

*'Do you know how hurtful it was when Katie said she'd invited me to her birthday to make up the numbers'.*

*'When she wasn't interested in my present or when I saw my dad for the first time since I was a teenager'.*

*'And he didn't even ask about Sapphire or when uncle Richard turned up at the party'.*

*'Now I believe our mother when she said she didn't know he was coming but Katie she knew I was abused by him'.*

*'And she doesn't care none of you do that for years all I wanted to do was forget him and yet I can't'.*

*'Because he's there at her party and then he tells me my dad was never my real dad'.*

*'Which no-one else bothered to tell me and now I'll be expected to go to uncle Richard's funeral'.*

*'Because if I don't it'll look bad so that's how things are'.*

*'Oh and do you know what it's like to feel second best'.*

*'Because I can never compete with special Katie the golden child that our mother adores I hate her'.*

*'And that's the truth not just because she's the favourite'.*

*'But because she's a nasty piece of work she called Corey a pikey bitch I hate everything about her'.*

'From her fake tan to her bitchy comments so guess what
I never want to see her again!'.
'Or have anything to do with her Katie said to her friends
that things were better before I came into your lives'.
'She probably didn't mean it you know what she's like'.
'Saying things' 'yeah I do she said she knew about
Corey being my sister for ages no-one told me'.
'Mam was just waiting for the right time to tell you'.
'And you're happy now' 'yeah I am because Corey
would never treat me the way everyone else does!'.
'I know Katie can be a bitch' 'I can't stand her!'.
'You know I thought it was great having two sisters
after spending my childhood alone'.
'All the time Katie secretly hated me when I met our
mother I was twenty nine I was looking forward to it'.
'Finally getting to see her after all those years all the
things I'd planned to talk to her about then I met her'.
'Katie was there then I learned after a while Katie
was always there because she's the favourite'.
'Nothing I ever do will be good enough she even said
I was never part of the family and it's true'.
'I can tolerate the fact she's the favourite that I never
grew up with our mother'.
'But what I can't accept is her denial of me being abused'.
'By that bastard! at her fortieth birthday party'.

'Acting like it was ok that a child abuser a rapist
was at her party without a care in the world'.
'Sipping champagne!' 'Victoria' 'no listen Corey and
Sapphire are my family they look out for me you don't!'.
'None of you do acting like I don't exist well from now
on I don't you and Katie are welcome to each other!'.
'I hate Katie as much as you do sometimes' 'I thought
you were the best of friends' 'we were for years'.
'What happened?' 'your right about her she thinks
she's better than anyone else she's the favourite'.
'Always has been you think it hasn't been hard for me'.
'Being second best' 'try being third best' 'mam misses you'.
'She really does the thought of you never speaking to her
again' 'it's for the best' 'she loves you whatever you think'.
'She said she came to your school when you were fifteen'.
'I don't remember' 'she wanted to see you she came to
your room to talk to you it was supposed to be a surprise'.
'Then she overheard a conversation you with a friend'.
'Saying you didn't need a mother because she never cared
about you so she got upset and left' 'we all say things'.
'At fifteen we don't mean but you have to understand Nina
she left me when I was eight she said she'd come back'.
'And she never did' 'she wanted to he wouldn't let her
your dad step-dad he was controlling abusive'.
'She had to leave him she hid all their fights she told me'.

'So you could have the perfect childhood he was the
protective older man but he abused her emotionally'.
'Physically she said it was eight years of abuse'.
'Mam could have come back for me' 'she wanted to'.
'Then dad took you abroad and by the time you came back
things had happened he wanted you to himself'.
'He wanted you nowhere near her she sent letters
and Christmas presents when you lived in Canada'.
'She heard nothing back whether you'd got them'.
'Until one Christmas he wrote back he said he was
giving them to a children's charity'.
'And would make sure you never got them that's what
he was like controlling obsessive even after they split'.
'He would make threats get his friends to find out
what she was up to' 'I know what he's like'.
'But why was he at Katie's birthday party?' 'because'.
'She always loved him thought he was great he was
the only dad she ever knew depsite what he was like'.
'If mam had her way she would never have to see him
again but Katie wanted him there' 'how can she'.
'So our mother was abused by him and yet she forces
her to see him have contact' 'like you said'.
'Katie's the favourite always has been I always hated him'.
'He was never a father to me only to Katie' Nina said.
'Well he was a terrible father when I was a child'.

'I loved him' Victoria said 'he gave me presents'.
'I was his favourite mam loved me but not like Katie
then when they split I thought it would be ok'.
'Because he loved me but when we moved to Canada he
changed he promised me it would be a great adventure'.
'That I didn't need my mother because I had him I believed
him then after a while it was like he got sick of me'.
'He sent me on these adventure camps with other kids
let me stay over at friends so I wasn't in the house'.
'We lived near the lake at first it was great I made friends
there then he started disappearing for days'.
'Weeks at a time I never knew why I missed him'.
'We had a housekeeper he had money he was a
businessman then later became a politician'.
'After a while I missed having a mother then a father'.
'I felt alone so I started comfort eating I always loved food
so I put on weight and before I moved back to Ireland'.
'He noticed he got angry at me said I needed to lose
weight else I'd get bullied for being fat but I loved food'.
'It was hard I had this red dress he brought me a year
before for Christmas it fitted fine'.
'Then after I gained weight it was tight on me I felt
ashamed like I'd let him down he didn't care'.
'He put me on a diet dad said we were moving back to
Ireland that if my mother saw how fat I'd got'.

'She wouldn't be happy I agreed I should lose weight
I hated dieting but I wanted him to love me again'.
'I thought if I did he'd be happy he was a bastard'.
'He weighed me every day until I could wear clothes for
my age again it continued after we moved back to Ireland'.
'Weighing me not every day but once a week banning
me from ever having ice cream or McDonald's'.
'Even fast food anyway we moved to outside Dublin'.
'This house he named The Castle it was more like a
prison' 'why?' 'because of them Mrs Harvey'.
'And Mrs O'Donnell the two housekeeper's cook's they
looked after me after I turned eleven he was always away'.
'On business trips I later learned he was a womaniser'.
'They were after his money his girlfriends I rarely
saw him they the two bitches ruined my life'.
'They never fed me properly for years I lived off soups
stews I had an eating disorder not a proper one'.
'But I was obsessed with food from my early teens
to my mid-twenties food was the enemy'.
'If I even gained a few pounds I was told off by them'.
'They said no-one would want to marry a fat girl I used
to bully Polly at school mock her for her weight'.
'But really I was jealous because even though she was
overweight she could eat what she wanted and not care'.

'Not like me they controlled everything they never let me
out the house they controlled me not even to a disco'.
'Except at school where they couldn't get to me they
only let Marion my best friend come to the house'.
'Once a month they told me what clothes I was allowed
to wear' 'they sound terrible' 'they were'.
'The house was always cold and when I asked to have
the heating on they said it would cost money'.
'So I tried to find a blanket or jumper Christmas was
always rubbish I hoped our mother would get in contact'.
'She never did or any other family members'.
'Anyway worst of all they used to invite him to the house'.
'Uncle Richard I think Mrs Harvey had a crush on him'.
'At weekends sometimes once a week once a month'.
'They never questioned why he spent ages in my bedroom'.
'Or if they did know they ignored the abuse they didn't
care even after he was asked to leave my school'.
'They made out the victims were lying because he was
such a nice person now you know everything about me'.
'He abused me too' 'what? when?' 'I was fifteen'.
'Richard had just got out of prison he tried to convince me
he was innocent and your dad anyway'.
'One night we were chatting in my room he raped me
mam was out I reckon he waited for his chance'.

'I couldn't tell anyone I felt ashamed like maybe
it was my fault for believing he was innocent'.
'And dad he raped me too he visited me at College'.
'I was too traumatised to ask for help I tried to kill myself'.
'When I was twenty one I couldn't do it I've never told
anyone Katie loved him idolised him'.
'I suppose I didn't want to ruin her image of him and
I was worried I wouldn't be believed' 'I believe you'.
'It took me years to have a boyfriend I was like
twenty three they ruined my ability to have relationships'.
'Same as me I had boyfriends they never lasted'.
'Because I never really enjoyed having sex I thought there
was something wrong with me now I know it was him'.
'I would have flashbacks' Victoria said 'same as me'.
'It took me years to tell people I told Corey at school
but when I told mam Katie just mocked me'.
'Like nothing happened' 'screw her' 'anyway you telling
me uncle Richard is dead is the best news'.
'Because even though I'll always have trauma'.
'I'll never have to see his smug face again'.
'Fancy some vodka and tonic to celebrate his death'.
'Why not sounds good I'm sorry if you ever felt left out
the family I don't want you to' 'it's fine'.
'Would you consider seeing mam again?' 'maybe I will'.

*'Anyway at dad's funeral' 'your going' 'do you think*
*I should?' 'I don't know I'm not sure' Nina replied.*
*'He didn't give a toss about me since I was a teenager'.*
*'Even then he wasn't nice to me what about you?'.*
*'I'd rather not go Katie wouldn't be happy' Nina said.*
*'I'd never hear the end of it I'm sure mam would rather*
*not go all he put her through'.*
*'Maybe we can think about it and then make a decision'.*
*'Sounds good' Nina agreed.*
*After she left Victoria thought about the fact neither of*
*them wanted to attend her father's funeral.*
*That they felt obliged because of Katie that Nina had*
*been abused by both her uncle and father.*
*That their mother wouldn't have wanted their father*
*anywhere near them.*
*Was that why Katie was their mother's favourite?.*
*Because if she received enough attention and presents*
*she would forget about their father.*
*Victoria also wondered why she hadn't been abused*
*by their dad he'd obviously targeted Nina.*
*She still couldn't forgive her mother for her behaviour.*
*Waiting so many years after leaving school to make*
*contact always putting Katie first.*
*Did their mother know Nina had been abused?.*

*Her sister had told her about her life Victoria would have*
*to attend her father's funeral even though she hated him.*
*After all she'd loved him once as a child.*
*It was a rainy June 17th in Dublin Victoria was attending*
*her father's funeral she had mixed feelings.*
*About the man she'd once called her father as a child*
*she'd been his favourite a real daddy's girl.*
*Later she'd seen him for who he was a womaniser*
*and gambler who palmed her off to other people.*
*To look after who didn't really care about her*
*who never got in touch after she left school.*
*She'd been estranged from her mother it meant she was*
*an orphan at least until she met her mother and sister's.*
*Despite this somehow it felt wrong if she didn't attend.*
*And deep down Victoria still cared what her mother*
*thought she'd chosen a black jacket and skirt.*
*Gold earrings Nina had driven them to the church.*
*She couldn't stand Katie but for one day she'd have*
*to be civil as Victoria got out the car she could see people.*
*A group of men no doubt her father's work colleagues.*
*And she also recognised his brother Katie was with their*
*mother sobbing uncontrollably she wanted to go over.*
*But felt her mother should come to her especially as*
*she'd been made to feel unwelcome in the family.*

*Finally she looked over 'Victoria Nina said you were*
*coming I didn't want to believe it' 'well I'm here'.*
*'I know I hadn't seen him since I was fifteen but he*
*was the only father I knew' 'we're glad you're here'.*
*'I'm glad you decided to turn up!' Katie said angry.*
*'Why wouldn't I' 'because you don't want anything to*
*do with me or mam!' 'Katie's upset I do want you here'.*
*'I came to pay my respects' Victoria said.*
*'The service will be starting soon' they watched as the*
*hearse arrived.*
*Victoria found herself strangely emotional at a man*
*she had loved and hated for most of her life.*
*They made their way inside the church Katie sat on the*
*front row with their mother as she held her in her arms.*
*As if she was a child not a woman in her early forties.*
*Victoria sat a few seats back with Nina 'back soon'.*
*Nina went to chat to Katie & their mother as they hugged.*
*She soon returned 'shall we go sit with them?' Nina asked.*
*'You go I'll be fine sat here' 'but we're all family'.*
*'I'm not moving' 'well I'll come see you after the service'.*
*Victoria watched as Nina re-joined her mother & Katie.*
*She'd never felt so removed from her family she knew*
*it was her own fault she could have sat with them.*
*But then she would have to have put up with Katie*
*giving her looks her family ignoring her.*

*Making her feel second best as they always did she*
*saw her mother and Katie coming towards her.*
*'Please sit with us you'll regret it if you don't'.*
*Her mother said 'why?' 'because we're a family'.*
*'And we want you to be part of it' 'well I'm not'.*
*'As I said I came to pay my respects to a man*
*I once loved my father'.*
*'But I don't know how you can pretend he didn't abuse*
*you' 'I'm not pretending I'm here for Katie'.*
*'And he was her father' 'my real dad not like yours!'.*
*'Katie she didn't mean it' 'yes I did!' 'it's not helping!*
*please you can't be sat apart' 'I want to sit apart'.*
*'Because I don't want to be anywhere near Katie!'.*
*'I'm fed up of pretending we get on when we both*
*know we hate each other go back to the front row'.*
*'While the black sheep of the family sits away!'.*
*'From her own family isn't that how you want it!'.*
*'Your sister needs you' 'there's so much I can say'.*
*'But I won't I'm staying here and neither of you are my*
*family!' 'you don't have any other family' Katie said.*
*'I have Corey how can you say those things to me and*
*how can you let her!' Victoria said angry at her mother.*
*'We all need to calm down just come and sit with us'.*
*'No way! after today I want nothing to do with any of you!*
*the way you treat me' 'stop making this about you!'.*

Katie said 'I thought you were upset or is it just an act to get attention!' Victoria said angry.
'The only attention seeker in this family is you!'.
'If you change your mind you know where we are we want you to feel part of this family all you do is reject us'.
'You don't get it do you Katie!' 'no I don't!'.
'Victoria I try and be a mother to you but you make it hard we're all upset' 'of course you are!'.
'About the fact my father left me to be brought up by the housekeepers who were both vile to me!'.
'I'm here because I want to remember dad as he was'.
'Kind and caring when I was a child until things changed'.
'And he didn't love me anymore maybe he never did'.
'And you've never been a mother to me only to her!'.
'I don't know why you bother with me pretend I don't exist' 'maybe we can chat another time' April said.
'When your feeling yourself please come to the wake'.
'I'll think about it' Victoria watched as they went to the front row how she hated her family the funeral began.
'We are here to celebrate the life of David Hutchings an upstanding member of the community'.
'A local businessman and politician a man who spent his life serving others a devoted father to his daughter's'.
'Katie and Nina uncle to his nieces and nephews a wonderful man' Victoria couldn't believe it.

*She hadn't been mentioned in the speech she had heard*
*enough when Katie got up to speak through the tears.*
*She found it hard to listen not when she knew he had*
*abused Nina criticized her as a child.*
*And her own mother how could she even attend his*
*funeral let alone listen to all the lies and glowing tributes.*
*Her family meant nothing to her now she no longer*
*idolised the mother she had growing up for so many years.*
*And she no longer thought Katie was fun to be around.*
*And Nina hadn't been there for her as they sang a hymn*
*she decided to leave as she shut the church door quietly.*
*Victoria called a taxi as she put up an umbrella as she*
*waited in the rain she'd made the effort with her outfit.*
*And make-up it hardly seemed worth it now 'Victoria'.*
*It was Nina 'don't go' 'I have to it's for the best do they*
*know? what he did' 'no it wasn't the right time'.*
*'To tell them' 'when is the right time they all think he's*
*a saint I mean I know you shouldn't trash someone'.*
*'At a funeral but even I came out worse than him'.*
*'According to them' 'I'm sorry' 'that I'm left out as usual'.*
*'I don't want you to be' 'I don't need anyone I never have'.*
*'I'm used to being let down by my family I couldn't do it*
*anymore make out like me and Katie get on'.*
*'I couldn't listen to what was said about him I should*
*never have come' 'I never wanted to either'.*

*'I came because I wanted closure peace but I realised
I can't have it it was wrong what Katie said'.
'It doesn't surprise me' 'so what will you do when
you get home?' 'not much I might call Corey later'.
'What's she like?' 'nice the best friend you could ever
have and her mother Carol taxi's here' 'I'll call you'.
That afternoon when Victoria returned home to her
apartment she didn't cry she didn't feel anything.
She texted Corey who had asked about the funeral.*
'Funeral wasn't great I left before the wake on the
plus side I'm speaking to Nina again speak soon xxx'.
*What would she do without Corey a few days later she
received a call to attend the reading of her father's will.
Victoria didn't see the point of going but apparently
she'd been left something.
Somehow she managed to get out of it according to Nina
Katie had been left numerous gifts.
But not much in the way of money apparently their father
had been almost bankrupt before he died.
Nina had been left nothing and she had been left her
old house The Castle Victoria thought about things.
She didn't want to live there it had been a home
with unhappy memories being emotionally abused.
By her housekeepers the people who should have
been caring for her when her family was absent.*

*Victoria decided she would sell it the following day*
*she contacted a solicitor about the will.*
*And within days photos had been taken that Friday*
*afternoon she decided things were looking up.*
*Now she could try and make a new future for herself.*
*No more bad memories it was a sunny day outside*
*she heard the buzzer ring she opened 'Victoria hello'.*
*'It's been years since we saw you' it was Mrs Harvey.*
*The woman who had ruined her life as a teenager and*
*controlled her 'how are you?' 'I'm great' Victoria replied.*
*Angry that somehow she knew where she lived.*
*'That's good are you free to talk?' 'yes course' 'great'.*
*'I know your house is on sale' 'The Castle' 'yes anyway'.*
*'Since you have this lovely apartment I was thinking*
*instead of waiting for a buyer you could sell it to me'.*
*'It would be easier what do you think?' 'I can't' 'but why'.*
*'You live in a new apartment and do you really want to*
*wait up to a year to sell that's what happens these days'.*
*'You want me to sell to you' 'yes I don't see why not'.*
*'It's an easy option' 'you want The Castle' 'yes I do'.*
*'Where do you live now?' 'in a cottage it's ok but not*
*like where we used to live'.*
*'How did you find out where I live?' 'I just did anyway'.*
*'Tell me will you sell to me?' 'anyone but you' 'I know we*
*didn't always get on' 'I will never sell this house to you!'.*

*'You mentally and emotionally abused me! you took advantage of me because I had no parents'.*
*'When you should have been looking after me!'.*
*'You controlled me! every aspect of my life!'.*
*'Maybe we went too far we were just looking out for you'.*
*'What use could you have for that house! it was a home to me Mrs O'Donnell' 'it was never a home to me!'.*
*'You nearly starved me to death you made me live in a freezing cold house because you refused to light the fire'.*
*'For heating and you stopped me going out having friends round controlled what clothes I wore'.*
*'And numerous other things I'm not a child anymore!'.*
*'You can't tell me what to do no-one can ever again!'.*
*'So you can take your offer I'm not selling to you I don't care who I sell to but it won't be you!' 'you'll regret it!'.*
*'When your house is still on the market cause no-one wants to buy it because it's too expensive please'.*
*'I'm sorry about everything sell it to me at a reduced price it's the least you can do'.*
*'Since we spent years looking after you!' 'abusing me more like please leave my apartment!'.*
*'Before I call the police!' 'if you change your mind'.*
*'I won't trust me!' 'if that's how you feel!' 'it is!'.*
*As Mrs Harvey left Victoria felt relieved.*

*Coming face to face with the person who ruined her*
*childhood she phoned her solicitor.*
*Instructing her not to sell to Mrs Harvey Victoria also*
*thought she might send someone to view the house.*
*On her behalf she would make sure every viewer was*
*checked out before Victoria wanted the house sold quickly.*
*So she could move on with her life but she also didn't*
*want to give Mrs Harvey the satisfaction.*
*Of thinking she could get hold of the house just to*
*get back at her for telling the truth.*
*According to them they'd looked after her treated her*
*well Victoria knew they had ruined her life.*
*Taken advantage of her when she was vulnerable.*
*That afternoon Polly was happy she was expecting a visit*
*from Christian her parents had gotten back together.*
*And were now living outside Chester she knew Wendy*
*wouldn't like it.*
*Since she'd hoped she could get back with her dad.*
*Which wasn't going to happen she still thought of the row.*
*At Emily's birthday party she still felt angry at what had*
*happened the things that had been said.*
*That Wendy thought it was ok that Emily had told her*
*their dad might not be her biological father.*
*At least she still had Christian she heard a knock at the*
*door 'hi' he smiled Christian hugged her.*

*'I've missed you' he said 'I missed you too' she said
she'd always loved Christian.*

*Aside from her brother he was one of her best friends.
She'd known him since she was twenty four and he
was nineteen there had never been a falling out.
They'd always had a lot in common both actors who
loved going to the theatre & cinema Art & History.
They even liked a lot of the same music somehow things
didn't feel the same since she'd found out the truth.
Stacey had said nothing had to change but it had Polly
wished she'd never attended Emily's birthday party.
Never found out about her dad 'drink?' Polly asked 'yes'.
'I've got a new Slush Puppy machine' 'flavour?' 'any'.
'I don't mind' 'how are you after everything?'.
Christian asked 'I'm fine you know' 'how could Emily
do that just say that at her birthday' 'it's Emily'.
'She enjoys the drama playing us off against dad at least
he can see her for what she's really like unlike Wendy'.
'Sounds like it didn't go well I couldn't go with work'.
'Trust me it was a disaster me and Stace looks like
we've been cast out of the family'.
'At least where Wendy's concerned' 'surely she should
realise by now what Emily's really like' 'not yet'.
'Her precious daughter who she won't hear a word said
against' 'I don't like her'.*

'I told her how homophobic and racist Emily is you
can imagine how that went down' Polly explained.
'Maybe she needed to hear the truth' 'it's sad really'.
'I told Wendy how much I loved her when I was a teenager
she was the mother I never had'.
'I never realised we'd end up never speaking'.
'I want you to know that even though we might not be
biologically related I'll always be your brother'.
'And dad will always be your dad nothing has to change'.
'But it has' 'it doesn't have to I love you' 'thanks'.
'Have you thought about finding out if he's really your
dad' 'me and Stace we sent away for DNA tests'.
'She found out Andy was her dad it wasn't such a big deal
like she's known for years'.
'Her mum slept with both Paul and Andy at the same time'.
'And she was fine about things I couldn't do it'.
'When did you get the results?' 'a few weeks ago'.
'I know I need to know the truth wait here' Polly went to
get the envelope with her letter.
'Stace said I should do it when I'm ready I wasn't that day
but maybe I am now' 'only if you want to' 'shall I do it?'.
'But don't tell Emily if he's not she'll only use it against
me' 'forget about her'.
Polly took the letter out the envelope 'I'm doing it'.

*She opened the letter as she looked at the words 99.9 per
cent not the biological father 'I really wanted him to be'.
'But I knew he might not be' 'like I said our dad has
always been the only father you've ever known'.
'Nothing Emily or anyone else says will change that'.
'I know why do I feel so down' 'because it's all been
a shock' 'why did mum wait so many years to tell me'.
'I think from what dad said she was protecting everyone'.
'But it wasn't the truth I wouldn't have minded that dad
wasn't my biological father to lie all these years'.
'I'm here for you I hate the way you found out'.
'Did you know?' 'I had no idea until dad told me'.
'Your still my sister' 'I know' 'dad's been your dad for
forty two years and he's not gonna stop' 'thanks'.
'Look on the positive side at least your not related to
Emily like I am' 'that's one good thing'.
'I always thought I looked nothing like her' they laughed.
'I'll tell you something else amusing Sue sold Shaun's car
for fifty quid on Ebay people couldn't believe it'.
'The price for a car worth twenty grand' 'no more than the
bastard deserves for what he did to Kaleigh and Sue'.
'I've got something to tell you you might hate me never
want to speak to me again' Christian said 'tell me'.
'I haven't had a relationship for a while I'm seeing Corey'.
'It wasn't planned it just happened' 'it's fine' 'really'.*

'You don't hate me' 'I'm not completely happy but I don't hate you your still my brother I hated it when we split'.

'But everyone's got a right to move on' 'I wouldn't want us to fall out' 'don't worry everything's fine'.

Polly assured him 'oh I'm seeing Marley again'.

'That's great' 'yeah he's a lovely baby' 'don't worry about dad not being your dad'.

In a few months everything will be fine' 'I know'.

'I just need to get over everything' 'I'll help you'.

Polly loved her brother he was a kind person she couldn't help feeling jealous of his relationship with Corey.

She didn't know how serious it was they'd been together before she got back together with Corey.

Had she been second choice? had she and Christian been in a serious relationship? was it really a summer fling.

As Corey had said all she knew was she didn't think she could trust another woman again after Margie.

And now Corey it was a warm afternoon as Polly got ready to attend a radio interview she applied her make-up.

Selecting her outfit carefully it wasn't like years ago most radio interviews were now filmed to be shown online.

So she had to look good she selected an emerald green blazer under a white T-shirt and matching green skirt.

Some four leaf clover earrings that matched her red hair.

As she looked at her watch she was running late.

*Her taxi was waiting outside to take her to Manchester*
*as Polly arrived at the studio the receptionist said hello.*
*She went upstairs to check her appearance happy she was*
*going to be interviewed by Martin Harrison.*
*Who always did afternoons as she finished checking*
*her appearance in the toilets full length mirror.*
*An older actress arrived blonde tall thin looking amazing.*
*Polly guessed she was in her late sixties but looked a*
*decade younger 'hi' 'Polly I love the jacket' 'thanks'.*
*'I've just finished my interview' 'Martin Harrison' 'no'.*
*'It's Charles Russell on today filling in' 'I like him'.*
*'He's lovely they both are' 'is Martin on holiday?' 'yeah'.*
*'I personally think once these DJ's get older they need*
*more time off it must get waring sometimes'.*
*'Three hours of news reports travel and chatting'.*
*'And you know half the time they get told what to play'.*
*'I know I feel like a lot of music today sounds the same'*
*Polly said 'I agree I thought it was just me'.*
*'There are exceptions I like La Roux and Mabel'.*
*'I love them too shame there's not more great music out*
*there like there was in my day have a good interview'.*
*'I will' 'see you soon' Polly watched as the actress*
*walked away she'd been a fan of hers for years.*
*But didn't want to act like an overexcited groupie.*

*So tried to keep her calm around her favourite celebrities
especially the older legends 'Polly'.
'Can I have your autograph?' a teenager asked 'course'.
'That's my son' a man said Polly scribbled on a piece of
paper 'here for an interview?' 'yeah Charles Russell'.
'He's started filling in for Martin I wasn't sure at first'.
'But he's actually good in the afternoon slots apparently
this week he's been getting higher ratings than Martin'.
'Oh really' 'don't say anything' 'not a word' 'it's his
own fault taking endless holidays' they laughed.
'Good meeting you' 'and you I must go' 'bye Polly'.
As Polly left she hoped she'd have a good interview
especially as it was a Friday afternoon.
As she made her way to the main booth for the interview.
She could see Charles he was wearing an orange & green
Hawaiian shirt she opened the door he smiled.
He seemed happy to see her 'now for a disco classic'.
'Diana Ross Upside Down' 'hi' he said as he turned
towards her 'hi' she replied 'like the shirt' 'thanks'.
'Oh me and Stace we listen to your Friday night disco
show' 'oh that's great'.
'Is there anything you don't want me to ask in the
interview?' 'no ask me anything I'm an open book'.
'I only asked because the other day we had a
big American star and there was a list of questions'.*

*'That I couldn't ask' 'I'm not like that' he smiled Polly thought he seemed nice she knew he'd done a lot.*

*In his thirty year career and had started out in TV presenting and was now a successful radio DJ.*

*She had never met him before they were both from Liverpool as she put on her headphones.*

*Ready for the interview 'that was Diana Ross Upside Down now I am very excited about my next guest'.*

*'She is an Oscar, BAFTA and Golden Globe winning actress'.*

*'Since quitting acting she has now gone into making documentaries and has a show on channel five this week'.*

*'To tell us all about it is Polly Patterson' 'Polly how are you?' 'good*

*'You started your career as a glamour model how was that?' 'I enjoyed it at the time it was fun'.*

*'For me like a lot of girls it's a stepping stone on to other things I did it almost four years'.*

*'And then I wanted to do other things like acting or TV'.*

*'You had such a successful career as an actress did you ever think you'd win an Oscar or a BAFTA?' 'no'.*

*'I tried to do projects films that suited me because when I started out I had no confidence as an actress'.*

*'It was something I wanted to try it was Stacey who said I should do it' 'really?' 'yeah'.*

'She said your quite funny but your sensitive as well'.
'I had a great run of films when I started a lot of the roles
were extensions of my personality but I think that's ok'.
'I never thought I'm gonna be this character actress'.
'Except there was this one film called Psychedelia
where I played a drug addict which I enjoyed'.
'Because it was a different type of role' 'I can relate
because when I started out I was doing comedy sketches'.
'And I didn't have much confidence either but over
the years I got more confident as time went on'.
'That's the same as me' 'would you go back to acting?'.
'I did a movie not long ago but the odd role which I enjoy'.
'I wouldn't do back to back films again I like being able
to do things I like I set up my TV production company'.
'I would see things on TV and think why don't they do a
documentary about that so I started writing down ideas'.
'And this documentary on channel five tell us about that'.
'It's got a very Jerry Springer esque title it's called
'Coming out the closet leaving the wife' 'I love it'.
'It's about people who are gay or lesbian who had to
leave their partners because of their sexuality'.
'It was based on my own experiences because I still feel
guilty to this day about splitting with my ex-husband'.
'Even though I know it wasn't my fault' 'it's weird to think
you were married to a man because you've been out'.

'For most of your career was it hard coming out?' 'yeah'.
'Especially my career being a glamour model selling sex
to men I had a great marriage I married at sixteen'.
'And he was twenty two years older my step-mum's brother
you can imagine how that went down'.
'We were together five years a year before we split'.
'I knew I preferred women so I had to tell him the truth'.
'Was that hard breaking it to him?' 'he found my stash of
Diva magazines under my bed'.
'Which is the UK's biggest selling lesbian and bi magazine
so when I told him he wasn't shocked'.
'And we're still good friends' 'I feel like you've been
such a great role model for gay people'.
'I feel like your sexuality never really affected your
career' 'I was lucky'.
'I was out of the beginning of my film career'.
'I just wanted to be a good actress management wanted
me to keep my sexuality quiet in America I said ok'.
'But if someone asks who my partner is I'm not gonna lie'.
'I was asked on a chat show if I had a boyfriend I said no'.
'I've got a girlfriend so I was out from the beginning and
people were curious cause it wasn't the done thing'.
'I think because I'm feminine and I'm quite accessible
to people it wasn't an issue like it could have been'.

'I know you'll have helped so many people Polly I've really enjoyed chatting to you' 'thanks for having me on'. 'It's ok before you go what song can I play?' 'I love the Pet Shop Boys and there's this song that I love'. 'It was the theme to The Clothes Show called In The Night' 'I know that song I love it too'. 'So we're gonna play it now thanks Polly' she took off her earphones she was going to say goodbye to Charles. As she watched as he ran off she said goodbye to everyone else as she left her taxi was waiting as she got in. It was raining the good old British weather. When she returned home Polly felt happy with how the interview had gone. That evening she watched the news then Emmerdale. Surfed the internet when she got ready for bed she looked outside the window a breeze was blowing. It was windy outside she didn't feel herself finding out her dad and brother weren't related had been a lot to take in. The fact she would probably never get to meet her biological father and other siblings. Emily had heard the news her dad wasn't her father. No doubt another private conversation she shouldn't have heard she had texted Polly to say she was happy. They weren't related and wasn't part of the family anymore how she hated Emily.

*She had never considered her her sister due to the fact they'd never gotten along.*

*How could anyone be so cruel then her falling out with Wendy and Aunt Hilary.*

*And the fact Christian was dating Corey she tried to make out she was ok about it and she didn't blame her brother.*

*For wanting to find love it still hurt everything in her life was going wrong Polly couldn't tell anyone how she felt.*

*She had always been expected to be outgoing and bubbly. Like her celebrity image Polly Patterson who turned up on the red carpet wearing glitzy outfits.*

*Pretending everything was ok sometimes she just wanted to be Susan her real name a deep thinker.*

*Who liked to read going to the theatre and was a bit quieter than her stage image.*

*But she felt people would be disappointed at the real her. They wanted Polly not Susan the celebrity character she had created it was part of her the glamorous side.*

*Who never turned up to any interview or red carpet event without full make-up jewellery and sparkly outfits.*

*But it wasn't all of her the following morning she received a letter through the post she'd been invited to a charity do. In Chester to do with a homeless charity she supported. Usually she'd have said yes the way she felt she wasn't sure she could go.*

*That afternoon Maggie was coming round maybe it would lift her spirits after feeling so down for the past few days. At 4pm she heard a knock at the door she opened.*

*'Love the T-shirt' Maggie said Polly was wearing a Coca Cola T-shirt 'thanks new the other day drink?'.*

*'What do you have?' 'coke, lemonade, lime juice' 'I'll try some lime juice' 'coming up so any gossip with you?'.*

*Polly asked 'you'll never guess who's been in contact'.*

*'Katie' 'not your ex-girlfriend' 'yeah that's the one'.*

*'Asking if we can get back together' 'I hope you told her where to go' 'course she was persistent'.*

*'Her career isn't going well her last album didn't sell well she's been dropped by her record company'.*

*'No more than she deserves' 'kind of she was cocky'.*

*'Understatement of the year I remember her saying how she was the greatest singer the UK had seen in years'.*

*Polly said 'and the rest' Maggie agreed 'she annoyed lots of people in the music industry she only lasted two years'.*

*'They put up with cause of her talent but they only put up with so much she said she wants to come out as a lesbian'.*

*'Especially since it's cool to be sexually fluid as they say these days she wants to be true to herself'.*

*'All bulls**t! I hated her when she turned straight ignored me said being bi was a phase'.*

*'Now I pity her cause she doesn't know what she wants'.*

'Your much better off out of it' Polly said as she brought the drinks into the living room 'I know it's alright'.

'Being single I do miss her sometimes things happen'.

'Don't they' 'think you'll date again?' 'maybe I want to take my time find someone nice'.

'And I like my own company what about you?' 'not much gossip Christian's seeing Corey' 'oh right'.

'Didn't they go out together before you got back together with Corey' 'yeah apparently it was a summer fling'.

'I don't hate Christian he is still my brother' 'think you'll meet your real dad' 'I doubt it can you imagine'.

'Guess what remember that girl you slept with at the youth club back in the eighties well she had a child'.

'And she's come back to haunt you forty two years later'.

'It wasn't your fault and didn't you say your mum and him were good mates' 'yeah he's got a family a son'.

'And daughter they'd hate me' 'no they might be happy if they knew about you' 'I googled stories of people'.

'Meeting their real families this girl met her real dad it started out fine' then the sisters got jealous'.

'She never spoke to them again and there's others'.

'I couldn't deal with being rejected' 'you must be curious'.

'What he looks like' 'I'd love to see a photo all I know is he's mixed-race and a DJ'.

'I guess I'll never get to meet him I could track him down'.

'What if he didn't want to know me' 'your Polly Patterson
famous celebrity' 'we're still dealing with people's lives'.
'His family might hate the idea of another person coming
into the family' they might not' 'I guess I'll never know'.
'Mum said she doesn't want me getting hurt' 'I guess she's
looking out for you' 'I know dad will always be my dad'.
'I know but somewhere out there you have another family'.
'I know Mags oh I've been invited to this charity do in
Cheshire I'm not sure I'll go' 'why?'.
'I've not felt myself lately life gets too much finding out
dad's not my dad then splitting with Cor'.
'I suppose it's easier to hide myself away' 'it's normal
to feel down I would after splitting up with someone'.
'And finding out about your dad and Christian'.
'It says I can invite one other person'.
'Stacey's spending time in Ireland and I don't think it
would be Kaleigh's thing' 'I could go' 'I'm not sure'.
'I'm up to it' 'go on it might make you feel better'.
'And if it's rubbish we'll drink champagne go out on
the pull' 'I'm not sure I'm up to dating' 'you should go'.
'Just for one night you can forget your troubles'.
'I suppose it is a good charity for the homeless' 'exactly'.
'We'll find something to wear and I've just brought this
great eye palette so make-up will be sorted' 'alright'.

*'I'll go' 'we'll have a great time you'll see' Polly*
*was glad Maggie had called round.*
*She had been such a good friend to her making her*
*feel better when she felt down.*
*The following Friday afternoon Polly began getting*
*ready to go to the charity do with Maggie.*
*She had selected a glittery navy blazer matching skirt*
*gold dollar earrings and a gold heart locket.*
*Polly knew she looked good but even so didn't feel herself.*
*Somehow she knew she'd be fine once she got to the venue*
*it was the fact she had to be all showbiz chatty sociable.*
*Pretend like everything in her life was ok when it wasn't.*
*Keep calm and carry on like people always expected her*
*to 'looking forward to it?' Maggie asked 'yeah'.*
*'It'll be great' 'if it's not we can always leave early'.*
*'I know how down you've been lately and I thought it*
*might cheer you up' 'I'm sorry I've not been myself'.*
*'It's fine I don't know how I'd react if I found out*
*my dad wasn't my dad at the age of forty two'.*
*'Actually I wouldn't mind since I hate my real dad so*
*much' 'Shaun was never a decent father to any of his kids'.*
*'He was a bastard glad he's gone' 'so am I I still wish you*
*know… that I'd had another dad'.*
*'You've been lucky with yours he's so lovely'.*

*'I know I have that's why I wonder if I shouldn't meet*
*my real father but then I'm curious what he looks like'.*
*'Whatever you decide I'm always here for you' 'thanks'.*
*At 6pm their taxi arrived to take them to Cheshire.*
*It was beautiful summer's evening they arrived at the*
*venue a posh hotel as they saw other people arriving.*
*A man with a clipboard stood near reception 'hi Polly'.*
*'You'll be on table five about three tables from the front'.*
*'I hope that's ok' 'it's fine' 'shall we go find the table?'.*
*Maggie asked 'yeah' all the tables had purple cloths on*
*them with table numbers a bottle of champagne.*
*In an ice bucket and champagne glasses along with*
*posh napkins 'listen I need the toilet I'll be back soon'.*
*Maggie said 'ok take your time' Polly looked around*
*as she saw people laughing together.*
*She wondered if she'd made a mistake in coming*
*everyone looked so happy she didn't feel happy.*
*She knew she possibly had the start of depression and*
*couldn't tell anyone she'd stopped going out as much.*
*And didn't feel herself she reminded herself why she*
*was there to support the homeless charity as a celebrity.*
*Polly saw two men coming towards her who looked*
*familiar she realised it was Charles and another man.*
*Who she was sure she had seen on TV before.*
*'Hi' Polly said 'hello it's great to see you here'.*

*Charles said smiling he seemed happy Polly thought.*
*'And we're sat on the same table' 'like the shirt'.*
*Charles was wearing a purple satin shirt 'it's a few years*
*old' 'it's nice' 'my wife wasn't too sure about it'.*
*'Are you here alone?' Charles asked Polly 'no I'm here*
*with someone she's just gone to the toilet' 'this is Bobby'.*
*'Hi' Polly looked over as Maggie arrived 'brought you*
*a coke' 'thanks Mags this is Maggie my date for the night'.*
*Polly joked 'hi I'm Bobby and this is Charles which you*
*probably already know' 'I'm a big fan of yours'.*
*Maggie said 'I used to watch that show you used to*
*present' 'that was years ago' Bobby said.*
*'I always loved it I used to watch it all the time' 'it's great*
*to meet someone who's such a big fan of my work'.*
*"He's a great TV presenter' 'thanks these days I focus*
*more on script writing' Bobby said.*
*'I think you should be back on the box' Maggie said.*
*'Maybe one day soon if I find the right project besides*
*Charles is the bigger star than me' 'no'.*
*'I don't do much presenting these days they put me on*
*channel five or Sky' 'I like channel five' Polly said.*
*'So do I and you can say what you want things you*
*wouldn't get away with on the main channels'.*
*Charles said 'anyway I can't believe we're sat on the*
*same table as an Oscar winning actress' Bobby said.*

'I don't think of myself like that' 'Bobby drinks'.
Charles said waving his hand in the air 'what did your
last slave die of' 'go on get us a pint and one for yourself'.
 Charles asked 'back soon girls' 'you two look very nice
tonight' Charles said to Polly 'well so do you'.
 'I look ok for fifty seven' 'you look ten years younger'.
Polly said 'so do you' 'it's the botox' Polly joked 'no'.
'Seriously I don't smoke or take drugs and I stay out
the sun when I can' 'I've always been a smoker'.
'I tried to pack it in a few times I've used patches'.
'You name it I've tried it' 'what about vaping?' Polly asked
'I'm not sure my brother died a few years ago'.
'From a heart attack so I need to give up' 'don't be hard
on yourself' we've all got our addictions' 'thankyou Polly'.
'Shame my wife doesn't see it like that I try and live the
best life I can but I'm not perfect it's what she wants'.
'The perfect man and the lifestyle to go with it'.
'Ordered you a beer' Bobby said 'oh thankyou' 'have
I missed any interesting conversation' Bobby joked 'no'.
'I was just saying how May wants the perfect man
which I'm not anyway...we have an arrangement'.
'An arrangement' Polly asked curious 'yeah'.
'Charles can have sex with other women as long
as no-one is ever brought back to the house'.
'It wasn't planned we haven't had sex for years'.

'We stay together because of my daughter Martine'.
'She's still young nineteen I don't know how she'd feel
if me and May got divorced' 'I don't agree with it'.
'I said to Charles you shouldn't stay in a loveless
marriage' Bobby said 'I agree' Maggie said.
'If I let her she'd try and take everything she could'.
'Maybe one day I'll try and get a divorce what about
you?' Charles asked Polly.
'I've got two biological children Kaleigh and Louie'.
'He's eight and two girls with Corey' Polly got out her
phone as she showed Charles Louie 'he's sweet' 'he is'.
'Polly's done a great job with him' Maggie said 'I watched
that documentary I enjoyed it' Charles said to Polly.
'Thanks I watched the travel one you did' 'I didn't know
if anyone watched I'm not Joanna Lumley'.
'Or Michael Palin' 'I liked it' 'well I liked that remake you
did of Rita, Sue and Bob Too' 'it was years ago now'.
Polly said 'it was great and the Christmas movie you did'.
'Martine loves it she watches it every Christmas we both
do can I get you a drink?' 'a vodka and tonic thanks'.
'Mags' 'the same' 'coming right up' 'he seems nice'
Maggie said to Bobby 'he is he's one of my best mates in
showbiz I only have a few'.
'But he's always been there for me' 'so are you married?'
Maggie asked Bobby 'yes for twenty years'.

*'Never really been anyone else I mean I had a few*
*girlfriends but anyway she's been the love of my life'.*
*'I think it sounds romantic' 'so is Maggie short for*
*Margaret?' Bobby asked 'yeah I always hated it'.*
*'It doesn't suit me it's always been Maggie'.*
*Charles returned 'drinks for the ladies' 'aren't you*
*he perfect gentlemen' Maggie said.*
*'We were just discussing names Maggie's name is*
*Margaret originally I was Robert I always hated it'.*
*'Sounded like a lawyer or a banker so it's always been*
*Bobby' 'well Polly's real name is Susan' Maggie said.*
*'Really' 'Susan-Marie I used to hate it as a child so*
*I changed it to Polly and it sounded better for showbiz'.*
*'Well I've never changed my name' Charles said.*
*'You've got a great name for showbiz Charles Russell'.*
*Polly said 'thanks' 'so making anymore documentaries?'.*
*Charles asked 'yeah I am I've got loads of ideas but*
*I'm always working on my lingerie range' 'lingerie'.*
*'Polly's done well she designed this ice-cream bra*
*sold out and some of the other designs' Maggie said.*
*'If your daughter ever wants anything not that I'm trying*
*to flog my products' 'thanks for the offer'.*
*'And an ice-cream bra that sounds interesting'.*
*Charles said 'is your daughter at College?'.*
*'Yes she's studying Art' 'I love Art me and Mags'.*

'Do you have a favourite artist?' Charles asked.
'I like Edmund Blair Leighton David Renshaw'.
'I've got a few favourites' 'I like those artists I've got
a David Renshaw' 'I find them quite romantic' 'me too'.
Polly agreed 'so how long have you been going out
together?' Charles asked 'me and Maggie' 'yeah'.
'We're not together we're best mates' 'really I'm sorry'.
'It's fine Mags is bi-sexual but she's not my type it would
be like going out with my sister' 'I just assumed'
'I'm single' Polly said 'wish I was single' Charles joked.
'Divorce the bitch and then you can be' Bobby joked.
'You know that's not an option' 'maybe you could make
it an option' Bobby said 'you know I can't right now'.
Polly was glad she had decided to come out she enjoyed
Charles company 'listen I'm sorry'.
'About the first time we met at the radio interview'.
'I didn't mean to rush off I really needed the toilet'.
'I really wanted to say goodbye' 'it's fine I know how
busy you must be doing the radio show'.
'Sometimes I fill in for people anyway some of the people
I interview are really nice charming'.
'Other times how can I put it when someone comes to
promote some play you've never heard of'.
'And they don't have any other conversation it can be
hard' 'I know how you feel I once met this actor'.

'He was a nice person but he'd been acting since he was
a child he didn't have any other topic of conversation'.
'Except acting I've seen him interviewed on telly you can
tell they want to talk about other things but anyway'.
'I kind of understand how you feel I hope I wasn't too
boring' 'no you were one of my favourite interviews'.
'You're just saying that' 'no I'm not can I get you another
drink?' 'ok then I'd love a vodka and tonic' 'coming up'.
'So do you have any children?' Bobby asked Maggie.
'One son Thomas he's the same age as Polly's son'.
'They play together which is nice and I once had another
son I was only seventeen I was too young to have a baby'.
'I had him adopted' 'Mags you never said' 'for years
I wondered if I made the right decision now I know I did'.
'I wasn't ready to be a mum I was barely out of school'.
'And my ex Arron let's just say he wasn't the settling down
type it would have been a disaster'.
'In fact my son would have ended up in care probably'.
'It was for the best' 'would you ever track him down?'.
Polly asked 'maybe if he wanted to hopefully one day
it'll happen' 'I'm sorry it must have been hard'.
'Having a baby then giving it away' 'I couldn't cope'.
'That's the truth I've had a great life' 'Mags worked as
a celebrity PA for years' 'really' 'she met everyone'.

*'I did but now I'm mostly a photographer and I do a bit of acting plays mostly' 'that's great I've written a few plays'. Bobby said 'what kind?' 'all sorts comedies dramas'. Charles returned as he almost tripped over 'are you ok?'. Polly asked 'I'm all the better for being with you'.*

*He joked 'you do know Polly's a lesbian' Bobby said.*
*'I know it's just a bit of harmless flirting'.*
*'He gets like this when he's had a few drinks jolly'.*
*'He even flirts with me when we're together they think we're a gay couple'.*
*'Me and Bobby have known each other what thirty years'.*
*'We have what's known as banter we even know what each other is gonna say we're good mates'.*
*'Me and Polly we met on a cruise in our late twenties in New York so it must be what fifteen years now'.*
*'That's great let's have a toast to friendship' Bobby said*
*'To friendship' Charles said 'you know I wasn't gonna come out tonight Mags said I should come I'm glad I did'.*
*'So are we I can't believe we never met before when we've both been in showbiz so long' Charles said 'I know'.*
*That evening it was 1am when the girls returned home to Polly's house on The Wirral they'd had a great time. With Bobby and Charles 'I can't believe I met Bobby I've been a fan for years' Maggie said.*

As they changed into their pyjamas 'and Charles he's
a radio legend' 'glad you went out now' 'yeah I am'.
Polly said 'I had a good time' 'me too he took a shine
to you Charles' 'I liked him he's easy to talk to'.
'I know it's his job but you know' 'so are you gonna call
him? he left you his mobile number' 'I'll text him'.
'Good idea' Maggie agreed 'night Sue' 'night Mags'.
Maggie went to her room down the corridor as Polly
thought about her night out she'd felt so down lately.
But spending time with Charles had lifted her spirits.
He was sweet, kind, funny and even a little bit camp.
She was sure he was one of those metrosexuals straight
men who liked fashion and grooming products.
Ok so he was a bit of a naughty boy who cheated on his
wife but it was great to meet someone you clicked with.
She hoped she would see him again Polly texted him.
'I had a great night tonight with you and Bobby'.
'Thanks for the company' a few minutes later she received
a reply 'I had a great night too'.
'Hopefully we can do it again Charles XXX' Polly smiled.
As she turned off her phone and went to bed the next day
Polly woke at 1pm in the afternoon.
She didn't do mornings especially after a night out that
evening she would be going out bowling with Harmony.
For her birthday Maggie was coming too.

*She was looking forward to it Polly put on Loose Women.*
*They were talking about adoption 'should you seek out*
*a birth parent?' they asked.*
*Suddenly Polly thought about her biological father.*
*And her half-siblings that she'd never get to meet if*
*only her mother had told her the truth years ago.*
*Maybe it wouldn't make a difference she wondered*
*what her real father would think about her.*
*If he knew who she was would he love her?.*
*Or would he reject her because she was the product of*
*a one night stand? would her siblings want to meet her?.*
*Or would they hate the idea of her existence? there were*
*times she wished she'd never found out the truth.*
*Somewhere out there she had a family she would probably*
*never get to meet Polly felt sad.*
*But knew the situation wasn't her fault why couldn't her*
*mother have told her the truth years ago.*
*There had been too many secrets over the years.*
*That afternoon Harmony arrived at the house with*
*Maggie Polly was happy to see them.*
*She was looking forward to their girlie night out.*
*They walked in as they sat down on the sofa.*
*'you look great' Polly said as Harmony sat down.*
*'I can't believe your turning twenty' 'neither can I'.*
*'I can't wait to go bowling tonight' Harmony said.*

'I haven't been bowling for ages' Maggie said 'listen can I
get anyone drinks?' 'please can I have a soda streamer?'.
Harmony asked 'course give me a few minutes'.
Polly went to make the drinks as she returned 'so been up
to anything?' Harmony asked 'we went to this charity do'.
'Last night in Cheshire I wasn't gonna go but Maggie
insisted I ended up enjoying it we saw Charles Russell'.
'I don't know who he is' 'he's a famous DJ and
TV presenter he's been around for years'.
'Did you text him?' Maggie asked 'yeah I did I said that
I had a great night I don't want to bother him' 'you won't'.
'He wouldn't just give out his number to anyone you could
always just send an emoji if you don't know what to write'.
'I guess you're right I've got your present' Polly said.
As she gave Harmony a big box 'thanks' 'I hope you like
it' Harmony undid the hot pink wrapping paper.
As she opened the box 'I love it!' it was a giant Care Bear.
Harmony collected them 'it's the latest' 'I love him'.
'I've got you another two presents' 'more'.
'Your my granddaughter and when else am I gonna get
a chance to spoil you' 'what did your gran get you?'.
'A Mariah Carey picture disc and a new clock'.
'That's great tell her I said hello' 'I will do Maggie got
me a new I phone' 'Mags always gives the best presents'.
'I try it'll be fun having a girlie night'.

*A few hours later they left for their night out Polly*
*still felt a bit tired from the night before.*
*But was determined to try and keep her energy levels up.*
*She had chosen a white shirt with ruffles black trousers.*
*And star earrings she looked nice but casual she thought*
*Harmony wore a Phase Eight emerald green dress.*
*Which matched her mahogany coloured hair.*
*Maggie drove them to the bowling alley as they arrived.*
*Harmony met her friends Evelyn and Frankie Stacey's*
*daughter Tahilia and Harmony's boyfriend Robert.*
*They collected their bowling shoes as they chose*
*their bowling lane they were having a great time.*
*Kaleigh couldn't be there as she had been ill.*
*And had picked up a summer virus Maggie took her shot.*
*As she landed a strike 'well done Mags' Polly said as*
*she sat down she looked around the bowling alley.*
*In the next aisle she was sure she recognised the people.*
*Then she realised it was Charles he saw her as he smiled.*
*'Polly hi fancy seeing you here' 'I know'.*
*'It's my granddaughter's birthday' 'you don't look old*
*enough to be a grandmother' 'Kales was only thirteen'.*
*'Harmony this is Charles' 'hi' 'hello happy birthday'.*
*'Thanks' 'she's just turned twenty' 'I thought you were*
*great on TV' 'thanks' 'so are you here with mates?'.*
*Polly asked 'it's my daughter Martine's birthday'.*

*'She's just turned twenty as well she's over there'.*
*'Is your wife here as well?' 'no we're not on great terms'.*
*'Marty I have someone I want you to meet she's a big fan'.*
*'Hi I love your films' Martine said starstruck by meeting*
*Polly 'thanks it means a lot' 'I can't believe you're here'.*
*'I've not been bowling for a while' Polly said 'me neither'.*
*Charles said 'I think I've done my back in' Charles joked.*
*'He's joking' Martine said 'no I'm not I'm not used to*
*carrying heavy balls' 'as long as your careful' Polly said.*
*'I like your blouse' Martine said 'thanks I'm channelling*
*Prince in Purple Rain' 'I love Prince' Charles said.*
*'Stacey got me into his music' 'listen you'll have to come*
*round the house sometime' Charles said.*
*'Your welcome anytime listen I'm doing Sunday lunch*
*next week I haven't eaten properly for weeks'.*
*'You know with my DJing gigs anyway please say*
*you'll come' 'I'd love to' Polly said.*
*'I wouldn't want to ruin your family lunch though'.*
*'You wouldn't I promise' 'in that case I'd love to come'.*
*'Good listen I'm just going to get a drink would you like*
*one?' 'I should really buy you one for the other night'.*
*'No it's fine what would you like?' 'just a coke'.*
*'I'll be back soon' 'thanks he's nice your dad' Polly said.*
*'He's the best we can't wait for you to come round' 'Polly'.*
*'I'm being called I'll see you Sunday' 'ok'.*

*Polly returned to her bowling aisle 'was that Charles?'.*
*Maggie asked 'yes it's Charles's daughters birthday'.*
*'She seems nice he's invited me over for Sunday lunch'.*
*'That's nice of him apparently he lives in a Cheshire*
*mansion his house was on Through The Keyhole' 'really'.*
*'He must earn a lot from his DJing gigs' Polly said.*
*'I reckon anyway you'll have to give me all the gossip'.*
*'I will' 'look over there' Maggie said 'group of lesbians'.*
*'Fancy anyone?' 'possibly but I'm happy being single'.*
*'What about you?' Polly asked 'I quite like the one*
*with purple hair' 'chat her up' 'she might be taken'.*
*'She just kissed another girl' 'there's me thinking I could*
*pick someone up at a bowling alley' Maggie joked.*
*Charles came over to Polly with her coke 'thanks'.*
*'Anytime' 'hello again' he said seeing Maggie.*
*'So about Sunday lunch do you like a roast?' he asked.*
*'She loves a good roast' Maggie joked 'she's being*
*naughty I don't eat meat but I love all the rest'.*
*'Roast potatoes and vegetables stuffing' 'that's great'.*
*'I haven't had a roast dinner for ages' Polly said.*
*'Me neither I've been on the road eating too much fast*
*food I'm trying to eat well again' Charles explained.*
*'I'm trying not to put on weight' 'well I'm the queen*
*of yo-yo dieting' 'May tells me off'.*
*'If I put on too much weight' 'you look fine to me'.*

'Thankyou' 'I've realised now I'm older that in winter
it's good to have a bit of weight on' Polly said.
'Keeps you warm' 'that's true listen come round
next Sunday I'll text you my address' 'that'll be great'.
'Bye' Charles said 'see you next week' 'it's nice of him
to invite you round do you think he cooks?'.
'Or does his wife do it?' Maggie asked 'I don't know'.
'I'll have to see when I go round' 'I've got a strike'.
Harmony said happy 'well done your better at bowling
than me' Polly said 'your turn' Polly picked up a pink ball.
As she took her shot 'half a strike' Polly joked she was
having a good night with Harmony and Maggie.
It was the first time in ages she had felt happy.
She wanted to hold on to that feeling if she could.
The following Sunday Polly got ready to have
Sunday lunch at Charles's house.
She knew his wife and daughter would be there.
And wanted to make a good impression she had
selected a dark green blazer a colour that suited her.
Matching three quarter length skirt black tights
black high heeled shoes her make-up perfect.
As her uncle Sam arrived to pick her up he had a friend
in the same area as Charles.
And had agreed to take her there 'hello gorgeous'.
He said as he arrived 'jump in your taxi awaits' 'thanks'.

'For doing this' 'I haven't seen my friend for a while'.
'So it's all good' 'how long have you known Charles?'.
'Not long we only met recently at a charity do in Cheshire'
'I think he's great on radio' 'yeah he is I saw him again'.
'Last week at the bowling alley it was his daughter's
birthday I was with Harmony and Mags'.
'I was thinking I wish I'd had kids' 'you still could'.
'I don't think I'd have the energy' 'think of the freedom'.
'You've had no school runs peace and quiet' 'I guess
your right such is the life of a gay man'.
'No responsibilities' 'except for the dog' 'Haven he's
my best friend Jim treats him like a child' Polly laughed.
'I'll have to come over see him' 'he loves his auntie Polly'.
'So what's his house like?' 'Charles I've never been'.
'Mags says he lives in a mansion' 'a mansion'.
'Personally it would be too many rooms to clean'.
'I'm happy with my seaside house' 'you must tell me
what it's like inside' 'I will I promise' 'you look nice'.
'Very dressed up for Sunday lunch' 'I want to make
a good impression I've not met his wife before'.
'Besides they'll be expecting...' 'expecting what?'.
'You know Polly Patterson celebrity not Susan
who prefers T-shirts and jogging bottoms'.
'Sometimes I feel like I have to be a persona'.

'That I can't always be myself but then lots of celebs
are like that' 'maybe they would like Susan'.
'Well today I'm Polly' 'I hope you enjoy yourself'.
They arrived for 11.30pm as Charles had asked
she arrived at the house as Sam drove away.
She felt slightly nervous especially being single
when you were married or part of a couple.
You could turn up at events together Polly hoped his wife
would like her she walked over to his front door.
As she knocked there was no reply what if they'd forgotten
they'd invited her she waited as she saw someone.
Coming to open the door Charles opened as he smiled.
'You look nice found it alright' 'yeah my uncle Sam
brought me he has a friend in the same area' 'come in'.
He kissed her on the side of the cheek 'dinner won't be
long' 'Polly hi' it was Martine as she greeted her.
'Hi' Polly said 'I'm so glad you're here mum and dad
have been rowing all morning they've stopped now'.
'Come let me show you round the house' Polly decided she
liked Martine she had dark brown almost black curly hair.
She followed Martine as she showed her round the house.
It was big with lots of Star Wars and pub memorabilia.
Which she guessed belonged to Charles outside
was a tennis court and swimming pool.

Martine's room was painted lilac on the walls with lots
of pink hearts around as well as inspirational quotes.
On the wall was a poster of Little Mix as Polly entered
her room she was transported back to being a teenager.
'I love the poster' 'thanks you like Little Mix'.
'I think their great' Polly spotted a picture of the seaside.
'I love the sea where is it?' 'Brighton' 'I've spent time
there over the years' 'dad says you live on The Wirral'.
'I love living by the sea I used to have a house in Malibu'.
'In L.A right by the ocean' 'sounds great how come
you moved back to the UK?' Martine asked
'Well I stopped doing movies and I missed England'.
'And I split from my ex it wasn't a good relationship'.
'So I moved back and Stacey so it was for the best'.
'I've still got an apartment in New York' 'I'd love to go to
New York' 'it's great lots to do museums, art galleries'.
'Restaurants' 'I bet you've been lots of places'.
Martine said 'a few I liked Greece actually' 'I've been'.
'I loved it too' 'so do you have any brothers or sisters?'.
Polly asked 'one and my half-brother Gerry'.
'He's a jazz musician I don't see much of him he's always
either in the studio or playing gigs he's nice though'.
'Are you at College?' 'yeah I'm doing Art and Design'.
'I'd love to have my work on display like do a show'.
'One day' 'sounds great Corey went to Art College'.

'She paints' 'I love it if I'm having a bad day I forget
everything' 'that's how I feel if I'm singing' Polly said.
'I sing' 'what about your dad?' Polly asked 'he can carry
a tune he's not a singer' 'dinner's ready' a voice called.
'You'll love mum's roast potatoes' 'I can't wait'.
Polly ventured downstairs she felt at home already
Martine was a nice girl she reminded her of Harmony.
As Polly ventured into the dining room she looked around.
At pictures on the wall of various paintings 'Polly hi'.
'I'm May' 'hi you've got a lovely house' 'oh thankyou'.
'We love it Polly can I get you a drink?' 'mum I'll get it'.
'What do you have?' 'juice or cloudy lemonade'.
'Sounds great' 'sit down make yourself comfortable'.
Polly sat down as Martine handed her a glass of lemonade
'thanks' 'it's ok' 'she likes playing hostess' May joked.
'So do I I love having people round' 'so do we when
Charles makes an appearance he's on the road a lot'.
'Too much' 'I've got to work' 'you don't have to take
every job that comes your way you do have a family'.
'How can I forget I enjoy my work' 'you take on too many
DJing gigs you need to spend more time at home'.
'I agree' Martine said 'I spend enough time at home'.
'It's not like I'm out everyday but who else is gonna
pay for the bills things cost money'.
'Like your designer wardrobe' 'that's rich!'.

*'Your obsession with designer shirts and other expensive*
*hobbies and your drinking!' 'I don't drink that much!'.*
*'You do if I let you you'd drink the bar dry which you do*
*anyway!' 'I like a drink' 'your borderline alcoholic!'.*
*'Is it any surprise living with you!' 'don't talk to mum*
*like that!' 'she says I'm an alcoholic!' 'you do drink a lot'.*
*'What about you and your college mates that time you*
*got so drunk I had to go pick you up'.*
*'In the middle of nowhere!' 'ok but I don't drink much now*
*you do though' 'you expect me to go do a DJ set sober'.*
*'When everyone else is drunk how else would I get the*
*crowd going' 'you could just have one drink' 'no May'.*
*'I can't just have one drink because who's gonna employ*
*a sober DJ you know I'm getting on now'.*
*'I've got younger DJ's competition I'm lucky I'm still*
*working at my age' 'bit sad though a man of your age'.*
*'Getting high' May said mocking Charles 'I don't get high'.*
*'I don't do drugs anymore!' 'anyway I'll go serve dinner'.*
*'You do that!' 'please don't row' Martine said.*
*'I'll try not to' 'it's normal they always row these days'.*
*'I love your paintings' 'thanks' 'I'm glad you're here'.*
*Charles said quietly Polly felt sorry for him clearly*
*trapped in a marriage he hated.*
*Trying to pretend to be happy for the sake of his daughter.*

May served dinner roast potatoes, carrots,broccoli &
stuffing 'looks lovely' 'mum's the best cook' Martine said.
'I wish I had more time to cook' Polly said 'I love it'.
May said as she sat down 'lovely potatoes' Polly said.
'Told you mum did the best potatoes' Charles seemed
quiet as he ate his food 'so Polly'.
'Charles said you met recently at a charity do' 'yeah'.
'I wasn't gonna go but my best friend Maggie said
I should as I hadn't been out for a while'.
'And then we met again bowling it was Harmony
my granddaughter's birthday' 'Harmony'.
'The girl from X Factor' 'yeah she turned twenty'.
'Same age as Martine' Charles said 'so are you single?'.
'Or with anyone?' May asked 'I've been single a while'.
'No-one since me and Corey split' 'how old were you
when you knew you liked women?' 'Martine'.
'That's Polly's business' May said 'no it's fine'.
'I was nineteen twenty I was married to my ex-husband'.
'I thought there was something wrong with me anyway
turned out I preferred women' 'I think it's great'.
'It's not like years ago no more hiding in the closet'.
May said 'I agree it was hard at the time being
a glamour model' 'I can imagine Polly'.
'I love your name Polly it's not too common now'.

'My real name's Susan O'Malley' 'I knew a girl called O'Malley once' Charles said 'her name was Sarah'.
'That's my mum's name' 'I used to hang out at this youth club called Whites in Liverpool'.
'Does your mum have dark hair?' 'yes' 'did she wear a four leaf clover necklace?' Charles asked.
'I'll have to ask' 'if it's her she was a nice girl'.
'We were more mates than anything' 'so what does your mum do for a living?' Charles asked.
'She did used to work in a bakery she works in a café now in Chester' 'what about your dad?' May asked.
'He was a hairdresser all his life he's retired now'.
'It must have been hard for you finding out he wasn't your dad' 'yes it was at the time'.
'I went through the same thing in my twenties' May said.
'I never had any idea it's one of those things everything's good now' 'do you think you might find your real dad?'.
Martine asked 'I'd love to all I know is apparently he's mixed-race and a DJ mum wouldn't tell me anything else'.
'Stace says that's where I get my curly hair from no-one on mum's side has curly hair' 'I love your red curly hair'.
May said 'thanks I used to hate it when I was a child'.
'But now I know what products to use I quite like it'.
'When I was younger I wanted to be everything I wasn't'.
'Blonde and slim' 'I think you look great' Charles said.

'I was thinking dad's mixed-race and a DJ what if he's
your dad and your mum and him knew each other'
Martine said 'she said he was a boy she knew from the
local youth club and they were mostly mates'.
'But slept together once' 'Polly' Charles looked at her.
'You don't think it's me' 'I could ask' 'I think you should'.
Martine said 'imagine if I was' 'we would be sisters'.
Martine joked 'I'll ask mum I promise' Polly stayed a
few hours as they chatted before it was time to leave.
As they waved her goodbye Charles agreed to take
her back home even though she said it was ok.
And she didn't want to inconvenience him they arrived
home around 7pm 'would you like a drink?' Polly asked.
'I'm ok I have to be up early tomorrow for an interview'.
'But you must come round again' 'you'll have to come
round here I'll cook you something' 'I'd like that'.
'Bye darling' Charles kissed her on the cheek 'bye'.
Polly said as she left waving him goodbye she'd had
a good day. she couldn't stop thinking about things.
The possibility Charles might be her dad it seemed
too much of a possibility her mum had the same name.
They had been mates and hung out at a youth club
together unless there were other mixed-race boys.
At the club that night Polly looked on Google images
at photos of Charles he may have looked black.

*And she white but she was sure she could see*
*a close resemblance.*
*They seemed to have the same facial expressions she*
*was sure she could even see it in Kaleigh and Louie.*
*She had to ask her mum about Charles she had to get*
*answers a few days later Polly went to Chester.*
*To see her mum as she knocked on the door she wondered*
*what her mum would say 'Susan you're here' 'yeah'.*
*'I needed to see you' 'needed or wanted' 'I want things*
*to be ok between us now' 'me too'.*
*'I need to know something about my dad' 'which one?'.*
*'My real dad' 'Susie I told you before I never told you*
*anything about him because he has a family'.*
*'And I don't want you getting hurt' 'ok I know that'.*
*'I respect the fact he has a family please answer*
*one question' 'go on' 'is Charles Russell my dad?'.*
*'Yes how did you find out?' 'we met I mean I've only*
*just found out he interviewed me on radio'.*
*'Then we went to a charity do together I went round*
*his house he invited me Sunday lunch anyway'.*
*'We got chatting I said my real name was*
*Susan O'Malley he said he knew someone'.*
*'With that surname and her name was Sarah and that*
*you'd hung out at a youth club'.*

'Then he asked me to ask you did you wear a four leaf clover necklace?' 'yeah' 'and he's definitely my father?'.
'Yes I never slept with anyone else and since it came back negative the DNA test you had done there's no-one else'.
'Who could possibly be your father trust me' 'I know'.
'But we should still have a test done' 'if it's what you want' 'I do and I'll have to tell Charles do you think he'll be ok about me being his daughter?' 'I don't know'.
'But if you've become mates' 'I Googled some photos'.
'I'm sure I can see the resemblance' 'course you can'.
'Because he's your real dad' 'does dad know he is?' 'no'.
'I'll tell him' 'hopefully everything will be ok' Polly said.
'Everything happens for a reason I guess you were meant to meet him now' Polly's phone buzzed with a text.
'Hi it's Charles I'm visiting a friend on the Wirral can I come see you tomorrow night? x' 'yes of course'.
'Can I cook for you?' 'who's that?' 'Charles he wants to come see me tomorrow night I'll tell him everything'.
'Tell him hello from me' 'I will' 'don't worry about food".
'Ok well if you want a drink the fridge is well stocked xxx'.
'I'll see you about 8pm xxx' 'what did he say?'.
'That he's coming over for eight I hope he takes the news I'm his daughter ok' 'I'm sure he will' 'yeah'.
The following evening it was a Friday night as Polly got ready for Charles's arrival.
She wanted to look good for when he visited.

*As she selected a white T-shirt with a bee on and*
*gold heart earrings her make-up perfect.*
*As she sipped lemonade she felt slightly nervous.*
*Polly wondered how he'd take the news she was his*
*biological daughter she had Googled photos of his son.*
*Who he was close to she was sure Martine wouldn't mind*
*that they were sisters but what about her half-brother.*
*What if he hated the idea of another person coming*
*into the family or his wife.*
*Polly knew she didn't have it in her to keep it a secret.*
*Not after twenty eight years of keeping Kaleigh a secret.*
*She had to do it tell Charles the news at just before 8pm*
*she heard Charles's car arrived as she opened the door.*
*Ready to greet him 'hello' he said he seemed in*
*good spirits 'hi' she said he hung up his coat.*
*It was raining 'come on I'll get you a drink' 'thanks'.*
*'What would you like?' Polly asked 'a coke if you have*
*one' 'of course' Polly got out the coke as she added ice.*
*'Ooh lovely so what have you been up to?' he asked.*
*'Not much I saw mum the other day she said to say hello'.*
*'It was her you were mates with and she did wear a*
*four leaf clover necklace' 'it was Sarah'.*
*'I haven't seen her since we were teenagers I met her*
*mum once she seemed nice' 'gran' 'yes' 'she's lovely'.*
*'I get on better with gran than my mum' 'how come?'.*

'It's the way it is we have a love hate relationship'.
'I've always been closer to dad I don't hate mum but we
always end up rowing so we don't see much of each other'.
'I've got something to tell you this might come as a shock'.
'I hope you don't hate me when I tell you this'.
'I could never hate you' 'remember that conversation'.
'Where I said that all mum told me about my real dad'.
'That he was he was mixed-race and a DJ'.
'Anyway I went to see mum I was curious in case it
was you I asked mum she told me you were my dad'.
'And that she never slept with anyone else I had a DNA
test when I first found out dad might not be my real dad'.
'There's no-one else it could be I understand if your
angry' 'why would I be?'.
'You know that one night stand from all those years ago'.
'Has come back to haunt you I wouldn't want to upset
your family I'm still in shock you know'.
'I swear I had no idea' 'I know you didn't I remember
when we had that conversation at dinner'.
' couldn't stop thinking about it either for days after'.
'Me too we can have a DNA test just to confirm'.
Polly suggested 'I think that's a good idea'
Charles agreed 'so what have you been up to?'.

*Polly asked 'I've just been doing a few DJ gigs'.*
*'In Manchester' 'sounds great' 'it is I'm just a bit tired*
*lately hard to keep up the energy level at my age'.*
*'What does May do for a living?' 'not much she was*
*training to be a florist before that a waitress'.*
*'She doesn't do anything now not now she can live off*
*my money'.*
*'You don't wanna hear about my marriage problems'.*
*'It's fine you know that saying a problem shared'.*
*'The marriage is dead no amount of counselling*
*could save it now I'd love a divorce but I can't'.*
*'Wouldn't Martine understand the relationship has broken*
*down' 'I don't know she's only nineteen if she left home'.*
*'Maybe we could it's hard if it wasn't for Martine'.*
*'We would have split years ago I was married once before*
*in my twenties that went badly but it gave me my son'.*
*'I don't think marriage has ever been for me it took me*
*till my fifties to realise that'.*
*'I'm not the womaniser people think I did go with a lot of*
*women but one day I realised it doesn't make you happy'.*
*'Sleeping around because it makes you feel empty'.*
*'I just wanted to be with someone I clicked with the first*
*few years were great with May I thought I found the one'.*
*'We had a great marriage then one day I realised we had*
*nothing in common that she just liked the lifestyle'.*

'I gave her by then it was too late then one day
I was lonely I felt trapped so I cheated'.
'Was it a serious relationship?' 'it was ok it wasn't love'.
'There were a few girls at first it was for the sex'.
'I thought it would make me feel better'.
'About the breakdown of my marriage it never did
so I turned to drink I'm not making excuses'.
'Anyway looks like I'm no good at relationships'.
'I've had bad luck with women my ex-wife before Corey
cheated then me quite a few times'.
Me and Cor got back together that didn't work out'.
'I've had my heart broken too many times so I'm gonna
stay single unless someone special comes along'.
'You are special hopefully one day soon you'll find
someone' 'I hope so now I'm in my forties'.
'I feel like you can become jaded in love' 'try being not
far off sixty I feel old now' 'you look good for your age'.
'So do you I was thinking about the age gap mum was like
fourteen when she had me' 'I would have been a teenager'.
'I would have been a terrible dad at that age maybe
everything happens for a reason' 'I agree'.
'Look I know you said you've eaten I've got some crisps'.
'Snacks if you want' 'sounds good' Polly brought in the
crisps 'I like your house' Charles said 'thanks'.

*'I always wanted to live by the sea' 'it's nice I lived in*
*London for a few years but it was too busy for me'.*
*'So I came back up north' 'same as me I was there in*
*my early twenties but it was never for me' Polly said.*
*'It seems nice here' 'it is and Stace and Kaleigh are*
*only ten minutes away' 'how old's Kaleigh?' 'thirty'.*
*'She looks twenty one though she's small only 5'1'.*
*'My mum was small' Charles said 'is she dead?' 'yeah'.*
*'Years ago she had breast cancer it was too late'.*
*'I'm sorry' 'it was a long time ago now twenty years ago'.*
*'What about your dad?' 'he went back to live in the*
*Caribbean he does visit occasionally you'd love him'.*
*'Lots of fun' Charles looked over at some photo frames.*
*'Is that little boy your son?' 'Louie yeah he's eight'.*
*'He's the best I'm really lucky he's well behaved'.*
*'Do you think I might be your dad?' 'mum says she never*
*went with anyone else I Googled some photos of you'.*
*'When I found out' 'do you have a mirror?' Charles asked.*
*'In the bathroom' Polly replied 'come with me'.*
*She followed Charles as they looked in the mirror.*
*'I'm dying to know we must get that DNA test' 'I thought*
*you'd hate me finding out you have another daughter'.*
*'Polly you're a lovely person and if you are my daughter*
*I'll be happy and if not we'll just be good mates'.*
*'I'd like that' Polly agreed 'me too this coke is lovely'.*

'Stacey's the coke expert every brand flavour out there'.
'She's tried it' 'that's like me with beer' 'I don't mind a pint but I'm only an occasional drinker'.
'I used to have a problem when I was younger'.
'I've had my issues I'm ok now I think May hates me drinking she hates me doing anything I have cut down'.
'And the cigarettes I used to be on forty a day now it's twenty I'd love to give up I can't'.
'I gave up when I was twenty one' 'what's your secret?'.
'I don't know I met Cor she gave up drugs I stopped smoking it was a good relationship'.
'I couldn't smoke now when I was a teenager I was addicted I was like eleven when I started'.
'I was the same age I wish I never started Bobby used to smoke these Cuban cigars but even he's given up'.
'I worry about having a heart attack with my brother dying' 'you'll give up one day when you're ready'.
'Maybe I've got an addictive personality' 'well my addictions are food and shopping' Polly confessed.
'It's like chocolate digestives I can't just have one'.
'I have to have the whole packet' 'that's the same as me'.
'I love my food my weight's up and down' 'you look fine'.
'Thanks I'm glad I met you' Charles said 'me too'.
That evening they watched TV together until late in the evening Polly felt as if she'd known Charles for years.

*Not just a few weeks it was too late for him to drive home*
*so he stayed overnight in the en-suite.*
*The next day Polly made him boiled eggs and soldiers.*
*He even met Louie after Margie dropped him off*
*a few weeks later she found out he was her dad.*

To be continued...

## English Girl Irish Heart

*Polly has grown up in Liverpool without her parents one*
*day when she is thirteen she is rescued from a life in care.*
*And sent to live in Ireland for a better life.*
*After her mysterious uncle Craig pays for her to go to*
*an all-girls private school outside Dublin Angelsfields.*
*There she meets best friends Stacey and Romina.*
*Together they navigate their way through school,*
*relationships and life.*

## Glamour Girl

*Polly is seventeen and is training to be a hairdresser*
*when she is spotted on Oxford Street in London.*
*As a glamour model as she becomes a celebrity.*
*It changes her life forever but life in showbiz is not*
*all she thought it would be.*
*When manager Adrian tries to control her career*
*music boss Steve offers her the chance to manage her.*
*And a new start Polly must decide*
*if she still wants to be a star.*

## Spotlight

Polly has a successful career as a glamour model.
When she gets a role in a hit movie it takes her career
to another level and she becomes a Hollywood star.
Unhappy in her marriage she leaves her husband
for close friend Corey.
And she must start another chapter in her life with
Corey's parents refusing to accept her sexuality.
And secrets from her past about to be revealed.
Can they have the happy ever after they deserve?.

## Love

Polly and Corey are happily married when Corey
is tempted by an affair their marriage is threatened.
Corey is trying to build a relationship with her
teenage son her mother's jealousy threatens to ruin
everything.
When Corey clashes with her brother's fiancée
will it damage their close relationship?.
Stacey is ready for true love but is her new boyfriend's
secret past and soon to be
mother-in-law about to come between them?.

## American Dreams

*Polly is living the American dream with
a successful acting career and a house in L.A.
When she and wife Corey divorce they must start
a new chapter without each other.
Corey feels lost after her divorce when she finds love
with a close friend she begins to heal.
But finds hiding a family secret harder than she thought.
Stacey has a successful career in Hollywood after
a major film role happily married to Christian.
Her mother-in-law is making things difficult.
She begins to wonder can love conquer all or
is real happiness just around the corner?.*

## *Chasing Rainbows*

*After divorcing husband Christian Stacey begins
a relationship with best friend Corey.
When Polly Stacey's step-sister Corey's ex-wife and
the person closest to her finds out she isn't happy.
Has it ruined their relationship forever?
Kaleigh is in an abusive relationship with girlfriend
Casey she sees no way out until Stacey helps her.
And they become good friends when Kaleigh starts to have
feelings for her she wonders does Stacey feel the same?.*

*Polly has fallen out with Stacey.
When she tries to take her own life Polly knows
she must repair their broken relationship.
When Polly survives an abusive relationship
when new love Margie comes on the scene.
Is she willing to take another chance on love?*

*Rainclouds*

*Corey has never stopped carrying a torch for her
ex-boyfriend Steve when they reunite.
Her brother Daniel does everything he can to come
between them and when she is pushed to the limit.
One night changes their relationship forever.
When Polly finds out her sister had a secret daughter
adopted as a teenager she tries to find her.
But when Harmony's adoptive mother finds out who
Polly is and the truth about Harmony's adoption.
Is she ready to have her heart broken?.*

*Out now in paperback & PDF*